Millie Criswell

Sweet Laurel

WARNER BOOKS

A Time Warner Company

To Larry, who's made my dreams come true for
the last twenty-six years. I love you!

WARNER BOOKS EDITION

Cover design by Diane Luger
Cover illustration by Ron Broda
Paper sculpture by Gregg Gulbronson
Hand lettering by Carl Dellacroce

Warner Books, Inc.
1271 Avenue of the Americas
New York, NY 10020

W A Time Warner Company

Printed in the United States of America

First Printing: March, 1996

10 9 8 7 6 5 4 3 2 1

"THAT SCENT YOU'RE WEARING IS PRE-VENTING ME FROM CONCENTRATING, ANGEL. YOU KNOW THAT, DON'T YOU?"

❧

His lips were so close to her neck that she couldn't think straight. He smelled of tobacco from the cheroots he was fond of smoking, and the manly scent played havoc with her emotions. When he blew gently into her ear, she pushed herself away from him instantly. "Stop that at once, or I'll be forced to quit this establishment. Do you hear me, Chance Rafferty?"

His answer was a devastatingly handsome smile. "What are you so frightened of, angel? Me?"

"Not a thing! And certainly not you, Mr. Rafferty. Now let's get back to work. Time's a' wastin', and I don't intend to be late for my lunch engagement."

"I can think of far more pleasurable ways to idle away the afternoon than having lunch, angel."

"That's good," she retorted. "Your appetite is much too large as it is."

❧

PRAISE FOR THE NATIONAL BESTSELLER, *WILD HEATHER*

Also by Millie Criswell

Wild Heather

PUBLISHED BY
WARNER BOOKS

CHAPTER 1

Denver, Colorado, 1883

"She ain't got no tits to speak of."

"Shut up, Chance!" Rooster Higgins, stage manager of the Tabor Grand Opera House, glared at the tall man seated next to him. "You and Whitey ain't even supposed to be in here during this audition, and you're going to get me fired. You know if Mr. Witherspoon finds out, I'll be back sweeping up at your saloon again." He mopped droplets of nervous perspiration off his brow with his handkerchief.

Chance Rafferty smiled that winning, self-assured smile that was known to melt the hearts of ladies—well, maybe not *ladies*—but women in general. It was a smile that could soothe the disgruntled patrons of his first-rate gambling saloon, the Aurora Borealis, and charm the angry mamas whose sons were, more often than not, found drinking and gambling there.

"Pardon me for saying so, Rooster, but if you're going to

1

be showing off your wares at an opera house, and you can't sing worth shit, then you'd better have a pair of hooters the size of Texas to make up for it. That's all I'm saying."

"Well, don't be saying it here." Rooster snorted indignantly, glancing up at the stage and praying that the innocent young woman singing hadn't heard Chance's insensitive remark. Chance could be pretty thoughtless when he put his mind to it. Of course, he was so damned good-looking that most women overlooked that little flaw.

"She sure is purty," Chance's cousin, Whitey Rafferty remarked, a childlike smile lighting his face. There was a vacancy behind that smile, behind his blue eyes, that had been there since birth. Though to look at the six-foot four-inch giant, you wouldn't consider him less than a man. Many had made that mistake, and many had lived to regret it.

Whitey Rafferty wasn't playing with a full deck, as Chance was wont to say—though Chance, who was as protective as a mother hen when it came to his dimwitted cousin, didn't tolerate anyone else saying it. Whitey dealt faro and monte at the Aurora with the best of them, but no one was absolutely certain he understood the rudiments of those games.

Chance stared intently at the stage, and though the hairs on his neck were standing straight up at attention—the little blonde had hit a note known only to God and his band of angels—as Whitey pointed out, she was a looker.

She had a face that could soothe the savage beast, and there were plenty of them to be found at the Aurora. Most hair he'd seen of that particular shade of blonde had come straight from a peroxide bottle, but he knew hers was the genuine article.

Chance prided himself on the fact he could spot a cardsharp, a con artist, or a virgin at first glance. The little woman on stage had *virgin* written all over her angelic face.

Damn shame about the tits! A woman needed a healthy pair to interest the customers, especially those inclined to spend their money on drinking and gambling and whatever else took their fancy. Without 'em a woman wasn't likely to get a job anywhere in the bawdy city of Denver, let alone at the Tabor Opera House.

Old man Witherspoon was a stuffy, tight-assed son of a bitch, but Chance would have bet his last silver dollar that old Luther liked bodacious women. All women, for that matter.

Chance shook his head in disgust. Every gambler knew that women were just plain bad luck.

"You guys better clear out now," Rooster told Chance. "Miss Martin's almost finished her song, and Mr. Witherspoon's due back from the bank at any moment." He looked over his shoulder toward the rear door of the theater, peering into the darkness. There was no sign of the old bastard yet, and Rooster breathed a sigh of relief.

Rooster could never figure out what Chance found so damned amusing about these auditions he insisted on attending. It was hard as hell for Rooster, having to tell all those poor unfortunates like Laurel Martin that he wouldn't be offering them a job with the company.

Mr. Witherspoon had pointed out numerous times that only the finest voices with absolute clarity and resonance would perform at Tabor's Grand Opera House. Rooster had heard the cantankerous bastard say it a thousand times if he'd heard him say it once. Of course, if the woman auditioning was willing to give Witherspoon a little "extra attention," she'd get the job quicker than Rooster could spit. Witherspoon was a lecherous old goat.

"That's no way to treat friends, Rooster." Chance leaned back against the velvet-covered seat and crossed his arms over his chest, as if he had all the time in the world and absolutely no intention of leaving. "If it weren't for me, and a certain lady opera singer who shall remain nameless, you wouldn't have your present job."

Rooster look chagrined. "I know that, Chance, and I try to

accommodate you and Whitey as best I can. But this here ain't no meat market. You come in here every week, inspecting these sweet young things like they was sides of beef hanging in Newt Lally's butcher shop.

"That ain't right, Chance. Even Whitey knows it ain't right, and he don't know a whole hell of a lot." The stage manager smiled apologetically at the big man, but fortunately Whitey had taken no offense at the comment.

Shooting Rooster a disgusted look, Chance made a rude noise, muttered an invective, and stood to leave; like a shadow, Whitey followed his movement.

At that precise moment the lady on stage hit the final note of her arpeggio, and Chance covered his ears against the screech. "Jesus, Mary, and Joseph! You'd better shut that woman up, and quick, Rooster," Chance said loudly enough to be heard above the wail, "or you're gonna have every goddamn cat and dog within a fifty-mile radius in here."

From her position on the stage Laurel peered out over the footlights and barely made out the men who'd been talking during her performance. The rudest of the three had even covered his ears. Of all the nerve!

She knew that the slight-built man was Mr. Higgins, the stage manager in charge of hiring for the theater, so she couldn't very well find fault with him. But the other two were as unwelcome and loud as they were big, and she wished they'd just leave.

Nervous as she was, auditioning for the very first time in her life, Laurel sure didn't need an audience. And a boisterous one at that.

She'd arrived in Denver two days before, weary but determined to get hired as an opera singer. She hadn't taken the time for lessons, certain that she could perform adequately without them. Her many beaus back home had told her that her voice was a gift straight from Heaven.

For as long as Laurel could remember, singing was all she had wanted to do. Her father's death last May had been the impetus for her journey west, and she was finding Denver a far cry from the sleepy farming community of Salina, Kansas, where she'd spent the entire twenty years of her life in a ramshackle soddy on the prairie.

All three of the Martin sisters had respected their father's deathbed wish that they leave the farm to pursue rich husbands, though none had the least desire to do any such thing.

The eldest sister, Heather, had gone to San Francisco to find a job as an illustrator. Rose Elizabeth had remained on the farm awaiting the new buyer before attending a finishing school back East. Heather had arranged for her enrollment, much to Rose's dismay.

Laurel doubted that Mrs. Caffrey's School for Young Ladies would have much luck "finishing" Rose. She had so many rough edges that Laurel thought it more likely that it'd be Rose who finished off Mrs. Caffrey instead!

Having finished her song, Laurel stood waiting nervously, watching with no small amount of disgust as Mr. Higgins pushed the shorter of the two men out the door. A shaft of sunlight poured in as the door opened, and she caught a glimpse of dark hair and broad shoulders. She thought she heard the man bellow something about cats and dogs, but she couldn't be certain.

Mr. Higgins's effusive apology for not hiring her for the opera company hadn't made the rejection any easier for Laurel to accept. She'd been positive that once he heard her sing, he'd fall over himself to sign her to a contract.

Though the man hadn't said as much, she thought his refusal to hire her might have had something to do with her lack of experience. She wouldn't try to fool herself into thinking that her first audition hadn't revealed a lack of polish. But she was determined to practice and try again.

"Practice makes perfect," her mama had always said. It

seemed that Mama'd had a trite cliché and adage to suit every occasion.

Having worked up an enormous appetite, Laurel went to the Busy Bee Café for lunch. Her large appetite was incongruous with her small frame, and her papa used to remark teasingly that filling her up was like filling a silo with grain. Smiling sadly as she remembered her father's words, Laurel seated herself at one of the blue-gingham-covered tables by the window. A terra-cotta vase graced the center, holding a lovely bouquet of wildflowers.

The restaurant was fairly crowded and hummed with the chitchat of enthusiastic diners. If the delicious odors she smelled were an indication of the food, she was in for a treat. Fresh-brewed coffee filled the air with a heady aroma, and the scents of cinnamon and nutmeg held the promise of apple pie for dessert. Her stomach growled loudly at the thought, and she glanced about to make sure no one else had heard it.

Laurel had just taken her first bite of steak and gravy-covered mashed potatoes when a nattily garbed gentleman in a garish green suit approached her table. A gold watchfob was attached to his red brocade vest. He had a thin, black mustache, and he stared down at her with the most peculiar look on his face, sort of like a predatory animal on the prowl. Immediately she chastised herself for the unkind thought.

"Excuse me, ma'am," he said in a very nasal tone. "But I was wondering if we could chat for a moment?"

Laurel had been warned not to talk to strangers, but this man looked harmless enough. He had asked politely, and they were in a very public place. Deciding to throw caution to the wind now that she was on her own, Laurel inclined her head and smiled. "Of course. Please have a seat. I hope you don't mind if I continue eating my lunch, but I'm absolutely famished."

Across the room, Whitey caught sight of the pretty lady from the Opera House and knocked Chance in the arm.

"Look at that lady over there. It's the purty one from the thee-á-ter."

Chance's eyes narrowed at the sight of Albert Hazen, Denver's most notorious pimp. No doubt he'd smelled the woman's virginity from clear across the restaurant. She'd make an attractive addition to the slimy bastard's stable of whores; there was little doubt about that.

Hating to be interrupted during the best fried chicken dinner he'd eaten in a month of Sundays, Chance heaved a deep sigh and shook his head. It seemed that an aura of bad luck surrounded him. Like scum skimming the surface of water, it needed removing at once. If there was one thing a gambler didn't need, it was bad luck.

"I doubt that little gal knows what she's letting herself in for, Whitey. We'd best go over and get rid of the creep."

Approaching the table, Chance placed a warning hand on the man's shoulder, touching the brim of his hat with the other in greeting to Laurel. "Beat it, Hazen. The lady's eating her supper, and I don't believe she wants your company."

Laurel stared wide-eyed at the giant who accompanied the handsome, dark-haired man. She'd never in all her born days seen hair as white as that. It was as if the sun had bleached all the color out of it, like wheat left too long in the field.

"That's all right," she said, realizing that she was staring quite rudely. "I was just explaining to this gentleman that if he wanted to talk, he'd have to do it while I ate. I'm quite hungry."

"Who I talk to is really none of your damn business, Rafferty. Now why don't you . . ."

As Whitey took a menacing step forward, Al Hazen shut his mouth and pushed back his chair, trying to ignore the drops of nervous sweat trickling onto his mustache. Turning toward Laurel, he bowed his head in apology. "Sorry about the intrusion, ma'am. Perhaps we'll meet another time."

"Over my dead body, Hazen." Chance's voice rang cold and deadly as the derringer in his coat pocket.

"That can be easily arranged, Rafferty." The man smiled maliciously before walking away, and Laurel gasped aloud, her hands flying up to cover her cheeks.

"My goodness gracious! I guess I should thank you, Mister . . . Rafferty. But that man wasn't really bothering me. He just wanted to talk. I realize I shouldn't have spoken to someone I hadn't been properly introduced to, but he seemed harmless enough and very polite."

"So you won't make the same mistake twice, ma'am, my name's Chance Rafferty, and this is my cousin, Whitey. And you're . . . ?"

"Laurel Martin."

"Now that we've been properly introduced, Miss Martin, I thought you might like to know that the man you were conversing with so politely is the biggest pimp in the state of Colorado."

"Pimp?" Laurel stared blankly, shaking her head. "I'm afraid I don't . . ."

Chance looked up at Whitey, shrugged in disbelief, then sat down at the table. "Ma'am, a pimp is someone who procures whores," he said quietly. When there was still no reaction, he added, "You know—prostitutes? Women who sell themselves for money."

"I had no idea. Why . . . how dreadful!" As the meaning of his words grew clear, Laurel's big blue eyes widened. "You mean that nice man thought I was . . ." Intensely mortified she felt her cheeks redden.

Chance shook his head. "No. He was hoping you'd want to come to work for him, though."

"But that's preposterous! Why on earth would I want to do that? I don't even know how to be a prostitute. And besides, I've come here to sing at the Opera House."

A virgin, just as I figured, Chance thought.

"We know," Whitey blurted before Chance could signal him with a kick in the shins. "We heard you singin' today."

Laurel studied the two men closely. She couldn't recall

having met them before, but there was no mistaking Chance Rafferty's massive shoulders. She was positive she'd seen them before, and she suddenly knew where. "That was you!" There was definite accusation in her tone, and her eyes narrowed slightly.

Chance had the grace to look embarrassed. "That your first time auditioning at the Opera House?" he said, trying to change the subject. The comely blonde was definitely not cut out to be an opera singer. Her voice was too grating— earthy, even. He could picture her belting out a barroom ditty. But an aria from *Aida*? He thought not.

"You sure sing loud," Whitey remarked, and received a scathing look from his cousin.

"You'll have to excuse Whitey, Miss Martin. He tends to speak off the top of his head."

"I guess that's better than covering his ears during a performance." She pushed away her plate, her appetite gone. Somewhere on the other side of the dining room a waiter dropped his tray of dishes, and his curses could be heard above the clatter of broken glassware.

"Yeah. Well, ah . . . You new in town? I don't recall seeing you around before."

"I arrived two days ago."

"Where're you staying?"

"I fail to see how that's any of your business, Mr. Rafferty." Laurel was beginning to like this handsome man less, the more she got to know him.

Chance turned on his winning smile, but it didn't erase Laurel's frown. His brows drew together as he filed away her very unorthodox response for future reference. Rejection wasn't something Chance was accustomed to when it came to members of the opposite sex.

"We just thought you might need an escort back to your hotel, Miss Martin," he explained. "Sedate as it's become, Denver can still be a pretty rough-and-tumble place. A lady should take heed where she goes unescorted, especially in this neighborhood."

Laurel had already had that lecture from Heather before leaving Kansas but had totally disregarded it, knowing her sister's overprotective nature. Perhaps there had been some truth in Heather's warning after all, she decided. And she couldn't help that she'd been forced to seek accommodations near the Opera House, which was just a few blocks away from the vice dens of the city. Her funds were limited, and she certainly couldn't afford to put herself up at the ornate and expensive Windsor Hotel.

"There does seem to be an inordinate number of saloons in this town," she said, her lip tight. "I can't believe people don't have better things to do with their time than sit in a saloon all day long. When on earth do those men have time to get their chores done?"

Chance swallowed his smile at her naïveté.

"Chance's saloon is the best one."

Laurel arched a blond eyebrow at the big man's comment. "You have a saloon, Mr. Rafferty?" She stared at the impeccable cut of his black broadcloth suit, the flashy gold and silver rings on his fingers, the ruby stickpin in his tie, and wondered why she hadn't put two and two together. "You're a gambler, aren't you, Mr. Rafferty?"

Chance grinned, and her heart nearly flipped over in her chest. "Hell yes, little lady. I'm the proud owner of the Aurora Borealis, the finest gambling and drinking establishment in the whole state of Colorado."

"Chance is honest."

Chance patted his cousin's shoulder affectionately. "Thanks, Whitey." He turned back to Laurel. "I pride myself on running a straight game, ma'am. I don't water down the drinks, and my dealers don't cheat the patrons. If a man loses his hard-earned winnings in my place, it's because he's not good enough to beat the house."

"And do you also pimp, Mr. Rafferty?" Her expression

was wide-eyed and innocent as she waited for him to answer, and Chance nearly choked on the water he sipped.

"No, ma'am." He shook his head, the dark strands of his hair glinting like brown satin in the sunlight streaming through the window. "The Aurora ain't a brothel, just a gambling house and saloon. Of course, what the customers do on their own time is their business." He wasn't a policeman. If the women in his employ wanted to make a little extra money on the side, who was he to interfere?

It was hard enough making a living these days, what with those do-gooders from the local temperance league breathing down everyone's neck.

The Denver Temperance and Souls in Need League, they called themselves. A bunch of self-righteous, teetotaling hags who had nothing better to do than harass a hardworking saloon owner and his employees and patrons.

Laurel took a moment to digest all Chance had told her. After a moment she said, "If you'll excuse me, Mr. Rafferty ... Whitey," she smiled kindly at the larger man, "I'd best be on my way. I have hours of practice ahead of me if I'm to audition for Mr. Higgins again."

"Did Rooster ... Mr. Higgins offer you another audition?" Chance was damned surprised to hear that. After all, he'd heard the woman sing, and he knew Witherspoon would never hire her. Not without big bosoms to recommend her.

On the other hand, Chance knew he could use another songbird at his saloon. Even if Laurel Martin's voice was as grating as sandpaper and shrill as a cat's in heat, most of his patrons would be too busy gambling and drinking to notice. And her looks would add a breath of fresh air to the place. Most men were suckers for the sweet, innocent-looking types. Most men. But not he.

"Well ... no," she admitted, her smile so sweet he could fairly taste the honey of her lips. "But my mama always said that practice makes perfect, and I know he'll want to hire me just as soon as I'm able to perform a little better."

Hell'd freeze over before that ever happened.

Wondering how any woman could be so innocent, Chance took Laurel's hand in his own, and the jolt of electricity shooting up his arm at the contact startled him. Enough to make him say, "Good luck to you, Miss Martin. And if it don't work out with Rooster, you come see me at the Aurora. We can always use a pretty gal like you to sing for the customers."

Whitey nodded enthusiastically, but Laurel found the suggestion shocking, and she yanked her hand away as if she'd been burned. Which she had. Her fingers still tingled from the brief contact.

"I am a respectable artist, Mr. Rafferty, not some dance-hall girl. I would never consider working in an establishment such as yours."

"Never's a long time, angel. I'm sure you and me will be seeing each other again." In fact, he'd have been willing to place a pretty hefty wager on it.

"I wouldn't hold your breath, Mr. Rafferty."

"Chance holds the record for breath holding," Whitey informed her proudly, looking at his cousin with unconcealed adoration. "Last year at the Fourth of July celebration he held it for two and one-half minutes."

Chance smiled smugly at Laurel, tipped his hat, and walked back to his table, leaving the little want-to-be opera singer staring openmouthed after him.

CHAPTER 2

His eyes were green. That revelation hit Laurel like a stroke of summer lightning as she stepped into the wide, unpaved street and was nearly run down by a passing beer wagon.

"Hey, watch where you're going, lady!" the disgusted driver yelled, shaking a fist in her direction. "Are you trying to get yourself killed?"

Pale and shaken, Laurel jumped back onto the sidewalk. Her heart was pumping so hard that she could feel each beat in her ears.

She'd been daydreaming. About *him* of all people. That man—that Chance Rafferty—was not only rude and obnoxious, he was going to be the death of her if she didn't pay closer attention to what she was doing.

And what difference did it make if his eyes were green? She wasn't going to see him again.

"Never's a long time, angel." His words, uttered with so much self-assurance, made her breath catch in her throat.

13

"Stop it, Laurel Martin. You goose!" she muttered as she made another, safer attempt to cross the street, looking both ways this time. "The man is a gambler, for heaven's sake. And no doubt a defiler of young women, such as yourself."

But what a handsome defiler!

Shaking her head in disgust, Laurel made her way to the imposing tall brick structure she'd spied upon leaving the café. Hudson's Department Store with its big storefront windows and pretty latticed grillwork was a world apart from Mellon's Mercantile back home. No doubt the scented soap she adored would be much costlier here. But after using the horrible lye concoction Graber's Hotel provided, she thought it would be worth paying the difference.

"May I help you, Miss?" a mustached gentleman inquired as she entered the store. He wore a white carnation in his left lapel and a pair of round wire-rimmed glasses that magnified his eyes and enhanced his puffy cheeks. He reminded Laurel of Lester, the pet bullfrog Rose Elizabeth used to keep in a box under their bed.

"Yes, thank you," she replied, wondering if he just stood at the door all day and directed traffic or performed some other, more useful function. "I'm in need of soap."

"Soap, Miss?" He seemed perplexed, as if he'd never heard the word before.

"I assume people here in Denver use soap to wash, same as they would anywhere else, don't they?"

He was about to reply when the bell over the door tinkled and an attractive red-haired woman entered. She was stylishly dressed in a long-sleeved, bustled gown, though her taste in fabric—red satin—seemed a bit garish to Laurel's eye. She carried a parasol of the same color with pretty white lace edging that Laurel thought was absolutely adorable.

The doorman's face immediately flushed and his expression changed to one of disdain. Stepping in front of the woman to prevent her from proceeding into the store, he said, "We don't allow your kind in here, madam. You'll have to leave at once."

The woman in question looked resigned rather than mortified by his comments, and she gave Laurel an apologetic glance. She couldn't have been much older than Laurel; if Laurel guessed right, the woman was probably even a couple of years younger.

As the woman turned to leave without so much as an argument, Laurel blurted, "Wait!" Then turned to the frog-faced man, "Why can't this woman come in here? Aren't you open for business?"

"You don't understand, Miss," the doorman explained, his voice lowered to a conspiratorial whisper because the other customers were beginning to stare. "Her kind aren't welcome here."

" 'Her kind?' " Laurel looked at the woman again but saw nothing unusual about her, other than the flaming color of her hair, which Laurel found very attractive. "Just because she's got red hair doesn't mean you shouldn't allow her to shop here. This is a free country, after all."

He sighed deeply. "I wouldn't expect a lady, such as yourself, to understand, miss, but this woman isn't fit to be in the same building with a *lady*." His bulging eyes seemed to implore her to understand.

But Laurel didn't. "Why not? If I don't object to her being here, why should you?"

"It's all right, miss," the young woman said in a soft voice, reaching out to touch Laurel's arm. "I can take my business elsewhere."

"But why should you? There's no sign on the door that says redheaded women can't shop in this establishment. And even if there was, it'd be against the law. Colorado achieved statehood in 1876, which makes it part of these United States. And to the best of my knowledge, that means it's part of a free country." Thank goodness Heather had been so insistent that her sisters keep up with current events, Laurel thought. Of course, she hadn't been so grateful all those evenings when she and Rose had been forced to read the newspaper before going to bed.

Astonished, the woman stared at Laurel.

"Miss," the man said with as much patience as he could muster, placing gloved hands on his slender hips. "This woman is an adventuress." His gaze skimmed insultingly over the woman, his lips thinning beneath his mustache. "She isn't fit to consort with decent young ladies like you."

Laurel turned to face the woman and had a difficult time believing the man's accusation. *Adventuress* meant "whore" where she came from. And this woman looked too sweet and fresh to be any such thing.

Laurel had seen a whore once, when she was eight and peeked under the swinging doors of the Rusty Nail Saloon. That woman had been fleshy to the point of being fat. Her bosoms had looked like watermelons about to explode, and her face had been painted up like a clown's.

No, Laurel thought, this woman couldn't be a whore. But even if she was, she still had a right to shop wherever she wanted.

The young woman's face turned bright red. "He's right, miss. I shouldn't have come in here."

Ignoring the obviously painful admission, Laurel grasped her hand. "If this woman isn't welcome in your store, then I shall be forced to take my business elsewhere."

"But, miss! Decent department stores don't allow women of the evening to frequent their establishments. It just isn't done."

"That's the stupidest thing I've ever heard," Laurel replied, squeezing the woman's hand to bolster her resolve. "Her money's as good as the next person's. What's her occupation got to do with anything?" Laurel knew it had everything to do with everything—prostitutes weren't considered socially acceptable in Salina, either—but she was out to make her point. "If I'm not offended by her presence, why should you be?"

"It's store policy, miss. I think you should know your facts before you go defending people of her persuasion. You're obviously new here in Denver."

"Obviously I am. But we have adventuresses in Kansas, too, and I never saw Mr. Mellon turn one away from his mercantile. Mr. Mellon's a practical man, you see, and is of the opinion that if you start turning everyone away that's committed a sin or two in their lifetime, you're not going to have much of a clientele to shop in your store."

Laurel brushed past the doorman, clutched the startled young woman's arm, and dragged her into the store with her, completely ignoring the man's attempts to protest. Fortunately, he was too stunned to stop them and could only emit croaking sounds like the creature he resembled.

"Miss, you really shouldn't have done that," the woman claimed, staring over her shoulder at the furious man standing guard at the door. "You're probably going to get thrown out of here with me."

Laurel shrugged. "I don't really care. I only came in to buy a bar of soap, and I can probably find that just about anywhere."

The young woman smiled gratefully. "My name's Crystal . . . Crystal Cummings. And I thank you from the bottom of my heart. No one's ever taken up for me like that before."

"Really?" Laurel shook her head, as if the notion were completely impossible to believe. "Where I come from, people treat each other a little bit nicer. I'm not saying there aren't those who are narrow-minded and rude, like Mr. Frog Face over yonder. But they'd rather talk behind your back than in front of your face." Euphenmia Bloodsworth came to mind. Old beak-nosed Bloodsworth, the sisters had called her—Salina's most notorious gossip.

Crystal giggled, and that made Laurel smile. "My name's

Laurel Martin." She held out her hand. "I'm new in town and I can use all the friends I can get."

"But, Miss Martin," Crystal whispered, clearly taken aback by the offer of friendship, "you're a lady. And ladies don't consort with women of my kind."

"I don't know a soul in this town, save for Mr. Higgins at the Opera House and another gentleman," she frowned, "who I'm sure has known his share of many different kinds of women. I doubt either one of them will mind that we are consorting. At any rate, I don't really care. I judge people for who they are and how they treat me, not for what they do to make a living." It was a lesson she'd learned from her parents, one of many she'd taken to heart.

When they finally reached the counter that contained various soaps and cosmetics, Laurel began picking up bars of soap and sniffing them. Then Crystal reached out, choosing one with pretty floral paper wrapped around it.

"Try this one. It's imported all the way from Paris, France, and it smells divine."

As Laurel inhaled the enticing fragrance of jasmine, her face lit with pleasure. The scent evoked images of the elegantly gowned southern belles she'd read about in books; of warm summer evenings in Salina, sitting on the old wooden glider her father had lovingly fashioned for his three daughters; of the sachet her mama had hidden in her unmentionables drawer and thought no one knew about.

"I love it," she sighed. Then she saw the price sign marking it at fifty cents, and her smile melted slightly. "But it's rather expensive."

"Al . . . that's my, er, friend . . . always says that you got to pay for quality."

Laurel wasn't sure whether Crystal's friend had been referring to soap, considering the woman's occupation, but she refrained from saying so. "I'm sure that's wise advice. I'll get this one."

Laurel made her purchase, then the two women headed for

the door. When they reached the doorman, who still stared daggers at them, Laurel turned on a brilliant smile, which threw him completely off guard.

"Thank you so much for your help, sir." She patted his arm. "You've been more than kind."

"Of . . . of course, miss," he stammered.

Laurel didn't burst out laughing until they reached the wooden sidewalk. "I don't think Monsieur Froggy knows what to make of me."

Crystal's eyes widened in admiration. "You speak French? How elegant. One of the girls I work with, Monique, claims to be from France. But I heard she's really from the French Quarter in New Orleans."

"I don't really speak French. But I want to sing opera one day, and they're sung in all sorts of foreign languages— French, I-talian—so whenever I can use a foreign word, I do. Practice makes perfect, you know."

"Do you have a place to stay? Because I'm sure my friend will put you up if you need a room." Seeing Laurel's cheeks fill with color, Crystal added, "I know you aren't walking the line, Miss Martin. You wouldn't have to work off your room and board. I'm offering as a friend, to repay you for your kindness."

Swallowing her embarrassment, Laurel smiled in gratitude. "That's really very kind of you, but I have a room at Graber's Hotel."

"That place is a dump, if you don't mind me saying so, Miss Martin." Crystal wrinkled her nose in disgust.

"Please, call me Laurel. And no, I don't mind you saying so. It's the truth. But my funds are limited and it was the cheapest and closest hotel to the Opera House I could find."

They began to walk in the direction of the hotel. The sun shone brilliantly, reflecting off the plate glass windows they passed, but even its warm shower of rays couldn't wash away the gloom of Laurel's present circumstances. "If I don't get hired by the opera company, I don't know what I'm going to do."

Crystal's expression held a great deal of empathy, and Laurel guessed that the young woman had faced similar circumstances herself. She didn't doubt for a moment that Crystal's solution had led her into her present occupation. It was a road many destitute women traveled—a road Laurel vowed never to take. Besides, she was immensely unsuited for prostitution.

She hadn't been exaggerating when she told Chance Rafferty that she didn't know the first thing about being a prostitute. Virgins didn't have much chance to hone their skills in matters of the flesh. And all the Martin sisters of Salina, Kansas, were virgins, to the best of her knowledge.

If there was one thing her mama used to counsel, it was that men didn't buy the cow when they got the milk for free. Laurel wasn't sure what that meant when she was ten, but she sure knew what it meant now. Her papa and Heather had made sure of it.

It was necessary for the women to step around two drunken men who lay sprawled on the sidewalk in front of the hotel, and Laurel clucked her tongue in disapproval. "There're far too many saloons in this town. Mama used to say that too much alcohol made men crazy as June bugs in January."

"Your mama was right. My pa was like that. You'd think he was a different person after he'd drunk a whole bottle of corn whiskey." Crystal's eyes filled with sadness. "I suppose he's as dead as Ma by now. I never stuck around to find out." She didn't elaborate, and Laurel thought it best not to press for details.

A loud cry of outrage made the women stop and look back over their shoulders. Laurel spied two dowdily dressed matrons taking the inebriated men to task.

"Those ladies are giving those men what-for," Laurel said to her companion. "Do you think it's their wives?"

Crystal shook her head. "They're from the temperance

league. They're trying to put all the saloons out of business. Al's furious. They've marched in front of the Silver Slipper a few times."

"They must be awfully brave to stand up for what they believe." Though Laurel doubted that men like Chance Rafferty would think so. No doubt the ladies were a thorn in his side.

"Bravery and good intentions don't put money in my pocket or food in my stomach," was Crystal's reply, and the women resumed their walk in silence.

Pausing before the sagging brick structure that was Graber's Hotel, Laurel said, "Well, this is where I'm staying. I appreciate your walking me home." *Home.* That was a joke. She glanced at the sad-looking building, then reconsidered. After all, her previous home had been nothing more than a sod hut, so she couldn't be too critical of Mr. Graber's establishment, deplorable though it was.

"I know we probably won't be seeing each other again, Miss Martin," Crystal said, her voice tinged with sadness. "But I'm working over at the Silver Slipper on Holladay Street, if you need me for anything."

Laurel's eyes widened at the mention of the infamous street. Holladay Street was known as the Street of a Thousand Sinners. Supposedly within its four blocks were more prostitutes, wickedness, and sin than in the whole city of San Francisco. But Laurel reminded herself that it wasn't her place to judge Crystal. As the Bible said, "Judge not, that ye not be judged." Her mama had often quoted that bit of wisdom.

"Since you're the only woman here whose acquaintance I've made, Miss Crystal Cummings, I think we're going to be seeing each other again. That is, if you want to." Crystal's childlike, enthusiastic smile touched Laurel's heart, making her glad she'd made the offer. "Why don't we plan to meet at the Busy Bee Café? That's where I've been taking my meals. The food's pretty decent."

"I work most nights." Crystal's face turned almost the

same shade as her hair. "But I could meet you sometime for lunch. I'm usually up by noon."

Laurel tried to keep her face impassive, as if conversing with a prostitute and discussing her schedule were common occurrences for her. "That'd be fine. Perhaps I'll see you there tomorrow."

Crystal frowned and shook her head. "Not tomorrow. Al's got a special client for me to see tomorrow, and he'd get angry if I wasn't available. But I could meet you the next day."

Masking the sadness she felt for Crystal Cummings and her unfortunate set of circumstances, Laurel set a date and time with her new friend. As she waved goodbye, she couldn't help thinking that prostitution wasn't all that different from slavery. The only appreciable difference, as far as she could see, was that you got paid for your labors.

Midafternoons at the Aurora Borealis were generally quiet, and today was no exception. In the evening the roulette wheel would whir and click, and the rattle of dice against the green felt tables would fill the gaming parlor with familiar noise. But for now it was blessedly quiet.

Jupiter Tubbs, the piano player, tinkered with the electric lighting fixture above his upright piano. It had been flickering on and off for days and was driving him to distraction. His wife, Bertha, took the opportunity to satisfy her penchant for neatness by sweeping up the many cigar butts and deck wrappers left carelessly beneath the gaming tables last night.

There were no customers, save for Henry Dusseldorff, who was sleeping it off on a cot in the back storage room. Bertha would be checking on that rascal directly to make sure he wasn't drinking all of Mr. Chance's profits.

In Bertha's opinion, Mr. Chance was too kind and too trusting and was liable to be sorry for it one day. There were only two people in this world Bertha trusted besides herself—Jupiter, her man of twenty years, and Mr. Chance, who'd hired her and Jup all those years ago when hiring niggers wasn't a fashionable or very wise thing to do.

"Where Mr. Chance be, Bertha?" Jupiter called out from his position atop the ladder. "I don't recall him sayin' he had no appointments today."

"And why should he be tellin' you his business, you old fool? Mr. Chance be all growed, case you hadn't noticed. And I doubt he need another daddy."

Jupiter smiled to reveal a set of ivories every bit as impressive as the ones on his piano. "You surely is one sassy-mouthed woman, but I loves ya anyway." His brown eyes twinkling, he winked at her. "How's about we go up them stairs and make us some fine music together? You knows how talented I is with my fingers, woman."

Bertha's chuckle spread all the way down her massive body, quivering like mounds of gelatin, and though she shook her head at her husband's outrageous comment, secretly she was pleased that after all these years and all her additional pounds, Jup still desired her. "I's bein' paid to clean and cook, not to make the hootchy-cootchy with you, you black devil. Now leave me be. I gots to go drag Mr. D. out of the back room before that wife of his comes looking for him with the rollin' pin."

"That wife is one ugly woman."

Bertha nodded. "And she's uglier on the inside than out."

"She's ugly." Squawk. *"She's ugly."* Squawk. *"Black devil. Black devil."*

Jupiter shot a forbidding look at the parrot perched in the wooden cage in the corner. "Shut your mouth, you stupid bird, or I pull all them feathers outta your hide."

Jupiter took a menacing step toward the bird, and Bertha, fearing the worst, rushed forward to throw a dusting rag over the cage. "Now hush up, bird," Bertha said, "or we'll be havin' parrot stew for supper tonight."

"I hates that bird," Jup said, scowling. "I wish Mr. Chance would up and get rid of it. He's too . . ." Before he could finish, the etched glass front door swung open and Chance walked in, shadowed by his cousin.

"Howdy-do, Mr. Chance," Jupiter said, his warm smile melting suddenly at Chance's fierce expression. "You surely gots the look of the devil on your face today." The man looked ready to spit nails.

"That ain't none of your business, you old fool," Bertha scolded, shaking a pudgy finger at her husband. "Leave Mr. Chance be. Can't you see he's plum wore out?"

"Chance is mad, mad, mad," Whitey informed them. He liked to repeat things three times to make sure he was understood. It was thought that he'd picked up the annoying habit from the parrot, but no one knew for certain.

"But not at me, so it's okay. Ain't that right, Chance?" he continued. The big man dropped heavily onto a nearby chair and busied himself with a stack of poker chips, waiting for the reassurance he constantly needed.

"Right, Whitey," Chance said, trying to keep his temper in check. Which wasn't always easy when it came to answering Whitey's multitude of questions. For someone who was considered simpleminded, Whitey could gather more information than the *Encyclopedia Britannica*.

Whitey was his only family—the only one he claimed, anyway—and he loved him like a brother. And sometimes like a father would a son.

He'd been the only buffer between Whitey and the cruelty of the world—his guardian and protector. And he took his duties seriously. At times it was difficult having such a large responsibility. Chance himself had been only a child when the two had fled their home in St. Louis. But over the years he'd come to rely on Whitey's companionship and love as much as Whitey relied on his.

"Why don't you go with Bertha and she'll fix you something to eat," Chance suggested to his cousin. "I need to talk with Jup a minute." He looked pleadingly at his housekeeper, who understood immediately and grasped the gentle giant's hand.

"Come with Bertha, Mr. Whitey. I got cookies in the kitchen fresh out of the oven." Because Whitey absolutely adored sweets, he offered no argument, trailing behind Bertha eagerly.

Behind the bar, Chance filled a mug with beer and took a swallow before speaking. "I had another run-in with Hazen. That bastard should be run out of town on a rail."

" 'Bout that woman you done told me about?"

"No. It didn't have anything to do with the little opera singer this time." Chance sipped thoughtfully at his brew, wondering how Laurel Martin fared. She'd been on his mind since he'd met her, and he wondered if she'd had any luck persuading Rooster Higgins to hire her. He made a mental note to ask the man about her audition the next time he saw him.

"Mr. Hazen be a bad sort. He don't treat his people nice a'tall." And Jupiter knew what that was like all too well. His memories of bondage, and the cruel treatment he'd received at the hands of Jubilation's overseer, were still fresh in his mind even after all these years, and that pain was reflected on his face.

The beer went down smooth and cold, and Chance sat down next to his friend. "There're always going to be bullies, Jup. That's just the nature of things in this world." He squeezed the older man's shoulder, wishing he could take his pain away, but he doubted that pain would disappear until Jupiter Tubbs was laid out in his coffin. The former slave had suffered unspeakable horrors at the hands of his owners, and it had taken years of kindness and patience on Chance's part to earn the man's trust and respect.

"Hazen's up to his usual tricks," Chance explained. "It's not bad enough that he runs the crookedest games in town and has more water in his drinks than whiskey. Now he's trying to get Mayor Fuller to give him another business license—despite the moratorium that's in effect on saloons and brothels—so he can open another bordello; one with twice as many whores."

Jupiter whistled and shook his head. "The mayor most often thinks with what's between his legs, not what's in his head."

"Hazen's not above using his girls as an incentive to make Fuller see things his way. I'd be hard-pressed to say who's the sleaziest of the two."

"If that fancy man get his way, that could hurt business. We gots us enough competition."

That sure as hell was the truth, Chance thought. Denver was as steeped in sin and corruption as any painted harlot. Holladay, Larimer, and Blake Streets were the gayest and gaudiest and certainly the most brazen tenderloin districts west of the Mississippi.

The Aurora Borealis, which didn't employ any whores to entice its customers, had to compete with brothels owned by Mattie Silks, Lizzie Preston, and, of course, Al Hazen's Silver Slipper.

Making money off women wasn't Chance's style. He preferred to earn his riches employing the skills he'd learned from the gamblers in the mining camps where he and Whitey had worked in their youth.

"It's just bad luck, that's what it is," Chance said, removing a deck of cards from his pocket. He fingered the cards with one hand until he extracted the queen of hearts to lay before Jupiter.

The black man's eyes filled with wonder, as they always did when Chance performed one of his card tricks. "You surely is good with a deck of cards, Mr. Chance. You surely is. And you done pulled out the queen of hearts. That be about the luckiest one of all."

Chance stared down at the card and another queenly vision came to mind. A vision with hair as blond as corn silk and eyes as blue as a summer day. He smiled, patting the card thoughtfully with his finger. "I got a feeling, Jup, that my luck's about to change."

"Queen of hearts is the lucky one, that's for sure," Jup said, and Chance nodded, his eyes intent with purpose.

CHAPTER 3

Laurel never failed to be awed when she entered Tabor's Grand Opera House—and she'd entered quite a few times, this being her fourth audition in the past two weeks.

Cherrywood from Japan and mahogany from Honduras gave the interior walls a rich, elegant look. A huge crystal chandelier shimmering like a thousand diamonds was suspended from the ceiling, and elegant private boxes—one reserved for the theater's builder and benefactor, mining millionaire Horace Tabor—sat to the left and right of the stage, affording an excellent view of the evening's entertainment.

How Laurel wished she could be part of it all. But Mr. Higgins had continued to decline her requests for employment, citing a multitude of reasons, none of which Laurel had fully understood since that first time when lack of experience had felled her chances.

She'd practiced diligently since then and felt confident that her voice and presentation were much more polished, but Mr. Higgins kept on presenting her with excuses ranging from her having the wrong color hair to the size of her shoes—the latter having something to do with costuming.

Nervously pleating and repleating the folds of her best yellow dimity gown, Laurel waited at the back of the theater, hoping Mr. Higgins hadn't forgotten their appointment. When the gilt-embossed clock on the wall chimed ten and the door opened, Laurel turned and breathed a sigh of relief, only to have her breath catch in her throat at the sight of Chance Rafferty framed in the doorway.

There was no sign of Mr. Higgins or any other theater employee. He was alone, and he looked every bit as handsome as she remembered. A tiny fluttering began in the lower regions of her midsection as he approached.

"Well, if it isn't Miss Martin," Chance said, tipping his black bowler hat. "I was hoping to find Rooster, but finding you is even better. I've been curious as to whether you'd been hired here yet."

She took a deep breath to quiet her nerves. "Good morning, Mr. Rafferty. I didn't think a man of your occupation would be up and about so early in the day."

He grinned to display even white teeth. "The early bird catches the worm, Miss Martin. Isn't that how the saying goes?"

"It is. It was one of my mama's favorites."

"I take it you have another audition set up with Rooster? You're persistent, if nothing else, Miss Martin; I'll give you that."

"Not that it's any of your business, Mr. Rafferty, but yes, Mr. Higgins and I do have another appointment. And I certainly hope you will not remain behind to snicker at my performance, as you did the first time." The image of him covering his ears still made her blood boil.

"I don't know what you mean, angel."

The look of pure innocence on his face almost made her laugh. "You should be the one auditioning, Mr. Rafferty. I think your talents lie in the theater."

"I'm a man of many talents, angel." He trailed his fingertip down her cheek. "You should let me show them to you sometime."

Laurel pulled back, shocked by the man's familiarity, and tried her best to ignore the butterflies flapping wildly in her stomach. *Stop it, you goose!* she chastised herself. *He's merely toying with you. Didn't Heather warn you about men of his kind?*

"You, Mr. Rafferty, are a man who is too full of himself. My mama used to say that a bag with too much hot air is bound to burst its seams."

Chance threw back his head and laughed, and the pleasing sound rippled along Laurel's spine like a feather on bare skin. "I think I like your mama."

"She's dead. As dead as your chances to seduce me," she informed him bluntly, ignoring his raised eyebrow. It was best to set him straight from the beginning, Laurel decided.

Heather and Rose had always accused her of being naive, but she wasn't stupid!

Rather than be put off by Laurel's bluntness, Chance was amused by it. He found it refreshing to meet a woman who was immune to his charms—refreshing and challenging. "You're not the only one who's persistent, angel. I'm a gambler, remember? When the cards are stacked against me, it only makes the game more interesting. The harder the win, the sweeter the pot, or so the saying goes."

Suddenly the huge theater seemed too small with Chance Rafferty standing in it. And much too dark and intimate. There were few lights on, and those that were on, up by the stage, were a good distance from where they stood.

"I really should be going, Mr. Rafferty. It appears Mr. Higgins has forgotten our appointment."

Chance stepped sideways to block her exit. "I doubt it. Rooster's always late. He most likely overslept. He was out late last night."

"Gambling at your place, I take it?"

"How'd you know?"

"Just a lucky guess, Mr. Rafferty. I'm beginning to think that your appearance here this morning wasn't totally coincidental."

"Are you always this suspicious of men?"

"Most of my beaus back home are gentlemen, Mr. Rafferty. They wouldn't think to accost a woman in a public place."

"No doubt they're boys still wet behind the ears." Her cheeks crimsoned, and he laughed. "I take it you haven't met too many grown men as yet, Miss Martin. Am I your first?"

She tried to brush past him, but he maneuvered his body so that she couldn't get by. The feel of his legs against her own made her throat feel tight. "Please let me pass, Mr. Rafferty."

"And if I won't?"

"Then I'll be forced to demonstrate just how loud my voice really is."

That unpleasant memory was vivid enough to make Chance step back. Not that he was afraid of the consequences, mind you, but he wasn't sure his ears could stand such punishment first thing in the morning. After all, he'd heard the young lady sing.

"Your wish is my command, angel." He bowed in an exaggerated manner, indicating with an outstretched arm that she was free to go.

Laurel had the urge to kick him right in his pompous backside. She'd never struck another human being in her life—except for Rose Elizabeth when they were children, and that didn't count—but she was certainly tempted to do bodily harm to the man standing so arrogantly before her. She didn't know what it was about Chance Rafferty that made him so infuriating, but he definitely had the ability to raise her hackles.

"If that were true, Mr. Rafferty," she finally retorted, "you would disappear right off the face of this earth."

His eyes twinkled. "Now, angel, is that any way to treat a friend?"

"We are not friends, Mr. Rafferty, and I sincerely doubt that we're ever going to be. Never in a million years. Do you hear me, Mr. Rafferty?"

He grasped hold of the finger pointed at his chest and pulled her to him. "I told you, angel, never's a long time." He kissed her long and hard, then he released her.

Before Laurel could catch her breath long enough to haul off and slap him across his arrogant, delicious mouth, Chance Rafferty had disappeared.

"Why are you wasting my time, Higgins?" Luther Witherspoon demanded, staring up at the stage where Laurel had just completed another audition. He pointed a cigar at Rooster's chest as if it were an extension of his hand, which it might as well have been, considering the number of cigars the man smoked in a day. "That woman's voice is atrocious. Mr. Tabor would fire us both if I hired her to perform here."

Rooster hated these confrontations with Witherspoon. The man relished making him feel like an incompetent fool, but he couldn't afford to lose his job. Not unless he wanted to go back to work at the Aurora sweeping up cigarette butts and washing dirty glassware.

"I feel sorry for her, Mr. Witherspoon. Miss Martin is a very persistent young woman. I've given her every excuse I can think of for not hiring her, but she just won't take no for an answer. She thinks she'll improve with practice."

The manager's eyes narrowed shrewdly. "I should live so long." He stared long and hard at the stage, rubbing his chin thoughtfully. "She's too flat-chested," he said, mostly to himself, but Rooster heard the comment and had to bite the inside of his cheek to keep from saying what was uppermost on his mind: Luther Witherspoon was a pig. It was no secret that Witherspoon judged a woman's talent by the size of her breasts, whether or not she could carry a tune.

"Miss Martin's a real lady, Mr. Witherspoon. Very kind and sweet."

Witherspoon frowned. "Lady or not, she's got no tits, she's got no talent. As far as I'm concerned, she's got nothing to recommend her. Now get rid of her or I'll be forced to tell her myself. And I doubt I'll be as gentle with her as you, Higgins. You've got to toughen up if you want to survive in the theater. Send Miss Martin packing."

Rooster was incensed by the man's callousness. "Please, Mr. Witherspoon! Just give her one more try. I tell you Miss Martin's improving. She's . . ."

Witherspoon's voice turned as glacial as the snow-capped peaks of the Rockies. "If you value your job, Higgins, you'll do as you're told. I make the decisions at Tabor's Opera House, and I'll decide who's fit to work here. If you're not careful, you'll be out on the street along with your precious Miss Martin." Witherspoon then yanked the cigar from his mouth, threw it on the floor, and squashed it beneath his shoe like a bug.

Rooster didn't miss the implication. He looked with unconcealed disgust at the spittle running down the man's jowly chins. The bastard enjoyed humiliating people. He thrived on controlling others' destinies. Rooster hated him, but not enough to quit. And he guessed that showed a lack of character where he was concerned.

How on earth was he going to tell Miss Martin that Witherspoon wasn't impressed with either her voice or her figure? The young woman had such hopes and aspirations of becoming an opera singer. How could he squash them and live with himself?

Rooster sighed, knowing that he would fabricate more excuses to spare Miss Martin's feelings. He just couldn't bring himself to tell her the truth. And maybe in time Witherspoon would change his mind.

That possibility seemed as unlikely as Miss Martin developing larger breasts.

The Reverend Augustus Baldwin was doing his best to look pious, despite the fact he was seated at a card table in the middle of Chance's saloon, surrounded by half-naked women serving drinks, and holding a pair of queens and three deuces.

"Come on, Gus," urged Chance, taking a drag on his cheroot. "We're all waiting for you to place your bet."

Reverend Baldwin's blue eyes twinkled as he stared at what he knew had to be a winning hand. His gaze lifted to Chance, to the other two men at the table, then down to survey the very handsome pot sitting in the center. "I'll venture ten dollars," he said, hoping he'd not just lost all of last Sunday's contributions. He could ill afford for that to happen, especially considering the poor attendance at services of late.

Chance whistled. "Sounds like you got some hand there, Reverend." Chance looked down at his own hand, a full house, then back up at Gus, who was grinning like an errant schoolboy. The man definitely did not have a poker face.

Knowing that the Reverend Augustus Baldwin gambled only to enhance the meager contributions his church received each Sunday, Chance hated like hell to deprive him of a winning pot. The other two men, he knew, had nothing to speak of. Chance had already calculated the cards they held and decided they weren't in the running this time around. He was proven correct a few minutes later when they folded.

It was just he and Gus now, and by his practiced deduction he guessed that old Gus was holding a pair of ladies and three deuces, which wouldn't be enough to beat his pair of kings and three aces. But he threw in his cards anyway.

"It's too rich for my blood, Reverend. I guess you'll be able to keep that building you laughingly refer to as a church open for another week."

"The Lord blesses you, my son," Gus said, pulling in his winnings and breathing a sigh of relief, hoping God would forgive him for his many transgressions.

"Looks to me like you're the one God blessed, Reverend," Pete Woolsey declared, pushing back his chair. "I don't much like playing cards with a man of God. It seems you got better connections than most."

The blacksmith, Nate Moody, who preferred gambling to holding down a steady job, nodded in agreement. "Me and the missus will see you Sunday, Reverend. But it don't look like we'll be putting much in the collection basket, seeing as how you won all my money."

Reverend Baldwin's face filled with concern, and he began to cough—deep racking sounds that shook his entire body. Discreetly he removed a handkerchief from his coat pocket and coughed into it.

Augustus Baldwin was what was commonly known in those parts as a lunger. The tuberculosis ravaging his body left him weak and pale, but he was determined to overcome the irksome affliction. Three years before, he'd left Boston and his well-paying position as minister of the Redeemer Methodist Church, moving west to the mile-high city of Denver to avail himself of the dry air and sunny climate.

But Augustus knew, as he sat there breathing in the smoke-filled, rancid air of the saloon, that he wasn't helping his condition any, only his wallet.

"If you're in need, Nate, I'll be more than happy to give some back to you," he said when finally he was able to talk.

Nate shook his head, trying to keep his eyes averted from the bloodstained handkerchief that had become as much a part of the reverend's costume as his clerical collar. "Nah. I'd just lose it somewheres else, or spend it on some piece of—" He stopped abruptly when he realized what he'd been about to admit to a man of the cloth. A man who knew his wife. "I gots to go, Reverend . . . Chance." Nate practically ran out the door.

Chance laughed at the man's nervous antics, and the reverend *tsked* several times, shaking his head sadly. "I'm afraid I haven't done a very good job of saving these men's souls."

"Most of 'em don't want to be saved, Gus. They're happy like they are."

"True. But I doubt we could say the same for their wives and children. And it's my sworn duty to help those lost souls." He picked up his whiskey glass and downed it in one gulp, welcoming the burning liquid into his body. Strong drink seemed to quiet the coughing, though he was ashamed to admit it. "Hard to save others when I do such a piss-poor job of saving myself."

Jupiter was playing a rousing rendition of "Little Brown Jug," and Chance kept time to the beat by drumming his fingers on the table. "You're only human, Gus. Just because you got the calling to serve God don't mean you don't have needs and desires same as the next man. God must have had a good reason for putting cards, whiskey, and women on this earth. Besides, if there weren't no sinners, you'd be out of a job."

The reverend smiled thoughtfully. "You've missed your calling, son. You should be the one consoling others. You do a pretty good job of it."

Chance leaned back in his seat and signaled to the pretty brunette, Flora Sue, to bring over another bottle of whiskey. "I've served my share of drinks over the years, Gus, tending bar and serving whiskey to the loneliest cowboys and dirt-digging miners. And I can tell you that there's nothing more depressing on this earth than talking to a miner whose luck's run out. I guess I got to be pretty good at what you call consoling. Some people've got a gift for doctoring or lawyering, but I got a gift for gab."

"I know you let me win tonight, Chance, and I can't tell you how much I appreciate all you've done for me and my poor flock of sinners. Installing that parson's box by the door was very considerate. Though I'm not sure how many of

your customers would willingly part with their winnings, I
thank you anyway."

Embarrassed, Chance waved away the reverend's thanks.
"Not many in this city would tend to those you do, Gus. I
don't know many preachers who'd allow prostitutes, drunks,
or opium addicts to attend their church, but you do. Helping
you out now and then is the least I can do. My needs get satisfied. Most of them, anyway."

Laurel's image came to mind. She'd been haunting his
dreams at night, filling him with a restless desire until the
idea of possessing her consumed him. He'd never backed
away from a challenge before, and having Laurel in his bed,
passionate and willing, was one challenge he aimed to meet.

"Heard you been spending more time than usual hanging
around the opera house. Heard there's a new woman in town
who's sparked your interest."

"Pretty women always spark my interest, Gus. You know
that."

"I've heard this one's a lady. That's not your usual cup of
poison, Chance."

Damn Rooster, Chance thought. *The man has the biggest
mouth this side of the Rocky Mountains.* "No harm in looking, now, is there?"

Pushing back his chair, Gus's piercing blue eyes never left
Chance's face for a moment. It was said that the Reverend
Baldwin could stare at a man and see all the way down to his
soul. Chance moved restlessly in his chair, giving credence
to that notion.

"I'm not going to preach to you, son. You'll have to come
to church for that. All I'm saying is to let your conscience be
your guide. There're plenty of loose women in this town to
occupy yourself with. Leave the nice ones alone. Unless, of
course, you're planning to settle down and get married.
That's not such a bad idea, considering you're not getting
any younger. A good woman can be a real comfort to a
man."

Chance snorted indignantly, but he didn't reply that he had absolutely no intention of ever entering into the overrated state of matrimonial bliss. After observing how marriage had turned his uncle Theodore into a spineless shadow of a man, Chance thought he'd sooner have his fingernails plucked out one by one than be saddled with a wife.

Marriage was a death sentence for all men. Especially being hitched to a *good* woman. Good women brought responsibility to a man. And change. They were never content to let a man just be. A good woman didn't allow a man to drink or gamble, or raise hell with the boys. A good woman's husband became henpecked. He'd seen it happen all too often.

Hadn't Aunt Aletha done that very thing to Uncle Teddy?

And who was to say that after a few years of marital bliss, any woman he married wouldn't turn into a prune-faced old biddy like his aunt and expect him to toe the line? He shivered at the thought.

Flora Sue arrived with the whiskey, and Chance, grateful for the interruption, pulled the buxom brunette down onto his lap, trying to ignore the flighty woman's annoying giggles and the veiled condemnation in Reverend Baldwin's words.

"Like you said, Gus, there're plenty of women to occupy my time with."

CHAPTER 4

Laurel could barely see through the mist of her tears as she hurried to the Busy Bee Café to keep her luncheon appointment with Crystal.

Her eighth and, apparently, final audition had just taken place at the Opera House, where the odious Mr. Witherspoon had told her in no uncertain terms that he would never hire her for the opera company. He'd been cruel and condescending and had made several insulting references to her lack of womanly attributes.

Ever sensitive about being flat-chested, Laurel's reaction to his insulting remarks had been anything but ladylike. Especially in light of the fact that those remarks had come from someone fat, disgusting, and pompous, who smelled as if he hadn't bathed for a number of years.

She wasn't about to take his verbal abuse, and she'd told him so in no uncertain terms, emphatically and loudly enough to make Mr. Higgins come running to her rescue.

Fortunately, it had been Mr. Witherspoon who needed rescuing, for she'd bopped him rather soundly on the head with her reticule before dashing out of his office.

Laurel's stomach was growling by the time she spotted Crystal at the corner table by the window. She shook her head ruefully, thinking that she might have lost her chance at becoming an opera diva, but she sure hadn't lost her appetite.

"Laurel honey, what's the matter? You look lowlier than a whipped dog. You're not sick, are you?"

Laurel wiped her wet cheeks with the back of her hand and took a seat next to her friend. "Nothing as drastic as that. I've just been told by Mr. Witherspoon that my chances of getting hired at the Opera House are nil."

Crystal placed her hand over Laurel's in a consoling fashion. "I'm sorry, honey. Witherspoon's a smelly old goat. I'll make sure Hattie fixes him real good next time he comes into the Silver Slipper."

Laurel's eyes widened. "You mean he goes there to . . ."

"I doubt there's a woman in this city who'd give it to him for free. I heard that rich wife of his kicked him out of her bed years ago. Can't say as I blame her, knowing how bad he smells and all."

"You've never . . . ?"

"Lord, no!" Crystal said, shaking her head emphatically. "I told Al flat out that I would leave if he ever gave me a customer like that. Hattie's older and not too thin herself, so she can't be too choosy about who she lays down for. And she's got a kid to support."

"How dreadful! I can't imagine having to bed someone I disliked." At the hurt in Crystal's eyes, Laurel amended, "I mean, I've never even been with someone I like, let alone someone I dislike."

"We all have to lose our virginity, Laurel. But we hope when we do it'll be with someone we care for, or at least like a little bit."

"Did you lose yours with someone . . . I mean was it

with . . . ?" Blushing, Laurel shook her head. "I'm sorry. It's really none of my business."

"If I told you who took my virginity, I'm sure you'd get sick to your stomach. Nice girls like you, who come from normal families, don't know about the evils going on in the world, and I'd just as soon you didn't learn them from me." Years of sadness hovered in the girl's eyes.

Laurel swallowed with a great deal of difficulty and changed the subject. "I guess I'm in a fix now that I have no chance of getting hired by Witherspoon. My money's almost gone, and I've got no skills to speak of." She paused while the waiter took their order. "I might have to return home to Kansas, though I dread that idea."

Farm life bored Laurel to tears. Unlike Rose Elizabeth, who could sit all day and watch wheat grow, Laurel craved excitement and adventure. She wanted a challenging career. Unfortunately, the only challenge she was likely to face now was to make ends meet.

Crystal appeared horrified by the suggestion. "I don't want you to leave. You're the only friend I've got besides the girls at the house, and most of them are jealous of me. Isn't there anything else you can do?"

"Singing's about the only thing I'm good at."

"There are lots of saloons and gambling halls in this town that could use a good singer."

Laurel swallowed her pride, along with the lump in her throat. She knew of one that was looking for a singer. "Do you know a man by the name of Chance Rafferty?"

"Intimately." Crystal's smile held a great deal of satisfaction. "And I didn't charge him a thing. Which is one of the reasons Al hates him so."

Understanding punched Laurel right between the eyes. "Is your friend Al's last name Hazen by any chance?"

"Yes. Do you know him?"

Wondering how she could possibly have been so stupid not to have put two and two together, Laurel nodded. The facts seemed obvious; Crystal was a prostitute, and Al Hazen was her pimp. "We've met," she finally replied. "And not under the most pleasant of circumstances."

Giggling, Crystal covered her mouth. "You must be the one Al told me about—the one Chance defended. That really made Al mad. He doesn't like to lose, especially to Chance. I think Al's jealous of him, though he denies it."

"The day I made Mr. Hazen's acquaintance, I met Mr. Rafferty as well. He . . . offered me a job singing in his saloon."

Crystal's face lit with pleasure. "Laurel honey, that's great! Chance is real nice. He'll treat you good if you work for him."

"If he's so nice, how come you never worked for him?"

"Chance doesn't deal in prostitution, just gambling. Didn't he tell you?"

"Yes. But I didn't know whether or not to believe him. He seems a bit of a scoundrel." Laurel thought that was the understatement of the century.

"Laurel honey, you shouldn't look a gift horse in the mouth. If Chance is willing to hire you to sing at the Aurora, you'd be able to do the one thing you love most in the world—entertain. And you wouldn't have to work on your back the way I do. It'd be strictly legitimate. And I'm sure you'd make lots of money in tips."

Taking a bite of ham, Laurel shook her head, uncertainty in her expression. "I don't know. I'm not sure I'd fit in in a place like that. I've been raised on a farm. We don't even have alcohol in Salina."

"Really? How come?" Crystal asked, astonished.

"They passed a bill in Kansas a couple of years ago prohibiting the sale of it."

"What does everyone do for fun?"

"We go to church socials, barbecues, barn dances, that sort of thing. I guess it's not too exciting compared to what you're used to."

A wistful sigh passed Crystal's lips. "I'd give anything to

go to a church social with a nice young man. Someone who'd look at me with adoring eyes and love me for who I am, not just what I can give him. But that'll never be. Not anymore."

"You mustn't say that, Crystal. Just because you're in this occupation now, doesn't mean things won't change in the future."

"Laurel, don't be naive. What man wants a woman for a wife who's been to bed with so many men she can't even remember?"

Laurel considered the question, the anguish on her friend's face, then replied, "At least you've got experience to recommend you. Look at me. I don't know the first thing about pleasing a man in bed."

"But that's the thing of it, Laurel. Men don't want wives who are experienced. They want to teach them about lovemaking themselves."

Men were contrary creatures, that was for certain, Laurel decided. "I still say that one day you'll meet a man who won't care."

"And I say you'd better go over to the Aurora as soon as we're done with our lunch and tell Chance Rafferty that you'll accept his job offer."

"You don't understand. I can't."

"You've got three choices as I see it, Laurel. One: You can go to work for Chance and earn a decent living. The man's handsome as all get-out, and it wouldn't be that difficult a chore seeing him every day. Two: You can hightail it back to Kansas, which doesn't sound all that exciting a place to be. Or, three: You can lie on your back all day and night like I do."

"Oh, I couldn't do that, Crystal! I'm sure you're very good at it, but I'd be just terrible. I don't have any experience, and I'm not much for lying abed all day. It gives me a terrible headache to be in a prone position for too long. I'm sure there must be some other type of job I can get."

"Don't think I didn't try to find honest work when I first

came here. But most men weren't interested in my skills, only my figure and looks. I'm afraid it's going to be the same for you. Beauty can be a curse to a nice girl."

"But . . . but what if Mr. Rafferty makes advances toward me?"

"You can be sure as shooting that he's going to, Laurel. Chance is a known womanizer in this town. But he usually sticks to whores. He seems to have a thing against decent women. It has something to do with the woman who raised him. I've heard him say that marriage and respectability are a one-way ticket to hell."

Laurel's eyes widened at the revelation, and though it did make her feel a tiny bit better, it still didn't explain anything about that kiss. And she couldn't bring herself to tell Crystal about it.

"I don't know if he'd still be willing to hire me."

Crystal laughed. "Honey, if you think that, you don't know much about men."

Amen to that, Laurel thought. She didn't know a blessed thing when it came to men. And she sure as heck didn't want Chance Rafferty for a teacher!

"It's quieter than a cemetery right now, sugar. Why don't we go upstairs and have us a little fun? You know how good Pearl can make you feel."

"My dick's hard, woman. Give me a poke."

Chance reached for the parrot perched near his elbow, ready to throttle him, but Percy was quicker and scampered away, squawking his victory the entire time.

"Damn bird! See if I ever take in another bird or animal as a wager." For two years he'd put up with that loudmouthed parrot, and he'd cursed himself daily for his stupidity in taking Percy as a bet from a down-on-his-luck miner. The bird had picked up every ribald expression the miner knew, plus many he'd overheard in the saloon.

"I bet your dick's hard as Percy's," Pearl remarked, licking her lips suggestively. "I got me a clever tongue, sugar."

Chance's smile never reached his eyes as he undraped the saloon girl's arm from around his neck and swatted her playfully on the behind. He and Pearl had had a few laughs in the past, and she did know a million and one ways to pleasure a man—some he hadn't even been acquainted with—but he wasn't in the mood right now for anything the woman had to offer.

"Sorry," he said, "but I've got to inventory the liquor supply. This place doesn't run itself, you know."

Her lower lip protruding in a pout, she ran her hand up the inside of his thigh, unwilling to take no for an answer.

Pearl had her mind set on winning Chance Rafferty. The handsome bachelor had the looks, the money, and the prowess in bed to keep a woman happy for a long, long time, and she was determined to be that woman. She'd thought long and hard about becoming his wife, but decided that there were far more benefits to becoming his mistress: nice clothes, a comfortable house, spending money. And no brats to care for, no meals to cook.

She had all the assets to interest a man like Chance and she fully intended to use them to her advantage.

"You don't mean that, sugar. I can tell you're hard as a brick for me. Why don't we go upstairs and take care of it?" She licked the whorls of his ear, but Chance jerked his head and pushed her away.

"I'm not interested, Pearl. Let someone else take you up on your offer. Besides, I don't like fraternizing with the help. It's bad for business."

"That's not what you said a few weeks ago, sugar. You said it was nice having me around."

Chance sighed, recalling the incident and how drunk he'd been that night—the same night he'd made the acquaintance of the little would-be opera singer. "That was then and this is now. I'm busy. Why don't you go upstairs and take a nap . . .

by yourself. It's going to be busy tonight, and you're looking a little tired."

Her dark eyes sparked fire, and with hands on ample hips, she thrust her breasts in Chance's direction, giving him an enticing view of the pendulous globes she was famous for. "I look better right now than any of those other cows you've got working here, and you know it, sugar." With a flip of her brassy, shoulder-length blond hair, she marched toward the stairs in a huff, swishing her curvaceous behind as she walked.

Chance breathed a sigh of relief. Pearl was definitely a hot number in bed, *insatiable* was more the word, but he didn't have the time or the energy to devote to her needs, or his own, right now. He was up to his elbows in paperwork and inventory.

Who would ever have thought, when he'd had the bright idea to go into the saloon business all those years ago, that he'd be pushing a pencil as often as he shuffled a deck of cards? This was the one part of the business he detested.

Bull Collins, the barkeeper, tapped Chance on the shoulder to get his attention, then nodded in the direction of the door. "There's someone to see you, Chance. She says you and her are acquainted. If that's the truth, you're one lucky son of a bitch."

Chance looked up from his mound of paperwork and turned to see Laurel Martin standing there. She was fidgeting with the strings of her reticule, looking hopelessly conspicuous and out of place, and he wondered what the hell had brought her to him.

Pushing himself away from the end of the bar, he walked purposefully in her direction. The closer he got, the redder her cheeks grew. She was gnawing her lower lip nervously, and Chance fought the urge to replace her lips and tongue with his own.

"Good day to you, Miss Martin. What brings you to this side of town?"

"How about a poke, sweetie?" Squawk. *"Fire in the hole."* Squawk. *"My dick's hard."*

Shocked by the outrageous comments, Laurel spun around to find a large green parrot perched on the end of the bar. His brightly colored wings were flapping wildly, and she thought that if birds could have a naughty expression, this one did.

Chance swallowed his smile at her outraged expression. "You'll have to excuse Percy, Miss Martin. He's definitely lacking in manners."

Considering his owner, Laurel wasn't at all surprised by that.

"Percy wants a kiss." Squawk. *"Give me some tongue, sweetie. Spread 'em, sugar."*

"Shut up, you stupid bird," Chance ordered. "Bull, take that damn bird and stick him in his cage. And cover him up, for chrissake!"

"Sure, boss." Chuckling, Bull grabbed hold of the protesting bird. "Looks like Percy ain't used to being around ladies," he said, casting Laurel an apologetic smile.

Turning his attention to Laurel, who stared after the bird, Chance asked, "What can I do for you?"

Unsettled by the vulgarity of the parrot, and knowing that was just a sample of what she could expect from working in a saloon, Laurel took a deep, fortifying breath.

She was unsure of what to say or how to say it. You just didn't blurt out that you needed a job, especially to someone you'd gone out of your way to insult on numerous occasions.

Oh, why hadn't mama and papa blessed her with more tact, like they had Heather? Her sister always knew the right thing to say or do.

"I . . . I need to talk with you about something, Mr. Rafferty. I hope you don't mind my intruding on your afternoon." She looked about, grateful to find that the saloon was relatively empty, save for the barrel-chested bartender and an elderly black man near the piano.

The Aurora was much nicer than she'd expected. Brass and crystal lighting fixtures cast a warm glow over the paneled walls and long mahogany bar, behind which hung a huge beveled mirror. Colorful oriental carpets covered the areas of shiny oak flooring under the gaming tables. The elevated stage, framed by a red velvet curtain, projected from the far wall, and Laurel knew this was where she'd be expected to perform if she was hired. At the moment, that was a big *if*.

"It doesn't look as if you're too busy at the moment."

"Looks can be deceiving," he said, thinking of the mountain of paperwork awaiting his attention. He escorted Laurel to a nearby table. "We do most of our business in the evenings, Miss Martin. Contrary to your previous opinion, many of our clientele do work for a living during the day."

Her face flushed as her words were thrown back at her. "Work is what I've come to talk to you about, Mr. Rafferty. I'm in need of employment, and I seem to recall you offering me a job the first day we met."

His eyebrow arched. "I take it your auditions at the Opera House haven't gone well?"

"Not well at all, I'm afraid. Mr. Higgins is kindness itself. In fact, we've become very good friends. But the other man, Mr. Witherspoon . . ." She shook her head, her lips thinning in disdain. "Let's just say he didn't appreciate my talent as a singer."

"Luther's a real hard-ass. He can be a son of a bitch when the occasion calls for it."

"He was rude and . . . Why, I've never been so insulted." But she wasn't about to tell him why.

"What is it you want from me, Miss Martin? I thought you said you weren't interested in working in a saloon. How'd you put it—you weren't some dance-hall girl?"

"I know what I said, Mr. Rafferty, but that was before, when I thought I could get a job at the Opera House. How was I to know that vile man wouldn't . . ." She swallowed her anger. "I need a job, Mr. Rafferty, and I have nowhere else to turn. I'm almost out of funds. I have enough money for one or two more night's lodging at the hotel, then I'll be put out on the street."

Chance leaned back in his chair, his face perfectly schooled not to reflect the exalted emotion he was feeling at the moment. The queen of hearts was in a fix, and she'd come to him for help. That conjured up all kinds of possibilities. "What kind of job are you looking for? You're a bit . . . ah . . . small to be serving drinks and such. The customers prefer a woman with a bit more—"

"I want to sing!" she interrupted. "I don't care to display my wares for your customers. And I can't help the fact that God chose not to endow me with large . . . bosoms." There! She'd said it.

She felt it had been her greatest misfortune in life to have been deprived of the asset of large breasts. Heather had them, even Rose had decent titties, as she called them, but not Laurel. Her breasts were flatter than flapjacks. And she'd done everything in her power to develop them, including the regular ingestion of Egyptian Regulator Tea, but nothing had worked.

Chance rubbed his chin thoughtfully. "What kind of songs can you sing besides those operatic ones? Do you know anything else? 'Oh, My Darling Clementine'? 'She'll Be Comin' Round the Mountain'?"

"Of course I know popular songs, Mr. Rafferty. I merely chose to perform opera because it was what I felt I was best suited for. If you'd rather I sang other tunes, I'd be perfectly willing."

"You'd have to wear something more appropriate." His gaze skimmed over every inch of Laurel as he inventoried her assets, and the admiration she saw reflected in his eyes made her squirm nervously in her seat.

"Your clothes are better suited for church, not a gambling parlor." He eyed the green gingham gown, which was hopelessly out of fashion, with a great deal of distaste. "I suppose I could find you a few things to wear."

Her eyes widened. "You mean—like what the saloon girls wear? Satins and feathers and all that?"

"Would you object to showing a little more skin?"

Her face flamed in mortification. Of course she should object! But she couldn't. Her finances being what they were, she wasn't in the most enviable position at the moment. Grateful that her mama wasn't alive to witness this degradation, Laurel found herself saying, "I suppose if it was a required costume, it would be appropriate. After all, the theater requires many different types of costumes."

"I guess we could pad you a bit in the front." He stared at her chest, and Laurel's face flamed anew. "To make you look a little bit larger."

"I fail to see why that's so important, Mr. Rafferty. I do have other assets to recommend me."

He folded his arms across his chest. "Such as?"

"Well, my hair is rather pretty. It's long. And I can wear it down if you'd like."

"Let's see it."

"You mean now? Right now?"

Before she could protest, he reached out and pulled the pins from her chignon, releasing the cascade of long honey-blond curls and sifting them through his fingers. It was soft, incredibly soft, like spun gold, and smelled of jasmine. "*Hmmm*. Very nice, Miss Martin. Very nice indeed." Thoughts of those soft curls trailing over his naked chest and abdomen were beginning to arouse him.

"Th-thank you."

Clearing his throat, Chance shifted in his seat. "What else?"

"Well, my voice is very loud. I'll be able to be heard above the roar of the crowd."

No doubt about that, Chance thought, dreading the prospect.

"How are your legs?"

"My . . . legs?"

"You do have legs beneath that dress of yours, don't you, Miss Martin? There's nothing deformed about them, is there? The skirts you'll be required to wear are much shorter than what you're used to. Perhaps I should take a look at them."

Her cheeks turned as red as the ruby in his stickpin. "Really, Mr. Rafferty! I assure you that my legs are perfectly fine. If they don't meet with your approval when I'm costumed, you may fire me on the spot."

He grinned. "Angel, you've got about as much grit and sand in your veins as many a miner I've met. I was afraid you wouldn't be able to handle yourself around some of my more enthusiastic customers, but I think you'll do all right."

"I won't be expected to entertain the customers, other than singing to them, will I? Because I'm telling you here and now, Mr. Rafferty, I won't prostitute myself under any circumstances."

"I don't much like paying for it myself, Miss Martin."

What on earth did that mean? "Mr. Rafferty . . ."

"You're hired, Miss Martin. I can't pay you much, but you can keep all your tips. And I'll throw in a room and some meals. Be here tomorrow morning."

Her eyes widened. "You want me to move in here? Live above the saloon?" She shook her head, her face filled with uncertainty. "I don't know about that, Mr. Rafferty. I've heard about what goes on in those rooms."

"What my girls do on their own time is their business, Miss Martin. I'm not here to judge them. And I don't profit from their skills. Your room will be your room. Who you invite to share it is your business." Of course, he'd be only too happy to make a few suggestions.

She reviewed her options. Her room at the hotel was awful and rat infested. And staying here in the saloon would prevent her from having to walk back and forth alone at night in this horrible section of the city. Plus, she'd be able to save her money and perhaps find herself another job that much more quickly.

Moving into the Aurora Borealis seemed the sensible and most practical thing to do for the time being. And her mama had always said that a pound of practicality was far more valuable than a pound of gold. Though at the moment, Laurel thought, she'd gladly have settled for the gold.

"I accept your offer, Mr. Rafferty. I'll be here bright and early tomorrow morning."

"Not too early, angel. We're open late most nights. And don't call me Mr. Rafferty. The name's Chance. From here on out I'll be Chance and you'll be Laurel. Agreed?"

"I suppose that will be fine, Chance."

He grinned. "You learn fast, angel. I think you and I are going to get along just fine and dandy."

She rose to her feet, not liking the self-assured look on his face one little bit. "As long as you remember that you're my employer and nothing more."

He lifted her chin with his forefinger and looked straight into her eyes—eyes filled with suspicion and uncertainty. "You're the one, angel, who's going to have to remember who's boss around here. And let me assure you, there's only one boss at the Aurora. What I say goes."

She pulled back her head. "And if we disagree about something?"

"I doubt we will, angel. You and I seem very compatible. I think we're going to get along just fine."

Laurel sincerely doubted that, after the few conversations they'd had, but she refrained from saying so. She needed this job. And if she had to put up with Chance Rafferty's teasing remarks, then so be it.

After all, the man was used to dealing with whores. Once she made it perfectly clear that she was a lady and expected to be treated as such, she had no doubt that he'd grow bored with her and leave her alone.

She looked at his wide shoulders, the dimples in his cheeks, and sighed inwardly.

He was a man few women could ignore.

She was a woman.

The conclusion to be drawn wasn't the least bit comforting.

CHAPTER 5

"God damn that bastard!" Al Hazen smashed his whiskey glass down on the bar, sending shards of glass flying everywhere, barely noticing the cuts to his hands. "Rafferty knew the girl was a virgin, and he wanted her for himself."

Pulling a clean towel from behind the bar, Zeke Mullins handed it to his boss. "Take it easy, Al. You're bleeding all over the place."

"Shut up!" He wrapped the towel around his hand like a bandage. "Where's Crystal? I want to talk to her."

He knew all about Crystal's friendship with Laurel Martin, but he hadn't objected to it, thinking it might serve him well to entice the little virgin to work at his establishment. But now she'd gone and hired on with Rafferty.

Zeke paled at the look of fury on Al's face, knowing it boded ill for Crystal whenever Al was in a rage. He usually used the little gal for a punching bag in order to take out his frustrations. It just didn't seem right to Zeke. Crystal was a real nice girl.

"I ain't seen her," he lied, knowing damn well she was upstairs in her room taking a bath. She was the cleanest whore he'd ever met, and she always smelled real good. "Maybe she went out for a spell."

Al's lips thinned. "You sure about that, Zeke? I wouldn't like it if you was to lie to me." He stroked his mustache, his brown eyes glittering dangerously.

Swallowing the lump in his throat, Zeke wiped his forehead with the back of his hand. "Crystal might be upstairs, boss. I'm not sure. You could check."

"I think I'll do that, Zeke. And we don't want to be disturbed . . . for any reason. You got that?"

The bartender nodded, watching the man's retreating back, wishing he could stick a knife into it. But he wouldn't. He didn't have the nerve. At least none that didn't come from a bottle. Reaching beneath the bar, he grasped the whiskey bottle that helped him through times like this and took a long swallow, thinking he'd be needing more of its courage before this day was through.

The bedroom door crashed loudly against the wall, and Crystal spun around, retreating a step when she saw the fury on Al's face. She remembered the other times Al had worn that look. God, how she dreaded these times, when anger and frustration turned the usually passionate man into a monster she hardly recognized.

Crystal dropped the damp towel, hoping her nakedness would take his mind off whatever was bothering him. Al usually couldn't resist her when she was naked. "What's the matter, honey?" She looked down at his hand and frowned. "Did you cut yourself? Is that why you look madder than a March hare?"

"Shut up, bitch, and come here." He slammed the door shut behind him, allowing his eyes to feast on Crystal's pink-tipped, plump breasts. She was a beauty, Crystal was. Pity she'd have to suffer for her friend's lack of judgment.

Fear clouded her pale blue eyes. "Why are you mad at me, Al? I didn't do anything wrong."

He struck her hard across the face, cutting her lip open with his ring; it began to bleed profusely. "No. But your little friend Laurel did. She's going to work for Rafferty. Did you know about that?"

Her throat filled with silent screams, and she shook her head, her hand going to her swollen, bloodied lip. "No. I—"

"Liar!" He struck her again, marring her flawless complexion with an ugly red welt that was sure to leave a bruise. "You were supposed to convince her to come to work for me. Instead she's gone over to the enemy."

Crystal raised her hands against the next blow and was successful in deflecting part of it. "Laurel's not whoring for Chance. She's going to be singing in his saloon."

"All women are whores," he said, pinching her nipples cruelly until her eyes filled with tears. "You're only good for fucking and nothing else. You hear me, Crystal?" He cupped her mound and squeezed hard, until she cried out for mercy.

"Please, Al! Don't hurt me any more."

"I'm just getting started, bitch." Grabbing a handful of hair, he yanked back her head. "I could break your lying neck and no one would do a thing about it. You belong to me, like a dog belongs to his master. When I say fuck, you fuck. When I say jump, you say 'how high, Al.' You got that, bitch?"

Crystal nodded, though the effort proved costly, her scalp burning as if her hair had been pulled from its roots.

"I can't hear you, Crystal."

"Yes," she whispered. "I understand."

He pushed her down on the bed, his smile evil and twisted, his eyes filled with lust as he reached for his belt.

Laurel stared at herself in the long, cracked cheval glass. She looked practically naked! How on earth was she going to go downstairs in a few short hours and face all those people—all those howling, women-crazy gamblers?

She couldn't possibly. Not dressed as she was.

The black satin gown cascaded off her shoulders, displaying a large expanse of creamy white skin. It was cut indecently low, and somehow the boning inside the costume pushed up her breasts, making them look much larger than they were. Why, she actually had cleavage! She poked at the plump protrusions, truly amazed by the discovery.

Her waist looked ridiculously small, thanks to the way the skirt had been pulled back and fastened with a saucy bow. Of course, it was done that way to expose her legs, which were now housed in black net stockings.

"Lord have mercy," she declared, shaking her head in dismay. "I look just like a harlot."

The knock on the door startled her. "Laurel, it's Chance. I've come to see if the dresses I brought fit. There's still time to alter them if they don't."

"What there is of them fits fine," came her muffled reply, making Chance smile.

"Open the door, angel. I have to approve of the costumes. And you did say I could make up my mind about your legs. I wouldn't want to be scaring away any of my customers."

Laurel flung open the door and stood there, looking every bit the enraged goddess. "I doubt you'll have any complaints about my legs, Mr. Rafferty. They're perfectly fine, as you can see."

So great was the transformation from prim little miss to femme fatale that Chance was stunned. Laurel did indeed have gorgeous legs, shapely calves, trim ankles, and no doubt firm thighs. An enticing thought that made him shuffle his feet restlessly. "I had no idea . . ."

"What? That I had legs? I assured you I did."

"You sure as hell do, angel. And you've got a decent pair of bosoms, too."

"Really! That is a terrible thing to say!" Though she was secretly pleased that he'd noticed the alteration. No man had ever stared at her bosoms with such appreciation before. "I admit to being a bit shocked myself. I have cleavage."

Chance's eyes were glued to that cleavage. "Jesus, Mary, and Joseph. The men are going to go wild tonight." That thought made him frown. Those filthy bastards were going to ogle Laurel's body, and for some inexplicable reason, that didn't sit well with him.

Clearing his throat, and trying to ignore the uncomfortable thought, he said, "You look absolutely dazzling. I'm sure your debut tonight will be well received. Is your room all right? Do you need anything else?"

Laurel took a quick glance around the room, noting the brass bedstead, the colorful patchwork quilt, the red velvet draperies at the window, and nodded. It was a far better room than the one she'd occupied at the hotel.

"Thank you, Chance. It's very nice. And thank you for the flowers." She pointed at the large bouquet of blue columbines in the vase on the walnut dresser. "They're lovely." She'd been touched by the gesture, for it seemed out of character with the Chance Rafferty she knew.

Chance stuck his head into the room and saw the arrangement. He smiled sheepishly. " 'Fraid I can't take credit for those, angel. Most likely it was Bertha who brought them up. She takes care of things around here."

A stab of disappointment shot through her. An unreasonable stab, she knew. Nonetheless, it still registered as disappointment. "Well, please thank Bertha for me. It was very considerate of her."

"May I come in? It's getting tiring standing out here in the hall."

"No, you may not! What would people think if I allowed a man into my room? I certainly wouldn't want to give anyone the impression that my favors are free for the taking."

It was bad enough that she was living in a saloon; she certainly wasn't going to provide more grist for the mill. Though she was sure that whatever was left of her reputation was already in tatters. Theater folk were considered no better than prostitutes by some. And her choice of friends and living arrangements had already condemned her by the Sacred Thirty-six—the town's socially elite females.

Chance grinned. "No doubt most men would be willing to pay a hefty sum for your favors, angel."

She gasped, and tried to slam the door in his face, but he wedged his foot in the opening. "If there's nothing else, Chance, I'd like to rest before this evening's performance. I still have some unpacking to do, and someone named Flora Sue offered to fix my hair for me."

His eyebrows shot up. "Really?" Flora Sue wasn't usually so generous with newcomers. "I thought you were going to wear it down," he reminded her.

"Well, well, if it isn't the boss ogling the new girl."

Pearl stood by Laurel's door, sizing up her competition. The girl was pretty in a vapid sort of way, but she wasn't Chance's type at all. He liked seasoned women; he'd told her as much. And this girl looked green as newly cut firewood. And as thin. Still, Pearl decided, it wouldn't hurt to scare her some.

"Watch out for Chance, sugar. He likes to sample all the new girls; don't you, Chance?" Laurel was shocked by the woman's effrontery. "Though by the looks of it, you don't have enough tits to interest Chance. He's really quite a breast—"

Chance shot Pearl a dangerous look as he cut her off. "That's enough, Pearl. Don't you have something else to do? I'm sure Bertha could use some help in the kitchen."

"I'm paid to serve drinks and keep the customers happy, not to dice vegetables and make biscuits. Let the new girl do it. She looks the type." With a throaty laugh that made the hairs on Laurel's neck stand on end, Pearl sashayed down the hall.

Never in all her born days had Laurel seen breasts as large as that woman had. They made her newly enhanced ones look pitiful by comparison. Sort of like an apricot standing next to a watermelon.

"I take it that was one of your bar girls?"

Still frowning, Chance nodded. "Her name's Pearl. She's a bit taken with herself, so don't mind her comments. Pearl thinks she's better than any of the other girls working here."

"Bigger maybe, but not better," Laurel was surprised to hear herself remark.

Chance laughed. "Definitely bigger than most, and she revels in it."

Laurel looked down at her bosoms. "Thank goodness I won't be required to entice the customers. I doubt they'd be impressed after seeing that woman's . . ."

He lifted her chin, fighting the urge to strip her out of that gaudy gown and throw her down on her back. Laurel's honesty and innocence made her far more enticing and sensual than most of the experienced women he'd known. A man could drown in those wide, trusting pools of blue, and Chance had never been much of a swimmer.

Clearing his throat, he said, "You've got nothing to worry about, angel. You're going to wow them tonight."

Laurel's heart accelerated at the comment; her skin grew warm, and she tingled in places she'd never even known existed. "Thank you. And if your Bertha needs help with the chores, I'd be only to happy to oblige. I'm sure I'll have plenty of time on my hands during the day, and I know my way around a kitchen."

"That's considerate of you. Bertha's getting on in years, and though she'd die before admitting it, I know she'd appreciate some help."

"Then consider it done."

He skimmed his finger lightly over her cheek, then down her neck, and felt the rapid beat of her pulse. "There's a lot about you that fascinates me, Laurel Martin. I think I'm going to enjoy getting to know you better." He traced the outline of her lips before parting them with the tip of his finger, inserting it gently into her mouth until it touched her tongue.

Laurel was totally and utterly shocked by his actions, and

by the delicious sensations he was creating. The feel and taste of Chance's finger in her mouth was the most erotic experience she'd ever had. Fighting the instinctual urge to suck, she grasped his hand and pulled it down to his side.

"You'd better leave, Chance." Her nipples were starting to pucker, and she knew she'd be mortified if he noticed, which he was sure to, the way her breasts were starting to swell up over the edge of her gown.

Turning her hand over, he kissed her palm. "Welcome to the Aurora, angel," he said, then walked away.

Closing the door behind him, Laurel felt the strangest stirring between her legs. Her nipples throbbed, and she had the strongest desire to touch herself in that forbidden area nice women never talked about.

"Laurel have mercy," she muttered, not knowing what to make of these foreign feelings. She decided that the scandalous costume was having an undesirable affect on her. She didn't want to consider what else it might be.

"Watch out for Chance, sugar. He likes to sample all the new girls . . ."

Pearl's words of warning made her blush, and Laurel was suddenly filled with unease—an unease that soon turned to indignation.

Chance Rafferty was a rake and a womanizer, and he had a wealth of experience when it came to seducing women. An inexperienced woman, such as herself, would be easy pickings for him.

Laurel drew herself rigidly erect and sucked in her breath, fortifying herself against the unfamiliar, unwelcome arousal Chance's touch had elicited. She'd be easy pickings for no man, she vowed. And that included that arrogant, scurrilous gambler.

The noise was deafening. Laurel peeked out from behind the red velvet curtains, swallowing with a great deal of difficulty at the sight of the raucous men who comprised the audience, and wondered how she'd ever be able to make herself heard.

"Be just a few more minutes, Miss Laurel."

Laurel smiled kindly at Jupiter, the piano player she'd met at rehearsal earlier in the day. Besides a piano, her accompaniment consisted of a banjo, a cornet, and a fiddle.

Chance's idea of an orchestra was vastly different from her own. She'd imagined violins, guitars, and the soothing strains of a concert piano, not the lively thumping of a honky-tonk piano and the twanging of a banjo.

This was not the Opera House, Laurel reminded herself; a fact made clear a moment later when a beer glass smashed against the stage, making her jump back.

"Gentlemen, gentlemen, quiet down!"

Chance's voice rang loud and clear as he prepared to introduce her, and Laurel swallowed again.

Dear Lord, give me the courage and strength to go through with this, she prayed, tugging the bodice of her dress up a bit. Never in her life had she imagined being worried about showing too much cleavage. Heather and Rose Elizabeth would laugh themselves silly if they could see her now.

The curtains were suddenly pulled aside, leaving Laurel to stand facing the crowd of ogling men. The orchestra was playing "Oh! Susanna," and Laurel belatedly realized that she was supposed to be singing.

She started in a small voice that suddenly grew louder when a redheaded man in the back yelled out, "Louder, cutie pie. We can't hear you."

But it wouldn't have made a lick of difference if she'd been shouting at the top of her lungs. Few paid her any attention. Chance was occupied at the roulette wheel, while his cousin, Whitey dealt faro. The serving girls, dressed in a fashion similar to her's, were laughing and playing up to the customers, encouraging the men to drink and spend their money at the gaming tables. Most of them, Laurel decided, were probably family men who could ill afford to lose their hard-earned cash.

"Let's see some leg, girlie," an intoxicated man seated right below the stage shouted, as he attempted to look up her dress. Laurel wanted to kick him right in his grinning mouth.

Doing her best to maintain her composure, she began a grating, off-key rendition of "I'll Take You Home Again Kathleen," a song her father had frequently sung at the top of his lungs while bathing. Suddenly the room quieted, and the men stopped what they were doing and listened. Several were shaking their heads in disbelief, and a few snickered behind their hands, but Laurel was too nervous and too caught up in the moment to notice their disapproval.

Finally, she thought, *I have made an impact on this audience.* That notion was soon dismissed when a bearded man at the billiards table shouted, "Bring Pearl on. Let's see some tits worth lookin' at."

Catching Pearl's smug smile, and noting that the woman had sidled up to the bearded man and was offering him a personal glimpse of her assets, and Lord knew what else, Laurel silently chastised the fate that had brought her to this humiliating end.

CHAPTER 6

"I'm never going to get used to singing in this place, Bertha. No matter how hard I try to please the customers, they don't seem to care one way or the other." Laurel pushed the bowl of peas she'd shelled across the scarred oak table toward the black woman seated on the other side.

Bertha Tubbs, who ruled the kitchen at the Aurora Borealis with an iron hand, had been reluctant to accept Laurel's offer of help. But that had been a week ago, and now the gray-haired woman seemed to accept her daily presence, even welcoming it, though she hadn't said as much.

"You's too sensitive, honey. Why, those gambling men ain't hard to please a'tall. They's just preoccupied with the business of makin' money. And that's what Mr. Chance wants them to do anyway. You is just an extra bonus."

Laurel frowned at that. She wanted to be the main attraction, not just some ornament to decorate a saloon. "I don't fit in here, but I'm not sure just where I do fit in. The Opera

House didn't want me, I have no future in Kansas, and I don't want a permanent career singing in a gambling parlor."

Putting her hand over Laurel's, Bertha shook her head, an admonishing look on her face. "Honey, we all do what we gots to do in this world to survive. That's just the way it is. From what you already done told me, you didn't have much choice 'bout working here, so you might as well make up your mind to make the best of it."

"Some of the girls don't like me much." Pearl had gone out of her way to make Laurel's life miserable, making snide remarks about her bosoms, or lack thereof, and mimicking the way she sang her songs.

Bertha clucked her tongue. "You be thinkin' about that Pearl. She's trash, pure and simple. If she had a brain as big as them other parts, she'd be lots better off."

A fit of the giggles overtook Laurel. "You and my mama would have gotten along just fine, Bertha. She always gave such good advice, and everything she said seemed to make sense. I sure do miss her."

"Is your mama dead, child?"

Laurel nodded. "She died when I was small. My sister Heather raised me and my younger sister, Rose Elizabeth."

"That's what family's for. Family looks out for one another."

"You and Jupiter never had any children, did you, Bertha?"

"No." Her expression grew sad. "The good Lord never blessed us with a child. But we got Mr. Chance, and Whitey's real childlike. Though he be fully grown, that man don't have all his wits about him, if you get my meanin'."

Picking up a sweet potato from the pile Bertha had placed in front of her, Laurel began to peel. Bertha was planning to prepare some of her famous sweet potato pies for dinner, and Laurel couldn't wait to sink her teeth into one. Her mouth watered just thinking about it.

"You get a real motherly look on your face whenever you

talk about Chance and his cousin. Have you been working for Chance long?"

Bertha nodded, wiping the flour from her hands on her apron. "Been here what seems like forever, honey. Me and Jup came to this place when there wasn't much here 'cept ramshackle wooden buildings, which was mostly saloons catering to the miners.

"Back then there wasn't none of them cottonwood trees like you see planted on the streets. Men brought in those trees and planted them for shade, and watered them with ditches they dug. It was the damnedest thing I ever did see. Never saw no one pay such attention to trees before. Course, where I come from down in Georgia we got lots of trees."

Trees were a rare commodity on the plains, that was for certain, Laurel thought. And the cottonwoods now gracing most of Denver's streets were large and lovely.

"Did Chance always own a saloon?" It was hard to imagine him without a deck of cards in his hands. From what she'd observed this past week, he was more skilled than most of those who tried their hand at poker or faro. Those who "bucked the tiger" inevitably lost.

"That boy and Whitey ran away from home when they was still wet behind the ears. Mr. Chance don't talk much 'bout the family they left behind. I think it pains him too much.

"They roamed about, doing different things, but mostly they mined for silver. That's where Mr. Chance learned his skill with the cards. There's a whole lot of sportin' men and women in them mining camps."

Speaking of sportin' women, Laurel thought, glancing up as Pearl strolled into the kitchen.

"Well, I see you've finally found the right job for your talents, Laurel. I guess Chance came to his senses and put you to work in the kitchen instead of on the stage."

"You hush your mouth, Miss Pearl, and leave this child

be. She's been a big help to me, and we don't need your sassy mouth ruinin' our day."

"Why, Bertha Tubbs! I'm so surprised. You usually don't cotton to anyone except your precious Chance. You should feel honored, Laurel, that Bertha's taken you under her wing."

Bertha reached for the rolling pin, and Laurel felt the inclination to keep quiet and let the woman bash Pearl's brains in. But she didn't. Owing mostly to the fact that she didn't think Pearl had any brains.

"I enjoy cooking, and Bertha's been kind enough to teach me how to prepare some of the dishes she's so famous for. I understand her sweet potato pie is just fabulous." Her comment elicited a boastful smile from the black woman.

Pearl patted her hips. "Not that I have to worry, mind you, but pie makes a body run to fat."

"Humph! Body wouldn't have to be fat if it didn't loll about all day doing nothin' but complaining. Work is good for the soul and the body. Didn't your mama ever teach you that, Miss Pearl?"

"My mama earned her living lying on her back, servicing the miners up in Leadville. The only thing she taught me was how to survive by using what the good Lord gave me."

Laurel was saddened by Pearl's lack of moral upbringing, but it didn't keep her from saying, "Not every woman has to be a prostitute, Pearl. The good Lord also gave us brains, so we could use them to help ourselves."

"If that's true, Miss Smarty, why are you working in a saloon surrounded by drunks and whores? If you're so smart, why ain't you got yourself a rich husband? Why ain't you living in one of them fancy mansions up on Brown's Bluff?"

"This job is merely temporary. And I don't believe marriage is the only choice for a woman. Plenty of women own businesses or have professions. My sister is in San Francisco working as an illustrator at a large newspaper." That wasn't quite the truth, for she had no idea if Heather had found a job, but Pearl didn't need to know that.

"Mark my words: You'll be in Chance Rafferty's bed before you know it." Pearl snapped her fingers, startling Laurel. "That man could charm the drawers off half the female population of Denver." She laughed seductively. "In fact, I think he already has. Chance has a big appetite when it comes to women, and if you think he's not going to come sniffing around your skirts, you're wrong. We've all bedded Chance at one time or another. And, sugar, it's a damned fine experience that I wouldn't mind repeating on a daily basis." With that, Pearl left the room with a satisfied smile, knowing that her comment would put Laurel on the defensive where Chance was concerned.

"That woman is pure trash," Bertha said. "Never you mind what she says, Miss Laurel. A man treats a woman the way she asks to be treated. If you's easy, a man's going to take what's offered. Men bed women like Pearl, but they don't marry 'em."

"Don't worry, Bertha." Laurel patted the concerned woman's arm. "I've got no plans to get married anytime in the near future, and I've certainly got no plans to bed Chance Rafferty. As my mama was fond of saying: 'She didn't raise no fools.' "

Dearest Heather,

I trust this letter finds you well and situated in the position of your choice. I've no doubt that you succeeded at becoming an illustrator . . .

"What're you doing, Miss Laurel? Are you puttin' words down on paper?"

Laurel paused in writing her letter and turned to see Whitey peering over her left shoulder. She smiled at the inquisitive man and offered him a seat. "Why, yes, I am. I thought it was high time to let my sister in San Francisco know what I've been doing here in Denver." She also intended to let Heather know that Rose Elizabeth still remained on the farm. The brief note she'd received two days before had alluded to some trouble with the new buyer.

Whitey stared at the marks on the paper and frowned. "I don't know how to make my mark. I never learned to read and write, 'cept Chance taught me how to read the cards so that I could deal, deal, deal."

"It's not hard to learn, Whitey. I'd be happy to teach you, if you'd like to."

His face lit with childlike pleasure. "If I could write a letter like you, Miss Laurel, I could tell my mama where I am and what I'm doing."

Remembering what Bertha had said about Chance and Whitey running away from home, Laurel guessed it had been a good while since Whitey had seen his mother. "Do you miss your mama, Whitey?"

He shrugged. "Sometimes I do. Sometimes I think about her holding me when I was real small, but she wasn't always nice. She used to call me stupid. And sometimes she'd hit me for no reason. Chance didn't like her when she did that."

"No, I don't imagine he did." In the short time she'd been at the Aurora she'd already seen that Chance was very protective of his cousin. Not that she could blame him. Whitey was a little boy in a man's body, and he needed someone to look out for him. Folks weren't usually tolerant of those who possessed a weak mind or body.

"Sometimes people say and do things they don't mean, Whitey. I used to call my sisters names, and sometimes we'd even get into fights, but I never stopped loving them. And I bet your mama never stopped loving you, in spite of what she may have said or done."

"Do you really think so, Miss Laurel?"

Her answer seemed very important to him, and that tugged at Laurel's heart. "Yes, Whitey. I most definitely do."

"You think you could teach me to make my letters, Miss Laurel? Then no one could say I was stupid, stupid, stupid."

Laurel reached for a fresh sheet of her lavender-scented stationery, then handed Whitey a pencil and showed him the correct way to hold it. "We'll start with the letter *A*." She showed him how to form the letter, waited patiently while he attempted it, then praised his first effort. "My mama always said that practice makes perfect, so you'll need to practice, practice, practice," she said three times, just like he always did, "over and over until you can do this letter right."

He looked up, wide-eyed and eager. "And then will I be able to write?"

She shook her head. "This is just the first letter of the alphabet, Whitey. There're twenty-six letters altogether. You'll have to learn each one, then we'll begin putting the letters together to form words. Once you can do that, you'll be able to write."

"And no one will call me stupid, stupid, stupid. Right, Miss Laurel?"

She patted the big man's hand. "You're not stupid, Whitey. You're just a little slower to learn than some other folks. But I've seen the way you deal the cards, and I'm very impressed by what you can do. I could never do that. We all have gifts God gave us. That's what makes each one of us special."

"God gave you a real purty voice, Miss Laurel. I just love it when you sing."

Laurel beamed at the praise. "Why, thank you, Whitey. That's the nicest thing anyone's said to me in quite some time."

"Chance thinks you sing like a screech owl, but I don't. I like it when you holler real loud and wake the dead."

*   *   *

Chance, who'd been listening to the exchange, bit the inside of his cheek to keep from laughing at the outraged look on Laurel's face. It was obvious she didn't like being compared to a screech owl or being told that she hollered. Which she most definitely did.

"Whitey," he said, coming to stand behind his cousin's chair before the guileless man could get him into any more trouble. "Laurel's trying to write a letter. Leave her be and go see if Jup needs any help unloading the beer kegs."

Laurel's eyes narrowed at the amused expression on Chance's face. It rankled that he thought so little of her talent. Obviously, the man had absolutely no taste. "Whitey's not bothering me half as much as you are, Chance."

"Laurel's teaching me to write. I might even write my mama a letter when I learn, Chance. Do you think she would like that?"

Chance doubted that Aletha Rafferty would like anything having to do with her dimwitted son, but he refrained from saying so, especially in light of the hopeful look on Whitey's face. "She might."

The big man smiled. "I'll take this paper and pencil with me, Miss Laurel, and practice, practice, practice. I got to go find Jup now."

Chance took the seat Whitey had vacated. "I don't want to encourage Whitey about his mother, Laurel. The woman's a harridan. And she wouldn't welcome hearing from her son."

"How do you know that? Maybe she's sorry for the way she treated him."

Chance's face darkened as memories of his childhood washed over him. He'd gone to live with his aunt and Uncle Teddy after his parents had died of the influenza. Teddy had welcomed his brother's child with open arms, but Aletha had looked upon him as just another cumbersome burden.

Like Whitey.

How a mother could treat her only child so cruelly, Chance would never know. But Aletha never missed an opportunity to deride Whitey, slap him if he didn't do her bidding fast enough, or humiliate him in front of his friends and neighbors.

Chance had often come to his cousin's defense, which had usually earned him his own beatings with a large wooden spoon his aunt kept expressly for that purpose.

Though Uncle Teddy had disapproved of his wife's child-rearing methods, he'd been too weak of character to stand up to her.

Aletha had always professed to be a decent, Christian woman, and Chance had decided early on if she was an example of decency and morality, then he wanted no part of either. Give him a hardworking, honest whore any day. At least they didn't pretend to be something they weren't.

"Aunt Aletha is a bitch," he said finally. "She'd never be sorry for the beatings she gave or the cruel things she said. Aletha made Whitey's life a living hell."

"And yours as well?" She studied him intently, and though he shrugged indifferently, Laurel thought he'd been just as affected by his aunt's cruelty as his cousin had.

"I was a normal kid. I could handle my aunt's nastiness. Whitey was the one who didn't understand the name-calling and the beatings."

"Is that why you ran away?"

"I see Bertha's been running her mouth again."

"I was curious about your background, so I asked her a few questions."

He smiled to hide his unease, running his index finger up her arm, causing gooseflesh to erupt wherever he touched. "I always knew you were interested in me, angel. I'd be happy to satisfy your curiosity, or whatever else is itching you. Just name the time and place."

When Laurel pulled back and looked at him with disdain, Chance knew he'd succeeded in deflecting her probing questions. Discussing his miserable childhood was something he found intolerable and uncomfortable. He wasn't a man who laid his feelings, or his cards, on the table. Unless, of course, he was absolutely certain he'd come out the winner. He'd been told early on to keep his cards close to his chest and never to reveal a weakness.

"If you don't mind, I'm trying to write a letter to my sister. Since this time is my own, I can choose how I wish to spend it. And I've chosen not to spend it with you."

"You're hard on a man's ego, Laurel."

"With an ego as big as yours, I doubt you'll suffer much." She smiled sweetly, and he threw back his head, laughing loudly at the insult.

Indignant, Laurel quickly pointed out, "Only a moron laughs when he's insulted, which doesn't say much for you."

"The way I see it, angel, if you weren't interested, you wouldn't be making insults." He stood to leave. "Don't tarry now, Laurel. I can't wait to see you all decked out in your finery again. You've got the prettiest pair of—"

"Really, Mr. Rafferty! Have you no decency?"

"—legs I've ever seen," he continued without interruption. "And no, angel. I've no decency whatsoever. You'd do well to remember that."

Insufferable, rude, horrible man! she thought. Grabbing her half-written letter, she proceeded to tell her sister just that.

Laurel paused at the office door and studied Chance as he plowed irritated fingers through his mass of dark hair. He was cursing mildly under his breath, and she knew immediately what had put that frustrated look on his face. He absolutely detested going over the saloon's receipts and ledgers.

"Jesus, Mary, and Joseph!" he cursed, throwing the pencil at the wall and wadding up the ledger sheet with the columns of figures that didn't add up.

"Up to your elbows in paperwork again, I see, and not

looking the least bit happy about it," Laurel remarked with a smile as she stepped into the room.

"You don't know how much I hate keeping these books, angel," he admitted, swiveling about in his chair, his eyes widening at the sight of her. "You look incredibly lovely today. Are you going out?"

She nodded. "I'm having lunch with Crystal, but we're not meeting for another hour. I'd be happy to help you with your bookkeeping. I'm very good with figures."

The prospect of spending an hour in close proximity to Laurel brought a smile to Chance's lips. "That's an offer I couldn't possibly refuse." He pulled a chair over for her and pushed the pile of paperwork toward her.

Leaning back in his chair, he observed the way she nibbled the end of the pencil while she studied the figures; the way she caught the tip of her tongue between her teeth as she added the impossible columns. It was a stimulating sight, making Chance realize how downright erotic bookkeepers could be.

Bending forward, so that his cheek brushed her own, he asked, "Is there anything you'd like me to do?"

Laurel shook her head. The enticing fragrance of Chance's cologne was rendering her light-headed. The brush of his arm against the side of her breast sent waves of awareness darting through the most shocking places.

Admittedly, she found Chance Rafferty too attractive and altogether too darn appealing, but she had no intention of adding to his pile of winnings, or satisfying that large appetite Pearl claimed he possessed.

She might be foolish, but felt certain that somewhere out there was her Prince Charming. Someday she would meet the man of her dreams. He would be kind, considerate, and treat her with love and respect. He'd be all the things she'd always dreamed the man she'd marry would be.

Laurel didn't know who her Prince Charming was yet, but she was pretty sure that he didn't own a saloon. And she was darn sure that he didn't consider women vessels for carnal pleasure and nothing more.

"That scent you're wearing is preventing me from concentrating on the work at hand, angel. You know that, don't you?"

His lips were so close to her neck and ear that she couldn't think straight, let alone add up a column of figures. He smelled of tobacco from the cheroots he was fond of smoking, and the manly scent played havoc with her emotions. Swallowing hard, she replied, "Then I shall purchase another kind at once."

He blew gently into her ear, and she nearly vaulted over the desk. "Stop that at once, or I'll be forced to quit this establishment. Do you hear me, Chance Rafferty?"

"I can think of far more pleasurable ways to idle away the afternoon than having lunch, angel."

"That's good," she retorted, "for your appetite is much too large as it is."

Laurel spied Crystal waiting on the corner as soon as she stepped out of the gambling saloon. Waving in greeting, she hurried her steps, wondering at the large, wide-brimmed hat her friend had chosen to wear for their outing. It was plain and rather conservative, not at all in keeping with Crystal's flamboyant style.

"Sorry I'm late, but I've been helping Chance with his bookkeeping."

"I didn't mind waiting, honey," Crystal said.

Focusing on her friend's face, Laurel gasped. "Crystal! What on earth happened to you? Your eye is black and blue and your cheek is swollen." She moved to touch the affected area, but Crystal pulled back.

"It's nothing. I ran into a door. I'm not usually so clumsy, but . . . ." She shrugged. "I guess I wasn't paying attention. It'll be fine in a few days."

Now Laurel understood the reason for the hat, though she wasn't sure she believed Crystal's explanation. Crystal moved with an elegant, catlike grace. There didn't seem to be a clumsy bone in her entire body, though Laurel had seen evidence before of bruises and lacerations. "Are you sure that's all it is, Crystal? I'm your friend, and if you need help, you know you can count on me."

"There's nothing you can do. Now, let's go have lunch. I'm absolutely starved, and I don't have much time. Al wants me back at the club earlier than usual."

"Do you have a . . . ah, a special appointment?" Laurel felt her cheeks warming. Discussing Crystal's work always left her embarrassed and tongue-tied.

"Al's determined to build another saloon. One that will rival Chance's place. I'm to soften up the mayor, bring him around to Al's way of thinking, so to speak."

Laurel clasped her friend's arm, halting her in midstride. "You don't have to continue working for Al if you don't want to, Crystal. I'm sure Chance would give you a job at the Aurora, no strings attached. I'll talk to him if you like."

Fear entered Crystal's pale blue eyes, and Laurel cringed in response to it.

"You mustn't do that, Laurel. I appreciate your offer of help, but I'm content to stay with Al for the time being. I can handle him. Sometimes his temper gets out of control, but he usually treats me pretty good."

She knew Al would never let her go. He'd told her numerous times that he would hunt her down and kill her if she ever tried to leave him. Al was possessive, obsessively so, and she was his most prized possession at the moment. And if she were to leave Al to go to work for Chance, his biggest rival . . . She shuddered, unwilling to imagine the consequences.

"You didn't run into a door, did you, Crystal? Al put those bruises on your face, and the others I've seen from time to time."

Crystal looked embarrassed at having lied to her friend. "Al was angry, but he apologized afterward." Al was always sorry after the beatings. And though he swore on a stack of Bibles that he'd never lift a hand to her again, the beatings always continued.

Having never been subjected to such violence, Laurel was uncertain what to say, but she knew someone had to talk sense to Crystal, and she would have to be that someone. "I know you care for Al, Crystal. And maybe you even think you love him. But you can't allow him to treat you like this. It isn't right. Perhaps if you leave, he'll come to his senses and realize what a big mistake he's made."

"I can't leave Al. Please don't ask me for details. Just believe me when I say that I have no choice."

Laurel's eyes widened at the implication. "Are you saying that he might do more than beat you if you were to leave?"

Crystal's laughter was derisive. "He already hits me, so I guess the next step would be . . ." She paused, for they'd reached the café and there were customers milling about the doorway. "I'm not willing to find out, Laurel, if he'd . . . you know. He's threatened as much, but I'm sure he's just blowing off steam."

Nothing else was said about the matter, but Laurel was consumed both with fear for her friend's safety and with finding a way to get Crystal out of her present predicament and occupation.

CHAPTER 7

Al Hazen was having a bad day. Crystal had gone to meet the Martin woman for lunch; the mayor had canceled their meeting for later today; and Rafferty's business had doubled since the opera singer had gone to work for him.

Laurel Martin's fresh-faced innocence and obvious naïveté had attracted customers to the Aurora Borealis in droves. She was a memory of all things pure and unsullied—sisters, mothers, sweethearts—all rolled into one lovely little package. She was the promise of virginity—a rare and valuable commodity in Denver's tenderloin district. And even her association with Crystal, a known whore, had not besmirched her reputation. If anything, the oddity of their friendship had made her all the more fascinating.

Al's frown deepened. Things were not going well at all, and it was Laurel Martin's fault. Ever since she'd come to town his luck had changed. She was bad luck, that's what she was. The Martin woman had come to town and taken all his good luck and given it to Rafferty. He gulped down a tumbler of whiskey, ignoring the raucous music of the orchestra in the corner.

They were playing "Camptown Races" and a couple of the girls were stripping out of their skimpy costumes for the few customers in attendance, but even the sight of their naked breasts and plump behinds couldn't bring a smile to Al's face.

He'd been jinxed, pure and simple. And when a gambling man was jinxed there was only one thing to do: get rid of the curse.

But with Laurel under Rafferty's protection, she was out of his grasp for the moment. A head-on confrontation with Rafferty and his giant of a cousin was not his style. He preferred a more underhanded approach to exacting his revenge.

One day he'd get even with all of them. One day he'd have the Martin woman right where he wanted her—under his thumb. It was only a matter of time and patience.

Pouring another drink from the half-empty bottle on the table, Al acknowledged the seductive smile of the ebony-skinned whore who strutted her stuff with wild abandon. Her tits were bouncing to beat the band, and she kept rubbing her crotch and smiling at him in invitation.

He'd never had him a nigger wench before, Al realized, feeling his member harden at the thought of plunging himself between the woman's firm thighs. His eyes remained glued to her big breasts, and he suddenly had a craving to taste some sweet brown meat.

Knowing Crystal wouldn't be back for at least another hour, Al grabbed the whiskey bottle and headed for the stairs, motioning for the woman to follow.

"You're doing so much better with your letters, Whitey," Laurel said. "You've almost accomplished the *D*. I think you should feel very proud of yourself."

Pearl paused at the top of the stairs and looked down at the

two people seated at one of the card tables. Their heads were
bent in concentration, and she almost puked at the look of
pure adoration she saw on Whitey Rafferty's face. It was obvious that the dimwit was as taken with Miss Prim and
Proper as Chance appeared to be.

Well, two could play at that game, she thought, a calculating smile transforming her frown. She could just as easily in-
struct Whitey in learning the alphabet, and at the same time
ingratiate herself with his handsome cousin, earning Chance's
undying gratitude and perhaps his love.

"Looks like you two are hard at work," she said as she approached the table. "What are you doing, Laurel, making out
a grocery list for Bertha?"

Laurel sucked in her breath, doing her utmost not to lose
her temper. She knew she should be used to Pearl's nasty
comments by now, but still the woman managed to get her
dander up.

"Miss Laurel's teaching me my letters, Miss Pearl. I'm
learning to write the alphabet," Whitey informed her
proudly.

Pearl leaned down close to the man, placing her hand on
the back of his neck. "Well isn't that nice, sugar. But you
should have come to me for help, if you wanted to learn your
letters." She toyed with the hair at his nape, then the lobe of
his ear, almost laughing aloud when he squirmed restlessly
in his seat. "We've been friends a whole lot longer, sugar.
Pearl would be happy to teach you anything you'd like to
learn."

Whitey stared at the buxom woman and beamed. "Really,
Miss Pearl? You'd do that for me?"

Patting his cheek, the whore smiled. "Of course, sugar.
After all, what are friends for?" With a spiteful smile at Laurel, she spun on her heel and headed for the bar.

Laurel relaxed the fingers she'd curled into fists as she
watched the bar girl walk away. It was all she could do not to
say something vile about the woman. But judging by the

look of pure delight on Whitey's face, she doubted that it would make a bit of difference to him. Obviously he was entranced by the woman's offer of friendship.

"We'd best get back to work, Whitey," she urged. "We've got lots more work ahead of us."

Whitey tore his gaze from Pearl's retreating figure and nodded. But his concentration was definitely not on learning his letters.

"You did real fine singin' tonight, Miss Laurel. I finally think you's gettin' the hang of this job."

Laurel smiled widely at Jupiter, who always went out of his way to praise her efforts, whether they'd been good or bad. Tonight she thought he was telling her the truth. The customers had actually seemed to enjoy her performance, except for the man in the front row who kept shouting vulgarities at her. Laurel frowned, thinking of the bearded giant.

His name was Shooter Davis, and he'd earned his nickname for shooting off his mouth at the least provocation. He was a frequent customer, always sitting in the row directly in front of the stage, especially on those occasions when Pearl entertained.

Several times in the past he had tried to grab on to Laurel's skirts when she ventured too close to the edge, but tonight he had lunged for her, nearly toppling her to the stage floor, and it had taken three men from the audience to haul him back to his seat.

She'd been terrified, and though Chance had given the man a tongue-lashing and a dire warning, Shooter had been drunk, and Laurel doubted if he'd paid much mind to the rebuke.

"I's going to turn in, Miss Laurel. There ain't many customers left, and Bertha be waiting. That woman can't keep her hands off me." Chuckling, Jup winked at Laurel, who couldn't help smiling as she watched him saunter away.

Jup and Bertha were truly in love, just like her mama and papa had been, and she hoped someday she'd have the same type of loving relationship with a man. She didn't intend to settle for anything less.

A quick glance about the room showed Laurel that Chance was still occupied in a card game with two of the customers. Whitey was standing at the bar talking with Bull, and most of the girls had either retired or had taken up with one of the customers for the evening.

Laurel considered going to the kitchen for a glass of milk and some of Bertha's oatmeal cookies, then decided instead to go upstairs and rest.

Tomorrow was Sunday, and she'd promised Flora Sue she would attend Reverend Baldwin's church service with her. Actually the invitation to church had surprised Laurel, for she didn't think Flora Sue was the spiritual type. The woman had practically gushed at the prospect of earning thirty dollars to spend the entire night with a miner.

Immersed in thought about her evening's performance, Laurel climbed the stairs. As her foot hit the top step, she was suddenly hauled up against a rock-hard chest and flattened against the wall, her mouth covered by a whiskey-smelling, callused hand. The man's beard brushed against her cheek, and she was immediately consumed by fear, for Laurel knew without a doubt that Shooter Davis had been lying in wait for her.

Panicked, she twisted her head from side to side, attempting to break the contact. She would not allow this foul-smelling creature to touch her.

"Calm down, little girl. Shooter just wants a peek at your titties. That ain't too much to ask for, now, is it? All them other girls show 'em to me. Don't think you're too good for Shooter, 'cause you ain't. And I know you've been wanting me to take a look-see."

With his free hand he began to tug on the bodice of her

gown, and Laurel heard the material rip as he yanked harder on it. Bile rose thickly in her throat.

He was going to rape her. If she didn't do something, he was going to rape her. Trying to remember all the things her papa had taught her about defending herself, Laurel brought her knee up, attempting to thrust it into the man's groin. It didn't hit the mark, but Shooter was startled enough to release her momentarily, which gave Laurel the chance to scream.

And scream she did. She screamed loud, long, and hard, praying that her voice, which had been accused of being able to wake the dead, now would.

"Shut up, little girl." Shooter tried to smother her cries with his lips, and Laurel tasted stale cigars and whiskey and thought she was going to retch. Twisting her head from side to side, she kicked at the man's legs, fighting him with every ounce of strength she possessed.

Why, oh why, didn't anyone hear her? There were people inside these rooms, yet no one came out to help. As if he could read her mind, Shooter laughed, placing his hand over her mouth again.

"They're all screwing their brains out, little girl. Just like you and me are going to be doing in a minute. I can't wait to get my hands inside that sweet little crotch of yours. I heard you ain't never been with a man, and I can't wait to bust your cherry." He reached up under her dress to cup her mound, and Laurel squeezed her eyes shut, shaking her head and silently screaming, *No!*

In the next instant, she found herself tossed flat on her back, and Shooter was no longer touching her. She opened her eyes to see Whitey holding him down, his knee lodged against the man's throat.

"You shouldn't be bothering Miss Laurel, Shooter," she heard the big man say.

A moment later Chance appeared. His expression was so

lethal it gave Laurel pause, and she swallowed at the sight of the derringer he pointed at Shooter.

"Are you all right, Laurel?" he asked, his voice as cold as tempered steel. "I heard your screams from downstairs and came as fast as I could."

"Yes." She sighed with relief, finally giving in to the tears of fright hovering in her eyes. "Thanks to Whitey, and now you." She smiled gratefully at the gentle giant.

"Did he hurt you, Miss Laurel?" Whitey's eyes were filled with concern for the woman who had befriended him. "I'll hurt him bad, if he did."

"I didn't do nothing, Chance," Shooter declared. "I was only having some fun with the little girl. I heard she wanted to . . ."

"Shut up, you bastard, or I'll pull this goddamn trigger." Chance hauled Shooter to his feet and handed him over to his cousin. "Take this bastard down to the police station, Whitey. Tell them he attacked one of the girls, but don't tell them which one." Having Laurel's name smeared all over the newspapers would serve no purpose, and he wanted to spare her further humiliation.

Whitey stared wide-eyed at Laurel, who was sobbing and clutching the edges of her gown together. "Is Miss Laurel okay, Chance? She's crying. Don't cry, Miss Laurel," the big man said, trying to comfort her.

"I'll tend to her, Whitey. You just take care of that piece of filth."

With a final concerned glance at the distraught woman, Whitey hauled Shooter down the stairs.

Chance knelt before Laurel. "Don't cry, angel," he crooned, caressing her cheek with his fingertip as he wiped away her tears—tears that seemed to go straight to his heart. "You're safe now." He pulled her into his arms, clutching her tightly to his chest, patting her back and head as if she were a small child. "He can't hurt you anymore."

"I'm . . . I'm all right," Laurel said, embarrassed to have

lost control. "He frightened me, that's all. I tried to defend myself like Papa taught me, but he was too tall and I couldn't reach his . . ."

Chance looked at her in surprise, then hauled Laurel to her feet, noting the rip in her gown. The bodice had been split, exposing her small, pert breasts to his view. The knowledge that Shooter had looked upon those breasts filled him with renewed rage. "Come on. I'll take you to your room."

"He ripped my dress," she said in a small voice.

"I'll buy you another. I'll buy you a dozen new dresses."

"There's no need. I can sew this one."

Pushing open her door, he escorted her inside and deposited her on the bed. "I'm going to burn this dress. I won't have any memories around to remind you of this night."

The vehemence in his voice surprised Laurel, and she looked up to find him staring intently at her. Concern flickered in the depths of his green eyes, as well as anger. But she knew his anger wasn't directed at her. "I'm all right now, truly I am. He didn't have time to . . ." She shivered violently, consumed with the aftermath of her ordeal.

Chance sat down next to her on the bed. "Turn around and I'll unhook your dress for you. I want you to get into bed." Laurel shook her head. "It's all right. I'm not going to do anything. I just want to help you undress."

Despite the impropriety of his suggestion, she couldn't bear the thought of him leaving just yet. He'd been so much kinder than she'd ever thought possible.

She turned her back to him, allowing him to unhook her gown. When he was finished, she ordered, "Now you turn around, so I can slip on my nightgown."

Peeling down the last of her undergarments, Laurel caught Chance's reflection in the mirror and sucked in her breath, realizing that he'd been watching her the entire time. Her cheeks crimsoned immediately at his ungentlemanly behavior, but her heart couldn't help but accelerate at the look of pure appreciation on his face. Obviously he liked what he saw.

Pretending she hadn't noticed, she slipped beneath the covers and pulled the quilt up to her chin. "All right. You can turn around now. I'm decent."

"I'll stay with you until you fall asleep."

This suggestion alarmed her. How on earth could she fall asleep knowing Chance was sitting next to her on the bed? Despite everything that had happened tonight, she was already too aware of him as a man. And as vulnerable as she felt, she didn't know if she could trust herself not to ask him to stay with her the entire night.

"There's no need, Chance. You can go. I'll be fine now."

He kissed her forehead in a brotherly fashion, but his lips soon trailed to her mouth and caressed her lips lightly. When she didn't protest, he deepened the contact, thrusting his tongue into her mouth. Laurel moaned, and he withdrew, a look of apology on his face.

"I'll go now," he said in a hoarse voice, gathering up the torn dress and heading for the door. "Good night, angel. Sleep tight. I'll be right down the hall if you need me."

Too afraid to speak, lest he hear the desire in her voice, she nodded, watching him slip out the door.

Closing her eyes, Laurel lay there listening to the sounds coming from the adjoining room where Flora Sue was entertaining her miner friend.

The headboard banged against the wall, there were cries of ecstasy punctuated by heavy breathing, and the bedsprings were twanging louder than Bert Swanzey's banjo strings. Laurel covered her ears, willing the noises to stop, praying that the uncomfortable tightening in her loins would go away, for it wasn't Flora Sue and her miner friend she pictured in the throes of ecstasy.

It was herself and Chance.

CHAPTER 8

She'd almost been raped.

The image of Shooter with his bearlike hands all over Laurel's small body still lingered, bringing Chance's simmering rage to the forefront and making his hands shake with uncontrollable fury.

The memory of Laurel vulnerable and afraid brought a wealth of protectiveness surging through him. He cared about her, much more than he wanted to admit even to himself. He knew that a woman like Laurel had no business working in a rowdy saloon like the Aurora. Instead, she should be married and have a passel of children clinging to her skirts. He knew instinctively that a nurturing, loving woman like Laurel would want lots of children.

His frown deepened. Even if he considered taking on the responsibility of a wife, he could never handle having to care for more children. Whitey, who was responsibility enough, was Chance's first priority. As helpless as his cousin was, he had to be.

And what kind of husband and father would he make anyway? He was a gambler. His friends were whores, cowboys, and other ne'er-do-wells. His lifestyle didn't lend itself to providing the right atmosphere for raising a family. And he certainly wasn't the kind of role model young children needed. Children needed a proper upbringing and a father they could look up to for guidance and respect. And Chance realized that he just wasn't that someone.

Gambling as a profession wasn't something he wanted to pass on to his kids. He didn't want to fool innocent, impressionable youngsters into thinking they could get by on their wits and skill like he had. He was fast becoming a dinosaur, soon to be extinct. A child growing up these days needed a good education, a vocation, a reliable way to earn a living.

Times were changing. The temperance movement was proof of that. And the movement was growing stronger, making it increasingly harder for men like him to earn a decent living. Soon, if things continued the way they were, his way of life would cease to exist, and then how would he meet the responsibilities of a wife and family?

He couldn't. He wouldn't. No matter how tempting, how much he desired Laurel, he just wasn't suited to marriage. But he wanted her, dammit! He wanted her.

Clutching the neck of a whiskey bottle as if it were a man's throat, Chance replaced it on the shelf and began to count the liquor stock. But halfway through the first row he lost count and had to start over.

Memories of last night washed over him again, making his temper flare anew. "Goddamn son of a bitch!" What had possessed Shooter to try such a thing? The man had been drunk, there was no denying that—Shooter drank himself into oblivion almost every night. But he'd never, to the best of Chance's knowledge, assaulted a woman before. He clawed at their skirts and made rude remarks, but it had never gone beyond that.

What if I hadn't heard Laurel's screams?

What if Whitey hadn't arrived in time to prevent Shooter from raping her?

What if . . . ?

"Chance."

At the sound of the feminine voice, he spun around so quickly that the whiskey bottle he held plummeted to his feet, splashing over his brand new calfskin boots.

"Laurel. Shit!"

"Oh! I'm sorry I startled you." The storage room was dimly lit, casting eerie shadows on the walls and floor, but there was still enough light for her to see Chance's irritation. He had a peculiar habit of cracking his knuckles when something bothered him, and he was cracking them like walnuts at the moment.

She had heard the note of surprise in his voice, as if he'd just conjured her up because he'd been thinking so hard about her. That notion pleased her. In fact, there was a lot about Chance that pleased her.

Last night had brought about that realization. And it wasn't just his handsome looks, the mischievous twinkle in his eyes, or the dimples when he smiled, which was often. Chance had been kind to her in his own way.

Sure, he teased her a lot. And maybe he didn't appreciate her singing—she frowned at that—but he had given her a job, a place to live, and a new wardrobe. And he was easy to talk to. Not stuffy or pompous like that smelly Mr. Witherspoon, but genuinely interested in what she had to say.

Chance had a big heart, though she doubted he'd ever admit it, and she found that awfully appealing in a rough-and-tumble gambling man.

Still . . . he just wasn't what a woman like her would consider marriage material. She needed someone hardworking and steadfast. Not a man who lived life according to the roll of the dice.

"Was there something you needed, angel?"

"Jup said I could find you here. I wanted to thank you for what you and Whitey did last night."

"Thank us?" Incredulous, he shook his head. "For saving you from that animal? That's hardly necessary. Besides, your screams are what saved you. I doubt I'll be making any more snide remarks about the shrill pitch of your voice."

Laurel should have been insulted, but she smiled instead, remembering how gentle he'd been with her. "I doubt you'll be able to restrain yourself from making nasty comments, Chance. Rudeness seems ingrained in you."

He ignored the jibe. "Are you feeling all right? You weren't injured . . . or anything?"

"No. I'm perfectly fine. And I'm even willing to forgive Shooter for what he did. I realize he was drunk last night."

"What Shooter did wasn't like him. Oh, he's loud and obnoxious, don't get me wrong. But I've never known him to hurt a woman before."

"*I heard she wanted to . . .*" Shooter's words picked at his memory, and his frown deepened as he tried to make sense of them.

"He was intoxicated. Mama always said that too much liquor made a good man mean and a mean man too stupid to remember he was mean."

He smiled at that. "Are you a lot like your mama, angel? Was she pretty like you?"

" 'Pretty is as pretty does,' Mama always said. Mama's prettiness stemmed from within. I guess she was what you'd call a handsome woman. She wasn't beautiful like my sister Heather, but more substantial like Rose Elizabeth.

"Rose is the most like Mama. She's a homebody who'd like nothing better than to stay on the farm and raise a passel of young'ns." Laurel wondered how her sister was faring with the new owner in residence. No doubt Rose Elizabeth was making his life unpleasant as all get-out. Rose didn't cotton much to strangers, and she was awfully possessive when it came to the farm.

Chance took a seat on the edge of the desk, eager to learn more about this enigmatic woman-child who fascinated him so. "But not you?"

"I wanted a career. Excitement." She laughed in a self-deprecating manner. "I guess I had my share of that last night."

He grasped her hand, pulling her toward him until she was standing between the vee of his legs. "You're something else, angel, you know that? Most women in similar circumstances would have gone to pieces, but you kept your head and held up admirably under the circumstances."

"I screamed my fool head off."

"But kept your wits. I seem to recall you saying last night that you had aimed your knee at Shooter's privates and missed."

"Papa taught us girls how to defend ourselves. He also taught us to fish, swear, and play poker. But only Rose Elizabeth curses. I think she does it most for the shock value."

"Poker, huh? My, you are full of surprises."

"There's a lot about me that would surprise you." No doubt it would surprise him to know that warm, tumultuous feelings emerged whenever she was near him. But, of course, she'd rather die than admit that to him.

Chance thought of the way her naked body had looked in the mirror last night—breasts that were tipped pink as spun cotton candy and probably just as sweet to the taste—and smiled. "You're right about that, angel. And I'm a man who enjoys a good surprise now and then." Drawing her into his arms, he kissed her, his lips playing over hers with nibbling caresses.

Though his kiss was gentle, almost restrained, it sent Laurel's stomach into a wild whirlpool of emotion. She leaned in to him, pressing her aching breasts against his chest, opening her mouth just a fraction to allow his tongue to slide in and mingle with her own. She felt giddy, drunk with passion, as if she'd just consumed the entire liquor supply in the storage shed.

When his hands molded her breasts, slowly circling the rigid points with his fingertips, Laurel could only gasp at the pleasure his touch elicited. But when they slid lower to cup her buttocks and pull her tighter to him, she felt the evidence of his desire pressing against her own. Sanity returned and she pulled away.

"You must stop. This . . . What we're doing is wrong."

"It felt pretty right to me, angel. In fact, it felt downright good."

She couldn't deny that. It felt too good even to admit! "Nevertheless, I'm not the type of woman who allows men like you to take liberties."

He released her, hugging his arms to his chest, willing his throbbing manhood to be still. He was hornier than he'd felt since he was an untried youth. "Do tell. What type of man am I?"

"You're experienced. And used to having women fall all over you. I heard you were insatiable and used to dallying with just about anything in skirts. Contrary to what you may think, I'm not an easy mark, Chance. I want more out of a relationship than a tumble in the hay."

The pulse in his neck started throbbing to match the one in his loins. "Really?" Like marriage, no doubt. Decent women always insisted on marriage before pleasure. Why couldn't a woman just learn to take her pleasure like a man and enjoy it, without the guilt, without the benefit of vows?

"I'm saving myself for the right man. Somewhere out there is my Prince Charming. I know it sounds silly," she said when his eyebrow arched so high it nearly touched his hairline, "but I know that someday he'll come along to sweep me off my feet."

"Will he carry a broom, or merely ride in on a white charger?"

"Now you're mocking me."

"There's no such thing as Prince Charming, angel. That stuff's just in fairy tales. I learned a long time ago that you take happiness whenever and wherever you can find it. If you wait for it to come to you, you'll be waiting the rest of your life." He caressed her cheek with his fingertip. "We could have a great deal of happiness, if you'd just give in to what you're feeling—act on your emotions."

She stiffened, her hands clenched at her sides. "I guess I don't equate happiness with a roll in the hay, the way you do."

His dimpled smile made her breath catch in her throat. "That's because you've never tried it, angel. There's much to recommend about a mutually satisfying relationship between a man and a woman."

"How would you know I've never tried it? A woman doesn't wear her innocence like a banner, flying behind her in the wind."

His laughter made her blood boil. "A man knows when there's a virgin in his midst. Why in hell do you think Al Hazen was so eager to talk to you that first day? He smelled your innocence clear across the café. A virgin brings a tidy sum to a man in his line of work."

"You're disgusting. And crude." She turned to leave.

"Grow up, angel. The world is an ugly place, and if you walk around with your head in the clouds, you're likely to lose it."

Pausing by the door, she turned to look back. "Better to lose my head in the clouds than to lose my virginity to you, Mr. Rafferty."

"Will you look at the way Pearl's fawning over Whitey?" Flora Sue remarked to Laurel later that afternoon. They had just returned from church and were seated in the gambling parlor, sharing a pot of tea and a plate of Bertha's corn muffins left over from last night's supper.

Since it was Sunday, the Aurora was closed for business, but those employees who didn't have families or anywhere else to go generally hung around the saloon to make their own amusements.

"It appears that she's trying to teach him his letters," Laurel replied, unable to keep the hurt out of her voice. "I started to teach him, but then Whitey said Pearl had offered, and he wanted her to do it."

Flora snorted. "Pearl thinks Whitey's as dumb as a box of rocks. The only reason she offered to help is to impress Chance. She's hot for him. And poor Whitey's always been a bit infatuated with Pearl. She teases him something awful."

"We shouldn't judge her too harshly, Flora. Perhaps she's really trying to do some good." And Whitey seemed to be reveling in the attention. The big man was hanging on her every word.

Flora patted Laurel's hand and shook her head. "I don't know what I'm going to do with you, doll baby. You're like a little lamb who's been thrust into a den of wolves. If you're not careful, you're going to get eaten alive. Even Sue Ellen, who's afraid of her own shadow and rarely speaks above a whisper, thinks you're naive."

Laurel tried her best not to feel insulted. Sue Ellen Turner worked alongside Flora Sue and was her best friend. She was a mousy, quiet girl, hardly suited to working in a noisy saloon like the Aurora. But the poor woman had been recently widowed with two small children to care for, and she hadn't been able to find work anywhere else. Chance had put her on a few weeks back to keep her and her kids from being evicted from their home.

It had been a nice thing to do, and Laurel realized that Chance often did nice things for others, like that parson's box he kept for Reverend Baldwin, and the frilly parasol he'd purchased one afternoon for Bertha. The black woman had blubbered like a baby over that blue satin parasol, insisting that it was the finest thing she'd ever owned in her life.

Remembering Chance's pleased expression brought a queer ache to Laurel's chest, and her hand went up to cover her heart.

"You look like you're a million miles away, doll baby." Flora's comment brought Laurel's attention back to the conversation at hand.

"You and Sue Ellen are entitled to your opinions, Flora. But I don't think you heard a thing Reverend Baldwin said at church services. We're to love our neighbors, and forgive those who sin against us. Remember?"

A seductive smile curved Flora's lips. "Just sitting in that man's church makes me feel sinful as hell. Gus Baldwin is a handsome man. And so, so dignified."

Laurel was shocked. "Is that why you wanted to attend church today? For shame, Flora Sue. The man is a preacher, for heaven's sake!"

"It ain't right for a man to be so moral and upright. I think it's my duty to introduce the reverend to some of the more delightful things in life . . . like myself."

Flora's smile was so smug that Laurel could only shake her head and laugh. Flora Sue had turned out to be a good friend, and Laurel wasn't about to ruin that friendship by lecturing to her about things she probably had never been taught as a child.

It made Laurel all the more grateful for the wonderful upbringing she'd had, and for the loving family who'd always supported, loved, and been there for her. Thinking about her sisters brought a lump to her throat. She missed them something awful, much more than she'd ever thought possible.

She had been so eager to strike out on her own, but she'd discovered the hard way that independence and loneliness were poor substitutes for the love of a family who cared.

"Am I doing it right, Miss Pearl? Miss Laurel says my *F*'s are improving."

"Pay no mind to what that woman tells you, sugar," Pearl

said, her eyes drifting to Laurel and that traitor, Flora Sue. "I'm your friend and I'm going to teach you the correct way to write the alphabet." She leaned in closer, so that her hair brushed his cheek.

"You sure do smell good, Miss Pearl."

Pearl's lips curved in a calculating smile, and she patted Whitey's slightly flushed cheek, wondering if impressing Chance was really worth all the effort she'd been putting out.

Teaching an idiot his letters was far beyond the call of duty as far as she was concerned. Though to be honest, Whitey Rafferty was a handsome idiot. There weren't many men with shoulders as wide or arms as powerful and muscular. He was almost as handsome as Chance, except for that vacant look in his eyes.

She had always enjoyed teasing Whitey, wondering if he had the same kind of sexual urges as normal men. She had an innate curiosity to see if Whitey's manhood was as big as the rest of him. But she knew if she overstepped her bounds and tried to find out, Chance would bounce her out on her rear faster than she could bat an eyelash. Chance didn't allow any woman to get too close to his precious cousin.

An incident had occurred a while back where one of the serving girls had kissed Whitey full on the lips on a dare made by one of the customers. Chance had witnessed the episode and fired the girl on the spot.

Pearl had no intention of allowing that to happen to her. She had plans to ensnare Chance Rafferty. And remembering those plans, she plastered a sweet smile on her face and waved at her employer, pleased when he accepted the invitation to join them.

"What are you up to, Pearl? I never took you for the studious type," Chance said when he approached, squeezing his cousin's shoulder affectionately.

"Why, I've volunteered to help Whitey learn his letters. The poor man was so disappointed when Laurel refused to help him anymore that I just had to offer."

"But . . ." Whitey began, but Pearl clasped his hand.

"There's no need to thank me, sugar. I'm happy to do it. Would you care to sit with us, Chance?"

Catching sight of Laurel across the room, the gambler shook his head. "No. I've got things to attend to."

Noting where his attention focused, Pearl smiled smoothly through clenched teeth. "You just run along, then. Me and Whitey have lots of work to do today. Don't we, sugar?"

Whitey's confusion was soon overshadowed by Pearl's willingness to help, and he nodded. "Yes'm, Miss Pearl. We surely do."

Once Chance was out of earshot, Pearl asked, "You like me, don't you, Whitey?"

He looked at her with adoration and undying affection, the way a puppy looks at his master. "I like you real fine, Miss Pearl. You're about the purtiest woman I ever did see."

"Does Chance think I'm pretty, too?"

"Sure he does. He said you got the biggest set of jugs this side of the Mississippi. What does that mean, Miss Pearl?"

Pearl laughed and squeezed his knee. "Perhaps one day I'll show you, Whitey. But for now we must continue with our lessons. You do want to learn to write, don't you?"

He nodded with childlike enthusiasm. "Yes'm. I want to write my mama a letter."

"And will you tell her all about me?"

"Yes'm. I'm going to tell her about how you taught me to make my letters, and how nice you been to me."

"And will you tell Chance, too, Whitey?"

She waited while he considered the request, knowing that Whitey's flattering opinion of her was sure to impress his cousin. Chance set great store by Whitey and was always pleased when anyone befriended him. He was sure to think she was far more generous and kind than Laurel.

"Yes'm, Miss Pearl, if you want me to."

"You're a lot smarter than I gave you credit for, sugar."

Whitey beamed under the praise. "Yes'm! I'm smart, smart, smart."

*   *   *

Gamblers were a superstitious lot, and Chance was no exception. He credited his recent winning streak to having Laurel close by, and it also gave him the opportunity to keep an eye on her, so there wouldn't be any repeats of what had happened to her the previous week.

He checked his cards, made his bet, then looked around to locate her. She was seated next to Jupiter on the piano bench, joining the musician in a duet about lost love, or some such drivel, and he breathed a sigh of relief.

Chance shook his head, wondering why women always had to fill their heads with sentimental bullshit. *Prince Charming, my ass.* Laurel would be a virgin till the day she died if she waited around for her prince to put in an appearance. And that would be a damn waste of prime womanly flesh.

"Your bid, Rafferty," Silas Tucker called out. "You gonna play poker or daydream? I swear I never seen you with your head so far up your ass before."

The men at the table laughed, and Chance felt heat rise above his white, starched collar. "I could beat you sorry sons of bitches with one hand tied behind my back and my head clean up my ass." He bet a twenty-dollar gold piece to prove his point, and somebody whistled shrilly.

"Too rich for my blood," one man claimed.

"You're a lucky bastard, Rafferty," Tucker said, throwing down his cards.

Chance smiled, his half-smoked cheroot dangling from the corner of his mouth as he pulled in the sizable pot. "Yes, I am, boys. Especially since I bluffed you with a pair of eights and threes. I am one lucky man."

But the next night, Chance's luck seemed to have run out. He lost the first three hands in less than an hour, accumulating losses of over three hundred dollars, and he wasn't at all pleased. He looked to find his lucky charm, but there was no sign of her, and he wondered where she was.

He'd discovered quite by accident that he seemed to win whenever she was nearby and to lose whenever she left the premises. It was the damnedest thing, but he was superstitious enough not to question it.

Irritated at having lost again, he threw down his cards, excused himself from the game with a promise to return shortly, and made his way to the bar.

"Where'd Laurel go, Bull? Isn't she supposed to be on stage soon?" He snapped open his pocket watch and realized she still had thirty minutes before her performance.

"Said she was hungry," the bartender explained over his shoulder, pouring two fingers of whiskey into a glass and pushing it across the bar toward a customer. "She's gone to the kitchen for something to eat."

That small woman could eat more than a herd of hungry bison, Chance thought, worried about how long she would be gone. "Well, fetch her quick. I'm losing my ass over yonder." He indicated the poker table by the window.

Bull scratched his head, a puzzled look on his face as he gazed across the smoke-clouded room, wondering why Chance was so on edge tonight. Business was good. The saloon was packed, with hardly an empty chair in sight, and the roulette wheel spun continuously, the click of the ball a reassuring sound. And liquor sales were brisk. They were making money hand over fist, as the saying went.

"What's Laurel got to do with your losing?"

Chance sighed, not about to reveal his latest eccentricity. "Just get her. I need to talk to her."

"You're the boss."

A few minutes later, Laurel stood to the left of Chance's shoulder, looking terribly ill-at-ease. "Bull said you wanted to talk to me."

"Just stand there a minute. I'm almost done with this hand."

"But I've really got to go, Chance." She shifted impatiently from one foot to the other, but Chance gave no indication that he noticed her discomfort.

Apologizing to the other players at the table, he leaned over to whisper to Laurel, "You can't go. I need to win this hand, and I want you here for luck."

"I'm flattered. Truly I am. But I wasn't kidding. I really have to go." She implored him to understand, biting her lower lip in anguish. If she didn't get to the privy soon . . .

"You can't leave!"

He turned back to the game, and Laurel stared daggers at his back, crossing her ankles to alleviate some of the pressure. She had to go. And she had to go now.

"I'll be right back," she said, dashing toward the rear of the building.

"Laurel!" Chance called out, cursing under his breath when his winning hand suddenly fizzled right before his eyes. "Goddammit," he cursed, shaking his head and ignoring the curious glances in his direction.

"Women!" They didn't understand a damn thing about poker.

"I refuse to stand here one more minute, Chance Rafferty," Laurel said four nights later. "This nonsense about me being tied to your luck has got to stop."

Everyone at the Aurora had gotten a real hoot out of Chance's latest superstition. Everyone except Laurel, who resented being tied to Chance's side night after night like a token cube of dice.

"Just keep quiet and blow on the cards for luck."

"I'll do no such thing! Why, that's disgusting. Not to mention downright ridiculous," she said.

Excusing himself from the game, Chance grasped Laurel by the arm and dragged her through the front door to stand outside on the sidewalk. The night air was chilled. Autumn had arrived and with it cooler days and brisk evenings. "I'm paying your wages, angel. I'm the boss, remember? What I say goes."

"You're paying me to sing for your customers, not to blow on cards and act stupid." Laurel shivered, rubbing at the gooseflesh sprouting over her arms, and cursed the skimpiness of her costume.

"Angel," he said, caressing her cheek, his voice full of entreaty. "A gambler's luck hinges on many things. Right now mine's hinging on you. Can't you just humor me for a while? I can't afford to lose. You wouldn't want me to have to get rid of some of the girls because I couldn't afford to pay their wages, now, would you?"

Sparks of blue fire flashed from Laurel's eyes. "That's blackmail, Rafferty. You're just trying to play on my sympathies to get your own way."

He picked up her hand, and Laurel's breath quickened. "Please, angel. I'm sure my winning streak can't last forever, and it's a small enough favor to ask. After all, I did come to your rescue not long ago."

She pulled her hand out of his grasp and stifled the urge to kick him where she tried to kick Shooter Davis. "Oh, all right. But I'm not going to blow on the cards. I'll stand at your side, place your bets for you. I'll even whisper sweet nothings in your ear. But I'll be damned if I'll blow on your stupid cards."

"I could think of something downright outrageous to say right about now, angel, but I doubt you'd understand." She had a mouth meant for pleasure, there was no denying that.

"I'm not sure I understand you at all, Chance Rafferty, and I'm not entirely certain that I want to."

His laughter followed her all the way back to the table.

Chance's winnings over the next few weeks added some "improvements" to the Aurora. Or so he thought.

Laurel certainly did not approve of the five-foot-long oil painting of a naked woman that hung on the back wall, right next to the sign that read: THESE DICE GUARANTEED TO BE SQUARE. She felt mortified every time she passed it on her way up the stairs.

There was also the matter of the stereoscopic device, which had just arrived. It was without a doubt the most shocking piece of equipment Laurel had ever laid eyes on.

If one looked through the eyepiece, which she had unknowingly done, much to Chance's utter delight and amusement, three-dimensional pictures appeared. Obscene pictures of naked women in various erotic poses.

"What do you think, angel? Isn't this the most splendid invention? You seem to be as taken with it as I am." He dusted the apparatus with his hankie, as if it were some prized piece of art from a museum.

Laurel's face flamed. "You are a vile human being, Chance Rafferty. Have you no shame? No morals? Why—there are naked women in those pictures!"

He'd seemed inordinately pleased by her observation. "Prime womanly flesh, each and every one."

"The men are going to love it, Laurel," Bull assured her, taking Chance's side as he always did when they disagreed in front of him.

"If this is what your good luck buys, Chance, then I'll be no part of it," she said with disgust, holding herself righteously erect. "I intend to inform the reverend about your depravity."

Both men laughed uproariously, fueling Laurel's temper even more, and she marched down to the makeshift church to make good on her threat.

CHAPTER 9

"Well, look who's here." Laurel was unable to keep the smug tone out of her voice as she watched Reverend Baldwin stroll into the Aurora.

The clergyman had been a good listener when she'd visited his church the previous day, and Laurel had no doubt that the good reverend would be able to persuade Chance to get rid of the hated stereoscopic device.

Having been raised a Christian, Laurel felt it was her duty to save the souls of those unwitting individuals who might be exposed to Chance's obscene painting and pornographic photos. It was one thing to condone gambling and drinking, but obscenity—never!

Although he'd made no guarantees of success in influencing Chance, she felt confident that the clergyman could make the gambler see the error of his ways.

Reverend Baldwin had a way with people. Even when he was shouting fire and brimstone from his pulpit, which was really just a modified beer barrel—the church was housed in an old, abandoned liquor warehouse—his parishioners knew he was their friend. He had a comforting, caring demeanor that Laurel found oddly refreshing in a man of the cloth.

Pastor Bergman back in Salina was so intimidating that no sinner would ever dare admit a transgression to him for the pastor was likely to condemn the sinner to eternal damnation. Pastor Bergman was very big on eternal damnation.

"Afternoon, Gus." Chance motioned the man forward to the bar. "Care for a drink?"

Removing his coat and tossing it on a nearby chair, Gus was about to reply in the affirmative when his gaze caught the painting Laurel was so incensed about. The subject of the painting, a well-endowed, fleshy woman reclined on a daybed of red velvet, wearing nothing more than a seductive smile. She reminded Gus of the subjects the Flemish painter Rubens had captured.

"I see you've acquired some artwork, Chance," Gus remarked, lifting his brow ever so slightly as he continued to study the painting, his hands clenched behind his back.

"I believe you'll agree with me, Reverend, that that horrible painting and awful device will corrupt the mind and soul of everyone who comes in contact with them. And I . . ." Before Laurel could say another word, Percy the parrot squawked loudly, flapping his wings against the cage.

"*Naked women!*" Squawk. "*Look at those tits. My dick's hard.*" Squawk.

"Shut up, you stupid bird," Laurel shouted, her face flaming as the bird's comments grew more outrageous.

"*Smart-ass virgin.*" Squawk. "*Smart-ass virgin.*" Squawk.

There was little doubt where the bird had learned that lovely ditty, and Laurel shot Chance a condemning look.

"Now, now, angel," Chance said, trying to hide his smile. "Is that any way to pick on a poor, defenseless parrot?"

Poor Percy." Squawk. "*Give me some tongue, babe.*"

"Oooh!" Laurel screamed, her fists clenched for battle as

she stepped toward the offensive bird. "I'll give you something else, you wicked feather-brained creature."

"I'd like to have a look at your stereoscopic device, Chance," Gus said quickly, hoping to save poor Percy from imminent death. "I'm not familiar with them, but Laurel informs me that they contain obscene renderings of unclothed women." He impaled Chance with a censorious look. "I hope that's not the case."

Chance had the grace to look embarrassed. "It's a harmless enough amusement, Gus. The customers love it."

Walking over to the device, which Laurel indicated with her outstretched arm, the reverend peered into the viewer. It seemed to Laurel that he took an inordinate amount of time to form an opinion about it.

"Isn't it the most evil thing you've ever seen, Reverend Baldwin?" she prompted. "My mama would roll over in her grave if she knew I was working in a place that had such a sinful contraption."

Gus removed his handkerchief from his back pocket, but rather than cough into it, as he usually did, he mopped droplets of perspiration off his flushed face. "I suppose in France one would call this type of thing art—"

"See, angel, I told you he wouldn't object."

"But this is not France, and I'm afraid I would have to agree with Laurel on this matter, Chance. This device smacks of obscenity and can no way be misinterpreted as art."

"But, Gus . . ." Chance's smile soured. He respected Gus's opinion, hated to go against it, but business was business. "I'm afraid I have to disagree."

Not about to give up easily, Laurel pointed a condemning finger at the reclining nude. "What about the painting? Aren't you going to mention that?" Crossing her arms over her chest, she waited for the good reverend to admonish Chance about his other disgusting diversion.

She was therefore quite shocked when he replied, "I rather

like it myself, Laurel. It's tastefully done, and I don't think it would offend anyone's sensibilities. Many great artists have sculpted and painted subjects in the altogether, my dear. It's very European in nature."

"Well, I guess I'm just a dumb farm girl, Reverend, because it sure as shootin' offends my sensibilities. If I want to see a naked woman I can look in the mirror."

"We all don't have that pleasure or privilege, angel," Chance quickly pointed out, and the look he gave her sent tingles down her spine . . . and lower.

Sensing that things were about to explode, Gus cleared his throat nervously. "This is Chance's establishment, Laurel, and he has every right to run it as he sees fit. I can only make recommendations and offer guidance. The final decision must remain his."

"How nice for someone to remember that." Chance stared daggers at Laurel, wishing he could pierce her prudish shell. The woman was rapidly becoming a thorn in his backside.

"I suppose you're correct, Reverend. And if Chance is going to be totally mule-headed about those obscenities . . ." She shrugged. "Well, it's his soul that's headed straight for eternal damnation."

"Yes, well . . ." Feeling vastly uncomfortable, but grateful that the ordeal was over, Gus loosened his collar and accepted the drink the bartender pushed toward him. Some sixth sense told him there was more to the animosity between Chance and Laurel than just a nude painting and a few obscene photographs.

"To show there're no hard feelings, angel, I'm going to call that painting *The Opera Singer,* as a tribute to you."

Laurel and Bull reached for the whiskey bottle at the same time, but Bull was quicker at anticipating Laurel's intent and prevented her from firing her intended missile at Chance.

Deprived of the pleasure of smashing the bottle over his head, Laurel walked up to Chance and, as hard as she could, kicked him square in the shin, feeling somewhat mollified when he winced in pain.

"Hey! What'd you do that for?"

"Kick his ass, girlie," Percy blurted, and Chance shot the parrot a lethal look, rubbing his bruised leg.

"There'll be more of that, Rafferty, if you so much as breathe my name in conjunction with that . . . that vile piece of so-called art." Turning on her heel, Laurel marched toward the stairs, ignoring the painting and the trio of men who looked after her with surprise and admiration.

"Well I'll be damned," Chance muttered, rubbing his shin, his eyes glued on Laurel's attractive backside as she climbed the stairs.

"There's not a doubt in my mind about that," the reverend agreed. "Not a single one."

Returning from the post office, Flora Sue smiled as she handed Laurel the letter that had just arrived. "Lucas asked me to deliver it, doll baby. I hope you don't mind, but I figured if you waited on him to deliver it, you might not get it till next month."

Lucas Willowby, the postmaster, was notorious for being inefficient at delivering the mail. A reputation well deserved, as far as Flora Sue was concerned. The last issue of the *Montgomery Ward Catalogue* she'd received had been at least six months out of date, and by the time she'd sent in her order for a dozen frilly garters and a black lace corset, the company had been out of stock.

"I think it's from your sister," Flora added. "The postmark reads San Francisco."

Laurel's eyes were lit with excitement as she saw the familiar handwriting. Grabbing Heather's letter, she headed up the stairs, eager to have an excuse to leave the parlor and Chance's annoying company.

Since the reverend's appearance that morning, Chance had

been making impertinent comments, accusing her of being prudish and a tattletale.

A tattletale! Of all the nerve! She'd never been a tattletale in all her life. It was always Rose Elizabeth who tattled on everyone. Laurel had usually been the one to get switched because of something Rose claimed she'd done. Most of the time it was the truth, but Rose still shouldn't have told.

Plopping down on her bed, Laurel tore open the envelope. It had been many weeks since Heather and Laurel had parted company at the train station in Salina, and she was eager to hear all about Heather's exciting job as an illustrator.

No doubt Heather had succeeded where she had failed. It had always been like that when they were growing up. Heather had received the better grades, the effusive praise from her parents, even the prettiest figure. But it was Laurel who had gotten the beaus. For some reason no one could ever figure out, Heather had never been all that successful when it came to attracting men. Even Rose Elizabeth, who was a tad overweight—her mama had called her "pleasingly plump"—had never lacked for suitors.

She turned her attention to the letter.

Dear Laurie,
　Your letter was a welcome interruption into my daily routine. San Francisco is an exotic place—a real melting pot of fascinating people—but I'm afraid that even as large and cosmopolitan a city as it is, male prejudice against women prevails and I have been unable to find a job as an illustrator.

Laurel felt a deep disappointment for her sister; she knew how much art meant to Heather.

　I have secured employment as a governess to a divorced man with two children.

Laurel reread the sentence. Divorced! How shocking.

Heather had always set the standard for the three sisters, and Laurel couldn't imagine her sister working for such an individual. Divorce was not an accepted practice, no matter how extenuating the circumstances, though Laurel knew that Heather was very open-minded about such things.

Brandon Montgomery could give your Mr. Rafferty lessons in the art of arrogance and stubbornness. His twin children—a boy and girl—are adorable, but he's too mule-headed to see how his strict regimen has turned them into sullen little people who crave their father's love and affection.

I have just nursed them all, including Mr. Montgomery, through a bout of the measles. Remember when you and Rose Elizabeth were covered in them?

Laurel nodded absently and scratched her arms, remembering only too well. What a misery that had been!

Mr. Montgomery owns one of the largest newspapers in the city, so I haven't given up hope that one day I'll be able to convince him of my abilities as an artist. Though that must remain a secret for the time being.

For now I must content myself with teaching his children to draw and instructing his Celestial cook in learning to read and write English. Mr. Woo is quite a challenge.

Rose's letter arrived shortly after yours, and I must say I am very disappointed in her behavior. The English duke will have his hands full trying to rid himself of Rose. No doubt she's burrowed into the farm like ticks on a dog. I intend to write her at once.

I pray your present situation is only temporary and that you'll be able to find work as an opera singer. I confess that when I try to picture you singing in a saloon, I cannot.

Laurel glanced at the walnut wardrobe filled with gaudy gowns and high-heeled shoes and wondered what her sister would think if she knew the kind of costumes she was required to wear. Heather had always been very conservative in her choice of dress and would no doubt be shocked by Laurel's attire.

Thank goodness she'd never told Heather about that sordid incident involving Shooter Davis. If she had, Heather would have been on the first train to Denver in nothing flat to drag Laurel back with her to San Francisco.

The rest of the letter was filled with motherly advice about eating properly and getting plenty of rest. It was signed with X's and O's, and Laurel's sigh was wistful as she refolded the note and placed it carefully in the drawer of the nightstand.

So far only one of the Martin sisters had succeeded in fulfilling her dream: Rose Elizabeth still lived on the farm.

Jup spotted Bertha at the kitchen sink, washing dishes and humming her favorite spiritual, and paying no attention to anything going on around her.

Slowly sneaking up behind his wife, Jup swatted her gently on the backside. "What you up to, woman?" He chuckled as she jumped in fright, then he stepped back to avoid the slap that was sure to follow.

Clutching wet hands to her heart, Bertha shook her head and glared at her husband. "You crazy old fool, Jupiter Tubbs. I done told you not to sneak up on me like that. I's goin' to have one of them heart seizures one of these days. Then where'll you be?"

His smile was mischievous. "I guess I'll just have to content myself with that there machine Mr. Chance done bought hisself. A man could keep mighty satisfied lookin' at that."

"Hmph!" She wiped her hands on her apron. "Mr. Chance got hisself in a lick of trouble with Miss Laurel over it. She was fit to be tied when he brought that contraption in here.

And I don't blame her one bit. Naked women struttin' their wares for all the world to see. Mm-mm-mm. What's this world comin' to?"

Jup picked up an apple and bit into it. "It ain't all that bad, honey. Men's got needs and some don't have the money to pay for whores."

"What's your excuse, you devil? I keeps you satisfied, but you couldn't keep from lookin' at those trashy white women in them pictures."

He encircled her waist from behind, pressing his face into her back. "Now, Bertha honey, none of those women can hold a candle to you. They's too skinny for my taste. I likes a woman with a little meat on her bones."

She chuckled. "Well, you gots that. I got me enough meat to stock Mr. Lally's butcherin' shop and then some."

"What you think's goin' to happen if Mr. Chance don't get rid of that 'scopic thing?" Jup asked. "You don't think Miss Laurel will up and leave, do you?"

Lowering herself into a slat-backed chair, Bertha heaved a dispirited sigh. "I likes that little gal a lot, Jup. She's about the sweetest thing around. Miss Laurel's gentle and kind. I don't think she's got a mean bone in her body. She'd be a good woman for Mr. Chance to hook up with. I prays to the good Lord that he don't scare her away. She's prideful, but so's he. Between the two of 'em they gots more stubbornness than a mess of army mules."

"You knows how Mr. Chance feels about women, honey. He's only interested in whores and the like. I don't think he's going to let no 'spectable woman get her clutches in him. Remember when that Sophonia Dusseldorff set her cap for him? Mr. Chance took off for Leadville and didn't return for a month."

Bertha chuckled at the memory. Sophonia Dusseldorff had attached herself to Mr. Chance like a shadow. It seemed that no matter where he went, she was there. If he left the saloon, she followed him. She constantly knocked on the Aurora's door to inquire about her father's whereabouts, even though she knew very well where he was—Mr. D. was always at the Aurora—batting her lashes the entire time she talked.

Mr. Chance feared the woman had some kind of eye disease, she batted her lashes so much.

When Sophonia had made it known that she wanted Mr. Chance to father her children, he'd found it the opportune time to travel to Leadville on business, giving Sophonia a chance to cool down her ardor or to focus it on some other unsuspecting suitor.

"Miss Laurel ain't nothing like Miss Sophonia. She's smarter, prettier, and she don't have no mean mama leading her by the nose.

"And you haven't seen him hightailin' it up to Leadville since Miss Laurel's come to town. In fact, he sticks around here like his feet is glued to the floorboards."

Jup rubbed his chin, assessing his wife's comments, and was about to respond when the door opened and Chance came in. He looked irritated.

"Have either of you seen Laurel? She went upstairs several hours ago to read a letter from her sister, but she hasn't come back down yet."

Bertha shot her husband an I-told-you-so look. "We ain't seen her, Mr. Chance. But I heard her tell Miss Flora that she was going to have dinner tonight with an old friend from the Opera House."

Chance's eyes widened. "Do you mean Rooster? Rooster Higgins?"

"Heard Miss Laurel say she had a hankerin' to keep company with a genteel sort of man." Bertha bit the inside of her cheek to keep the obvious lie from showing on her face.

"Genteel, my ass! Rooster Higgins?"

"Most likely she's upstairs primping for her outing with Mr. Rooster. He's taking her somewheres fancy. How come you never take Miss Laurel nowheres nice, Mr. Chance?

Maybe you should, the way you upset her with that nasty thing you done brought in here."

"You too, Bertha?" Chance began to crack his knuckles.

"Just 'cause I work in a saloon don't mean I'm not a God-fearing, churchgoing woman, Mr. Chance. The good Lord don't cotton to such goin's on."

Chance looked helplessly at Jupiter, but all he got was a shrug. Jup wasn't about to contradict anything his wife had to say on the subject of God-fearing.

"I guess I'll go find Laurel. Make sure she knows to be back here for tonight's performance."

"I's sure she knows that, Mr. Chance. Miss Laurel's a right smart girl."

"Well, she can't be too smart if she's going out to dinner with that dumb, worthless Rooster Higgins," Chance retorted, turning on his heel. But before he could escape, Bertha's parting words halted him in his tracks.

"Can't say Mr. Higgins's the dumb one, Mr. Chance. After all, he's the one spendin' the evening with Miss Laurel. And there's no tellin' what a fine meal and a glass of wine will do to a woman's mood. It makes a body mighty relaxed. Yes it do."

The door slammed shut, and Bertha and Jup looked at each other and burst out laughing.

Flora Sue rushed into Chance's office, where he'd been holed up all evening. It wasn't like Chance to miss an opportunity to gamble, but Jup had explained with a grin that "Mr. Chance couldn't seem to pay no mind to what he was doing this evening."

"Chance, you'd better find someone else to take Laurel's spot tonight. She's in no shape to perform."

Chance spun around in his chair, a mocking smile on his face. "What's the matter with her? Did cupid's arrow pierce her heart and make her too giddy to work?"

"I hardly think Rooster is Laurel's type, Chance. Though he is kind'a cute," she added, smiling thoughtfully to herself, which brought a disgusted snort from Chance.

"Oh, for chrissake! What's wrong with her then?"

"Laurel's drunk. She's up in her room half-naked, singing at the top of her lungs, not caring who hears or sees her. I haven't been able to talk sense to her, and she keeps threatening to crawl out the window and dance on the roof."

"Jesus, Mary, and Joseph! Little Miss Prude went and got herself drunk? I can't believe it. Wait until I get my hands on Rooster."

"He's up there with her now. He feels terrible about the whole thing. Said she only had two small glasses of champagne."

Chance catapulted from his chair as though there were springs attached to his bottom. "Rooster's up in Laurel's room and she's half naked?" He'd kill the son of a bitch if he'd so much as laid a finger on her.

"He's standing guard at her door." Flora Sue smiled. "It's really cute the way he's so protective of her, like a big brother or something. And Laurel seems equally fond of him. When she kissed his cheek in gratitude, I thought the poor man was going to drop her. Rooster's not very big, you know."

"I really am going to kill the son of a bitch."

Fearing the murderous gleam in her employer's eye, Flora Sue decided that Rooster needed protecting, so she followed Chance up the stairs, practically running to keep up with his longer stride.

"Rooster!" The name spewed forth like a curse when Chance spied the nervous man pacing in front of Laurel's closed door. "What the hell's going on?"

Rooster knew that Chance's temper could be a formidable thing when he was pushed. The gambler didn't lose it often, but when he did it wasn't wise to be in close proximity. Rooster took a sidestep. "You'd best get on in there, Chance. Laurel only had a couple glasses of champagne, but she's acting like a wild woman, threatening to climb out the window and dance naked on the roof like somebody named Mazeppa or something.

"I checked on her a time or two, to make sure she was still in there, but she threw the vase at the door when I opened it and then started laughing hysterically."

"Jesus, Mary, and Joseph! Why the hell did you ask her out in the first place? If you hadn't, none of this would have happened."

"You can't blame Rooster, Chance. He and Laurel are good friends. What's wrong with him taking her out for a nice meal?" Flora patted the stage manager's cheek. "I know I'd be pleased go out with him if he asked me."

Rooster's Adam's apple bobbed excitedly, doing a fair imitation of a cork on water, and his eyes rounded to the size of silver dollars. "You would, Flora Sue?" He'd had a crush on the pretty dance-hall girl for months but had been too timid to ask her out. Though he knew he could have bedded Flora if he had the right amount of cash, Rooster thought too highly of her to have suggested that.

Watching the two of them fawn all over each other like lovebirds made Chance sick to his stomach. He escaped into Laurel's room, stopping dead in his tracks.

Nothing could have prepared him for the sight of Laurel in a black satin corset, garters holding up a pair of black silk stockings on those incredibly long legs he'd been dreaming about of late. She was leaning back against the window sill, eyes closed, her hair fanning out in the breeze behind her. It was an awesome sight to behold and he sucked in his breath.

"Laurel."

Her eyes came open at once and she flashed him a brilliant smile, tilting her head coquettishly. "Well, hello, sugar," she said, doing a very credible impersonation of Pearl's syrupy drawl. "How nish of you to come by and see me." She batted her lashes, and Chance couldn't help but smile.

"Flora said you wouldn't be able to go on stage tonight."

She stood on coltish legs, wobbling as she made her way toward him. "Thash silly, sugar. I'm perfectly fine, as you can see." Draping her arms about his neck, she asked in a seductive voice, "Don't you think I'm fine, sugar?"

"I think you're drunk, that's what I think."

"Pooh. I am not. I only had two glasses of bubbly." She held up three fingers. "You can ask Rooshter if you don't believe me, but I hardly ever lie."

"I think it's time for you to go to bed, angel. You're going to feel like hell in the morning."

Her hands went to his chest, where she toyed with the buttons on his shirt. "I bet you can make me feel better, Chance. I like it when you kiss me . . . and do all those other things." She rubbed against him suggestively, and Chance stiffened like a tree limb.

"You're playing with fire, little one, and you're going to get burned. Now let me help you get out of that corset."

"I can do it," she said when his hands moved to the fastenings of her corset. But she was too intoxicated to work the hooks and eyes, and after a few agonizing moments of watching her fumble with her breasts, Chance slapped at her hands.

"Allow me. I'm pretty proficient at undressing a woman."

She cocked her head to one side and smiled. "You're a stallion, that's what all the women around here shay, Chance sugar."

"Do they now?" He laughed, continuing to unfasten her corset. When he had it completely undone, he peeled it away and feasted his eyes on her nakedness, and a lump formed in his throat. For a stallion, he felt damned awkward at the moment.

"You're beautiful," he whispered.

"I feel wonderful. So free and uninhibited. I've never drank champagne before." She ran to the window and stuck the upper half of her body out. "Hello, Denver!" she yelled, waving her arms wildly.

"Jesus!" Hoping no one had seen her, Chance rushed forward, grabbing Laurel about her waist and hauling her back inside. He shut the window with a bang. "In case you've forgotten, angel, you're as naked as the day you were born. I suggest you crawl into bed now and get some sleep."

She wrapped her arms about his waist, snuggling her face against his chest, listening to the rapid beating of his heart. "Your heart's thumping hard, Chance. Much faster than mine. See?" She placed his hand over her breast, and it was just too much temptation for one man to resist.

His heart wasn't the only thing thumping hard . . .

Laurel was tempting fully dressed in her Sunday church clothes. Naked, she was the personification of Eve in the Garden of Eden, and Chance knew without a doubt that poor old Adam hadn't stood a chance.

Massaging the plump little globes, he marveled at how satiny soft they felt, at how they filled his palms so well. Her nipples were pink, pert, and pebbled instantly when he flicked his fingers over them.

"Mmmm," she moaned. "I like it when you do that. Flora Sue said that small-breasted women have more sensitive breasts."

"I think Flora Sue might be right, angel." Pressing his lips to her mouth, he drank of her sweetness, trailing his hands down her back, her buttocks, and finally to the soft nest of curls between her legs. She was wet and ready.

"God, Laurel, you're killing me." He felt as if he might disgrace himself at any moment, he was so excited. He'd been with hundreds of women before, but none had affected him like this impossible, innocent virgin.

"Touch me some more," Laurel urged. "It feels good when you touch me like that. No one's ever done it before."

Chance moaned, drawing her to the bed to lay her down on her back. His mouth recaptured her lips, even as his fingers spread the damp golden curls to capture the tiny bud of her femininity.

Chance's hand on her most private of places set Laurel's

blood rushing through her veins like warm honey, heating her to a fevered pitch. Her breathing grew shallow, and she moved against him, urging him to continue the delicious torment. "Oh, God, please don't stop. That feels *sooo* good."

Her innocence touched him as nothing else could have, and he kissed her long and hard, knowing that she would hate herself and him in the morning if he proceeded any further. But when he tried to draw away, she pulled his head back down. "Don't go. Don't stop touching me."

"You're drunk, angel. I don't take advantage of drunk women."

Her legs gaped wider, showing him more eloquently than words could express how much she wanted him, needed him to love her. "Just touch me a little more. Please, Chance. I need . . . I need . . ."

The invitation was blatant and impossible to resist. Rolling on top of her, he covered her mouth once again, driving in his tongue while at the same time inserting his finger inside her and replicating the thrusting motion.

Trailing kisses down her neck, her breasts, he laved and nibbled at her swollen nipples, then sucked hard, while plying her engorged bud with his hand. When she began to buck wildly beneath him, he knew she was nearing her moment of completion, and he nestled his head between her thighs to taste her sweetness.

"Oh, oh . . ." Laurel cried out, clutching the quilt between her hands, as if it could keep her grounded to the earth.

She was flying, flying. . . . The incredible things Chance was doing with his mouth and tongue had ascended her to the heavens. Soaring, soaring . . .

Her climax came quickly and she cried out in joy, tears misting her eyes at the sheer beauty and wonder of it. Slowly she drifted back down to earth, the effort to open her eyes too great a task to undertake at the moment.

Cuddling Laurel to his chest, Chance was awed by her newly found sensuality, and his ability to arouse and satisfy it. He'd never made love to a virgin before. Never understood why men put such a store by a woman's innocence.

But now he knew.

He'd been the first man ever to touch Laurel in an intimate way. To taste the sweetness of her purity, and hear her satisfied mews of pleasure.

It humbled him.

It pleased him.

It made him think.

Laurel sighed with pure contentment. "That was wonderful."

"I hope you're not going to hate me in the morning, angel." He brushed damp strands of hair away from her face.

She could smell her musky scent on him; it was a strange scent, an evocative scent, and it made her feel womanly. "Why would I hate you? You've made me feel like an honest-to-goodness woman for the first time in my life. Thank you."

He kissed the tip of her nose, then helped her beneath the covers. "You're going to feel different in the morning, angel, but I'm not sorry for what happened. I only wish . . ."

"What?"

"Never mind. There's plenty of time for the other."

"Oh, you mean, like what Flora Sue and her miner friend did the other night?" She giggled at the memory, feeling warm and tingly inside.

"I guess you're getting quite an education listening to the goings-on around here."

She smiled seductively, caressing his cheek. "Mama always said that experience was the best teacher. I'm inclined to think she was right."

CHAPTER 10

"Hello, sugar." Pearl draped herself around Chance's neck, nuzzling his cheek as she eyed the cards spread out on the table before him. "Solitaire's such a lonely game. Are you feeling lonely this afternoon, sugar?"

Chance had been hoping to avoid another encounter with the determined bar girl. "Have a seat, Pearl, if you're bored. I'm just wastin' a little time until . . ." *Until Laurel returns from lunch.* "Until Whitey gets done stacking firewood for Bertha."

She accepted the invitation, pouring herself a drink from the half-empty whiskey bottle on the table. "I bet you're real pleased about Whitey's progress."

"I was never that crazy about him learning his letters in the first place."

Pearl did her best not to show how put out she felt by Chance's attitude. "That's not very gracious of you," she said. "I've been spending a lot of time teaching your cousin how to make his letters."

Chance looked up from the cards, searching her face. "Why'd you volunteer to teach Whitey, Pearl? I didn't think you were particularly fond of him. And it seems out of character for you."

"That's an awful thing to say, sugar." She dabbed at imaginary tears with her fingertips. "I'll have you know I'm quite fond of the boy. I had a brother once, you know," she lied. "He was killed in the war." She sniffed a few times, adding, "Just because I'm a whore, Chance, don't mean I don't have feelings." She clasped his hand. "You know how much I care for you and Whitey. You're like family."

Not entirely convinced, but unwilling to hurt Pearl's feelings more than he already had, he squeezed her hand. "Thanks for helping my cousin. I appreciate it, and I know Whitey does too. He talks about you all the time."

Pearl felt elated at the admission. "You're welcome, sugar. Why, you know I'd do just about anything for you." Her hand went to his cheek. "Just name it."

Not about to be led down a road he had no intention of traveling, Chance winked at the whore, then pushed the deck of cards toward her. "Then how about playing a game of poker with me, Pearl? If there's one thing I can never get my fill of it's poker."

Pearl forced a smile as she reached for the deck.

"Miss Martin, I'd like to talk to you if you have a minute."

Laurel paused in her conversation with Crystal and looked up to see Albert Hazen standing in front of the café. There was a thin smile beneath his mustached lip, and he looked as if he'd been waiting impatiently for her and Crystal to finish their lunch.

The glorious, sunny autumn day turned suddenly dark and gloomy, but it didn't have a thing to do with the weather.

"Al, is everything okay?" Crystal asked worriedly before

Laurel could respond to the request. "I was planning to be back as soon as Laurel and I finished our lunch."

Whatever was left of Hazen's smile disappeared, and his eyes narrowed. "I'm not here for you, Crystal. I've come to discuss business with Miss Martin, so why don't you hightail it back to the Silver Slipper and wait for me."

Crystal didn't miss the warning look Al flashed her, but concern for her friend made her say, "Laurel needs to get back to the Aurora, Al. She doesn't have time to talk to you right now. Do you, Laurel?" There was a great deal of entreaty in her voice.

Laurel's gaze moved between Al Hazen's angry expression and Crystal's pleading look. She sighed inwardly. If she refused to speak with Al, it would bode ill for Crystal. He was sure to take out his frustration on her, and Laurel couldn't allow that to happen. Crystal was her best friend, and she had to protect her at all costs.

Clasping Crystal's arm, she said, "I'll be fine. Why don't you go on back to the saloon? I'm sure Mr. Hazen will only detain me a minute."

Crystal bit her lower lip, a pensive shimmer in the depths of her eyes. "Are you sure? Because I'll stay if you want me to."

"That's not necessary," Laurel reassured her, relieved a moment later when Crystal nodded and began to walk away.

Hazen guided Laurel to a wooden bench near the street corner. The feel of his cold, reptilian hands on her person made Laurel want to shrink back in disgust. But she didn't. She wouldn't give Hazen the satisfaction of knowing how frightened she was of him.

"What is it you want to speak to me about, Mr. Hazen? Crystal was correct when she said I needed to get back to the Aurora." Bertha was expecting her to help with dinner.

Toying with the ends of his mustache, looking every bit as sinister as she now knew him to be, Hazen glanced over her in quick assessment. "I understand you're working for Rafferty now, Miss Martin. I've come to make you a better offer."

Rafferty's business had more than doubled since the blonde had gone to work there. Now he'd heard that Rafferty was offering a free lunch with the purchase of two nickel beers. The bastard was doing everything possible to put him out of business, and Al had no intention of sitting back and allowing that to happen.

Now that the mayor had refused his bid for another bordello, Al was going to have to make the one he had much more profitable. Hiring Laurel Martin was just the first step.

Laurel was shocked by the man's audacity. To think that he actually thought she would entertain the notion of working for him. It was insulting! The man made his living off innocent women's suffering. Not to mention the fact that he was a vicious animal. "I'm not at all interested in working for you, Mr. Hazen. I'm not a prostitute, but even if I were, you wouldn't be the kind of man I'd consider selling myself for."

"You haven't heard my offer yet, Miss Martin. I'm willing to double whatever Rafferty's paying you. I'll give you better accommodations. And you can keep whatever tips you make. Just to show you my heart's in the right place, we can split your services seventy-five–twenty-five, instead of the usual fifty–fifty. I'm not a greedy man, Miss Martin."

Bile rose thickly in her throat, and Laurel shot to her feet. Her anger was so palpable that it seemed as if the air around her were charged with electric current. "You're disgusting, Mr. Hazen. I have no interest at all in prostituting myself, for you or anyone else."

He stood, grasping her arm. "That's not what I hear. I hear you don't mind giving it to Rafferty whenever he's in the mood."

Guilt over what had happened the previous night made Laurel's cheeks flame in embarrassment. Surely no one could have known of her disreputable behavior with Chance.

Unless, of course, he'd been indiscreet enough to tell someone.

"You're mistaken, and I won't stand here another minute and allow you to insult me." She yanked her arm free from his hold. "Perhaps you're used to mistreating the women who work for you, but I'll not allow you to victimize me."

His face was taut with anger. "You think you're so goddamn high and mighty, but you're gonna find out different. I don't like losing to Rafferty. And I don't take no for an answer, especially from a woman." The way he spat *woman* made it abundantly clear that he held the entire female gender in contempt.

"One way or another, you'll come to me, and when you do, I'm going to make you sorry you ever went to work for Rafferty." The unnatural light in Hazen's eyes bespoke madness.

Laurel decided that she wouldn't allow him to intimidate her one more minute. "You're a despicable human being, Mr. Hazen. My mama always said a stench followed a skunk no matter where he roamed. You, Mr.Hazen, stink to high heaven."

Not giving him a chance to respond, Laurel turned and hurried down the street, ignoring the vile names Hazen called after her.

By the time she reached the Aurora, she was white faced and breathing hard, but she didn't stop to answer Jup or Bull's questions concerning her demeanor. Instead, she marched straight into Chance's office.

He looked up when she entered, a delighted smile crossing his face. It made her wish she weren't so furious with him.

"I need to talk to you, Chance."

His smile faded and he rubbed the back of his neck. "I knew you'd be upset about last night. Why is it women always—"

"It isn't about what happened last night." She turned various shades of crimson as she unbuttoned her coat. "Though I guess we need to talk about that, too."

He looked closely at her, noting the fear still lingering in her eyes, and rose to his feet. "What's wrong? You look scared to death. Has Shooter been bothering you again?" His hands fisted at his sides. *I'll kill the bastard this time.*

Laurel wanted to run to him, to throw herself into Chance's arms and beg him to hold her, to chase away the evil aura that Hazen's words had created. But she couldn't. Not after what had happened between them last night. That would only complicate things. And things were complicated enough already.

Laurel couldn't blame Chance for what had happened last night. She'd practically begged him to make love to her. She really should be grateful that he'd used some restraint in leaving her virginity intact. God! She had acted worse than any two-bit whore on Holladay Street.

Every disgraceful, delicious minute of their encounter was firmly embedded in her mind . . . and in her heart. She'd been drunk, she told herself. But it hadn't been the alcohol that had made her so brazen. She'd wanted Chance Rafferty with an intensity that frightened her, and she'd used the alcohol as an excuse to lose her inhibitions and beg him to make love to her.

"Was I right? Has Shooter been bothering you again? I'll rip him apart if he has," Chance said, stepping closer, bringing Laurel back to the other, more pressing reality.

"If I tell you what's wrong, you must promise not to behave in a rash manner." She didn't want to give Hazen an excuse to come against Chance. After all, this was her problem, not his.

Chance sighed and shook his head. "I don't like playing games, angel. Now, are you going to tell me what happened or not? You looked white as a ghost when you came in here and not the least bit content. Not exactly flattering to a man in my position, considering our recent encounter."

Needing to wipe the self-satisfied smirk off Chance's face, she blurted, "Al Hazen insulted me." It worked. The veins in his neck and temples began to bulge like a Yellowstone geyser.

"What! Did he hurt you?" He looked her over carefully.

She shook her head. "No. Crystal was with me at first. But she left when Hazen insisted on talking to me alone. I was concerned for her welfare, so I agreed to hear what he had to say."

"That was foolish."

"We were in broad daylight. I didn't think I was in any danger."

"You don't know Al Hazen."

"I know he abuses Crystal, and I couldn't allow my actions to bring any more pain upon her."

"What did the bastard want?"

"He wanted me to come to work for him." She explained in detail everything he'd said. "He thinks we're . . ." She swallowed. "He thinks we've been sleeping together. He said if I was giving it to you, then I shouldn't mind giving it to his customers." She covered her face with her hands, mortified to admit such a thing. "He acted as if he knew what had happened between us last night."

Chance drew Laurel into his arms, willing his fury at Hazen to subside for the moment. He'd deal with that bastard later, in his own way and time. "Nothing happened, angel. You're still a virgin. I merely helped you attain a little pleasure. There's nothing wrong with that."

She looked up at him, and the tears in her eyes shot straight to his heart like crystal bullets. "How can you say that? We're not even married. We don't even get along all that well, and I allowed you to . . ."

His kiss silenced her. Then he asked, "Didn't you enjoy it? Didn't you thank me for making you feel like a woman?"

"Well, yes," she replied in a small voice. "But I was raised on the doctrine of eternal damnation. Pastor Bergman would consider what we did a sin. And my sister Heather warned me about men and their animal urges."

"But she didn't explain about the urges women have, did she?" Laurel shook her head in dismay, and he smiled tenderly. "Trust me, angel, you're not going to hell in a handbasket just because you enjoyed making love. God wouldn't have made it pleasurable if we weren't supposed to enjoy it."

She looked up, noting the sincerity and kindness in his eyes, and knew in that moment that she was falling in love with Chance Rafferty.

But how can I be?

He was a gambler and a scoundrel of the first order.

But he's kind and gentle, and he makes me feel like no one ever made me feel before.

He wasn't the marrying kind. Everyone in the saloon had warned her that Chance was a man looking for pleasure, not permanence.

But he has dimples, and a most extraordinary smile.

He had a definite lack of morals and refinement.

But he can kiss the very breath out of me and make me crave for more.

He was in no way, shape, or form Prince Charming material.

But he's a man. All man. And a man can be changed.

Chance had just thrown the bolt on the front door and was about to turn off the lights when a frantic pounding sounded against the glass. Unlocking the door, he was shocked at the sight of Crystal leaning heavily against the door frame.

She'd been beaten so viciously that he barely recognized her lovely face, which was swollen to twice its normal size. The skin around her eyes was discolored, and there was dried blood on her lips.

"Jesus, Mary, and Joseph!" Grasping the woman about the waist, he scooped her slight form into his arms and carried her into the gambling parlor. "Jupiter!" he yelled out, and a moment later the piano player appeared from the kitchen.

"Lordy be!" Jup said as his gaze fell on the near unconscious woman cradled against Chance's chest.

"Fetch Bertha, Jup, then get Laurel. Tell her Crystal's been hurt bad."

Jup left to do his bidding, and Chance marched toward the stairs, the beaten woman held tenderly in his arms. Her lips were so swollen that she couldn't speak. She tried to form words, but could only nod her head in a gesture of what appeared to be thanks.

"Hazen," Chance said, the word sounding more like a curse than a question, and Crystal nodded slowly.

Bertha, Jup, and Laurel appeared all at once.

Seeing the shocking condition of her friend, Laurel clutched the edges of her wrapper together and ran forward, her eyes swimming with tears. "Dear God! Crystal!" she cried, taking the woman's limp hand in her own.

"She's fainted," Chance explained. "It's probably a blessing. She's been beaten pretty badly. I think her ribs might be cracked." Due to the pallor of her skin, he feared that she might be bleeding internally, but he refrained from adding more to Laurel's burden.

"Shall I fetch Doc?" Jup asked. "This woman might need some tendin' to." He stared at the lifeless form before him, remembering . . .

"Doc Toomey ain't going to be in any shape to help," Bertha said, shaking her head in disgust. "He was drinking to beat the band tonight. I wouldn't trust him to treat a horse, let alone this here child."

"I think we should get the reverend," Laurel said. "He told me he had a small amount of medical training before he became a preacher. And it wouldn't hurt to have someone praying over Crystal right about now." She had the sinking feeling that Crystal was going to need all their prayers before this night was through. *Damn Albert Hazen to hell!*

Jup left to find Gus, and Laurel ran up the stairs to ready the empty bedroom at the end of the hall. It was the farthest one from the noise of the main gambling parlor, and Crystal wasn't as likely to be disturbed there by drunken revelers looking for an evening's entertainment.

"Put her here on the bed." Laurel pulled down the comforter and smoothed the sheets. Her voice cracked when she said, "This is all my fault. If I hadn't been so rude to Hazen—"

"That's nonsense," Chance cut in. "The man's an animal. Always has been. If he hadn't taken his anger and frustration out on Crystal, he'd have taken it out on you." *And he'd be a dead man by now.*

"It ain't gonna do no good arguing about this now." Bertha turned to Laurel. "I'll get Miss Crystal undressed, honey, while you fetch one of your nightgowns for her to wear."

Laurel returned a moment later, carrying a soft flannel rose-patterned gown that was one of her favorites. She handed it to Bertha.

Feeling more helpless than he'd felt in years, Chance paced the small room, while Bertha and Laurel tended to the stricken woman. Crystal whimpered several times while they undressed her, but she didn't regain consciousness.

"I'll kill that bastard," Chance swore, and fear darted through Laurel's breast.

"That kind of talk's not going to help Crystal at the moment. There'll be time enough to deal with Hazen after she's taken care of."

"Miss Laurel's right," Bertha said, wringing out a damp washcloth and dabbing the dried blood from Crystal's lips. "We don't need no more trouble right now. We gots us enough to deal with. Why don't you go see what's keeping Jup, Mr. Chance? And you'd best make sure Whitey went straight to his room."

Chance's eyebrow shot up. "Whitey? Why wouldn't he be in his room?"

Bertha shrugged, not about to reveal her suspicions about Pearl. But she wouldn't put anything past that woman when it came to making trouble. "I'd just feel better, that's all."

Chance went down the hall and paused before the door to Whitey's room. He hadn't spent a great deal of time with his cousin lately. Whitey was always busy with Pearl and his writing lessons, and Chance had been preoccupied with a certain blond opera singer who he couldn't get out of his mind.

Laurel was becoming as necessary as the air he breathed. He could barely remember what his life had been like before she'd come into it. Her warm laughter never failed to draw his attention. Her radiant smile could light up a room on the gloomiest of days. She was gentle, kind, a woman who didn't fit into the mold in which he usually lumped all decent women.

Laurel wasn't calculating or greedy. She had a soft spot in her heart for anyone she perceived as less fortunate than herself: dimwits, prostitutes, down-on-their-luck preachers.

She was special. And if he'd been the kind of man who was looking for a good woman to marry, she certainly fit the bill.

But he wasn't, he reminded himself.

He knocked softly on Whitey's door before opening it to find his cousin diligently practicing his letters. Notepad on lap, his lower lip gathered between his teeth in concentration, Whitey looked like a schoolboy studying for a college exam, and Chance's chest swelled with pride.

"Howdy, Whitey. Just thought I'd stop by and see how everything's going."

The big man smiled proudly, holding the paper up for Chance's inspection. "I'm learning to make my *H*'s, Chance. Pearl says I'm doing real good."

The mention of the whore made Chance frown. He still

wasn't convinced of her motives in tutoring Whitey, despite her reassurances. Pearl never did anything nice without an ulterior motive. Generosity and kindness were not inherent in her nature. So why, suddenly, was she being so attentive to his cousin?

"She ain't causing you any trouble, is she?"

"Miss Pearl's purty. And she's been real nice to me, Chance. I think she likes me."

"I'm sure she does, Whitey. Pearl likes most men."

"I like her, too. She smells good."

Chance, however, found Pearl's gardenia scent cloying. "I guess." He took a seat on the chair next to the bed. "You mustn't mistake Pearl's friendship for anything else, Whitey. You know she likes to tease everyone."

Wetting the lead of the pencil with the tip of his tongue, Whitey drew several more letters. "She likes me, me, me. Pearl said I was handsome as you, Chance. Ain't that something? Most times women don't see me the same as they do you."

Chance scoffed inwardly. Did the whore think to make him jealous of his own cousin because he'd spurned her advances? The thought was too preposterous to even consider.

Pearl couldn't be interested in Whitey sexually. Whitey could never satisfy someone as insatiable as the whore. He was much too childlike to feel sexual yearnings and didn't have the urges normal men had. And Pearl definitely needed someone with an ardent sex drive to match her own. She'd bed just about anyone who wore a pair of pants and had a dollar to spend on her.

At any rate, he decided, he'd best keep a close eye on both of them. He had no intention of allowing Pearl to mislead his cousin or pretend a relationship that didn't exist. But for the time being he would leave things as they were. Whitey was content, and that was the most important thing, in Chance's opinion.

And he did have other, more pressing concerns on his

mind at the moment, like Al Hazen and his despicable treatment of women. Despite what Bertha and Laurel had cautioned, he was determined to exact his pound of flesh against the ruthless bastard.

Gus stood at the side of the bed, staring down at the helpless woman before him. She made whimpering sounds as she slept, probably reliving her ordeal in her subconscious, and the reverend reached out to caress her cheek in a gesture of comfort.

For three days and nights Crystal Cummings had clung to life. It was only by the grace of God, constant prayer, and a smattering of medical training on Gus's part that had gotten the woman this far. By all rights she should have succumbed to the vicious beating Al Hazen had given her.

What was wrong with a man who could abuse such a beautiful child? Why had God put such foul creatures on this earth?

These were the questions Gus could never answer, though he asked them silently every day. He didn't want to question his faith in a God who could allow an innocent young woman to be treated so shamelessly, to be forced at an early age to sell herself to the highest bidder so that she could have a roof over her head and a small amount of food to sustain her.

He sat in the chair next to the bed, clasping her small, clammy hand in his own. Crystal reminded him of a fragile porcelain doll. Her skin was smooth and unlined with age, unlike his, which was as creased as a well-used saddle.

She had an exquisite figure that a man could only dream of possessing, but he knew many men had possessed her.

It was difficult, even being a man of God, to avoid Crystal's allure. And though he tried to ignore the stirring of passion that seeing her naked had aroused, he hadn't quite been able to, and he prayed to the Almighty to help him resist the temptation before him.

His hands had trembled when placing the bandages around her injured rib cage, and his fingers had burned when they'd come in contact with the underside of her full, satiny breasts. And his eyes had not looked away from the sight of her nipples, dusky, rose-tipped beauties that poets could write sonnets about.

With her body bruised and her lips cracked and swollen, a man might not think the young prostitute all that enticing. But to Augustus Baldwin, who'd never before experienced the gut-wrenching emotion he felt every time he looked at Crystal, she was the most beautiful creature on the face of God's earth.

"Reverend Baldwin."

He looked up at the sound of Laurel's voice, his hand releasing Crystal's, feeling guilty at his own thoughts.

"How is Crystal doing today? Her color seems to be a bit better."

Gus forced a smile as he looked at his patient's black and blue face. "Only you would have such an optimistic opinion, my dear."

"Mama always said that a broody hen never lays many eggs. I try to see the best of things when I can, Reverend. And I know with your help Crystal's going to come out of this just fine."

"Your faith humbles me, my dear. Sometimes it's hard to keep my spirits up. It's a failing I have; one of many, I'm afraid."

Carefully, so as not to disturb the sleeping woman, Laurel lowered herself onto the edge of the bed. "Why did you become a preacher, Gus? You don't seem like the type. Why did you quit your doctoring lessons?"

Pain filled his eyes, and he looked away. "I thought once that I was infallible and found out I wasn't. Someone I cared very deeply about died because of my stupidity, my inflated sense of self-worth." Because he had failed to listen to men who possessed years more experience and knowledge than himself.

She placed a comforting hand on his arm. "Your wife?"

"No." He shook his head. "I've never been married. It was my sister. My sweet Adrianna. She died in childbirth, and I never forgave myself for not being able to save her."

"I'm sure it wasn't your fault, Reverend. Women die in childbirth every day. It's part of life on the prairie. My own mama died trying to bring forth new life." A baby boy who'd tried to be born before his time.

"I'm sure you did everything you could for your sister. My papa never blamed Doc Spooner for my mama's death. He did the best he could, doc did, same as you, but these things just happen. Nobody knows why. God's will, Bertha would say."

Gus brought Laurel's hand to his lips and kissed it. "For a young girl, you're very wise."

"You might not have been able to save Adrianna's life, Gus, but you did save Crystal's. I know she's going to be eternally grateful when she realizes what you've done."

Funny, Gus thought, as he stared down at the sleeping woman, a gentle warmth wrapping around his heart, it wasn't Crystal's gratitude he craved. It wasn't even her body. He realized, despite the vast differences in their ages and upbringing, and the fact that they hardly knew each other, that it was Crystal Cummings's heart that he desired above everything else.

But only God knew how he was going to satisfy that unreasonable yearning, for he doubted that a woman of Crystal Cummings's extraordinary beauty would see much worthwhile in a consumptive old coot like himself.

"Well, you're looking downright perky this morning," Laurel said, seating herself on the Windsor chair next to

Crystal's bed. "Funny what a week's worth of Bertha's good cooking can do to a body, and the attention of a handsome gentleman like Reverend Baldwin."

Propped up against the headboard, leaning against two fluffy down pillows, Crystal's blush could be seen quite clearly beneath the fading bruises. "The reverend has been very kind," she admitted, unwilling to look Laurel in the eye, lest she reveal too much.

"Why, Crystal Cummings! I do believe you're blushing."

Laurel's comment made Crystal giggle, and she grabbed herself about the middle to keep her sore ribs from hurting. Fortunately they weren't broken, only bruised. "Hard to believe a woman in my profession can still blush after everything I've seen and done."

"That's all in your past. After you're fully recovered, which Bertha assures me will be quite soon, Chance is putting you to work at the Aurora. You'll be expected to serve drinks, talk to the customers, and nothing else."

"Did Augustus . . . Reverend Baldwin have something to do with that?" Crystal asked, wondering how Al would react to her defection. No doubt he'd try to make good on his threat to kill her; he'd threatened to do it often enough. But she didn't fear him so much, now that she had friends. Now that Augustus Baldwin had come into her life.

"I believe Gus spoke to Chance, but Chance had already decided you weren't going back to the Silver Slipper. Chance paid a visit to Al with the intention of beating the living daylights out of him." Crystal's eyes widened. "But the coward had already left town—on business, he was told." A sigh of relief slipped through Crystal's lips.

Hazen's departure had allowed Chance's temper to cool somewhat. He rarely spoke of killing the man anymore, only of tearing him limb from limb. Laurel thought that was a great improvement.

"You've all been very kind. I don't know how I'll ever repay you."

"Posh! Don't be silly." She dismissed Crystal's gratitude with a flick of her wrist. "I've enjoyed having you around. Flora Sue's about the only female friend I've got around here, and she's been preoccupied with Rooster Higgins." It seemed that Flora had transferred her attentions from Gus to Rooster this past week, and Laurel was vastly relieved, since Gus seemed to have taken a shine to Crystal, and vice versa. Oh, they'd both tried to hide their attraction, but everyone had noticed how their faces lit up whenever they were in the same room together.

It was the same way she felt whenever she was with Chance. A heart-pounding, palm-sweating feeling, accompanied by strange tingling sensations centered low in her abdomen.

Some would call it lust, but she preferred to think of it as a love affliction. One, she hoped, that would not prove fatal.

There hadn't been any more amorous encounters with Chance since Crystal's illness, and Laurel hadn't quite decided if she was relieved or regretful about that. Chance's kisses and caresses were an addiction and she was finding it difficult to live without them.

"What's that letter you've got clutched in your hand?" Crystal asked, noting the white vellum envelope. "I know it can't be for me." There was a touch of sadness in the woman's voice, and Laurel wondered how one so young could have already experienced a lifetime of grief and heartache.

Forcing a gaiety she didn't quite feel, Laurel replied, "I nearly forgot. It's from my sister Rose Elizabeth. I figured if you were bored enough, you might enjoy hearing it. Rose's letters are always entertaining, and I'm sure this one's no exception."

Crystal's face lit with pleasure and she clapped her hands together. "Yes, please. I'd love to hear it. You're so lucky to have such a close-knit family."

"You wouldn't think so if you'd had to share a bed with

the two of them. Rose Elizabeth used to hog the covers something terrible."

Crystal sighed, wondering what her life would have been like had she had siblings. She urged Laurel to read the letter.

" 'Laurel, my dear,' she begins," Laurel said, laughing aloud at Rose's mimicking of the Englishman's way of speaking.

" 'His lordship, the Duke of Disaster, otherwise known as Alexander James Warrick, the Duke of Moreland, still resides on our family farm, much to my very great annoyance and disappointment. I've tried every way I can think of to convince the duke that he's ill-equipped for farming, but he refuses to listen to anything I have to say on the matter. Apparently a woman's opinion is considered trivial where he comes from. Isn't that appalling?!

" 'The man is arrogant and extremely rude and relishes ordering everyone about. But I've reminded him on countless occasions that the British lost control of the colonies some time back, and we Americans aren't interested in following British suggestions or instruction.' "

"Oh, my," Crystal said, shaking her head. "It sounds as if your sister is courting trouble. I've had occasion to entertain some of those British gents, and I can tell you firsthand that they're virile as all get-out. I doubt the duke's going to listen to anything Rose has to say about his leaving. They're used to gettin' their own way in just about everything. And I do mean everything."

There was a pregnant pause. "You don't think the duke will try to seduce my sister, do you?" Laurel asked.

"Honey, I'm saying that if it hasn't happened already, it probably will. Those Englishmen are animals. Why, on one occasion I'd prefer to forget, one of my customers, who said he was an English earl, bit my backside. I couldn't sit down for a week. And they call themselves gentlemen." She shook her head. "I never had any miner bite my butt before."

Blushing, Laurel continued:

" 'Folks here in Salina are pretty taken with the duke. He's flashed quite a bit of money around town, and he even made a donation to Pastor Bergman's church fund. I thought that was a pretty underhanded thing to do, but then I put nothing past Alexander Warrick.

" 'Though he's threatened to evict me on several occasions, I've made myself indispensable by cooking his meals and educating him about the farm. Though it galls me to do both!

" 'I've written to Heather to inform her of my situation here on the farm, but have not had a reply yet. I'm sure she'll be quite put out with me.' "

Laurel's eyes rolled heavenward. That was an understatement!

" 'Hope you are well and happy and that your difficult Mr. Rafferty isn't . . .' " Laurel stopped and looked up to see Crystal's eyes bright with mischief.

"Aren't you going to finish reading about *your* Mr. Rafferty?"

"She's just responding to a comment I made about Chance being a bit difficult, that's all."

"I bet you called him a royal pain in the ass."

"I did not!"

"Come to think of it," Crystal said, smiling, "it's your sister who's stuck with the *royal* pain in the ass, not you. You're just stuck with a sweet scoundrel. Ain't that right, Laurel honey?"

"And you're sweet on the Reverend Augustus Baldwin, and don't try to tell me any different, Crystal Cummings. You get giddy as a schoolgirl whenever he comes by to visit."

Her hands flying to her cheeks, Crystal couldn't contain her laughter. "We're a pair, aren't we, honey? You're stuck on a man who can't abide decent women, and I'm entertaining thoughts about a man who obviously requires one."

CHAPTER 11

Having heard from Jup that Al Hazen was still out of town—no doubt, hiding beneath the rock he'd originally crawled out from under—Laurel decided the time had come to sneak over to the Silver Slipper to fetch the remainder of Crystal's clothing.

Chance had expressly forbidden her to go anywhere near the saloon, fearing Hazen's impending return—the animal had a business to run and couldn't stay away forever—and had sent Whitey to fetch Crystal's things two days before. But Whitey had brought back totally inappropriate attire for a woman on the mend—a woman who needed to impress a preacher.

Checking to make sure the coast was clear, Laurel paused at the foot of the stairs. The bottom step creaked loudly as her foot came down, but no one was around to hear it, and she breathed a sigh of relief.

On tiptoe she crossed the Aurora's gambling parlor. She had just reached the front door when an irate voice that could only have been Chance's said, "Where do you think you're going, angel? It's not Sunday, so I know it's not church where you're headed. And why are you walking on tiptoe?"

He leaned over the bar, his eyebrow arched in question, motioning her toward him with the crook of his finger.

Chance thought Laurel looked guilty as hell, and too lovely for words in the blue taffeta gown and matching bonnet she wore, and he felt a familiar tightening in his loins.

Laurel gave an irritated sigh. *Does the man have eyes in the back of his head?* "I need to go out for a while," she explained, an innocent smile on her face.

He vaulted over the bar with the agility of a mountain lion and looked just as fierce when he came to stand next to her. "Where?"

She swallowed. Lying wasn't one of her strengths. Rose Elizabeth was the best liar of the three Martin sisters, a real fabricator of truths.

Rose had once convinced Euphemia Bloodsworth that she was dying of a rare blood disease and wasn't expected to live out the year. This coming from a woman who looked as robust as a horse.

Of course, dear Euphemia had spread the word faster than a Kansas prairie fire, and the concerned citizens of Salina had turned out in droves to visit the supposedly dying young woman. When Ezra Martin got wind of what Rose Elizabeth had done he'd paddled her backside so hard that she couldn't sit down for days, made her give a public apology to the townsfolk, and wouldn't speak to his daughter for over a week.

Knowing she'd never be able to equal Rose's silver-tongued fabrications, Laurel gave it her best shot anyway. "To the dressmaker's?" Seeing Chance's skeptical look, she decided that, all in all, it was not a very memorable performance. Rose was definitely not in any danger of giving over her childhood title of most convincing liar.

"Don't ever play poker, angel. You can't lie worth crap."

"Don't be crude. And anyway, it's none of your business where I'm going. I'll be back before tonight's performance, so you needn't worry."

Who was she kidding? Chance wondered. He worried about her constantly, more than ever since Hazen's beating of Crystal.

Rolling down his sleeves, Chance fastened the cuffs with a pair of gold links he extracted from his pants pocket. "Wrong on both counts, angel. It is my business, and you're not going anywhere alone. Hazen could return at any time."

Laurel had the childish impulse to stamp her foot in frustration, or at least to give Chance another swift kick in his shins. "You're my employer, Chance, not my watchdog. I'll go where I please, when I please."

He shrugged into his coat. "Fine. Since you obviously intend to go to Hazen's place, I'll go with you."

"How did you . . . " Laurel realized she'd been caught.

Linking her arm through his, he smiled down at her. "Anyone who lies as badly as you ought to be paddled within an inch of their life. But since I'm such a gentleman," he grinned, "I've decided to treat you to dinner instead. After we're done performing our secret mission to obtain more clothing for Crystal . . . ?" He paused, waiting for confirmation, which she gave grudgingly, much to his amusement. "We'll go get something to eat. How does that sound?"

It sounded wonderful, but she wasn't going to admit that to him. "It's not as if you're giving me a great deal of choice."

"True. But then I find that a woman tends to do better when her mind's not all muddled up with making choices."

"*Oooh!*" she screeched, attempting to kick him, but he merely laughed, sidestepped her attack, and escorted her out the door.

Crystal looked out her bedroom window to the alley behind the Aurora and wrinkled her nose in disgust. The smell wafting up through the open portal was foul, tainting the freshness of the crisp October day.

The narrow passageway known as Hop Alley was strewn with empty beer barrels, broken liquor bottles, and an assortment of garbage. Rats and roaches roamed over rotting vegetables and partially eaten pieces of food. Chickens and ducks hung on poles suspended between braces, their plucked skin devoured by millions of flies.

The sight was enough to make a body puke.

The building backing up to Chance's saloon was a Chinese restaurant called the Peking Duck, which served more opium than anything else to their customers, and obviously was not overly concerned with the unhealthy conditions it created for adjoining businesses such as Chance's.

The owner, Lee Poon, a wizened wrinkled little man who reminded Crystal of a dried apple, had visited Al's saloon on occasion, availing himself of the whores and paying for their services with the opium he'd addicted them to.

Fortunately, she'd never been one of the chosen, having made it abundantly clear that she wasn't interested in anything having to do with the white powder that took away a person's inhibitions and lulled them into a world of bizarre dreams that were more often than not nightmares.

The knock on the door—three soft raps made in quick succession—made her breath catch in her throat. She recognized the signal as Augustus Baldwin's. He came every afternoon at this time, and she eagerly awaited his visits like a schoolgirl in the throes of her first romance.

Shaking her head at her own stupidity—for what genteel man of God would want to saddle himself with a whore?— she called out for him to enter.

Though he wore a pleasant smile, he looked tired and drawn, his complexion pasty, and she worried that the tuberculosis plaguing his body had rendered him ill again.

"Why, you're up and about, Miss Cummings. I'm so pleased to see you're doing better."

"I wish I could say the same about you, Reverend. You're looking a bit peaked around the edges. Is your sickness worse today?"

Though they'd discussed his ailment, Augustus never felt comfortable dwelling on it. It made him feel weak and frail, and less than a man. He didn't want Crystal to think that way about him. "I'm fine, my dear. It's just the nature of the disease, I'm afraid. Some days are better than others."

"Come in and sit down." She motioned to the small round oak table that had been set with a ceramic teapot and two cups. "Bertha graciously supplied us with some refreshment." She made an effort to speak in a refined manner, though she felt awkward doing so. Genteel words were not going to make her any less a whore, despite what Laurel said.

Laurel had insisted that a change of wardrobe and a few etiquette lessons were all that was needed to smooth some of Crystal's rough edges. But Crystal was of the opinion that you couldn't turn a sow's ear into a silk purse, no matter how hard you tried. And she definitely had a great deal of "pork" still inside her.

Gus took a seat at the table, waiting while Crystal filled his cup with the hot liquid. "Has Bertha said when you'll be going back to work?"

His question made Crystal blush as red as her hair. "I'm not going back to that kind of work again, Reverend."

His own face colored dramatically. "I didn't mean to imply that you would be, Crystal. It is all right if I call you that, isn't it?"

She shrugged. "Many men have." She was purposely being rude, though she wasn't sure why.

If the reverend was shocked by her statement, he gave no indication. Smiling kindly, he patted her hand, and Crystal felt both comforted and stimulated by the innocent gesture. "I'm well aware of your former occupation, Crystal. There's no need to try to warn me that you're not suitable company for someone like me, because that couldn't be further from the truth."

"I don't want or need your pity, Reverend. I'm not ashamed of who I am." She felt that she needed to distance herself from his kindness. She couldn't allow herself to become entangled with someone as decent and kind as the reverend. It just wouldn't be fair to him, no matter how much she wished for it.

"Nor should you be. You're a lovely young woman who's had herself a run of bad luck. I doubt you chose your former profession willingly. Am I right?"

"I did what I had to do to survive. Besides, it didn't much matter. Not after . . ." She closed her eyes, trying to block the hideous image of her drunken father.

Aware of her uneasiness, he said, "I didn't mean to pry, my dear. I only wanted to assure you that I'm here because I want to be. I realize that I'm much too old for you. And not very pleasing to the eye . . ."

"Don't be silly, Augustus!" Crystal blurted. "Why, you're a very handsome man. I thought so the first time I laid eyes on you."

Shocked by her admission, his cheeks warmed. His tender feelings for her were multiplying rapidly. "I'm honored you think so."

Refilling their teacups, Crystal didn't flinch when she said, "I can't change what I am, Augustus, or what I did before we met. I'm a whore, and that's the truth. I've been with more men than I care to think about. I sold myself for money to put food in my belly and clothes on my back.

"I'm not proud of it, but it's a fact that can't be changed. I'm honored that you'd come to visit someone like me, but you should know that you'll probably damage your reputation by doing so."

He threw back his head and laughed at the idea that he had a reputation worth salvaging, but the laughter soon turned to coughing and he removed his handkerchief and pressed it to his mouth. "I can't change what I am either, my dear. I'm a consumptive old fool who's never been married, who's never even had himself a lasting relationship with a woman."

Crystal's eyebrow shot up at that. "You mean you're . . ."

He smiled and shook his head. "No. I'm not inexperienced. I've been with a woman or two, but I've never had what you would call a desire to get close to any woman before. At least, not until now."

Crystal nodded matter-of-factly. "If you're saying you want to bed me, Reverend, that's understandable. Men like you bed women like me all the time."

Clasping her hand, he drew it to his mouth for a kiss. "My dear Crystal, what I'm trying to say, and doing it rather badly, I'm afraid, is that I'd like to court you with the intention of marriage."

"Marriage!" Crystal jumped up from the chair. "Are you insane, Reverend Baldwin? Preachers don't marry whores. Decent men marry decent women. It's the way of things."

He rose to stand behind her, placing his hands on her shoulders. Dressed in the demure flannel robe and nightgown, her glorious red hair pulled back and tied with a green velvet ribbon, Crystal looked as virtuous and demure as any genteel lady of quality. She might have been a prostitute with her body, but he would have bet any amount of money that her heart was as pure and untouched as any virgin's soul.

Turning her toward him, he kissed her forehead. "My dear, I've never been a conventional sort of man. It's true I left Boston because of my illness, but I never really fit in there. It was much too staid, too bound in propriety and custom. I preach the word of God to those who need it—to those folks who might otherwise never have a chance to listen to His message of love and salvation.

"I wouldn't presume to think that you could ever love someone like me, Crystal, but I'd be honored if you would share what is left of my life. I'm not certain what kind of husband I would make, having lived a bachelor's existence.

But I would love, cherish, and protect you from the harshness of the world."

Crystal sank down on the chair, hardly able to believe what this gentle man was saying. He wanted to marry her, to make her his wife, to cherish and love her.

She gazed into his face—a faced marked by years, marked by illness, but she saw only kindness and love. There would be no beatings from this man, no cruelty.

But would it be fair to saddle him with someone like her?

And then there was Al to consider. Al wouldn't give her up willingly. One day there would be hell to pay. She knew that, just as she knew she was falling in love with Augustus Baldwin.

"I cannot commit to anything as serious as marriage right now, Augustus. Though I'm honored that you would even consider sharing your life with me." Noting the disappointment on his face, she patted his cheek. "But I would be willing to have you court me. Discreetly, of course. There's still a part of my old life that needs to be reckoned with."

"You're referring to Al Hazen, of course?"

"I thought I loved Al once. And maybe a part of me did. But I think it was mostly just the need to be loved by someone, anyone. And Al was handy."

"But if you're not in love with him anymore . . ."

"Al's not right in the head. The Bible speaks about an eye for an eye. Well, that's how it is with Al. He's going to want revenge for my leaving him. He'll come after Chance now that I'm here. I won't have him coming after you, too."

Her words wounded, and that hurt showed on his face. "You think Chance can take care of himself, but I'm just a weakling who needs to hide behind a woman's skirts?"

She kissed him softly on the lips, heard his sharp intake of breath, and smiled. "I care about you, Augustus. More than I've ever cared about anyone before. I don't want to be a widow before I have a chance to be a wife."

He drew her to him, caressing her back, her hair, kissing

her cheeks. "What makes you so sure Hazen will come after you? He's not in Denver anymore."

"Al's business is here. He'll be back, if only to get his revenge on me. There's not a great deal I'm sure of, honey, but one thing I'm certain of is the amount of hatred festering in Al's heart. He won't be content to let matters lie. Someday, some way, he'll be back to get me. And he won't be too particular about killing anyone who gets in his way."

The velvety black, diamond-studded sky twinkled with a million stars. The air was biting, stinging her cheeks, and Laurel nestled deeper into the jacket Chance had graciously provided, warming herself against the evening's chill as they walked briskly toward the Aurora.

The scents of brandy, tobacco, and bay rum rose from the woolen garment, teasing her senses. The feel of his hand, warm and strong, holding her own as he guided her across the street made her feel protected and cherished.

It had been a wonderful evening, and though the hour was scandalously late she hated to see it end, hated the thought of Chance going down the hall to his room while she went to hers, of lying in her cold, lonely bed and wondering what Chance was doing in his.

Laurel felt mellow, almost content, after the delicious dinner they'd eaten at Delvechio's Italian Restaurant. They'd supped on veal scallopini and mounds of spaghetti and meatballs, then Chance had surprised her with an invitation to see the perky songstress Annie Wiegel in the musical melodrama, *Bronco Kate*, which was being performed at the Opera House.

Next to her own nerve-wracking opening night, the evening had been the most exhilarating since her arrival in Denver. Chance was a witty and charming companion, always ready with an amusing anecdote or story, and Laurel had just about forgiven him for his earlier highhandedness about accompanying her to the Silver Slipper.

Their arrival at Hazen's establishment had been met with indifference, and they'd been able to procure most of Crystal's clothing thanks to the help of a woman named Monique, the New Orleans whore Crystal had once mentioned. Chance had hired a boy to deliver the clothing to Crystal's room at the Aurora before he and Laurel had gone to the restaurant for dinner.

"It looks as if everyone's already retired for the evening," Chance said, holding open the front door. A single lamp burned, casting eerie shadows over the walls and floors of the saloon. Percy's cage was covered and blessedly quiet, and their voices sounded strange as they bounced off the felt-covered tables and beveled mirrors in the tomblike room.

"I don't think I've ever stayed up this late before, " Laurel admitted. "Even on Christmas Eve."

Chance chuckled, bolting the door behind them. "You're becoming worldly, angel. Watch out you don't turn into a night owl." As if on cue, a distinctive *whoo-whoo-whoo* floated through the doorway, and Laurel smiled, shaking her head.

"If I didn't know better," she said, holding on to his arm as they climbed the stairs, "I'd think you'd arranged that."

When they reached her room, Laurel paused before the door and patted Chance's cheek in a tender display of affection and gratitude. "I guess I should thank you for a wonderful evening, even though I was coerced into it." She smiled impishly.

"What? You're not going to invite me in for a nightcap?" His attempt at looking wounded made her laugh.

"You know perfectly well what spirits do to me. I wasn't able to enjoy that wonderful Chianti you ordered with dinner, and I don't think it would be wise to tempt my luck now. Alcohol and I don't seem to mix."

Reaching behind her, he turned the knob. "So, who says

you have to drink? I'll just have a sip of brandy," he retrieved a silver flask from the hip pocket of his trousers, "and we can continue our pleasant conversation."

"It's late, Chance." But even as she protested, Chance was urging her backward through the doorway, following right behind.

Pearl dashed into the storage closet at the end of the hall to avoid detection, leaving the door cracked slightly to give her a better view of the approaching couple. Her eyes narrowed at the sight of Chance entering Laurel's room. She'd had her suspicions about the two, especially when she'd heard from Bertha, who hadn't bothered to conceal her delight, that Chance had taken Laurel out for an evening on the town. Apparently, her suspicions had just been confirmed: Chance was bedding little Miss Innocence.

Ungrateful bastard! After spending day after day tutoring that dimwitted cousin of his, you'd think Chance would have shown his gratitude by taking her out instead of Miss Goody-Two-Shoes.

Some virgin, she thought. They'd probably been fooling around under everyone's nose the entire time, and no one had realized it. Laurel had just pretended to be innocent, but she was really just as much a whore as the rest of the women working there.

Tiptoeing to Laurel's door, Pearl pressed her ear against it, listening to the soft giggles and sighs of a woman who was obviously enjoying a man's touch—Chance's touch.

And why shouldn't she? Pearl knew firsthand that Chance was a damn good kisser. She'd never fucked anyone quite like him, never felt as satisfied as she had after they'd done it that one time. And she wanted to feel that way again. She wanted it more than anything.

And she was determined to get it.

Chance was hers. She'd had him first, before Laurel had

waltzed into their lives, and she wasn't going to sit back and let Laurel ruin things for her.

If Laurel was out of the picture . . . Pearl tapped a long, lacquered nail against her chin. She'd almost succeeded that first time with Shooter, but he'd been too drunk and too stupid to carry out the plan of raping Laurel and scaring her off.

But Laurel might not be so lucky the next time. She wouldn't always be under Chance's watchful eye, and Pearl would be watching for the right opportunity.

The room seemed suddenly too small with Chance standing in it, and Laurel took a step backward, her eyes round with nervous trepidation. "You shouldn't be in here. What if someone saw you enter?"

He shrugged, stepping closer, until they were face to face. "Everyone's asleep, angel. And all we're doing is having a friendly little chat." He caressed the pounding pulse at the base of her throat.

"I . . . I think you should leave." Chance's touch poured through her veins like molten lava, leaving her trembling and weak kneed.

"Why do you fight what we feel for each other? You know you want me, and I definitely want you."

She pulled away, unable to think when he was touching her, when his lips were so close that she had only to reach out and press her own to them. "I admit I'm attracted to you, Chance, but I also know that women like me are easy conquests to a man like you. And it's no secret that you aren't looking to get married."

He hauled her against his chest, kissing her with all the pent-up passion being near her all evening had created. The jasmine scent of her hair, the feel of her warm breath on his face, and the innocent touch of her hand when she'd gestured to him had combined to play havoc with his emotions.

He wanted her. Wanted her in a way he'd never wanted a

woman before. Not just for sexual gratification, though that was high on the list. He wanted to possess her, make her his exclusively and irrevocably. He wanted to protect her, cherish her . . . .

But she was right: He didn't want to get married, to her or anyone else. Still, they could have a very satisfying relationship. If only she would give in to the natural desire she was feeling.

That desire should have been sending warning signals to Laurel's brain; instead it was shooting warmth to her nipples which were hardened with need, and to the achy area between her thighs, which begged for the feel of his warm hands.

"Let me touch you. Let me make love to you, angel. I want you." His lips never left her mouth, his hands never stopped their persuasive exploration of her now naked back and partially clothed breasts.

When did that happen? Laurel wondered. She couldn't concentrate on anything but the wonderful way Chance's touch made her feel. Her breasts were full, aching, needing to burst forth from their confinement.

When Chance unhooked her corset, removing the last barrier between them, there were no words of protest from Laurel, only soft mewling sounds of frustration and desire as she wrapped herself around his still-clothed body.

"Please," she heard herself say, but her voice sounded hoarse and strange even to her own ears, as if it were coming from a great distance.

"Come," he urged, pulling her toward the bed, his voice smooth and insistent as it lulled her into his silken web. "You're so beautiful." He stroked the satiny flesh of her inner thighs before lowering his head to kiss her there. Her soft moans of pleasure encouraged him to continue, and he toyed with rosy nipples now darkened with passion, laving them, rolling his tongue over the protruding buds, before sucking first one and then the other, while his hands moved to the area between her legs to find she was wet, throbbing, ready to take him.

He stood to remove his jacket and then his shirt, and Laurel watched as if dazed. But when his hands went to the fastening of his trousers, she saw his intent. Finally realizing that this would go much farther than the last time, she shook her head and sat upright.

"No! Please, you mustn't, Chance. I'm a virgin. I must save myself for marriage."

"You're just scared, angel," he crooned, sitting down next to her on the bed, caressing her cheek. "But you mustn't be. Surely you know I would never hurt you."

Not intentionally, Laurel thought. *And never physically.* But to love him, to make love to him, knowing that he didn't love her in return, would never marry her, would be the most hurtful of all things she could experience.

Laurel reached for a corner of the quilt, covering herself, noting the darkening of his eyes, the frustration on his face. She also noted his massive shoulders, the dark furring of hair on his chest, and she wondered if what she was about to do was wise. It certainly wasn't easy.

"Things should never have gotten this far, Chance, and I take full responsibility for what happened here tonight. But I can't go through with . . ." She shook her head. "I'm sorry."

He reached for his shirt, his lip curling disdainfully as he shrugged it back on. He'd never forced a woman in his life, and he wasn't about to start now.

"Why do you deny what you feel? Sex between a man and woman is a beautiful thing."

"Sex between two people who love each other is even more beautiful. And I don't believe you love me, Chance." Even though she wished with all her heart that he did. For there would be no hesitation on her part, if that were the case.

Aching with unfulfilled desire and a need to hurt, as he was now hurting, Chance lashed out at Laurel. "I guess I'm not the Prince Charming you're waiting for, angel. I don't live in a world of fairy tales and make-believe." He grasped her hand, placing it on his erection, ignoring her shocked gasp.

"This is reality, Laurel. I'm a flesh-and-blood man, and God knows you're all woman, if only you'd let yourself be. I'm offering you pleasure beyond comprehension. Passion that defies explanation. A chance to be loved, and loved well."

"But for how long?" Her eyes filled with tears, but she willed them back. She couldn't let him see how much this hurt her. "I want forever. You're only offering now."

"For as long as it lasts, angel. Nothing is forever. We take pleasure where we can and damn the consequences. Life's a gamble. If things work out, fine. If not, we go our separate ways."

Her heart was pounding so loudly in her ears that Laurel feared she was going to pass out. Biting her lower lip, she regained control of her emotions, and in as calm a voice as she could she replied, "You're forgetting something, Chance . . ."

Question replaced the anger in his eyes. "What's that?"

"I'm not a gambler."

CHAPTER 12

Unkempt, ill-tempered, and smelling worse than Zeke Mullins could ever have imagined, Al surreptitiously entered the rear door of the Silver Slipper and came up behind the barkeep, who was pulling whiskey bottles from the shelves while he whistled a slightly off-key rendition of "Buffalo Gals."

"What the hell are you so goddamn happy about, Mullins?"

Whirling about, wrinkling his nose in disgust at the offensive odor emanating from Al, Zeke nearly dropped the whiskey bottle he held. He took in his employer's torn checkered trousers and mud-stained shirt. The man looked as if he'd been dragged for miles behind a couple of angry mules, and he smelled a hell of a lot worse than he looked. "Jesus, Al! What's that stink?"

Scraping the horseshit from the soles of his usually immaculate shoes on the edge of a wooden crate, Al was none too pleased by the question or by Zeke's comment on his foul odor.

"Get someone to clean up that goddamn mess out back," he ordered. "And tell Luke to haul me up some hot water so I can wash the stench off me."

"Where you been? You've been gone almost two weeks. Everyone's been askin'. The girls were afraid you'd run off with their share of the profits."

"Tell them to get fucked—literally! We need to make up for lost time."

Nodding, Zeke turned to leave, but Al grasped his shoulder before he could avoid the inevitable question.

"Where is she?"

Zeke hated to be the one to break the news of Crystal's whereabouts, especially knowing that Al wasn't going to like it one bit. "Gone, Al. Crystal's gone."

A shattered look passed over Al's face, then was quickly masked by one of outrage. "She left town?"

The bartender shook his head, and Hazen's lips slashed thin. "Crystal's at the Aurora, isn't she? With that bastard Rafferty?"

"Crystal was bad off, Al. You nearly killed her. She had to go somewhere for help."

He sneered. "I shoulda killed the bitch. This is what I get for showing mercy. Now she's gone over to the enemy. Probably sleeping with the green-eyed bastard. She screwed him once, you know. Didn't even charge him. Rubbed my nose in it, she did."

"I'm sure Crystal ain't sleeping with Rafferty, boss. Monique claims Chance is hot for that little blond gal he's got singing for him. Says they came in together to gather Crystal's things, then went out for a night on the town."

"Pearl, that big-busted whore Rafferty's got serving drinks, says he's stickin' it to her, just like you figured."

Al kicked the crate clear across the room, breaking it into several pieces. "I'm gonna get even with that slick thievin' bastard if it's the last thing I do. And Crystal's gonna be damn sorry she betrayed me."

Rafferty might be having a lucky streak, but he wasn't going to win this time. The stakes were too high for Al to let that happen. The gambler had three things he cared deeply about: the Aurora, his simpleminded cousin, and the Martin woman. It'd be a pity if something were to happen to one or more of them, Al decided, rubbing his chin thoughtfully. Maybe if Rafferty lost what was important to him, he'd know how Al felt about losing Crystal.

She was his. Only his. And he meant to get her back, no matter what or whom he had to destroy to do it.

Pacing the confines of her sparsely furnished room, Pearl took several deep drags on a cigarette and blew smoke rings over her head while she planned and plotted the best way to get rid of scheming Laurel Martin.

Pearl had come to the conclusion that Chance deserved one more opportunity to realize that she, Pearl, was the better of the two women. He might be screwing Laurel—no doubt she'd snared him with her innocent act. Men were suckers for that shit—but once Laurel was gone, Chance would forget all about her. Pearl would make certain of that.

She knew dozens of ways to please a man. The Chinaman, Lee Poon, had instructed her years ago in the art of Oriental lovemaking. And she'd been an excellent, if not overzealous, student.

She liked sex. And often. She would have done it for free if she weren't intent on making a living. Some women were good at cooking or sewing, some had a knack for dancing or singing, but Pearl was just good at lovemaking.

She'd been introduced to it at fourteen when one of her mama's best customers had wandered into her room at the brothel by mistake, and Pearl soon discovered that a few seductive smiles and come-hither stares could earn her a lot more money than her mama was making.

The miner offered to pay her five dollars for a look at her

tits, which he'd said were the most beautiful things he'd ever laid eyes on, and fifteen more if she let him fuck her. Of course she had, and she'd enjoyed every delicious minute of it.

Standing in front of the long cheval glass, the sun glinting off the mirror and her long bleached-blond hair, Pearl stripped off her red satin wrapper to gaze at her reflection.

Her breasts had always been her best asset. She fondled the pendulous globes, admiring their lushness, pinching both nipples until they hardened into two pulsing points, all the while imagining Chance's lips upon them, sucking and teasing, and she sighed with pleasure.

Pearl liked it rough, hard, and fast. And Chance Rafferty had the equipment and the body to pleasure a woman long into the night. Just thinking about him made her hot, wet, and wanting.

Pearl's erotic fantasies were interrupted by a persistent knocking on her door, and she frowned. "Who is it?"

"It's me, Miss Pearl. You said to come to your room for my lesson."

Whitey. How intriguing, Pearl thought, smiling wickedly. He'd come for a lesson, and she wondered just what entertaining things she could teach him today.

"Come in, sugar. I was just resting a bit."

Whitey opened the door and his smile suddenly froze. Gasping, he covered his eyes. "You ain't decent, Miss Pearl."

"Come in and shut the door, sugar," she coaxed. "I was just about to get dressed."

Whitey did as instructed, but his hand remained firmly clasped over his eyes, though he could still picture Pearl, all white and naked, and his skin started to tingle.

Pearl noticed the slight bulge in the front of his pants and was pleased that the dimwit wasn't immune to her charms. "I thought you said I was pretty, Whitey. How come you're covering your eyes? Don't you like to look at me?"

Whitey felt a lump in his throat. "Sure I think you're purty, Miss Pearl. But Chance says I'm not to look at naked women. He says it ain't the proper thing to do."

She crossed the room to stand nude before him. "Chance has seen me naked, Whitey. He's even touched my breasts. Would you like to touch them?" She pulled his hand down to uncover his eyes, which were still shut tightly.

"I don't know if I should, Miss Pearl. What if Chance were to find out? He'd be mad, mad, mad."

She made the decision for him by placing his hand on her breast, and she felt his fingers tremble as they clasped the satiny globe in exploration. The innocent massage sent currents of desire racing through Pearl, and she smiled ruefully, thinking that even a simpleton had the power to turn her on.

"Chance wouldn't have to know, Whitey," she said. *"Mmmm,* that feels so good, sugar. I like it when you touch me. Chance touches me like that sometimes."

Opening his eyes, he stared at her large breasts, at his hands touching her pink rigid nipples, and he pulled back as if he'd been burned. "I ain't never touched a woman before."

Leading him farther into the room, like a lamb to slaughter, she pushed him down on the bed. "Do you like what you see?" Hands on ample hips, she posed and postured for him, delighting in the drool of excitement dribbling down his chin. His gaze focused on the dark patch of hair between her thighs, and his curiosity wasn't the only thing aroused.

"Can I touch that?"

Pearl smiled, stepped closer, and covered his hand with hers as she placed it on her mound and showed him the slow seductive movement that drove her wild. "How does that feel, sugar?"

"Funny. I feel funny, too. My Willy's hard as a brick," he explained, using the euphemism Bertha had taught him. "Is something wrong with it, Miss Pearl? It hurts."

She rubbed his long, hard shaft, running her tongue over her lips, anticipating. "All men's pricks get hard when they touch a woman, Whitey. Even your cousin's. Chance has put his deep inside me. It felt real good."

His look of confusion told Pearl it was time to end the lesson for today, though she silently bemoaned the fact that she wouldn't find out if he was really as huge as he felt. The thought of taking that hard shaft deep within her made her wet mound quiver.

Backing away, trying to regain her composure, she reached for her wrapper. "You mustn't tell anyone that I showed you my secret place, sugar. Chance wouldn't like it."

He scratched his head. "How come? If he's seen your titties, how come I can't?"

Securing her robe, she nestled herself on his lap, wiggling her bottom until she heard him moan. "Chance is jealous of you, sugar. If he knew we were together like this, that you had touched me here," she pointed to her breasts, "and here," then to her crotch, "he'd be mad at both of us. You won't tell anyone, will you, sugar? It has to be our secret."

He shook his head, wondering why his Willy was throbbing so much. "I promise, Miss Pearl. But if I do good with my lessons, do you think you'd show me your titties again?"

"Sugar," she said, caressing his cheek. "If you do real good, and do everything I say, I'm going to let you do a whole lot more than look. Would you like that, sugar?"

Staring at her breasts, now hidden by the red satin material, he nodded enthusiastically, giving her a hug of affection. "Yes'm," he said loudly. "I'd like it fine, fine, fine."

Still smarting over Laurel's rejection of him, and remembering how adamant she'd been about saving her virginity for a goddamn Prince Charming who wasn't likely to ever materialize, Chance cursed inwardly, paying scant attention to what Bull was anxiously trying to tell him.

"Are you listening, Chance? I said those women from that

temperance league are making a nuisance out front again. They're going to scare the customers away."

Chance gazed in the direction his barkeep pointed. Through the condensation-covered plate glass window he saw six women carrying placards and banners as they marched on the sidewalk in front of his saloon. For the past three days they'd been permanent fixtures, and he wondered why he'd been so blessed to attract their attention.

The Women's Christian Temperance Union, or WCTU, as they were called, were a bunch of frustrated old biddies who were hell-bent on ridding every town and city they settled in from "the ravages of alcohol," as they so eloquently and frequently preached.

"Repent, ye sinners!" they shouted. "Alcohol and demon rum will be your ruination!"

"Jesus," Chance said. "Why the hell don't they take their singing and chanting somewhere else? They give me the creeps."

Bull poured Chance a whiskey, figuring he could use something stronger than coffee long about now. "The leader's the worst of the lot. Her name's Hortensia Tungsten. She's formed some local group called the Denver Temperance and Souls in Need League. She called me a whoremonger the other day when I tried to get in the door, tried to knock me over the head with that sign she carries."

"I wonder if it would do any good to summon the police. Maybe they could get rid of them."

Bull shook his head. "Naw. Mort Fines over at the Hurdy Gurdy House tried that. Chief Stebbins said they was within their right to demonstrate, as long as they didn't do any damage to the premises."

Swallowing his whiskey, Chance welcomed the fiery brew into his gut. It was getting cold outside; the sky had the promise of sleet or snow, and he expected to see one or both before morning. "They'll most likely get tired of marching and go on home," Chance said. "And if the weather worsens, they'll surely give up then."

Bull didn't look nearly as confident as Chance sounded. "I don't know, Chance. I've heard of these temperance women making trouble in other parts of the country. They're like ticks that burrow beneath your skin and refuse to come out."

Chance knew that the WCTU reached every city and state in the country. The organization was comprised only of females—men were banned from voting membership. Through song and prayer, touted from church pulpits sympathetic to their cause and from makeshift bandstands wherever crowds would gather, they spewed forth their edict of salvation through sobriety.

Like an out-of-control prairie fire, their fanatical gospel had spread, and Chance feared that businesses such as his were likely to burn as a result.

Women! They're just not happy until they can change a man.

Plowing his fingers through his hair, Chance finally replied, "I got more important things to worry about right now, Bull." Like how he was going to get Laurel into bed without marrying her. And how he was going to exact his pound of flesh from Hazen's hide, now that the bastard was back in town.

Yeah, he had a lot more important things to think about than a bunch of man-hating harpies.

It had been a slow night, thanks to the inclement weather and those damn temperance women who hadn't allowed the light snowfall to interfere with their praying and singing of hymns. If he heard another chorus of "Nearer My God To Thee," Chance thought he might have to hurt someone.

The fact that Laurel was humming the hymn as she approached the bar didn't help his mood. "I'd appreciate it if you found some other tune to sing, angel. That one's getting on my nerves."

Noting his irritation and the way he kept popping his knuckles, Laurel smiled, knowing how annoyed he'd grown with the ladies of the temperance league. She actually found their singing quite refreshing and uplifting compared to the bawdy ditties she was asked to perform. "Really? I kind of like it."

"Was there something you wanted or needed?" His eyebrow arched as his gaze skimmed over her red satin costume. It hugged every delicious curve, presenting her lovely legs to definite advantage, and he wondered at his own stupidity in insisting that she dress so provocatively. Perhaps a change of costume was in order. Something high-necked and long-sleeved, that draped in folds down to the floor.

"I just thought you should know that the ceiling in my room is leaking like a sieve. I told Jup about it, but he said I should speak to you."

Chance sighed. He'd been neglecting things of late. The roof was merely one in a long list of things requiring his attention. Unfortunately his attention had been diverted elsewhere; he stared meaningfully at Laurel. "I'll have someone take care of it first thing in the morning. Will you be all right tonight? Because if you need something, anything, I'll be only too happy to accommodate you. My bed is large enough for two."

The suggestive remark made Laurel's knees wobble. Chance's caressing fingers on her cheek almost weakened her resolve, but she was determined to stand fast in her refusal to bed him.

Until she saw some indication that he loved her, there would be no lovemaking. It was that simple. She had no intention of giving the milk away for free; he'd take the whole cow, or nothing, as her mama had cautioned.

"I'm sure tomorrow will be fine. The leak is in the far corner of the room, away from the bed."

"Hey! That's some pair you got, sweetie. Give me some tongue. My dick's hard."

Laurel looked sharply at the parrot, her lip curling in disgust, then she stuck out her tongue. "There you go, you perverted bird. Have some tongue."

Chance threw back his head, and the deep, rich baritone sound of his laughter sent shivers down Laurel's spine. "The parrot's got the right idea, angel. Me and Percy are suffering from the same affliction."

Her gaze traveled down to the rather pronounced bulge at the front of his trousers, and her face flamed. "I'm sure you won't have any difficulty finding someone to ease your *affliction.*" She started to walk away, but he grabbed her arm.

"I don't want just anyone, angel. Don't you know that by now?"

If only that were true, she thought. "Save your seductive comments, Chance. They're not going to work."

"It's going to get mighty cold this winter in that big lonely bed of yours. How long do you intend to wait for that Prince Charming of yours to show up?"

She caressed his cheek, replying in her sweetest voice, "Someone once said that you have to kiss a lot of toads before you meet your prince. I guess I'm still in the toad-kissing stage of my life. Good night, Chance. Sleep tight."

Watching her walk away, Chance shook his head and reached for the bottle of whiskey on the bar, pouring himself a hefty shot. A toad, was he? He'd see about that!

Hoping she'd made Chance furious, Laurel glanced over her shoulder, plastering a smug smile on her face, only to have it dissolve at the sight of Pearl draping herself around Chance's neck.

Like a vulture circling its prey, it hadn't taken the whore long to swoop down on her victim. Though Chance didn't look like he minded in the least that he was about to be devoured.

A white-hot stab of jealousy knifed through Laurel, bringing unexpected tears to her eyes as she hurried to the kitchen. There was only one cure for the way she felt at the moment: Bertha's applesauce-spice cookies. Lots of them!

*   *   *

"Hey, sugar! What're you looking so glum about? I take it little Miss Priss rejected your offer?" Pearl caressed his stubbled cheek, smiling inwardly. She recognized the sexual frustration on Chance's face; she'd seen that look a thousand times on "happily" married men and on schoolboys on the prowl. "Some women don't know when they're well off, do they?"

In no mood for Pearl's flirtations, Chance's eyes darkened. "What's between me and Laurel is none of your business, Pearl. So why don't you run along?"

Ignoring the suggestion, she poured herself a drink. "Why, sugar, I didn't know there was something between the two of you."

Chance covered his mistake smoothly, unwilling to let Pearl's viperous tongue sully Laurel's reputation. "There isn't. But even if there was, it'd be none of your business."

"A woman in my profession can't help but notice when a man is getting all hot and bothered. And, sugar, I saw the bulge in your pants from clear across the room." She trailed her finger up his arm. "A man like you shouldn't have to suffer, sugar. I'd be happy to cure what ails you. We had a good time once."

The thought of bedding Pearl made Chance's stomach roil. Her coarse, oversexed demeanor wasn't the least bit appealing. And even if his dick was suffering a bad case of rejection, he sure as hell wasn't going to cure it by sticking it into someone who had been used as many times as Pearl. Even he had his standards.

The startling thought that whores and easy women weren't quite as tempting as a certain blond virgin made him wonder just what kind of spell Laurel had weaved around him. He hadn't had eyes for anyone else since she'd set foot in his place. And, he realized with a great deal of disgust, he hadn't had any womanly comfort, either.

No doubt he was destined to go through life with a permanent hardening to his male member. Damn, his luck was changing for the worse!

"What do you say, sugar? Let's go up to my room and get naked and sweaty. I'll let you do whatever you want to me; you know I'll make it good for you. Don't you remember how good it was between us?"

Her hand on his neck felt like a hundred pounds of cloying velvet, weighing him down, suffocating him. Shaking his head, he removed the offending appendage. "Thanks for the offer, Pearl. But no thanks. I'm not going to compound my previous mistake by repeating it. I was drunk, and you were insistent, if I remember correctly." *Very insistent, if memory serves.* "I admit to being weak, but as I told you once before, fraternizing with the help is not good for business."

Her eyes darkened at the rebuff, and her fingers curled like claws at her side. "I guess I'm not good enough for you anymore, is that it, Chance? You've only got eyes for that mealy-mouthed priss, who couldn't care less whether you live or die." She tossed back her head and laughed. "It's your loss, sugar. There're plenty of men who'd like to bed me." *Like your dear cousin, Whitey, who finds me irresistible,* she added silently, her lips forming a spiteful smile.

"There's never been anything between us, Pearl, so don't go pretending there is. You're a good barmaid, nothing more. What you do on your own time is your business. I just don't want you doing it with me."

"I'll make you sorry for the way you're treating me, Chance Rafferty. I'll make you all sorry. Just you wait and see if I don't."

"Anytime you're unhappy with our arrangement, Pearl, you can pack up and leave."

Like a snake, her hand darted out to rub the length of him before he could pull back. "I got bigger fish to fry. Much bigger than you, sugar." And it was time she tossed both into the fry pan.

CHAPTER 13

Bertha found Laurel seated at the kitchen table, one hand in the cookie jar, the other pressing the remainder of an applesauce-spice cookie into her mouth. There was a half-empty glass of milk in front of her and a mound of cookie crumbs on the floor beneath her chair, indicating she'd been at the jar for quite some time.

"Lord have mercy, child! What you doing stuffin' yourself like that? And look at the mess you done made." Scurrying to the closet, Bertha took out the broom and began to sweep, all the while mumbling about messy white folk.

She *had* made a mess of everything, Laurel realized. And she wasn't sure how she was going to fix it.

Why, oh, why had she fallen in love with someone as unsuitable as Chance Rafferty? And why, that being the case, couldn't the powers that be at least have made him love her back?

"I'm sorry about the mess, Bertha. I was planning on cleaning it up before I went to bed." The thought of bed made her cringe. Was Chance upstairs with Pearl at that very moment, enjoying what Laurel was unwilling to give?

Noting the misery on the young woman's face, Bertha set the broom aside and lowered her bulk into one of the chairs. "You going to tell me what's wrong, Miss Laurel? I knows you don't like my cookies that much."

Laurel reached across the table to grasp the black woman's hand, drawing strength and solace from it. "My life's a miserable mess, Bertha, and I don't know what to do about it."

"You's in love with Mr. Chance, ain't you, honey?"

Laurel's eyes widened at the woman's perceptiveness. "How'd you know? I thought I was doing a pretty good job of keeping my feelings hidden."

"Maybe from that thick-skulled man. But, honey, I's a woman. And a woman knows the symptoms of lovesickness."

"Well, it's likely to kill me if I don't leave here, Bertha. I can't go on pining away for a man who'll never think of me in terms other than a convenience, who other women fawn over, and who laps up the attention like a cat with a full bowl of cream."

"I thinks you is selling Mr. Chance short, Miss Laurel. He ain't been lookin' at no other woman since you came to work here."

"I'm just a challenge for him, Bertha. Something to win. You know how Chance loves a challenge. But once I give him the one thing he covets, he'll lose interest."

"You ain't got nowhere else to go, child. You can't just up and leave."

Mr. Chance would be devastated, Bertha knew. He might not act like Miss Laurel meant anything to him, but Bertha knew her boy. He was crazy about the young woman, even if he was too stupid and stubborn to know it himself. Bertha had never seen him so moody, except when he was on a losing streak. And he'd been off his feed lately. That just wasn't like him. Not like him a'tall.

Laurel sighed at the truth of Bertha's words. She'd

thought of going back to Kansas. But where would she stay? The duke had his hands full with Rose Elizabeth, and she doubted he would welcome another Martin sister with open arms. She supposed she could find a job at one of the other gambling parlors. But most likely they'd be run by men like Hazen, who'd want her to sell herself to the highest bidder. And having had a taste of Chance's lovemaking, she knew she could never be with anyone else.

"You mustn't fret so, Miss Laurel. Things have a way of workin' out for the best. You just gotta believe that."

"I'd miss you and Jup if I were to leave here, Bertha. You've been like family to me." Laurel's eyes filled with tears, which brought Bertha's anger to the forefront.

"I's going to talk to that thick-headed, no-account gambling man and set him straight about a few things."

Laurel shook her head. "Oh, no, Bertha! You must promise not to say anything to Chance about what I've told you. I'd be humiliated if he found out how I felt about him."

"But if you love him, honey, why don't you tell him? That could make all the difference in the world."

"Chance doesn't want to love anyone, Bertha. He likes being a carefree, happy-go-lucky gambler, with no strings attached and no wife to weigh him down. If he knew I cared for him, it would only add to his burden. I won't have a man care for me out of guilt or a misguided sense of duty."

"But at least talk to him, honey. Let him know that you're thinking about leavin'. Maybe the shock will bring him to his senses."

Laurel rose and circled the table. Kneeling beside Bertha, she wrapped her arms about the black woman's massive girth and hugged her fiercely. "I love you, Bertha, and I'll never forget you, no matter what happens."

Tears filled the old woman's eyes, and she sniffed loudly. "Lord have mercy! You're makin' me bawl like a baby, child. I loves you, too. And I don't want you leavin' here. Me and Jup thinks of you like a daughter."

Laurel's smile was almost apologetic as she said, "Between me, Chance, and Whitey, you've got yourself a very difficult trio of adopted children, Bertha."

"Yes'm. I knows that. But I wouldn't trade any one of you young'ns. I loves you all like you was my own flesh and blood. And that's a fact."

"What's a fact?" Jup wanted to know, walking into the kitchen with a big grin on his face, but pulling up short as he saw that the two women were crying.

Bertha shot him a quelling look. "Hush up, you black devil. This here's private talk between me and my baby. And you ain't invited to listen."

Laurel smiled inwardly at Jupiter's indignant expression, the way he drew himself up all stiff and fit to be tied whenever Bertha got his goat, which was often.

The old couple reminded her of her parents when they'd argued about something. Adelaide Martin had never let Ezra get the best of her in any disagreement either.

Laurel hadn't been exaggerating when she'd claimed that Bertha and Jup were like family. And she didn't know how she would cope with missing them, if she decided to leave.

And then there was the matter of Chance.

How would she be able to exist without seeing him every day, without hearing his voice, his teasing comments?

How could she go on with her life knowing that she'd left the best part of it behind?

But can I love a man who doesn't love me back?

"Do you see that young blond woman across the café? The one seated next to the red-haired woman?"

"You mean the prostitute?"

The heavier of the two women shook her head. "I don't think she's a prostitute, Gertie. I've made inquiries about her. Word has it that she merely sings for her supper."

"But we saw her dressed in that awful red satin gown. It

was indecent. And she was parading back and forth across the stage like a jezebel. No decent woman would behave in such a fashion."

Hortensia Tungsten clucked her tongue disapprovingly. "We are here to show these unfortunate souls the error of their ways, not to cast aspersions. Perhaps this young woman can aid our cause, and we can aid hers in return."

Gertie Beecham gasped, clutching the cameo pinned to her collar, which was as stiffly starched as her spine. "You can't be serious. Why, we'd lose our charter from the WCTU. Surely Miss Willard would never countenance such a thing."

"I'm in charge of the Denver League, and I will say what is appropriate and what is not." She inhaled the last bit of pecan pie, patting her generous stomach contentedly. "A fine meal. Surprising really, considering the location of this place."

Gertie sighed. Instead of waxing poetic over her food, Hortensia needed to be paying closer attention to the matters at hand. Gazing across the cafe, she noted that the woman in question was now standing. Her subdued and attractive gown of gray foulard silk was quite in contrast to her outrageous and sinful costume of the other evening. Her companion was decked out in a green velvet dress cut much too low for daytime wear. Or any other time, Gertie decided as an afterthought, pursing her lips.

"Hurry, Gertrude, " Hortensia urged, heaving her bulk out of the chair. "They're about to leave and I want to catch them before they go."

"You're not serious, Hortensia! Tell me you're not."

"I've never been more serious about anything in my life, dear. Pay the check. We have important work to do this day 'For God and Home and Native Land.' " The WCTU motto sprang easily from her lips, halting any further objection Gertie was about to make on the subject.

Stepping outside into the crisp November day, Laurel huddled beneath the new woolen cape she'd just purchased with some of her earnings. It felt good to have a measure of independence, not to be beholden to anyone for support. Though if she were completely truthful with herself, independence did come with a high price tag: loneliness.

"I'm completely stuffed to my seams." Crystal looped her arm through Laurel's. "Your suggestion to go out for lunch was a welcome one. Bertha watches me like a hawk, even though I'm fully recovered from my . . ." Her smile of a moment ago faded. She was going to say *accident*, but what Al had done to her had been no accident.

"Bertha likes to baby everyone. I guess it's because she has no children of her own to fuss over."

The mention of children brought a dreamy look to Crystal's face. "I'd like to have a child one day, wouldn't you? I couldn't think of anything more wonderful than to hold a mewling babe against my breast." Her sigh was wistful, touching a responsive chord in Laurel's breast.

She'd never given much thought to having children. She'd always thought that someday she would, but it had never seemed important until now. Until Chance Rafferty had waltzed into her life and given her a taste of passion, the feeling of possessing someone, and being possessed in return.

Yeah, you're possessed all right, Laurel Martin! she told herself. *But definitely not in the romantic sense.*

Trying to mask her unhappiness, for it didn't look like marriage and motherhood were in the cards, especially with Chance stacking the deck against her, she forced a playful smile to her lips. "Especially if that babe just happens to belong to the Reverend Augustus Baldwin."

Suddenly Crystal ground to a halt, gasping aloud, and Laurel looked up to see Al Hazen crossing the snow-encrusted street in their direction. Enraged by the sight of the pimp, she yanked hard on Crystal's arm. "Come, Crystal," she urged. "Hurry!" But Crystal stood fast.

"I'll not show fear to that piece of slime. Al feeds on fear; it's what makes him thrive."

"Good afternoon, ladies," Hazen said, tipping his bowler as if nothing were out of the ordinary. "How nice to see you both. You're looking well, Crystal." His gaze skimmed over her possessively.

"No thanks to you. What do you want? We're in a hurry."

"Is that any way to treat an old friend, after all that we've meant to each other?"

"You're a part of my past life, Al. I've gone on to bigger and better things." And she suddenly realized that what she had said was true. She had Augustus now, and Al no longer had a stranglehold over her emotions.

Crystal was released from his spell for the first time since she'd met him. Her new job, new friends, and newfound love had all blended together to give her strength. She was no longer the frightened child Al Hazen had "rescued" three years before. She was a woman. And she was free.

At the dark look passing over his face, a lump of fear rose in Laurel's throat. But instead of pleading with Crystal to leave, she allowed her to have her say. It was obvious that the woman needed to vent her anger.

"What was between us is over. I'm through allowing you to control me, to use me for your own gain. Your hold is gone, Al, and I want to be left alone."

Hands fisting at his sides, Al's face turned purple in rage. "Don't think you're so high and mighty now, babe, just because you're working for Rafferty. You're still a whore, Crystal, and that will never change. You spreading your legs for Rafferty, or is that honor reserved for Miss Martin?"

He turned to Laurel. "I've heard about you, sweetheart. Word has it you're fucking the boss. Well, it wouldn't be the first time, now would it? Crystal can tell you all about that, can't you, babe?"

Ignoring the taunts, and noting Crystal's ghostly pallor, Laurel grasped her friend's arm firmly. "Come along, Crystal. We don't have to stand here and listen to this foul-mouthed animal spewing forth garbage." They tried to leave, but Hazen blocked their path, refusing to step aside.

Incensed by the man's effrontery, Laurel felt her cheeks heat in anger. "Please remove yourself at once, Mr. Hazen. You're in our way."

"I'm not done talking to you *ladies* yet." He sneered as he said the word, and grasped their arms.

"Unhand those women at once! And remove yourself from these premises, sir."

Hazen's gaze slid to the two white-haired matrons marching determinedly toward him. Dressed in unrelenting black, they looked like buzzards swooping in for the kill. One carried a large, hand-lettered sign that read: REPENT YOUR SINS OR BURN IN HELL, and the other was wearing a familiar and very unwelcome white ribbon tied in a bow: the badge of the Women's Christian Temperance Union.

He forced down a curse and attempted a smile, not wishing to incur the women's wrath. The last thing he needed were do-gooders picketing the Silver Slipper. Business was bad enough as it was. "I was just having a word with these ladies," he explained.

"It's obvious, sir, that these young women don't wish to converse with you," Hortensia Tungsten stated, motioning her friend forward. "Gertie," she directed, "if this gentleman does not remove himself directly, please bash him over the head with your sign."

Wide-eyed, Laurel and Crystal looked at each other, then shared a smile.

Al's lips tightened. "I have every right to be on the street. You can't tell me who to talk to, lady."

A crowd was beginning to gather. The newsboy on the corner stopped hawking his papers, and the wooden cart loaded with vegetables stopped dead in the middle of the street, its driver leaning forward on his knee to take a closer look. People drifted out of the various businesses, pausing to see what all the commotion was about.

Hortensia couldn't have been more pleased. She loved a crowd. It was how she and her flock of women spread their word. And she fully intended to make good use of her audience. "What is the name of your establishment, sir? For as sure as I'm standing here, I know you're in the business of sin and corruption. You definitely look the type."

"He owns the Silver Slipper," someone standing on the sidewalk shouted.

"That's the gospel truth. The Slipper's a brothel, and a more sinful place you'll never lay eyes on," a sharp female voice proclaimed with contempt.

Noting the hostility on several of the onlookers' faces, and knowing that his saloon was sure to be targeted by these harridans, Al's eyes glittered with rage and vengeance. "Another time," he whispered to Laurel and Crystal before spinning on his heel to beat a hasty retreat.

Breathing a sigh of relief, Laurel held out her hand to the older woman. "I don't know how we can ever thank you, ma'am. What you did was very brave. Mr. Hazen is a terrible human being."

Crystal nodded, awed by the woman standing before her.

Hortensia Tungsten was an imposing sight to behold. Standing close to six feet tall, she was large boned and prone to excess flesh, due to the desserts she was so fond of eating. She wasn't particularly attractive; her hawklike nose and close-set eyes stamped her homely. But she had a lot of gumption, and a commanding voice that made people sit up and take notice.

She'd been recruited two years before by Frances Willard, the union's intrepid leader, who recognized in Hortensia the fortitude and tenacity so necessary to winning the battle against demon rum.

Gertie came to stand beside her friend and mentor. "We deduced as much. Hortensia knew at a moment's glance that horrible man was up to no good. She's very astute about such things."

"Allow us to introduce ourselves," the taller of the two

women said, holding out a gloved hand. "I'm Hortensia Tungsten, and this is my associate, Gertie . . . Gertrude Beecham. We're with the newly formed Denver Temperance and Souls in Need League, and I wondered, Miss Martin, if I might have a word with you, while my associate escorts your friend, Miss Cummings, back to the Aurora."

"You know where we work?" Laurel could barely contain her surprise. These weren't the type of women who frequented businesses on this side of town.

"Actually, Miss Martin, I know a great deal about you, which is why I'd like to talk to you privately, if you'll allow me."

At Laurel's hesitation, Crystal patted her hand reassuringly. "I'll be fine, Laurel honey." She looped her arm through red-faced Gertie Beecham's arm and said, much to the astonished woman's mortification, "Ready, Miss Beecham?" before giving Laurel a sly wink.

"Shall we go back inside the cafe? I fear the weather's not suitable for a civilized discussion."

As if on cue from a higher authority, a light snow began to fall, giving credence to the woman's words, and Laurel stared at Hortensia Tungsten with renewed admiration.

Once they were seated, Hortensia, who couldn't possibly miss the opportunity to sample the pumpkin pie she'd been eyeing at lunch, ordered two big slices and two mugs of hot coffee.

"I understand you perform nightly at the Aurora, Miss Martin," she said, dropping two heaping spoons of sugar into her coffee, then lacing it with a generous dollop of cream, unmindful that it was likely to add yet another fold to the pair of chins she now sported.

Laurel blushed. "Yes, I do. But probably not in the way you're thinking, Miss Tungsten. I'm not a prostitute. Financial constraints forced me to seek employment as a saloon singer after my efforts to find honest work at the Opera House failed. Believe me, Miss Tungsten, I endeavored to succeed at opera, but was told that my voice was unsuitable." Witherspoon's rejection still stung like hailstones against soft skin.

The older woman nodded, licking the gooey pumpkin pie off her fork before replying. "I heard as much, dear. Your experience working in a saloon and gambling parlor intrigues me. Though many of us know firsthand about the evils of drink—my own disreputable husband, Reginald, drank himself to death—it would help our cause immensely to have someone with your inside knowledge of saloon life . . . gambling and prostitution included."

"My knowledge? I'm afraid I don't understand."

"Our leader, Miss Willard, founder of the Women's Christian Temperance Union, believes that rather than dwell on the evils of drink, we should instead emphasize the moral and religious aspects of temperance and the impractical side of alcohol consumption.

"Men who spend money gambling and drinking deprive their families of necessities such as food, clothing, and education. I'm sure you have observed family men gambling away resources that could better be spent on their wives and children."

Laurel had in fact witnessed this many times over, but a sense of loyalty to her friends and co-workers at the Aurora kept her silent.

Hortensia touched the white ribbon pinned to her lapel. "This is our badge of courage, Miss Martin. It symbolizes purity, womanliness, God, and home. Miss Willard calls our group 'the great society,' and that is what we are. Through peaceful confrontation and the gathering of pledge signatures, we hope to unite women of this land to stand up for their rights and defy the abuses that men heap upon them. We also hope that through our efforts women will one day earn the right to vote."

Setting down her fork, Laurel shook her head in confusion. "That is all very noble, Miss Tungsten, but I don't understand what all of this has to do with me. I'm working in a saloon, undermining the very thing for which you stand."

Grasping Laurel's hand, Hortensia looked deeply into her eyes, trying to convey the conviction she felt in her soul. "But, my dear, that is the whole point. Your experience can be put to the good. You could join our cause and speak out for the downtrodden women of Denver, for the children who go to bed hungry every night, for those poor unfortunates who are beaten senseless by drunk and abusive husbands, lovers, and fathers."

"Crystal." Laurel said her friend's name aloud, not realizing she'd done so.

"We all have friends, my dear, who have been abused in one form or another. I, myself, was treated abominably and was not the least bit sorry when my husband succumbed to his failing.

"If, as you've led me to believe, your present employment is only temporary and unsuited to your true nature, then join us, Miss Martin. Speak out against what you have observed."

Speaking out against Chance, Crystal, Flora Sue, and the others who earned their living at the Aurora was unthinkable, and her concern shone on her face.

"I can almost read your mind, dear," Hortensia said. "You've made friends and feel you'd be betraying them by joining our cause. And I admire your loyalty. But think of the many you'd help."

"Miss Tungsten, I'm honored by your proposal, but loyalty aside, there is a practical reason for not joining you. I now have a roof over my head, and the ability to earn my own way. I cannot afford to walk away from my present job."

"We would supply you with whatever you need, Miss Martin. A room will be furnished, though it will be necessary to share your accommodations with others. Three meals a day will also be provided, without alcohol, of course!"

Thinking of her humiliating bout with a bottle of champagne, Laurel knew she'd never miss alcohol!

"And your salary will be provided by donations, which are gathered during speaking engagements."

Laurel's eyes widened. "You would expect me to speak?"

"Indeed, my dear. You'd be the featured speaker, the center of attention, so to speak. People will come from miles around to hear what you have to say on the evils of gambling and demon rum. You'll be given their undivided attention."

The center of undivided attention. How different that would be from what she was doing now. But as tempting as Hortensia Tungsten made it sound, Laurel knew she couldn't go against her friends. "I don't think I'm the right person for this job, Miss Tungsten, though I appreciate the offer."

Hortensia clasped Laurel's hand. "Think on it, Miss Martin. Don't give me your answer now. The Lord works in mysterious ways. If your destiny is to aid our cause, then He will provide the way. Just promise me you will think about all we have said here today."

"My mind is made up, Miss Tungsten. I will not speak out against people who have become my friends and family. I could not forgive myself for being part of their ruination."

"And what of your ruination? Surely your own family would be horrified to know what you're doing for a living. Surely you do not enjoy parading yourself night after night for a bunch of drunken men, who no doubt entertain lascivious thoughts."

There was only one man she knew of who entertained lascivious thoughts about her, but Laurel refrained from mentioning her esteemed employer's name. "Mama always said that if your heart is pure and your mind is clean, then no matter what you did, God would always love you."

"But . . ."

Laurel raised her hand to forestall the woman's objection. "I will think on what you've said, but it's doubtful that we will meet again, Miss Tungsten. Thank you for the pie and coffee; they were delicious. And good luck with your efforts to rid this town of sin and corruption. You have a difficult task ahead of you."

"We'll meet again, Miss Martin. I feel it in my heart."

Though Laurel did not respond to the persistent woman's prediction, as she crossed the street on her way back to the Aurora, she couldn't dismiss the sixth sense that warned her that Hortensia Tungsten could be right.

CHAPTER 14

Noting the Closed sign on the Aurora's front door, Laurel crinkled her forehead in confusion. It was highly unusual for the saloon to be closed for business so early in the day, especially considering the fact it was Wednesday and not Sunday.

She entered to find a celebration in progress. Colorful streamers of red, white, and blue hung from the ceiling rafters, bottles of iced champagne in silver buckets graced the center of tables, and platters of delicious-smelling food lined the mahogany bar.

Percy, that obnoxious creature, was pecking on a particularly delectable-looking tray of sandwiches, and even though she'd just consumed a large piece of pumpkin pie, Laurel felt her stomach rumble in response to the tempting sight and smell of Bertha's cooking.

She smiled in greeting as Augustus and Crystal came forward, holding hands and looking for all their worth like two people very much in love. Perhaps the celebration was for them, for their engagement, Laurel surmised. But surely Crystal would have said something to her if that were the case.

"There you are, " Crystal said. "I've been worried sick about you." They exchanged a meaningful glance, remembering Al Hazen's recent threat.

Shaking the snow off her cape, Laurel hung it on a nearby chair to dry. "What's all this? Is there something you two want to tell me?"

Crystal's cheeks flushed rosy. "Laurel honey, you do jump to conclusions. This party isn't for me and Gus." She smiled so sweetly at the reverend that his usually unhealthy pallor ignited. "It's for Chance. For his birthday."

"His birthday?" Laurel's eyes sought Chance and found him standing on the opposite side of the room, laughing with Jup about something. He looked boyishly handsome and very relaxed in his black superfine pants and blue cambric shirt, which had been left partially unbuttoned. Her eyes were drawn to the exposed area of flesh and the sprinkling of dark hairs at the vee of his neck.

"I didn't know," she said, hearing her heart pound loudly in her ears and wondering if her voice sounded as strange as she felt. "I would have bought him a gift if I'd known."

"Come join the party," Crystal urged, clasping her hand. "We've been waiting ages for you. Have you been with that temperance woman all this time?"

"Crystal tells me you've been approached by Hortensia Tungsten," Gus interrupted, a thoughtful look on his face. "She hasn't taken you to task for working here, has she?"

He'd already been visited by the Denver Temperance and Souls in Need League, and they'd urged him rather emphatically to aid in their noble, if not misguided, cause. But he knew that turning gamblers, whores, and drinking men into teetotalers wasn't a very practical solution to the problems existing in today's society.

He was certainly in favor of encouraging husbands to

cleave to their wives and to forego their other amusements—
many of which smacked of drunkenness and infidelity—and
he preached as much in his sermons every Sunday. But he
wasn't naive enough to think that a few prayers and hymns
were going to change overnight what had taken decades to
develop.

Laurel answered Gus's question but her attention was
fixed on Chance. When he turned his head in her direction
and his green eyes locked with hers, Laurel felt the magnetic
pull clear across the noisy room.

Ignoring the raucous music pouring forth from Jup's
piano, Flora Sue and Rooster's spine-tingling chorus of "Oh,
dem Golden Slippers," and Percy's vulgar comments about
the size of Pearl's breasts, she walked purposefully toward
him.

"Where've you been, angel? I was afraid you'd miss my
party." He handed her a glass of champagne.

Laurel stared at the bubbly liquid with a great deal of uncertainty, remembering the last time she'd indulged herself
with the intoxicating spirit. Never in her life had she felt so
uninhibited. It had been a wildly exhilarating, embarrassing,
and frightening experience.

"You're not going to refuse to toast me on my birthday,
now, are you?" Chance asked, a definite challenge twinkling
in his eyes.

She sipped cautiously, vowing not to have more than one
glass, and felt herself relax for the first time since her disturbing conversation with Hortensia Tungsten.

Here at the saloon, surrounded by Chance and all her
friends, she knew with a certainty that she'd made the right
decision in not joining the temperance league.

"I didn't know today was your birthday. I'm embarrassed
because I have no gift for you."

A dark eyebrow shot up. "No gift?" His gaze raked her
from head to toe, a devilish grin cutting his face. "I wouldn't
say that, angel. You've got the only gift I want."

Laurel's cheeks flamed, and she took a large swallow of champagne, but rather than cool her down, it only made her hotter. Thankfully, Bertha waddled forward, saving her from having to comment on Chance's suggestive remark.

Taking one look at her favorite couple, the woman decided that a little matchmaking was in order. "Lordy be! It's about time you done showed yourself, child. Jup and me was getting worried."

Laurel shook an admonishing finger at the cook. "I should take you to task, Bertha Tubbs, for not telling me about this party and not allowing me to help."

Chuckling, Bertha pinched Chance's cheek, as if he were a lad of ten and not a full-grown man. "My boy here wouldn't have allowed me to have this party if I woulda told him or anyone else what I was plannin', honey. Every year it's the same: Mr. Chance warns me not to go having a party, and every year I has one anyway. I's got a mind of my own."

A calculating gleam entered Bertha's warm, dark eyes. "Now why don't you two run along to the storage room and fetch me some more bottles of champagne and a bottle of that expensive Napoleon brandy. I'm fixing something special for dessert tonight."

Laurel followed Chance into the storage room at the back of the saloon, feeling extremely relaxed and just a bit woozy. It was pitch black inside when they entered, and she couldn't see a blasted thing in front of her, including Chance, who had stopped abruptly. "Ooops," she said, colliding with his backside. A very warm backside, she realized.

"I'll light a lamp. We never had this part of the saloon electrified."

A warm glow soon suffused the room and Laurel's heart as well. It'd been a while since she and Chance had had an opportunity to be alone, and she found herself wondering if this hadn't been Bertha's intention all along. She smiled to herself, unable to fault the older woman's meddling . . . not when she wanted Chance as badly as she did.

"I missed you today." The huskiness of his voice played along her spine like caressing fingers, hitting a responsive chord within her. "Did you enjoy your luncheon with Crystal?" He held out his hand to her.

She wouldn't tell him of her meeting with Hortensia Tungsten, or with Al Hazen, for that matter. It was his birthday, and she didn't want anything to spoil it. "Yes. We had a very nice time."

Pulling her against his chest, he snaked his arms about her waist. "You could make my birthday extra special, angel. You know that, don't you?"

She nodded mutely, knowing exactly what he was referring to, and wondering why she just didn't let him have what he wanted. It was what she wanted, too. To lie naked with Chance, feel his lips on her breasts and belly, to have him fill her with his masculinity . . .

Yes, it was definitely what she wanted.

His kiss was slow and gentle, sending delicious shivers of desire coursing through her and reaffirming her need for him. Wrapping her arms about his neck, she pressed herself to him, delving her tongue into his mouth, tasting and touching and wanting their kiss never to end.

Moaning deep in his throat, Chance forced himself to step back. "You'll unman me, angel, if you continue kissing me like you want me." He watched the conflicting emotions play across her face like words on newsprint, clear and easy to read.

"I do want you, Chance, more than you'll ever know. But I'm just not sure . . ."

"You think too much. Just let your body speak for you. It knows what you want." Her breasts knew, for her nipples hardened instantly at his touch. The very core of her knew, for it was dewy with need. Her heart knew, for it was bursting with the love she felt for him.

"Come with me," he said, leading her to the far corner of the room where an old cot stood waiting.

She went, knowing that if she was going to object, now was the time to do it. But no words of protest came forth.

It was time. She knew it. Her body knew it. Her heart knew it.

Having made the momentous decision, she lay down on the ticking and waited for him to follow. Her smile was anxious, his overjoyed.

"Are you sure?" he asked. "Because I want you to be sure. And I also want you to know that I haven't been with anyone else since you came into my life, angel." He caressed her cheek. "Other women don't seem to interest me anymore."

Stunned and delighted by the revelation, Laurel was filled with renewed hope that Chance did love her; she nodded, unable to find the words to tell him just how sure she was, or how much she loved him.

Not giving her the opportunity to change her mind, Chance's fingers went to the copper buttons on his jeans, unfastening them with a dexterity that surprised Laurel.

His fingers were long, tanned, and lean, much like the rest of him, and they fascinated her whenever she watched him deal cards or roll dice. The same fingers that could efficiently feel the nicks in a marked deck could also explore and bring exquisite moments of pleasure. She swallowed hard at the memory.

Those fingers were at the moment making short work of unbuttoning her dress and untying her drawers. "You won't regret this, angel," Chance said in a seductively soothing voice as he settled down next to her. "I promise."

Laurel wanted to believe that with all her heart and soul, but the fact remained that she was gambling her love on a gambling man.

None of that mattered at the moment, however. Only Chance's fingers massaging her hardened nipples, his lips and tongue ravishing her mouth, the hot skin of his bare chest pressing against her own, mattered.

Regret might come later. And so might tears. But now there was only pleasure. There was only Chance.

His hands and mouth were everywhere, on her sensitive swollen nipples, suckling the hardened nubs, sliding down her taut belly to tease, taste, and tantalize. To devour the very essence of her being.

"Chance," she whispered, grasping his head between her hands, urging him to continue the delicious torment his tongue inflicted. "Oh, God! Please!"

"You're almost ready, angel," he said, easing himself over her as his fingers parted her swollen nether lips, then slid in to ready her for their coupling. "I've never wanted anyone as much as I want you."

Absorbed in their pleasure, neither heard the frantic pounding on the door or the shouts of "Chance? Miss Laurel?" But as the caller grew more insistent, his voice louder, and they finally heard him shout, "Bertha sent me to fetch you," lips parted, hands stilled, and heads turned toward the door.

Laurel moaned. Chance groaned, then let out a string of expletives. "Jesus, Mary, and Joseph!" he said as he rolled off of her.

"I don't think so, Chance. It sounds like Whitey."

He looked at her, cursed again, then began putting on his clothes.

Her fingers flying, Laurel began refastening ribbons and buttons. "What if he comes in and finds us like this?"

"It's all right, angel," he said, kissing her cheek and sighing with a great deal of frustration. "He won't. I've taught Whitey that it isn't polite to enter a room without an invitation."

Regret plastered Laurel's face. "I guess we'd better get back to the party."

"I guess," he agreed, but his lips managed to find hers once more and for a moment they lost themselves in each other again. "Someday we're going to finish what we started, angel. But I guess it's not going to be today." But it had to be soon, or he'd die from want of her.

Flooded with disappointment and an ache so keen that rational thought was impossible, Laurel wanted to shout, to insist that the day wasn't over yet. But she couldn't make her lips say what her mind so brazenly thought.

Silently she rose to her feet.

It's bad luck, that's what it is, Chance thought, sipping thoughtfully on a mug of steaming coffee as he gazed out the window at the heavy wet snow that had been falling since late last evening.

It was November, for chrissake! Not even Thanksgiving yet. Snow didn't usually arrive until January or February, so why did this storm have to come now?

Bad luck.

Snow meant fewer customers, less revenue—something a gambling parlor could hardly afford. It also meant that his guests from the previous night's party would have to remain his guests. He could not in good conscience send Rooster and Gus out in the middle of a blizzard. And judging by the way the wind was howling and the cottonwoods were listing toward the frozen ground, this was definitely a storm of blizzard proportions.

"Snow ain't let up yet, I take it," Rooster said, standing next to Chance to take a look for himself. Wiping the condensation from the glass with the palm of his hand, he shook his head in dismay. "Witherspoon ain't going to like it if I don't get back to the Opera House. You know how cantankerous that old bastard can be."

"Why don't you quit that job and do something else, Rooster? You've hated it since the day you stepped inside that gawdy brick testament to Tabor's wealth."

"It ain't the job I hate, it's Witherspoon. And I figure he can't last forever. Him and Tabor had a terrible row just last week. He was almost fired then. I figure if I just hang on a bit longer, I might get the bastard's job. And I figure a married man needs a good job."

An icicle broke, hitting the sidewalk and narrowly missing a mangy mutt that had wandered outside to take care of his business.

Turning to his friend, Chance said, "I hate to be the one to point this out, Rooster, but you're not married."

"Not yet, I ain't. But the way things are progressing between me and Flora Sue . . ." His smile was boastful. "Well, I expect we'll be before too long. Flora Sue's got a hankering for respectability."

Flora Sue had a lot of hankerings, that was for certain, but Chance wasn't quite convinced that respectability was one of them.

And why would his friend want to get married if he didn't have to? That was like putting your neck in a noose and asking to be hanged, when you hadn't even committed a crime. It made no sense to Chance, but he clasped Rooster's shoulder anyway and offered, "You let me know if there's anything I can do, Rooster. If you and Flora Sue want to get hitched now and need a loan . . ."

Rooster shook his head, but his eyes were filled with gratitude. "I appreciate the offer, Chance, but I'm determined to do this on my own. I ain't never had me so fine a woman as Flora Sue before, and I aim to do right by her."

"Well right now you can do right by me and help me get those crates of whiskey out of the storage room and stacked behind the bar. Since you're stuck here anyway, you might as well make yourself useful."

"Heard you and Laurel were doing a bit of inventorying yourselves there last night," Rooster teased.

Chance grinned. "Can I help it if the woman can't keep her hands off me?" Damn! They'd come so close last night. A few more minutes and Laurel would have been his at last. But then Whitey . . .

He frowned. He hadn't seen his cousin all morning. "Have you seen Whitey today?" Chance called out to Jup, who shook his head.

"No, Mr. Chance, can't say that I have. Bertha was just askin' me the very same thing. Don't know where that boy's run off to."

Well, he couldn't have run very far, Chance figured, stopping at the foot of the stairs. Not with the way the snow was piling up. "Jup, would you help Rooster with the whiskey crates? I'll run up and check on Whitey. I'm sure he's still in bed. Maybe he's embarrassed about what happened last night." He'd done his best to reassure his cousin that no harm had been done, even though it had. Unfulfilled and stiffer than a two-week old corpse, he hadn't been able to lie on his stomach the entire night!

Jup and Rooster left to do his bidding, and Chance took the stairs two at a time, suddenly smiling to himself. Maybe he'd pay a visit to Laurel's room after he was done checking on his cousin. Maybe the weather was a blessing in disguise. After all, there was nothing cozier than lying in bed during a snowstorm, a fire blazing in the wood stove, two bodies snuggled next to each other for warmth. His grin widened.

Blowing a kiss to Laurel as he passed her room, and vowing silently to return, Chance paused before Whitey's door, hoping his cousin wasn't still asleep.

Pressing his ear to the wood, he listened for the distinctive sound of Whitey's snoring—snoring that was usually loud enough to wake a deaf man. At the sound of a woman's low moan, Chance stiffened.

"That's it, sugar. That's a good boy."

Pearl's drawl floated through the closed portal, and Chance almost choked with fury. He pushed the door open so hard it slammed against the wall, startling the couple.

His green eyes darkened at the sight of Pearl, her robe hanging open, standing at the side of the bed, Whitey's face pressed to her ample breasts. Her expression was nothing short of triumphant. She had threatened to get even, but he'd never thought she would stoop this low.

"You goddamn whore!" he bellowed, stepping farther into the room. "Whitey!" he screamed at his cousin. "Let go of that bitch and get yourself dressed."

Whitey's eyes widened with fear. Never in his life had he seen Chance so mad. Not even the times his mama had been mean to him and Chance defended him. "I didn't do nothing wrong, Chance. Miss Pearl was just letting me suck her titties. She said you do it all the time."

"You bitch! I ought to kill you with my bare hands."

Malice, not fear, entered the whore's eyes. "What's the matter, Chance? Are you jealous?" Though she knew without waiting for his answer that it wasn't jealousy but hatred that had put that dark, dangerous look on his face.

She had sullied his precious Whitey. Taken away the one thing he fussed and worried over. Seducing Whitey had been the perfect revenge against Chance's callous treatment of her. The innocent dimwit was now tarnished in Chance's eyes, and Pearl reveled in the satisfaction she felt.

Before Chance could reply, Laurel stuck her head through the doorway and gasped at the sight before her. She hoped that what she suspected was wrong. But from the lethal look on Chance's face, she wasn't. Her heart went out to the befuddled man on the bed, who obviously didn't understand the consequences of his actions.

"Is Whitey all right?"

"Sure he is. Ain't you, sugar?" Pearl's laughter was snide as she winked at Chance's cousin. "He was merely testing out his manhood."

Laurel's eyes darted around the room, taking in every sordid detail at once: the seductive smile on Pearl's face; the way her robe hung open to reveal her nakedness; Whitey's flushed face and bare chest; Chance's fists curling and uncurling, as if he were trying to get hold of his temper.

"How could you, Pearl? You know Whitey's little more than a child."

Belting her robe, the whore shrugged. "I've been tutoring him, and he's been liking his lessons real fine."

Chance stepped toward Pearl, a murderous gleam in his eyes, but Laurel, fearing his intent, clasped his arm. "Let her go, Chance. She isn't worth it."

"Is that what he told you? Why, you really are naive." With that parting shot, Pearl pushed past Laurel and left the room.

Frightened of Chance's fierce expression, Whitey pressed back against the headboard, hugging a pillow to his chest. "I didn't do nothing wrong, did I, Chance?"

In the space of a few seconds, a million conflicting emotions washed over Chance's face. Whitey was a child in a man's body, he told himself. Pearl was to blame for what had happened. But anger and disappointment at Whitey's behavior still festered inside like a canker. "We'll talk about this later. Come downstairs after you've dressed." With barely a glance at Laurel or his cousin, Chance stalked out of the room, slamming the door behind him.

"Chance is mad, mad, mad, Miss Laurel. He doesn't like me anymore." Tears filled the big man's eyes, and Laurel found her throat tightening up.

"Don't be silly, Whitey," she said, taking a seat next to him on the bed, with no thought to propriety. Whitey needed consoling, and she was the only one available at the moment. "Chance is just angry with Pearl and he's taking it out on you. What Pearl did was wrong. She shouldn't have . . ." How could she say *seduced*? He probably didn't even know what the word meant. "Chance doesn't like mixing business with pleasure."

Whitey scratched his head, clearly confused. "Miss Pearl said Chance touched her titties and that he stuck his Willy deep inside her."

Laurel didn't need a dictionary to figure out what that

meant, and she swallowed hard at the thought of Chance making love to the whore. What Whitey said was undoubtedly true—Flora Sue had said as much—but that had been a long time ago. "I think Pearl's exaggerating a bit, Whitey. Chance and Pearl are merely friends."

"No, ma'am," he said, shaking his head emphatically. "She said Chance comes to her room almost every night and sticks his Willy in her. That's why she said it'd be okay if I did. But I didn't, Miss Laurel. My Willy just wouldn't work right."

Tears filled Laurel's eyes. Chance had told her only last night that he hadn't been with another woman since she'd arrived, that he wanted no one else. And like a fool she'd believed him. Wanted to believe him. Needed to believe him. Obviously he'd lied to have his way with her. Whitey was too ingenuous to make up such a fabrication.

Had Chance gone to Pearl last night to relieve his frustration? Had he finished with Pearl what he'd started with her? And had he been doing so all along?

"You're not mad at me too, are you, Miss Laurel? I wouldn't want you to be mad. Why are you crying, Miss Laurel?" Whitey reached for her hand, patting it, trying to comfort her.

Like a dull-edged blade, pain knifed through her heart. "I'm not crying," she lied, pushing herself to her feet. "You'd better get dressed and get downstairs now, Whitey. Chance's anger is only temporary. He'll be fine in a little while."

"I guess I won't be getting any more writing lessons from Miss Pearl. Will you help me with my letters, Miss Laurel? I've been doing real good. I'm all the way to *M* now."

"I . . ." What could she say? After last night, after almost giving herself to Chance, and now, learning of his intimacy with Pearl, how could she stay on working at the Aurora as if nothing had happened? It would kill her to see Chance with

Pearl, to think about them being together every day. Every night.

"I don't know, Whitey. We'll talk about it later."

Laurel left Whitey sitting amid his tangled bedsheets, a look of pure confusion on his face, and headed back to her room. She had a lot of thinking to do, plans to make.

She was uncertain about a great many things, but one thing stood out in her mind with exacting clarity: She was thankful to God that she hadn't given herself to Chance Rafferty last night. That she hadn't given him the one gift, the one thing he wanted.

For what it was worth, she still had her virtue. She still had her pride. And she still had the offer from the Denver Temperance and Souls in Need League to put scoundrels like Chance Rafferty out of business.

Her mama had always counseled that no good could come of revenge, but Laurel wasn't listening to her mama's words right now.

CHAPTER 15

"But why are you leaving? I don't understand. I mean . . . I thought after the other night . . ."

Laurel was unwilling to think about "the other night" or to put any stock in Chance's heartfelt expression. "I've had another job offer."

"From who?" He shook his head, dismissing the question. "No matter. I'll double their offer, give you a larger room, decrease your working hours."

Laurel sighed. "It's not a singing job, Chance, and I'd prefer not to talk about it." Gripping her well-worn leather valise until her knuckles turned white, she said, "I'm sorry things didn't work out." *Sorrier than you'll ever know.*

"I guess this will leave you short-handed, what with Pearl's firing and all"—she had found some solace in that knowledge—"but I'm sure it won't take long to replace me. Singers in a town like Denver are a dime a dozen." She moved toward the door, then stopped suddenly.

"No matter what happens, I want you to know that I'm

grateful for all you've done for me. I . . ." There was so much more to say, but tears clogged her throat and the words couldn't pass. "Goodbye, Chance."

"Laurel, wait! If it was something I said, or did . . ." He held out his hands beseechingly, giving Laurel the satisfaction of seeing him grovel. But she took no pleasure in that.

"It's not you, Chance, it's me. I confused fairy tales with reality. You warned me not to, remember?"

"I don't understand."

"Neither do I."

And she still didn't. Not even after spending two weeks brooding over everything that had happened between them.

And everything that hadn't.

"Miss Tungsten would like to see you, Miss Martin," Drucilla Gottlieb, her new roommate, declared. She wore that smug expression Laurel had grown to hate in the short time she'd been in residence at Josephine Costello's boarding establishment for indigent women.

The small hotel was as spartan as Graber's but much cleaner. Two narrow beds lined bare gray walls, and two faded green wing chairs rested beneath the one, uncurtained window. It was a decorator's nightmare, and she wondered what Oscar Wilde, the British playwright who'd recently done a series of lectures on the art of interior decoration, would say if he could see it. "Utilitarian," no doubt.

She forced a polite smile. "Thank you. I'll be right down."

"You're never going to learn everything there is to know if you spend all your time staring out that window."

"I hardly think that's any of your business, Drucilla. Besides, I was merely checking the weather." The brief episode of snow had passed, leaving crisp days and frigid nights. Nights spent in lonely reverie.

"Miss Tungsten likes punctuality." Drucilla's lips pursed tightly, as if she'd just sucked a lemon dry. "I really don't understand why she chose you, of all people, to represent our cause. Why, you're nothing more than a—"

Laurel lifted her chin. "Yes? You were saying?"

"A saloon singer. Hardly a fit role model for the temperance league."

"Perhaps Miss Tungsten wanted someone who could relate to the masses." She sized up Drucilla Gottlieb and shook her head. "My mama always said that experience was the best teacher, Drucilla. At your young age, you haven't lived long enough to have any experiences worth sharing."

"Just because I'm chaste and prefer to remain that way doesn't mean . . ."

"What on earth is going on here?"

Both women turned to find Hortensia Tungsten standing in the doorway, and their faces reddened. "Your harsh words and very unprofessional manner can be detected all the way down the stairs. Drucilla," she looked directly at the mousy, brown-haired woman, "please leave your prejudices outside before you enter this house again. I'll not have dissension in the ranks. We have enough problems to deal with, without fighting among ourselves. Is that clear?"

It was, and Drucilla left the room, but not before shooting Laurel a look of pure hostility.

"Perhaps Drucilla is right, Miss Tungsten. Perhaps I'm not the best person for this job."

Hortensia shut the door, then took a seat in one of the chairs by the window, urging Laurel to join her. "We've been through all this before, dear. You're perfect for the job, and I'm delighted, as is Miss Willard, that you've agreed to join our noble cause.

"I realize dealing with narrow-minded young women like Drucilla will be a trial for you, but do try to remember all the good your contribution will bring."

Laurel had tried to remind herself of that each and every day for the past two weeks, but there had been no shortage of people trying to dissuade her from her present course.

Crystal had paid her three visits, urging her to return to the Aurora, citing their friendship and her loneliness. Even Augustus had come—at the urging of Crystal, she was sure—to counsel her against her decision. But the hardest visit had come from Bertha, who'd regaled her with improbable but nonetheless heart-wrenching stories of what her departure had done to Chance.

The once happy-go-lucky man had apparently turned quiet and sullen, listening to no one and speaking harshly to everyone. Bertha had said that she hardly recognized her boy anymore, and wouldn't Laurel please find it in her heart to forgive him for whatever he'd done and come back?

But Laurel couldn't. It was time for her to face the real world, to quit living a life of daydreams and Prince Charming. Chance had been right about that. There was no such thing.

"Are you listening to me, Laurel? I said your first temperance demonstration will be this Saturday. Are you ready? And have you decided on a suitable objective?"

Hortensia's words forced Laurel to make a decision—a very momentous decision. "Yes. I have. I will lead the ladies to Mr. Rafferty's gambling parlor, the Aurora Borealis, on Saturday night, Miss Tungsten. There, we will let Mr. Rafferty know that what he is doing to the good citizens of Denver is an abomination."

Hortensia's eyes widened, even as they lit with pleasure. "But, my dear, won't that be terribly difficult for you? Mr. Rafferty was recently your employer."

"Not as difficult as it's going to be for Mr. Rafferty."

"Angel's gone. Angel's gone." Squawk. *"Lordy be, Mr. Chance. My dick's hard."* Squawk. *"Give me some tongue, babe."*

"Shut your goddamn big mouth," Chance yelled, throwing his beer mug directly at Percy's cage and missing it by a mere fraction. It hit the rack of liquor bottles at the rear of the bar instead, breaking several and releasing the amber liquid onto the floor.

Percy squawked loudly and repeatedly, flapping his wings against the cage, trying to escape the irate gambler's anger.

"I won't miss next time," he warned, and the bird miraculously quieted, providing Chance a small measure of satisfaction.

It was midafternoon and it was quiet. Bertha and Jup had gone to secure provisions for tomorrow's Thanksgiving feast, Crystal was assisting Gus with the church decorations, Flora Sue had a luncheon engagement with Rooster, and even Whitey had opted for a nap, rather than face Chance's surly mood.

His frown deepened, as did his melancholy. Laurel was gone, he'd been on a losing streak ever since, and he could find no enjoyment in the little things that he used to take for granted.

Keeping the books was a chore without Laurel there to help. She'd always laugh and goad him into finishing his paperwork, then praise him for his efforts, as if she were the teacher and he the student. Dinners were quiet affairs now. There was no lighthearted banter around the table. No good-natured teasing remarks from Bertha, and no covert winks from Laurel. There'd been no new performer to replace his little angel.

As if anyone could.

What the hell happened?

In his mind he'd gone over that morning when he'd found Whitey with Pearl, gone over and over it again, but he couldn't make sense of what had occurred to drive Laurel from his arms.

Did she change her mind about making love with me?

No. He didn't believe that. She wanted him as much as he wanted her, and nothing could ever convince him otherwise.

What then? Did Pearl's disgusting behavior with Whitey shock her sensibilities?

But he'd fired Pearl that same day, and Laurel knew it.

He wished he'd fired Pearl months ago, then none of this sordid business would have ever taken place. He'd heard she'd gone to work for Al Hazen. *How fitting*, Chance thought. *Two pieces of slime working together in perfect harmony.*

Tomorrow was Thanksgiving, but in his opinion there was little to be thankful for. Revenues were down, hardly anyone spoke civilly to him anymore, Whitey had grown reclusive since the incident, and the temperance league was stepping up its efforts to rid the town of businesses like his.

He'd heard from Crystal and Bertha that Laurel was working for them now. In what capacity they didn't say. He supposed she was doing bookkeeping or some sort of secretarial work. Something respectable and boring. And totally alien to her nature. He knew what performing meant to her. Laurel used to say that a day without singing was like a day without sunshine.

And he knew what that meant now in spades. He missed her—missed her enchanting smile of innocence, her sweet, seductive jasmine scent that still tormented his senses, her tinkling laughter that cloaked him like warm, loving hands.

His life was empty without her.

But does that mean I love her?

No. He didn't love her; he couldn't. He would never love any woman that way.

But if I don't love her, then why does my heart hurt so bad?

And if I don't love her, then why has the sun stopped shining for me?

And if I don't love her, then why can't I get her out of my mind?

"Rock of ages, cleft for me. Let me hide myself in thee," the women sang.

"Holy shit!" Bull swore, staring out the window at the fire-lit processional. "Chance," he yelled, "come quick."

Staring at the first decent hand he'd had all evening,

Chance chomped down on his cheroot. "What is it, Bull? I'm fixing to take these gentlemen to the cleaners." He smiled through the smoky haze at the other two men at the table, but they obviously didn't find any humor in his remark.

"I've seen those biddies before, Bull, I'm not interested in seeing them again."

"Not these you ain't. These ones are different."

Chance pushed back his chair. "If you gentlemen will excuse me for a moment . . ." He stepped to the window and looked out.

"What's so damned important that you had to—" His mouth fell open, the cheroot dropping unnoticed to the floor. "Jesus, Mary, and Joseph!"

"I told you, didn't I? It's her; it's Laurel."

Even dressed as she was in a plain gown of gray cotton partially covered by the dark woolen cloak he'd helped her pick out, and a bonnet hiding her glorious hair, Chance had little problem recognizing the woman who'd haunted his dreams of late. "I take it she's not their secretary."

"She's leading them, for crying out loud. Don't you see that white ribbon she's wearing? God, she's one of *them*!"

Before Chance could reply, the door burst open and the group of women entered, Laurel heading up the column.

"Repent, sinners!" shouted a gray-haired woman with a large black mole on her nose. "Sign a pledge that you'll abstain from the evils of drink."

"Amen! Hallelujah!" chorused the others.

Laurel stepped farther into the room, scanning the premises until her eyes found Chance, who was standing by the window, a shocked expression on his face. "Mr. Rafferty," she announced, nodding perfunctorily, trying not to show that seeing him again made her heart ache. "We've come to ask your help in ridding this town of sin and corruption. Close down this den of iniquity, or we'll be forced to take harsher action."

Laurel's zealous speech irritated the hell out of Chance. So did the fact that she looked right through him, unwilling to acknowledge their previous relationship. That hurt, but he grinned to hide it.

"I liked you better in your red satin gown, angel. It's a damn shame to hide your legs like that."

Mole woman gasped audibly.

A chorus of male hoots and laughter followed. Then some drunken cowboy remarked, "Hey, it's the singer. The one with the small tits."

Laurel's face crimsoned. Though she'd mentally prepared herself for such verbal attacks, she hadn't counted on hearing them from lips she'd so recently kissed. But she held her ground and said, "Ladies, please pass out your pledge cards to these kind gentlemen."

Gertie Beecham was obviously uncomfortable at the prospect of walking farther into the room, but she did as she was instructed. Soon the other women followed, mingling with the gamblers and cowboys, passing out pledges, and urging them to sign a vow never to drink again.

"I recognize some of you men," Laurel stated. "Most of you have wives at home and little children to care for. Why don't you go home and be with them now, instead of squandering your money on liquor and cards?"

"My wife's a nag," Herb Porter, the druggist, admitted, taking a swallow of beer and wiping his mouth on his shirtsleeve—something he wasn't allowed to do when his wife was around. "This is the only taste of freedom I get. A man should be able to relax with a whiskey and a game of cards after a hard day's work."

"Yeah!" Nate Moody pounded a meaty fist on the card table, making the coins scatter every which way. "My woman's gonna have another kid soon. A man has a right to a little relief, if you get my meaning."

Laurel got it all right, and she wasn't buying it for a second. "Those are poor excuses for doing what you men do. You've responsibilities to your wives, and to that unborn child, Nate Moody, and to the ones you have at home. Surely you men wouldn't want your wives to be out doing the same as you. You shouldn't have married if you didn't want to remain faithful and accept the responsibility." Her gaze fixed on Chance, but if her words hit true, his expression gave no indication.

"Your speech is very pretty, Miss Martin," Chance said. Now why don't you take your little sewing circle and leave? We're trying to enjoy ourselves, and I don't appreciate the interruption. I've a business to run."

"Your business is the corruption of morals, Mr. Rafferty. You prey on the weaknesses of others."

"Are you talking about yourself, Miss Martin, or my customers?"

Laurel did her best to ignore the aspersion that hit too close to the truth. "You men are being victimized by Mr. Rafferty. Go home to your families, to the people who love you. Don't waste yourselves on a gamble that will never pay off."

"Life's no fun without risk, Laurel. Even you should realize that."

"Sometimes a woman needs a man she can count on. One she can trust. One who doesn't lie at the drop of a hat. A smart woman doesn't put her faith in a gambling man."

Chance's face paled. It was obvious that she was talking about him, about their relationship, and not about the others in the room. He stepped toward her, eager to find out the reasons behind her declaration, but she turned and fled out the door before he could reach her.

Bull shut the door behind them. "Good riddance," he said, wiping his hands back and forth with finality.

Nate Moody and Herb Porter stood and, with apologetic looks on their faces, headed toward the door, the pledge cards clasped tightly in their hands.

Chance, watching them leave, didn't say a word. A man had to do what a man had to do. He just hated like hell that Laurel had achieved even this minor victory.

"How come Miss Laurel don't like us anymore, Chance? She looked mad, mad, mad."

Wrapping his arm about Whitey's shoulder, Chance led him to a quiet table at the rear of the room. "She isn't mad at you, Whitey. She's mad at me. But I don't know why."

Whitey hung his head in shame. "I made Miss Laurel cry, Chance. I think she's mad at me."

"What do you mean, you made her cry?"

"I told her about what Miss Pearl said, about you sticking your Willy inside her every night. It made Miss Laurel cry real hard. But I didn't mean to make her sad, Chance."

"Jesus, Mary, and Joseph!" That sure as hell explained a lot of things about Laurel's behavior. But why would she believe such a lie? Why hadn't she come to him and asked if it was true? Why had she condemned him without knowing the truth?

Memories of Aunt Aletha washed over him, and his lips thinned. Aletha had always accused, blaming Chance for everything that went wrong in her life.

Women were quick to condemn. Chance had foolishly thought Laurel might be different, but she wasn't. She'd tried and convicted him without so much as hearing his side of the case.

Damn the woman!

"Are you mad at me, too, Chance?" Whitey wanted to know, fidgeting nervously with the bone buttons on his shirt. "I didn't mean to cause no trouble. You still like me, don't you, Chance?"

Clasping his cousin's hand, Chance squeezed it reassuringly. "You're the only family I've got, Whitey. I love you. And though at times I may get upset over something you do . . ."

"Like what happened with Miss Pearl?"

Chance nodded, wondering if the talk they'd had about male and female relationships had sunk in. "I'll always love you. That will never change."

"Miss Laurel told me that once. She said that even though people fight, they don't always mean the bad things they say."

"Laurel's right, Whitey." Too bad she didn't take her own advice to heart, Chance thought. For he had no doubt that

Laurel meant each and every one of the "bad" things she'd said to him this evening.

Pearl nuzzled Al's ear, sighing contentedly as she reached inside his shirt to caress his smooth chest. She'd just had the best fuck of her life, having found in Al Hazen a man with her own need for hard, driving sex.

"Didn't you get enough, babe?" he said, rolling out of the bed, then bending down to place a kiss on her large erect nipple. "I've got to get downstairs. This place doesn't run itself, you know."

"I'll never get enough of you, Al. You're the best."

"Better than Rafferty?"

She thought about it for a moment, delighting in the dark look that crossed his face at her hesitation, then smiled. "Much better. Rafferty was too much of a gentleman. I like a real man between my legs."

She splayed them to prove her point, and Al's eyes riveted to the dark thatch of hair that did nothing to hide her blatant femininity. He swallowed with some difficulty, annoyed that the whore could affect him so strongly.

"I hear Laurel Martin quit and went to work for the temperance league," he said, to take his mind off Pearl's tempting flesh.

Believing herself to be responsible for that occurrence, Pearl's eyes sparkled with pleasure. "Miss Goody Two-Shoes wasn't cut out to work in a saloon. Though she liked bedding Chance well enough." At least Pearl had the satisfaction of knowing that if she couldn't have Chance Rafferty, no one could.

"Laurel's pretty, but she's got no tits. Don't know what Rafferty saw in her."

"Speaking of Laurel," Pearl said, "there's something I'd like to discuss with you."

"Oh yeah? And what would that be?"

"I want to get rid of her, Al. I want Laurel Martin gone from here."

"Really? Now that is interesting." And a downright coincidence, since he himself would have liked nothing better than to get rid of the Martin woman. He'd gone over dozens of ways to do it but hadn't come up with any plan he felt would be foolproof—a plan that wouldn't tie him to her death or disappearance. "What's she done to you anyway?"

Pearl twisted the corner of the sheet. "My reasons are my own." She certainly wasn't going to confide that she'd been jealous of the bitch. "I'd think you'd want to get even with her, Al. After all, it was Laurel who lured Crystal away from you."

Al's eyes darkened, as they did whenever anyone mentioned Crystal. "I'll think about it."

Pearl patted the space next to her, smiling seductively. "I'm sure I can convince you, sugar."

"You're a great whore, you know that, Pearl? A man could almost forget that you make your living on your back and not on the stage. You're good. Real good."

"I'll be an asset to you, Al. But I want a bigger cut than the other girls. I figure with my experience and looks, I should get at least seventy-five percent of the profits."

Buttoning the silver buttons on his red brocade vest, Al threw back his head and laughed. "You're a good fuck, Pearl, but your pussy's not lined with gold. You'll take fifty–fifty like everyone else."

"Did Crystal get fifty–fifty? I heard she got a bigger split."

"Crystal was different. You're not like her." Crystal was a lady, despite the fact that she whored for a living.

Pearl rose from the bed and walked toward him. "I'm better than her, sugar." She cupped his genitals, pleased to find him erect and ready. Dropping to her knees, she unfastened his trousers, pressing her mouth to the naked tip of his shaft, and delighting in his low moan of pleasure.

"I'm not like anyone you've ever had before, sugar," she said, licking her lips. "I want you to remember that."

CHAPTER 16

"Mama always told my papa—'Ezra,' she'd say, 'if God had wanted man to drink alcohol instead of water He'd have put it in the clouds for rain and filled up the rivers and ponds.'

"To prove her point, she'd walk him out to the barn, where he kept a jug of whiskey hidden in the loft, take it outside, and pour the contents onto a patch of wildflowers. Those flowers would just shrivel up and die; their life sucked dry from the alcohol.

"And, folks, that's what alcohol is doing to the citizens of this town. It's drying up hopes and ambitions and sucking all the good out of decent folks, such as yourselves."

The applause surprised Laurel. She hadn't known what to expect from this crowd that had gathered in front of the Silver Slipper Saloon to hear her speak, but she was bound and determined that Al Hazen would feel the brunt of her wrath before this day was through. Chance Rafferty wasn't her only target.

Every saloon, brothel, and gambling parlor would receive a visit from the Denver Temperance and Souls in Need League. In the past week they'd signed up twenty-two new converts, and that was only the beginning. Soon they'd have hundreds of reformed drunks and gamblers added to their cause. A cause Laurel felt was more justified every time she saw a bruised and battered woman or child.

One such woman was standing next to her now. Lizzy Maxwell had come to bear witness against the evils of drink. Laurel urged the pregnant woman forward and introduced her to the crowd.

"My name is Elizabeth Maxwell," the drawn, older woman began. "Perhaps some of you know my man, Clifford, who used to drive the milk wagon. Clifford used to be a good husband and loving father." She patted her swollen belly. "But that was before the drink overcame him.

"We ain't married no more, 'cause he run off with a painted harlot, leaving me and my two young'ns and this here unborn babe to fend for ourselves."

The crowd murmured their sympathy and outrage, and one shrill voice in the back yelled, "Hang Clifford Maxwell!"

"I guess I should be glad he's gone, but to tell you the truth, I'm relieved. Hardly a day went by that Clifford didn't beat me and the young'ns senseless during one of his drunken rages.

"I bless this league of fine ladies, who've lent me a helping hand during my trials, and I hope you'll listen to what Miss Martin here has to say. Alcohol *is* poison. I know it for a fact. It killed my family."

Giving the courageous woman a heartfelt hug, Laurel thanked her. Then she turned to face the crowd and continued, "Salvation through sobriety is the only way to rid this town of the evils of drink and prostitution. I've seen many a married man with family squander his money on liquor, women, and cards, when he should have been paying his rent and putting food into his children's bellies . . ."

Chance stood hidden at the back of the crowd, listening in amazement to Laurel's speech. Her homespun stories and articulate delivery held the crowd spellbound, and he now understood why Hortensia Tungsten had recruited her to spread the word of the league. Laurel was a born orator.

He couldn't help the pride he felt each time he watched her speak, though her very words were putting a definite crimp in his business. The crowds at the Aurora had grown smaller every night, the customers fearing public retribution and condemnation for the enjoyments they sought.

He frowned when a particularly zealous woman threw up her hands in the air and shouted, "Hallelujah, sister!" The crowd joined in, chanting "Glory to God. Praise the Lord," as they placed money in the wicker basket being passed around.

The white-ribboned army looked more determined than ever to bring reform to Denver's red-light district as they marched toward Al Hazen's establishment.

"Better him than me," Chance mumbled and turned away, pulling his hat low over his brow to conceal his identity. He sure as hell didn't want anyone to think he was part of this fanatical gathering.

Stepping into the Aurora Borealis he pulled up short at the sight of Bertha coming toward him with a rolling pin. These days he couldn't be sure that she wouldn't use the thing as a weapon. The old woman blamed him for Laurel's leaving and had hardly spoken a word, civil or otherwise, to him these past few weeks.

"Don't have no help in the kitchen no more, Mr. Chance," she stated, accusation bright in her eyes. "Since Miss Laurel up and left, there's been no one to help me with the cookin' and cleanin'. Miss Laurel used to do a right fine job of it; yes she did." She slapped the rolling pin against her left palm, and Chance was tempted to take a step back.

"Kick his ass, girlie!" Percy squawked loudly.

Since the incident with the beer mug, the vociferous parrot

had stepped up his harassment of Chance. Or so it seemed to the much-abused gambler.

"Shut up, you stupid bird!" Chance said.

Bertha smiled. "That bird don't have a bad idea, Mr. Chance. Some men knows when they's well off, but not you. You had to run that sweet child off and break my heart."

He reached out to the woman, hating to see her so distraught. Bertha had been more of a mother to him than his own, who had died when he was young, or his aunt, who didn't have the slightest idea of what being a mother entailed.

He couldn't remember a time when his aunt had comforted him with loving arms, kissed him to show affection, told him she loved him. He'd been raised without nurturing, without loving, and he guessed it showed.

It was difficult for him to show emotion, to open himself up to a woman's tender words and ways. He'd been shown early on that tenderness bred rejection and that heartfelt emotion was scorned as weakness.

Bertha continued to look at him with condemning eyes.

"I didn't chase her off, Bertha. Whitey said some things to Laurel that she misunderstood. If she'd come to me, I could have straightened everything out."

"Hmph! And why should she come to you? Did you ever tell her how you felt about her? Did you ever own up to bein' crazy in love with her?"

"I'm not in love with anyone."

She raised the rolling pin over her head as if she were going to strike, then lowered her arm, shaking her head in disgust. "If I thought this here pin would knock some sense into that thick skull of yours, I'd bash you with it. But I doubt even that'd do any good. You don't see what's right before your eyes. Miss Laurel's in love with you . . . or was. Why you so thick-headed and stupid? I ain't never seen a man so mulish before." Turning, Bertha ambled out of the room, leaving Chance staring after her.

Laurel . . . in love with me?

"Stupid, Chance! Stupid, Chance!" Percy repeated.

Falling into the nearest chair, Chance felt as if the air had been kicked out of him. He stared at the bird, but there was no anger in his eyes this time. For once, Percy had said something right. He was probably the stupidest son of a bitch in the world. No. there was no "probably" about it. He *was* the stupidest son of a bitch, for having allowed Laurel to walk out of his life.

He'd been on a losing streak ever since she left. Nothing had gone right in his life. Bad luck surrounded him at every turn. And now even the damn parrot had turned against him.

Laurel was his lucky charm. He needed her, he told himself, not to love or to be loved by, but to bring back his luck.

Having convinced himself that this was his only motive, Chance set out to do just that.

> *"The man who drinks the red, red wine*
> *will never be a beau of mine.*
> *The man who is a whiskey sop*
> *will never hear my corset pop."*

Pearl's lusty parody of the popular temperance ditty brought a chorus of cheers and laughter to the Silver Slipper's patrons, and a smile to Al's lips. But that smile was fleeting.

Looking out the front window at the line of women, their arms linked to form a battering ram of self-righteousness, he frowned deeply. "That bitch!" Staring at the comely blonde in the forefront, his eyes narrowed.

Laurel Martin would rue the day she singled out the Silver Slipper. There was no way in hell he'd allow her to ruin business for him again. He was still smarting over how much he'd lost when she was singing at the Aurora, and he still resented her influence over Crystal, though the latter seemed less important now that Pearl warmed his bed. But once again the girls were complaining at their lack of customers, and even now, as he glanced about the saloon, it was nearly empty.

No one wanted to run the gauntlet and become a victim of lashing female tongues.

"Repent, ye sinners!" they called out, their voices raised as high as the placards and torches they held. "Jezebels, hear our words: You'll not enter the gates of Heaven by pressing your flesh for worldly goods."

"They at it again, sugar?" Pearl asked, coming to stand by the irate saloon owner and looking out at the processional that had become a familiar sight of late. "I see Laurel is right there spurring them on. I told you we needed to get rid of her, Al."

"She'll get hers. Believe me," Al promised and Pearl's eyes sparkled with satisfaction. "No one's going to put us out of business."

"I don't doubt for a moment that Chance put her up to this. He's always been jealous of you, sugar." She patted his cheek, pleased to see that her lie had hit its mark.

Al toyed with his mustache, contemplating. "I'm surprised I didn't put two and two together before. You're right. Rafferty probably put his whore up to harassing me. Notice whose saloon the league decided to target."

"I wouldn't let them get away with it, sugar, if it was me. What would we do if those harpies shut us down so we couldn't make a living?"

"We'll be ready for them next time. Laurel Martin and her band of cronies will not get off so easy, " he promised, his eyes darkening.

Pearl's lips curled in a smile of pure delight. Revenge was going to be sweet as spun sugar, she thought. Laurel Martin and Chance Rafferty were going to be the sorriest pair alive on the face of this earth.

Laurel clutched her sister's letter to her breast and allowed her tears to flow freely. If only Rose were here with her now, she wouldn't feel this desperate loneliness.

Christmas was only a couple of weeks away, and she'd no

doubt be spending it alone and as miserable as she had been on Thanksgiving.

What she wouldn't give for a taste of Rose's pumpkin pie. The miserable Thanksgiving fare they'd eaten at the boarding hotel was a far cry from the sumptuous holiday dinners she'd shared with her family on the farm. The chicken had been dry and stringy and tasted as if it were older than Mrs. Costello, who had to be nearing eighty! The mashed potatoes had lumps in them the size of boulders, and the rolls were so hard they could have been issued by the army for munitions.

It hardly seemed possible, but the company was worse than the food. Having to sit across the table from prune-faced Drucilla every morning and evening was enough to give a body indigestion. Laurel experienced heartburn each time the young woman stepped into the room and opened her mouth.

Rose's letter made her homesick and just a bit envious. It sounded as if Heather was deliriously content in San Francisco with the Montgomery family. And even Rose was finding her duke an enjoyable if not exasperating challenge. Rose always did love a challenge, and Laurel feared she'd met her match in Alexander Warrick.

Laurel needed to reply to Rose's letter and pen another to Heather. But what could she say? She was miserably unhappy with her present situation, despite the modest success she'd experienced with the temperance league.

She missed her friends at the Aurora. And she missed its owner as well.

Did Chance miss her, too?

Probably not, she thought. Especially since her last visit to his saloon when the ladies got a little carried away with their mission and began dumping the contents of beer mugs and whiskey bottles onto the floor and over customers' heads.

It was only after the police had been summoned and they'd all been dragged bodily into the street that she'd seen

Chance crack a smile. Of course, she'd been sitting in a mud puddle the size of the Pacific Ocean at the time.

The absurdity of the whole situation made her smile, and she tucked Rose's letter away in the drawer of her nightstand, vowing to answer it before the night was through.

A knock sounded on the door, and she tensed, then immediately relaxed, realizing the knock was too quiet and timid to be Drucilla's, who fairly pounded on the wood before she entered. "Yes?" she said.

Gertie Beecham stuck her head through the doorway, looking none too pleased at her mission. "A bouquet of flowers has just arrived for you, Laurel." She produced the arrangement from behind her back. "Hortensia asked me to bring them up."

"They're beautiful." Laurel eyed the mass of carnations and roses, a look of pure wonder on her face. "Who would have sent such a nice surprise?"

Gertie pursed her lips, her distaste clearly evident. "Since I'm not a reader of minds, I couldn't tell you. But there is a card attached." Handing her the bouquet, the older woman shut the door behind her.

Laurel sighed at the woman's odd behavior, then chalked it up to Gertie's penchant for propriety. No doubt the thought of a single woman receiving a gift from a stranger sent her sensibilities into an uproar. Gertie's rules of decorum had come straight from a book she'd purchased on the subject, and she never lost a chance to quote from it when the opportunity presented itself:

> *In the presence of others sing not to yourself with a humming voice, nor drum with your fingers or feet.*
>
> *Turn not your back to others, especially in speaking; jog not the table or desk on which another reads or writes; lean not on anyone.*
>
> *Use no reproachful language against anyone, neither curses nor revilings.*

Laurel especially liked the last one, considering the fact that Gertie had taken it upon herself to call poor Bull, the bartender at the Aurora, "a whoremonging, egg-sucking dog whose veins are flushed with sinful spirits."

Setting the flowers carefully on the chair, Laurel removed the tiny card attached to one of the stems. Never in her life had she received such a lovely gift, such an expensive gift, for she knew those roses and carnations would have to have come from a hot house. It was too cold in Denver to grow such plants outdoors.

"I want to see you," the card read. It was signed *Chance*.

Chance paced nervously in front of the Busy Bee Café, waiting for Laurel to make an appearance. Her note said twelve o'clock, but according to his gold pocket watch, which he'd checked five times in just as many minutes, it was ten minutes after the hour, and he'd half convinced himself she wasn't going to show.

A moment later he saw her rounding the corner, and he chided himself for acting like a schoolboy in the throes of his first passion. He was a businessman, for chrissake! An adult.

So why were his palms sweating?

"Sorry I'm late." Laurel held out her hand formally, as if they were meeting for the very first time. Then, realizing how stupid the gesture was, considering how many times his hand had caressed her naked breasts and other parts of her anatomy, she pulled her hand back sharply.

"There was a meeting of the board this morning, and it ran over." Mostly due to Hortensia's penchant for talking about things that weren't remotely related to temperance-league business.

"You look well," he remarked, then felt foolish at making the inane comment. Of course she looked well. She looked goddamn beautiful. And no doubt she knew it.

Entering the restaurant, they were seated in a secluded corner at the rear of the room. As she took her chair, Laurel felt relieved that no one from the league would be able to see whom she was dining with.

It wouldn't do to be seen in public with the owner of one of Denver's most popular gambling parlors. Hortensia would clearly disapprove, and Gertie would no doubt have herself a fit of the vapors.

To spare their sensibilities, and her own hide, Laurel had made up a lame excuse about picking up more pledge cards from the printer, though she wasn't certain that Hortensia believed the fabrication.

She'd never been a good liar, Laurel reminded herself.

"I wasn't sure you'd come."

Laurel glanced up from her menu to find Chance staring strangely at her, and her cheeks warmed. "Thank you for the flowers. They were most unexpected, especially considering the fact that some of my ladies got a little carried away at the Aurora the other night."

"Did you ever warm up?" he asked, grinning. "I imagine your backside was cooler than an ice cube after sitting in that mud puddle. A vigorous massage would have warmed you right up." And he was just the man to administer it.

As if she could read his lurid thoughts, Laurel shifted restlessly in her chair. "A hot bath achieved much the same result, but thank you for asking."

"I was hoping the flowers might be considered a peace offering of sorts. I'd like to be friends."

Friends. Lovers. But nothing more. Laurel willed away the moisture welling in her eyes. "Of course we can be friends. Haven't we always been?"

We've been much more than friends. We've almost been lovers, for chrissake! But he didn't dispute her contention. "I guess."

"How is everyone at the Aurora? I miss them all terribly."

"Do you?" *And do you miss me, too?* He sure as hell missed her. But of course he wasn't about to admit that.

"Bertha's given me what-for about your leaving, and Crystal only speaks to me when she has to."

"There's something to be said for loyalty."

"I guess," he said, choking back the bitter retort on the tip of his tongue. "How do you like your new job? I didn't think you'd enjoy a position that didn't afford you the opportunity to sing."

"*Singing songs other than Christian hymns is an abomination unto our Lord.*" Drucilla's words rang loudly in her ears and made her frown. "The position offers other rewards. I enjoy helping others too weak to help themselves."

"That's noble of you."

"I'm not doing it to be noble, Chance. I'm doing it because . . ." Why? Why was she doing something so alien to her? She'd never been involved in causes before. She'd never thought of herself as the preachy type to shout about fire and brimstone.

"Because?" he prompted, his eyebrow arching in question.

Because revenge seemed sweet at the time, she wanted to shout. *Because you hurt me, as no one has ever hurt me before. Because I wanted you to love me and you didn't. Because you took my dreams of a Prince Charming and snuffed them out like one of your wretched cheroots.*

"Excessive alcohol is ruinous to a person's health. It destroys families and brings unhappiness to a great many people."

"Now you sound like one of your pamphlets."

Her shoulders lifted, then sagged. "I'm being paid to spread the word of the league, and that's what I intend to do. And I also believe it to be a just cause."

"My luck's run out since you left, angel."

She still thought his belief silly. "I can't believe a grown man would be so superstitious. You were lucky before I came; you'll be lucky again. It's just the whim of the cards."

He shook his head. "I've gambled too many years to know the signs. Once your luck starts petering out like mine has, you never get it back. I need you, angel. I need you back with me."

Her eyes narrowed. "To bring back your luck?"

"Among other things."

Her heart hammered against her ribs. "Such as?"

He banged his hand down hard on the table, upsetting their water glasses, which fortunately were empty, and drawing unwanted attention their way. "I miss you, goddammit! Things haven't been the same since you left."

Her heart smiled this time, she was sure of it. "You don't have to sound so unhappy about it."

"Well, I am unhappy. I want you to come back to work at the Aurora."

Her joy faded a bit. "Back to work at the Aurora? Singing in a saloon?"

He nodded. "Everything will be just the same as it was. Bertha and Crystal will be happy. Whitey can continue with his writing lessons; he talks about you all the time. And we can pick up where we left off."

"You mean—I can become your lover, your kept woman, your whore?" She pushed back her chair, intending to end their conversation.

"Wait?" he said, reaching for her arm. "You misunderstand. I wouldn't expect anything like that from you." He *wanted* it, but he wouldn't expect it.

Noting the desperation in his voice, Laurel relented and sat back down. "Chance, don't you understand? We can never go back to the way we were. Things are different now, I'm different. I want more out of life. I was never cut out to be a saloon singer." *Or a gambler's whore.*

He was losing her again, dammit. And this time if she left he'd never see her again. She'd walk out of his life forever. He couldn't let that happen. So he said, "My intentions are strictly honorable."

"They are?"

"I'd like another chance, Laurel. I'd like the opportunity to put my money where my mouth is."

If this was a declaration, it was the oddest one she'd ever received. "Excuse me?"

He took her hand and kissed it. And though the words seemed to choke the very life out of him, he said, "I want to court you proper like, if you'll let me."

"Court? You mean as in keeping company?" She could hardly believe it. Chance Rafferty wanted to court her?

He was sweating so hard that he had to pull the handkerchief out of his back pocket to wipe up the droplets. "Uh . . . uh-huh." He nodded.

Leaning back in her chair, too stunned to speak, Laurel thought of all the ramifications of this turn of events. Chance wanted to court her. Why, he didn't say. And she lacked the courage to ask if he intended the courtship to lead to marriage.

And what would the ladies of the temperance league say when they heard she was keeping company with a saloon owner?

"This declaration is rather sudden, Chance. I'll have to give it some thought. Our relationship will put me in a very awkward position with the league."

"So quit. What do you want to work for them for anyway?"

Was that why he wanted to court her—so that she would quit? So that she wouldn't be in a position to demonstrate against him anymore? Well, he was in for a very rude awakening if that was the case. She had no intention of quitting her job with the league, but she had every intention of bringing Chance Rafferty to the altar. To his knees, if need be.

Rose had been right: She'd given up too easily. Chance Rafferty was only a man. If she could reform drunks and whoremongers, surely she could do the same to one charming gambling man.

How difficult a task could that be?

"I won't quit my job, Chance, but I will accept your calling on me at Mrs. Costello's boarding hotel." She smiled so sweetly at him that his heart nearly flipped over in his chest. "But first, I believe we have some unfinished business to discuss."

Pearl. The whore's presence stood between them. He could almost smell her cloying gardenia perfume.

"Pearl lied to Whitey," he blurted. "There was never anything between us."

Laurel looked skeptical. "Never?"

He sighed deeply and rubbed the back of his neck. "Just once. But it meant nothing. I was drunk, and Pearl took advantage of the situation. A man's allowed one indiscretion, isn't he?"

"Your own admission is as good an excuse for the prohibition of alcohol as any I've heard."

"Do you believe me then?"

She nodded. "Yes. Though I'm not quite sure why."

"And you'll still let me court you?"

"If you observe all the proprieties. Mrs. Costello is very particular about who comes to call."

"We have to keep company under the watchful eyes of all those biddies?" How the hell was he going to bed her under those circumstances? And persuade her to come back to work at the Aurora? This courtship business was going to be a lot tougher than he'd anticipated.

"I'm sure Mrs. Tungsten will expect us to be chaperoned at all times, considering my position and your occupation. That won't be a problem, will it?"

Dismayed, and looking as if he'd just consumed a whole bottle of castor oil, he shook his head.

"And, of course, we'll need to attend church every Sunday from now on. Mama always said that couples who prayed together bonded like glue."

Hope sprang eternal. "And did your mama say how long it

took to consummate . . ." he shook his head, "to complete this bonding process?"

"Why, that depends entirely on you, Chance," she said, patting his cheek. "Once your reformation is complete, the bonding can commence."

His face whitened. " 'Reformation'?"

She wanted to laugh at the expression on his face. She wanted to shout that for once Chance Rafferty hadn't gotten the best of her. She wanted to tell him how much she loved him, and that one day he'd thank her for all she intended to do.

But she didn't do or say any of those things. Instead, she merely nodded her head, squeezed his hand reassuringly, and said, "Uh . . . uh-huh."

CHAPTER 17

Minerva Whitefish tiptoed up behind Laurel and tapped her lightly on the shoulder. "Excuse me, Miss Martin," she whispered. "But there are some people at the front door to see you."

Feeling irritated, Laurel looked up from the speech she was writing. Minerva never walked, she tiptoed; she never talked, she whispered; and she never said plainly what was on her mind, she just alluded to it.

"By 'people,' do you mean ladies or gentlemen, Minerva?"

The slight woman wrung her hands nervously. "Well, they don't look quite like ladies, Miss Martin. They've got paint on their faces, and their bosoms are clearly displayed, and it's not even noon."

Smiling widely, for she now had an inkling of who had come to visit, Laurel patted Minerva's hand. "There's no need to be upset, Minnie. I believe the ladies you refer to are my friends Crystal and Flora Sue, from the Aurora."

Minerva's eyes bulged behind her thick-rimmed glasses. "Friends? Oh, my goodness!" She patted her cheek. "They look . . ." her voice lowered and Laurel had to crane her neck to hear, "disreputable."

"Having been in dire straits myself at one time, Minnie, I never judge others. One never knows when one might be required to—"

The woman's gasp was louder than any sound Laurel had previously heard from her. "I would *never*!" She shook her head emphatically. "I'd rather die first than lie with a man in sin."

Laurel suspected that the spinster would rather die than lie with any man, in sin or otherwise. "I truly think you would, Minnie. Yes, I do," Laurel said, smiling to herself as she made her way to the front door.

Opening it, the greeting she was given startled her momentarily. "We're freezing our asses off out here," Flora Sue declared, stomping her feet to get the circulation flowing to her toes. "Doesn't that dried-up prune know it's winter?"

Laurel's eyes twinkled. Crystal and Flora Sue were a sight for her tired eyes. God, she'd missed them! "Come in . . . come in. Minerva isn't used to entertaining guests."

"Judging from the looks of her, she ain't used to doing much of anything," Flora Sue concluded, stepping into the parlor.

Crystal giggled. "Shame on you, Flora Sue. Remember what Augustus said about speaking ill of others."

"Just because Augustus Baldwin is keeping your fires banked this winter, don't mean I can't speak the honest-to-God truth."

Laughing at her friends' bickering, Laurel held out her hands to both women. "I've missed you."

"We've missed you too, Laurel honey. Things just aren't the same at the Aurora without you. And the entertainment stinks. Bert Swanzey's delivery of 'Camptown Races' sets dogs to howling over a five-mile radius. Chance never did replace you."

Laurel was inordinately pleased to hear that. "What brings you two out on such a dreary day? I expect we'll have snow before this evening." The sky had darkened considerably since morning, the clouds now ominous and heavy with moisture.

"Bertha said as much. And," Flora Sue added with a searching look, "she also said you and Chance had yourselves a meeting yesterday. We came over to find out if that was true, and if you're coming back to the saloon like she's predicting."

"Bertha's getting ahead of herself, I'm afraid. It's true, Chance and I did meet for lunch." She looked about to make sure Drucilla wasn't eavesdropping; the woman was a notorious snoop. "But I'm not going back to work for him."

Crystal's face fell. "But why? It's almost Christmas, and I was hoping all of us could be together again. Gus is going to give a wonderful Christmas Eve sermon, and Bertha's planning to make a feast to end all feasts. Please say you'll come."

The league was having a big temperance rally on Christmas Eve. Frances Willard, the driving force behind the WCTU and its president since 1879, was expected to speak. She was currently touring the West with her secretary, Anna Gordon, and was considered the foremost female speaker of the day.

Laurel's presence would be expected for such an important event, and she was admittedly curious about the woman who inspired such devotion from her followers. Hortensia and Gertie hung on her every word and deed, and even dour Drucilla appeared awed when speaking about her.

"The league has something planned that night, but if it's possible, I'll sneak away to join you."

"You look happier than the last time we saw you," Flora Sue commented. "Did something happen between you and Chance?" She leaned forward and lowered her voice in a conspiratorial fashion. "Something physical, I hope?"

Feeling heat creep up her neck, Laurel shook her head. "No. Nothing like that. But Chance has declared himself."

Crystal screeched, then covered her mouth. "He's asked you to marry him?"

"Not exactly. But he has asked to court me. I guess that's a start."

Flora Sue's eyes widened. "Chance Rafferty asked to court you? I find that hard to believe, doll baby. That man is scared of anything smacking of commitment. He told Rooster he'd never marry, told him marriage was a death sentence for all men."

Crystal cast her companion a sharp look. "Hush, Flora Sue! Men have been known to change their minds. Look at Rooster. Who would have ever guessed he'd be whipped as bad as he is. The poor man practically drools every time you walk into the room."

Smiling like the cat who just swallowed the canary, Flora Sue patted her hair. "I know how to make my little Rooster crow, girls."

Laurel laughed. "I'm not offended by what Flora says. I'm well aware of Chance's sad upbringing, though I've not been privy to other details of his private life."

"No one knows much about those, doll baby. Chance has always been closemouthed about his past."

"And about his present, apparently. If we hadn't overheard Bertha grilling him after he came back from your luncheon, we wouldn't have known he went," Crystal confided.

"How are you planning to keep company with Chance under the noses of all these proper ladies?" Flora Sue wanted to know. "You'll never be alone to . . ." She patted Laurel's hand, hoping to spare her friend embarrassment. Laurel wasn't like the other women she knew; she was what her mama would call "decent." "Well . . . you know."

"I'm not planning to 'you know' until we're married. If Chance wants to bed me, he's going to have to put a ring on my finger."

"But not before you put one through his nose," Crystal added, giggling.

"Mama always said there was more than one way to skin a cat. I'll handle Hortensia and the other ladies of the league my own way." A secretive smile crossed her lips. "And I have some very definite ideas about the way to handle Chance."

Never having heard anything so outlandish before, Flora Sue decided to set Laurel straight about the ways of men, decent or not. "I don't understand how you can handle him if you're not fixin' to bed him. Surely you know that the way to a man's heart is straight to his crotch, doll baby. They do anything for you, once you give them a taste of the honey pot."

Before Laurel had a chance to respond; Crystal said, "Flora Sue does have a point. Chance is a man used to dealing in carnal delights, so to speak. It's going to be very difficult to keep such a man at bay."

"I realize you two have a different perspective on such matters, due to your extensive experience. But my mama always said that abstinence makes the heart grow fonder. She used to say that a man who had too many tastes of the honey pot usually got a stomachache from too much sweetness."

"But if that's the case, Laurel honey, why did Flora Sue and I have so many repeat and satisfied customers? That don't make a lick of sense."

The more Laurel thought about it, the less she understood, and the deeper her frown grew. Finally, she shrugged. "Mama didn't say anything about that."

Flora Sue laughed. "No, I bet she didn't. Because she wanted to keep you and your sisters drawers up for as long as she could. Your mama wasn't used to dealing with a man like Chance. His six-shooter's loaded and ready for bear, and it's pointing right between your legs, doll baby."

Untying the ribbons of Laurel's chemise, Chance nuzzled her soft breasts, placing kisses on her pert, rosy nipples. His fingers toyed with the waistband of her drawers, insinuating themselves lower and lower as he reached for . . .

"Isn't Augustus a wonderful speaker, Chance? I'm so pleased you consented to attend church service with me today."

Chance swallowed, expecting to be struck down by a bolt of God's vengeance. Here he was, seated in a house of worship, or in this case, Gus's makeshift church, thinking about making love to Laurel. He shifted to ease the growing discomfort between his legs, and a sharp splinter went right into his backside from the rough-hewn boards he sat on.

"Jesus, Mary, and Joseph!"

Laurel smiled contentedly and patted his hand. "You really are in the spirit today. Augustus will be so pleased."

"Isn't he ever going to shut up? He's been talking for almost an hour. I never figured Gus for such a windbag."

"*Ssh!* He's going to make an announcement about our next temperance meeting."

He leaned over to whisper in her ear, purposely placing his lips against the sensitive flesh, and was pleased when he heard her sharp intake of breath. "I'm inclined to believe that sin is a whole lot more fun than salvation, angel."

Laurel stared straight ahead, hoping the tingling feeling between her legs would cease, and fearing that Chance might be right: Eternal damnation loomed sharply on the horizon.

"Well, Mr. Rafferty, we meet at last. I'm Hortensia Tungsten, but I'm sure Miss Martin has already spoken to you of me."

From his position on the horsehair sofa in the parlor of Costellos' boarding hotel, Chance summed up his adversary: Formidable. Large. Homely as a bullfrog. Hortensia Tungsten looked like she ate steel for breakfast and spat out nails.

The delicate chair she sat upon was sure to collapse at any

moment. Her generous derriere spilled over the sides of it like foam overflowing a beer mug.

Laurel, seated next to him on the sofa, looked anxious but hopeful that he wasn't going to say something totally outrageous. He was tempted, goddammit.

"Pleased to make your acquaintance." He smiled his most charming smile, wondering if the old blubber-gut could be sweet-talked.

"Laurel tells me that we may be seeing a bit more of you around here, Mr. Rafferty. That you have declared yourself a suitor." Though she tried to keep her voice impassive, Chance didn't miss the underlying disdain.

"I have. And Laurel has consented to my suit." He winked at Laurel, ignoring Mrs. Tungsten's gasp.

"I'm sure you'll understand when I say that your present occupation leaves cause for skepticism where Miss Martin is concerned. We're doing our best to improve upon her previous reputation as a saloon singer, and I'm not sure her keeping company with a gambler is going to enhance that."

Laurel braced herself for the outburst, but all she heard was Chance's polite chuckle. "Come now, Mrs. Tungsten, even a gambling man has a right to reform. Laurel told me as much. Isn't that right, an— my dear?"

She nodded, wondering if Gus's sermon this morning really had made an impact on Chance. He certainly acted odd.

"Am I to understand that you will be shutting down your saloon, Mr. Rafferty?"

Chance nearly choked on the wretched tea he was sipping. A good shot of bourbon would have done a lot to improve the flavor. "Close the Aurora?" He shook his head. "No, ma'am. That wouldn't be possible. You see, it's how I make my living, and many people depend on me for their livelihood."

"But . . . but, Mr. Rafferty, how can you possibly court our Miss Martin if you're not intending to cease and desist your present avocation? I cannot allow her to sully our cause and confuse the issue."

Noting the reddening of Chance's cheeks, Laurel decided it was time to have her say. "Mr. Rafferty's reformation is likely to take some time, Hortensia. Rome wasn't built in a day, as you are so fond of saying." She smiled sweetly at the older woman. "Mr. Rafferty needs time to ascertain that what we're doing is the right thing for him."

Double chins *shook* as Hortensia wagged her head in confusion. "But, Laurel dear! He's a gambler, and you're a temperance worker. I fail to see how the two of you can reconcile such an impossible arrangement."

"You hired me to bring reformation to Denver's masses, Hortensia. Think of what others will say if I am able to reform Mr. Rafferty to our way of thinking."

When pigs fly, Chance thought, though he could see that the argument held great appeal for the older woman.

"Is Mr. Rafferty willing to be reformed? That is what I want to know before I give my blessing to this courtship."

Both heads turned to stare sharply at Chance, who was doing his best to look serious and repentant, as was expected of him. "I'm willing to do whatever it takes to make Laurel mine. I want her, Mrs. Tungsten." *In the most elemental way.* "And I'm willing to turn over a new leaf to achieve my objective."

Laurel's eyes softened, and she smiled tentatively.

Hortensia, however, was not so easily won over. "Mr. Rafferty, I fear that you will need to upend the entire tree. A leopard does not readily change his spots."

Chance did his best to look offended, though he really wanted nothing more than to dump the fat cow into the nearest river and drown her. No doubt she'd float!

"I must say I'm shocked, Mrs. Tungsten, that you put so little faith in Miss Martin's abilities. I happen to know that she possesses certain attributes"—*soft skin, pert breasts, kissable lips*—"to bring a man like me to heel."

Laurel's eyes rolled heavenward.

"Not being as thoroughly familiar with these attributes as I am, Mrs. Tungsten, you wouldn't know how inspirational they are to a man like me. I'm willing to go through hell"— and he certainly was—"to join myself—bond, if you will— to experience and revel in her divine being."

He clasped Laurel's hand, bringing it to his mouth for a kiss, and Hortensia's hand flew up to cover her heart.

"I had no idea how committed you were, Mr. Rafferty."

Chance's devastatingly handsome grin set Laurel's toes to curling and even brought two splotches of color to Hortensia's pasty complexion. "Dedicated and determined as I've never been before."

The enormous spruce tree gracing the center of the gambling parlor made Laurel's breath catch. There had been no Christmas tree at Mrs. Costello's. The league didn't hold with wasting money on unnecessary and useless items. "Why, bringing a tree indoors is just foolishness, plain and simple, that's what it is," Gertie had said.

Laurel, standing in the Aurora's doorway, her eyes glowing with pleasure as she stared at the gaily decorated evergreen, felt grateful that Chance didn't feel as Gertie did. The satin garters and costume jewelry hanging from the branches told her that Flora Sue and Crystal had lent a hand in the decorating of it. And they'd done a splendid job. She only wished she'd been there to help.

Bertha shouted with joy when she caught sight of Laurel, then admonished, "Shut the door, honey. You's letting all the cold in and the heat out."

All eyes turned in Laurel's direction, and she felt suddenly self-conscious to be back at her former place of employment. Did they blame her for their lack of business? Chance had told her that profits had been slim. And she knew the girls relied on tips to supplement their meager wages.

"Well, Lordy be! Howdy-do, Miss Laurel." Jup rushed forward, his toothy grin almost lighting up the room."You sure is a sight for these tired old eyes."

When the piano player engulfed her in his spindly arms, Laurel knew she'd come home.

That feeling was brought to her full force when Percy perched on Bull's shoulder, squawked excitedly, flapped his wings, and said *"Repent ye sinners. Angel's back!"*

The room erupted in howls of laughter, and none laughed harder than Chance, who came forward to take Laurel in his arms. "Welcome home, angel. As you can see, you've been missed."

"Let that child go, Mr. Chance," Bertha called out as she sliced ham for the buffet. "Miss Laurel needs to eat. She's scrawny as a bird."

Chance tipped up her chin, staring into eyes swimming with unshed tears of happiness. "I know I'm starved, angel. How about you?"

His wicked grin told her that he wasn't talking about food, and she felt a familiar fluttering in her midsection. For when it came to Chance her hunger knew no bounds.

"Everyone's delighted you could come this evening, Laurel," Augustus said between bites of his sandwich. "But I thought you'd be tied up with your temperance meeting tonight."

"Miss Willard came down hoarse, so it was canceled. I tried to act disappointed and concerned, but I was secretly overjoyed. I guess that was wicked of me, wasn't it, Reverend?"

"One has to follow one's heart, my dear." He set down his plate. "Come with me. There's something I want to show you."

She crossed the room with him, wondering at the mysterious smile lighting his face. She'd never seen him so happy and relaxed before, and she guessed that Crystal had a great deal to do with his new demeanor. "I admit you've piqued my curiosity, Gus. Did Chance go and buy another one of those lurid paintings?" Glancing across the room to where the now infamous nude hung, she shook her head. "It's no wonder those women want to shut him down."

Gus chuckled, pointing to the empty space where the stereoscopic device used to be. "He sold it, Laurel. Chance finally sold the thing to Mort Fines."

She could hardly believe her eyes. "But why? He was so determined to keep it, even after we had that terrible row."

"God works in mysterious ways. Apparently at church service last Sunday, Chance injured himself on one of the pews. You know how rough and splintery those boards are."

She nodded, suppressing her smile. So, Chance had gotten a splinter in his butt! Of course, he'd have been too embarrassed to mention it. And then he'd had to put up with Hortensia's inquisition. . . . She shook her head. Poor Chance. "I can't say I'm sorry it's gone."

"Chance took the money from the sale and started a church-building fund. We hope to start construction come spring."

"Oh, Gus! That's wonderful." She clutched his arm. "I'm so happy for you . . . for both you and Crystal."

A look of total contentment passed over his face. "I've never known a woman like Crystal before, Laurel. She's wonderful."

"So when are you planning to make an honest woman of her?"

"I've asked her. Believe me. But she thinks she'll be sullying my reputation by marrying me. I told her that was nonsense, that I would quit the clergy if need be, but she wouldn't hear of it. I admit to being a bit out of my league where women are concerned."

Laurel pecked him on the cheek. "Leave Crystal to me. I've always been able to talk some sense into her. I think she'll listen to me."

"I'm not certain, my dear, that someone doesn't need to talk some sense into you." At her wounded expression, he added, "Laurel, I admire you for what you're doing to help the ladies of this town. But I caution you to look into your heart and search your motives for your actions.

"I'm not saying that what you're doing is wrong, but I wonder if you're following your head instead of your heart. Think about it, my dear. We all love you and want what's best for you."

Augustus walked away to join Crystal, and Laurel took time to ponder his advice. Her feelings had been mixed from the beginning on whether she was doing the right thing. She hated bringing unhappiness and discord to her friends at the Aurora. They'd become as much a part of her life as her own family. But they also abetted the drinking and gambling that ruined the lives of so many.

And though at first she'd joined the temperance league merely to spite Chance, she'd since had the opportunity to observe the many good things they did for people—for children like Bud Foley.

Just last week, Will Foley's boy, Bud, had been brought to the hospital with a broken arm. Caused, his mother said, by his father, who had come home in a drunken rage and beaten the child senseless. The league had stepped in immediately, offering refuge to both Bud and his mother, and had even taken Mr. Foley under their wing for counseling on his addiction.

What was the answer, the right choice to make? She couldn't just abandon her work; it had become too important to her now. But how could she abandon her friends? They were important, too.

"You look awfully sad on such a happy occasion, angel." Chance came to stand before her. "And I think I have just the thing to cheer you up."

"Not champagne, I hope. It was difficult enough convincing Hortensia that I was coming here to offer counsel and spiritual guidance. I doubt she'd be too pleased if I returned to the hotel drunk and howling at the moon."

Chance laughed. "Your intolerance for alcohol has given me many amusing and titillating moments, but it's not drink I'm referring to." Reaching behind his back he retrieved a sprig of mistletoe and held it above her head. "I believe you're standing under the mistletoe, angel. And I'm sure you know what that means."

Laurel's heart began to thump louder than the sprightly tune Jup was pounding out on the piano, but uncertainty clouded her eyes. "I really don't think we should, Chance."

"But it's tradition, Laurel. You wouldn't want to break with tradition, now would you? And it's only one little kiss, though I'd be pleased with a whole lot more."

It was hard to argue with tradition, and with a man who had dimples. "One kiss, and that's all. Or I'll report you to Hortensia Tungsten."

A look of mock horror crossed his face before he drew her into his arms. "One kiss, " he promised, touching her lips with the tip of his tongue, leaving her breathless. "Just one little kiss."

But it was much more than a "little" kiss, and Laurel knew she was lost the moment his tongue pressed into her mouth, the moment she tasted the brandy on his lips, the moment her heart took flight, her legs grew leaden, and her body cried out for so much more.

It was one little kiss, but it meant everything to her.

CHAPTER 18

"They're coming! The goddamn bitches are coming," Al shouted over his shoulder as he sighted the group of women marching down the street. "Get ready. We won't let them get the best of us this time."

Pearl's face lit up with spite mingled with anticipation. "The girls are ready upstairs, sugar. Shall I give them the signal?"

"Damn right! Those bitches will know after tonight not to target the Silver Slipper again." He had a little surprise for Laurel Martin and her band of harpies. No one made a fool of Al Hazen.

"I hate demonstrating in front of the Silver Slipper," Gertie whispered to Laurel as they neared their destination. "That horrible man spat on me the last time we came here." Nervously, she wiped her cheek, remembering.

Laurel's breath clouded the frigid night air as she said, "Al Hazen is a pig, but we can't allow him to intimidate us, Gertie. He likes to bully women, beat them up. It makes him feel important."

The bawdy music from the saloon drifted out into the street, and the band of women raised their voices to be heard above the din. The first strains of "Onward, Christian Soldiers" were barely out of their mouths when the first missile hit Laurel smack in the eye. She screamed as the remnants of an overripe tomato slithered down her face and the front of her coat.

Before the women could take cover, the customers from the saloon poured out of the building, hurling rotten vegetables and epithets at them.

"Take that, you harridans!" one of the men shouted as he threw a cabbage at them.

"You frustrated bunch of virgins," a drunken cowboy claimed, testing the weight of an apple he palmed.

"Get outta here, you bitches!" Hazen ordered, stepping out on the wooden sidewalk in front of his place. "Beat it. You're not welcome here."

"We're not ready to leave, Mr. Hazen," Laurel shouted, wiping her face, and bringing an exasperated moan from her co-workers, who were eager to depart.

Minerva tugged at Laurel's skirt. "Please, Miss Martin. Let's do as he says and get out of here before they shoot us."

Ignoring her, Laurel shouted, "We're not afraid of you, Mr. Hazen. Your intimidating words won't scare us off."

"No?" An evil grin materialized beneath his mustache. "Well, maybe this will. Let 'er rip, girls."

The upstairs windows suddenly opened and screams and giggles of pure delight filled the air. Before the temperance women could flee, a putrid shower of human waste rained down upon them from ceramic pots and brass spittoons the whores held upended in their hands.

Laurel nearly gagged at the thought of what was presently adorning her hair and clothing, but she stood fast, shaking her fist in Hazen's direction. "You haven't seen the last of us," she threatened. But when she looked about her she saw that the other women had fled.

The group of men on the porch laughed, then went back inside to resume their amusements.

Standing alone in the dark street, Laurel knew real fear for the first time in her life. That fear was compounded by the sight of a large, burly man who stepped out of the shadows and came toward her. She couldn't see his face, but she thought she saw the glimmer of a gun barrel in the light of the streetlamp, and she gasped, shivering in panic.

Suddenly the man melted back into the shadows, and she heard a sound behind her. Turning, she saw Chance running toward her, and she breathed a sigh of relief.

Having heard from several of his patrons what was occurring at the Silver Slipper, Chance had run the short distance to Hazen's establishment.

"Jesus, Mary, and Joseph!" he yelled at the sight of the bedraggled temperance worker—his supposed intended. Sniffing the air a few times, he wrinkled his nose in disgust. "Is that smell what I think it is?" She smelled worse than the inside of a horse barn in the middle of a summer heat wave.

Laurel, who had never been so happy to see anyone in her entire life, wasn't the least bit offended by Chance's reaction. "I'm so glad you've come." Holding out both arms to hug him, she ran forward, then stopped suddenly as the horrified look on Chance's face finally registered.

"I guess I'm not too appealing at the moment."

"That bastard will answer for this, angel. I promise you that." He stared at the windows of the saloon, knowing full well, that Hazen was peering at them from inside. "You hear that, Hazen?" he shouted. "We're not done by a long shot." But the only response was silence.

"Don't waste your breath on him, Chance. Hazen's like a snake. He only strikes when he thinks no one's looking."

"Come on. I'll walk you home."

She shook her head as she dug her heels into the muddy

street, and a small piece of something Chance didn't want to think about landed on his boot. He shook it off, then gripped her by the elbow.

"No! I want to go back to the Aurora with you. I need to be with my friends tonight." She couldn't bear the thought of seeing her co-workers right now. She might just be tempted to tell them exactly what she thought of their defection. The cowards! And there was still that shadowy figure to consider.

Laurel's request pleased Chance. He had a few choice words to say to her, and he didn't particularly want to say them in front of her temperance-league cronies.

Picketing his saloon and some of the others was one thing, but harassing a man as dangerous and violent as Hazen was something else.

Laurel could very easily have gotten herself killed tonight. That thought made his stomach cramp and a searing pain enter his heart.

It was time he put a stop to all this nonsense.

Bathed, and dressed in a gown she'd borrowed from Crystal, Laurel waited impatiently in her old room for Chance to return. He'd gone downstairs to fetch something for them to eat, and her stomach reminded her with every growl that it hadn't been fed since early that morning.

The knock on the door had her bolting off the bed. "Come in."

"Are you decent?" Chance stuck his head in the doorway and scowled at the sight of her. "Goddammit! Son of a bitch!"

"What is it? What's wrong?" She looked down to make certain all her buttons were fastened; then, satisfied that they were, she hurried forward to assist him with the tray. "You'd think I'd grown two heads while you were gone, the way you're looking at me."

"What you've grown, angel, is the blackest and bluest

shiner I've seen in a month of Sundays. That bastard Hazen gave you a black eye."

At the mirror, she was shocked to see the discoloration around her right eye. "Oh, dear!" She looked as if she'd been the loser in a fistfight. She hadn't had a black eye since Rose Elizabeth had tackled her while playing Indian attack when they were small.

"Come here and let me take a closer look."

Chance's fingers were gentle as they probed the swollen area around her eye, and she winced only once, when he pressed too hard. "Sorry." His frown deepened. "We need to talk, angel."

"Can't it wait until we've eaten? I'm starved."

Chuckling, he shook his head. "You always did have a large appetite."

Removing one of the ham sandwiches from the tray, Laurel sat down on the edge of the bed, talking between bites. "Mama always said that ladies who have birdlike appetites usually have birdlike brains to go with them."

"If your mama knew what you'd been up to of late, I doubt she'd credit you with having too much brains."

"Just because things got a bit out of hand tonight is—"

He put up his hand to forestall her argument. "Don't mess with Hazen, Laurel. He's bad news. I'll take care of the bastard in my own way, but I don't want you putting your life in jeopardy."

"My life was hardly in jeopardy, Chance. I was pelted with some rotten vegetables, and other things I'd rather not remember." She'd already scrubbed her hair three times, but she still wasn't satisfied that she'd gotten out all the stench.

"Hazen won't stop with flinging insults and garbage at you angel. Don't you know by now that he's nuts? I want you to stop harassing his place. If you have to target someone, target me. I only get mildly irritated."

"I appreciate your worrying about me, Chance, but . . ."

"Dammit, Laurel!" He advanced on her, pulling her off the

bed and into his arms. "You could have been seriously in-ured tonight. What was to stop those men from raping you . . . or worse? You were all alone in the dark when I came along."

Her face whitened at the veracity of his words, and she swallowed, remembering the man with the gun and how close she had come to getting killed. "I . . . I'm committed to the temperance cause."

"Angel," he crooned, brushing back silken strands of her hair and placing kisses at her temples. "I wouldn't know what to do if something happened to you. I . . ."

She gazed up, hope shining in her eyes. "Yes?"

He looked longingly at her, then gave a deep sigh of re-gret. He knew what she wanted to hear, but he couldn't bring himself to say the words, to say what he felt in his heart: that he loved her and couldn't imagine a life without her in it. To say those words meant committing himself to her forever, and he just wasn't ready to do that.

Commitment meant marriage. Marriage meant children. He was ill-suited for the roles of husband and father. And even if he were to let his heart rule his head, it wouldn't be fair to Laurel. He could never give her the kind of life she deserved. Never make her fairy-tale world a reality.

He was a gambler, and that's all he was ever going to be.

Putting his arm around her, he led her to the window. The stars glimmered luminously, like sparkling diamonds against a backdrop of ebony satin, but they were no lovelier than the love shining in Laurel's big blue eyes.

"I love the stars," he said. "They're so mysterious, yet comforting to look at. See that brilliant one up there? That's the North Star. I remember sitting around campfires in the mining camps, looking up at the star and wishing me and Whitey would strike it rich."

"And did you?" she asked, trying not to let her voice re-veal the disappointment she felt because he hadn't declared himself, and wondering if he ever would.

"No. We made enough to get along but we never hit pay dirt. Mostly I played cards to earn my way. It was a lot less work, and a hell of a lot more fun than swinging a pickax."

"What's that group of stars?" she asked, pointing to the odd formation that looked like the shape of a hunter.

Chance's gaze followed her finger. "Orion. See," he explained, tracing his finger along the glass, "you can make out the Hunter's belt and sword."

Laurel stared intently, then nodded enthusiastically. "You're right! I never realized."

"To the naked eye the stars look blue-white in color, but if you were to view them through a telescope, you'd see that some are actually a deep red."

Laurel looked at him in wonder. "You've looked through a telescope?"

"Astronomy is sort of a hobby of mine." When he saw her surprise, he added, "Would you like to look at the stars through a telescope? I have one in my room." He tweaked her nose. "That is, if you're not too afraid to enter a man's bedroom."

"Your room can't be nearly as frightening as what I've already experienced tonight."

He wiggled his eyebrows suggestively. "Don't be too sure, angel. I can be downright scary when I put my mind to it." Without another word, he grasped her hand and led her to his room.

"It's so big!"

His grin was incredibly sexy, and it made her heart flutter. "Why, thank you. I like to think so."

"I meant your room," she chided, knocking him playfully on the arm. "Now behave yourself."

"What fun would that be, angel?"

While he went to the large bow window to ready the telescope, Laurel took the opportunity to look around. She'd never been in a man's bedroom before, except her father's and Whitey's, but she didn't think either of those counted.

Chance's room was much larger than the others she'd seen. There was a whole wall of windows, and the mahogany bedstead hugging the side wall was enormous. The blue-and-white gingham comforter matched the curtains at the window, and there was a colorful oriental carpet on the pine-planked flooring. By the wood stove stood two comfortable-looking blue leather wing chairs, and between them a table stacked with books.

A closer inspection revealed Chance's interest in astronomy and the surprising fact that he read Mark Twain and Herman Melville.

Not only was she seeing his bedroom for the very first time, she was seeing a whole new side of Chance that she hadn't known existed. His room spoke of refinement, of educational pursuits, and she found that somewhat daunting.

"I had no idea you were interested in so many different things."

He smiled, handing her a glass of sherry he'd poured from a crystal decanter. "I guess we've never spent much time really getting to know each other. There's a lot about you, for instance, that constantly surprises me."

She gestured to herself. "Me? Why, I'm as simple and open as they come. I doubt you'll glean many surprises from me."

"You've got an extraordinary talent for speechmaking, angel. I never realized that before." There were a great many things to love and admire about Laurel. Not only did she possess a generous heart, but her ability to inspire others to reform was extraordinary.

Her penchant for giving unselfishly of herself spurred him to do the same, and he found he enjoyed the charitable functions he'd taken upon himself. Soon Gus would have a new church, the public library would be able to purchase books with money he'd donated, the women's shelters would have regular deliveries of food, and all because Laurel had set an example to help her fellow man.

He might not be willing to give up liquor or gambling, but he could use part of his profits to help those less fortunate than himself. The great feeling he derived from his small contributions couldn't be measured monetarily.

Chance's observation surprised Laurel. "You've heard me speak? I don't recall seeing you in the crowds."

He motioned to one of the wing chairs, inviting her to sit. "I doubt it would have looked too good for a saloon owner to be seen at a temperance meeting. Trust me—I kept a low profile."

"Do you really think I'm good?" His opinion mattered more than she cared to admit.

"Good enough to put a crimp in my business, angel." He took a sip of sherry, and she followed suit, welcoming the sweet burning taste into her throat, but being ever mindful of the effect that spirits had on her.

"You're not trying to get me drunk, are you?" she said teasingly, but the look he cast her was serious and intent.

"When we make love, angel, I want you sober as a judge. I want you to feel every kiss, every caress. I want you to know that it's me who's putting a brand on you."

Sharp, tingling sensations filled her, and she practically launched herself out of the chair. "I'd like to see your scope now."

His eyebrow arched. "Really?"

The heat from her loins shot straight to her cheeks. "Quit twisting everything I say, Chance Rafferty, or I'm going to leave." The man was positively incorrigible.

He laughed, following her to the window. "Stand behind the eyepiece and look into it."

She did as he directed and was immediately awed. "Everything looks so close. I feel like I could catch a moonbeam in the palm of my hand."

"You should see what it's like to view an aurora."

"Like in 'aurora borealis'?" So that was where he had come up with the name for his saloon.

"I've seen the northern lights and they're breathtaking. They're like streamers of luminous light, beautiful and special. A rarity to behold."

"Like this saloon?" His expression was heartfelt, and she couldn't help but smile at his look of embarrassment.

"Come here," he said, hauling her into his arms. "I'm not usually so poetic about things, but with you sharing my enthusiasm for astronomy, I can't help it."

Tenderly, she caressed his cheek. "You're a different Chance than the one I met those many months ago."

He grasped her hand, kissing her palm. "Not different, angel, just more myself."

"I like this side of you."

"Enough to let me kiss you?"

Behind them the pine logs in the wood stove hissed and crackled, but Laurel could hear only the steady pounding of her heart.

Chance didn't wait for her answer. Instead, he drew Laurel into his arms and covered her mouth with his own. At first his kiss was urgent, demanding, communicating how desperate he was to possess her, then it gentled as he continued to explore the soft inner recesses of her mouth with his tongue.

At her soft moan of pleasure, he raised his lips from hers and gazed into eyes filled with uncertainty and wonder. "I want to make love to you, angel. I want to make you mine."

Desire twisted Laurel's heart, made her knees tremble, and it was difficult to form a coherent thought. Somewhere in the back of her mind she knew she should resist. But no words of resistance poured forth, and Chance took her silence as acquiescence, sweeping her up in his arms to carry her to the bed.

CHAPTER 19

In the space of two heartbeats, Chance's nimble fingers undid the row of buttons down the front of Laurel's gown as he gazed into eyes filled with passion and a touch of apprehension.

"I've waited a long time for you, angel. Longer than I've waited for anyone. I know this is your first time, but you won't be disappointed. I'll make it good for you."

Caressing his stubbled cheek, she sighed, knowing her only disappointment was that Chance hadn't said he loved her. But in time, and with patience, perhaps that would change. "You make me feel things I've never felt before. I . . ." She blushed as she stood next to the bed, naked before him. "I want you to unlock all of the mysteries for me. I want to feel it all."

Quickly taking off his clothes, he lifted her onto the bed and lay down beside her. The candles he'd lit cast her body in golden hues, and he traced over it slowly and carefully with his index finger. "I could gaze upon your naked flesh all day and never tire of it. You are perfection."

Her hand reached up to explore his massive chest, the dark hairs curling there, and she smiled. "You're pretty perfect yourself."

"God, angel, I . . ." He kissed her, thrusting his tongue into her mouth and as his hands explored, she arched toward him. His hand slid across her belly, then gently cupped the fullness of her breast, before his mouth and tongue began to tease her nipples.

"Chance!" she moaned, grasping the sides of his head, then caressing the strong tendons of his back.

His tongue trailed over every inch of her flesh, laving her swollen nipples, kissing the undersides of her breasts, delving into the sensitive area of her navel, until she felt she was about to fly off the bed. "I can't take any more. Please!"

"You're almost ready, angel," he promised, lowering his head until it rested between her thighs. Positioning her legs over his shoulders, he opened her to him, searching out her most intimate of places with his tongue, tasting and teasing the engorged bud until her rapid, shallow breathing told him she was ready.

Easing himself over her, he inserted his finger into her opening, stretching the silky taut flesh to make his penetration easier. "Just relax," he told her when she stiffened. "I'm going to go slowly." Her response was an instant arching of her lower body that made him smile. She was definitely ready.

As he began to ease into her, the fire in her loins intensified until she thought she would burst into flames. She felt hot, incredibly hot; every nerve ending in her body tingled with yearning. Finally, with one final thrust he entered, and she knew a brief moment of pain, then felt herself expand to accommodate his large appendage. Thrusting her pelvis off the bed, she rose to meet him, moving as his hands encouraged and his body dictated.

"Oh, God! Oh, God!" she said, as the movements grew faster and more intense and she tried to reach that indefinable conclusion she knew awaited her. In and out he pumped, taking her higher and higher with every powerful stroke.

"That's it." He cupped her buttocks, demonstrating how she should move. "You're almost there, angel."

Music played in her head. Drums pounded out the rhythm. Violins strained to reach the crescendo. And then at last, in one blinding stroke, she hit the final note and sang out her completion. Chance climaxed simultaneously, and they both floated back down to a calmer place.

Cradling Laurel against his chest, Chance kissed her cheek tenderly, noting it was wet. Tears filled her eyes, and he immediately grew concerned. "Did I hurt you?"

She shook her head, smiling widely. "No. It was wonderful. More beautiful than I could ever have imagined."

"Then why are you crying?"

"Because I'm so happy."

He smiled tenderly and kissed her again, and his heart felt full to bursting. "You'll stay the night?" He couldn't let her go. Not now. Maybe not ever.

She trailed her finger down his chest to touch the part of him that gave her so much pleasure, grinning when he sucked in his breath. "Only if you promise we can do that again."

"If I didn't know better, angel, I'd say my little temperance worker was becoming a wanton woman."

She stroked the hard length of him, watching his eyes darken with passion, and reveled in the power she felt. "Do you mind?"

He smiled slowly and shook his head. No, he didn't mind one little bit.

It was nearly dawn when the horse-drawn street car dropped Laurel off in front of Mrs. Costello's establishment.

As quietly as she could, Laurel tiptoed into the two-story house, grateful for the silence that greeted her.

Apparently everyone was still asleep, but she knew that in a short while Mrs. Costello would begin preparations for the morning meal, and the kitchen and dining room would be humming with activity. The proprietress might be older than Methuselah, but she was punctual.

Laurel had just reached the stairway when Hortensia came barreling into the hallway wearing a threadbare plaid wool robe and a look of anger and disappointment. Drucilla, two steps behind her, looked smug, as only Drucilla could look. The younger woman smiled spitefully, and Laurel knew in that instant she'd been found out. Drucilla had probably wasted little time in informing Hortensia that Laurel hadn't returned to their room last night.

"Laurel," Hortensia said, holding the edges of her robe together, her mouth pinched in a frown. "Why are you returning home so late? And where have you been?"

"It's obvious where she's been Mrs. Tungsten. Just look at her—she's positively glowing."

Laurel's cheeks filled with color, and she shot Drucilla a deadly look. "I stayed the night at the Aurora, as a guest of my friend Crystal. I deemed it too risky to come home after the trouble we had at the Silver Slipper, especially after everyone ran away like scared rabbits and left me alone to fend for myself." Her comment was directed squarely at her roommate, who, she was certain, had run faster than the rest of her cohorts.

"If Mr. Rafferty hadn't come to my rescue, I'm not sure what fate would have befallen me." She wasn't about to mention the one that had. Even now those memories stirred, turning her insides to mush.

"You're bringing shame upon our entire group by fraternizing with whores and gamblers," Drucilla claimed.

"At least I have friends to fraternize with, Drucilla Gottlieb, which is more than I can say for you. You're just jealous because no one wants to be around your vicious tongue."

Before Drucilla could reply, Hortensia stepped between the two women, holding up her hand. "Enough. Drucilla, please go upstairs and ready yourself for the day's activities. Laurel, I would like to speak to you in private."

"Of course, Mrs. Tungsten," the young woman replied, her chin held stiffly in the air as she turned toward the stairs. "Laurel certainly needs a good talking to and that's a fact."

Hortensia bit her tongue at the snide remark and shook her head in dismay. "I'm not sure which one of you needs talking to the most. Please come into my office, Laurel."

Laurel entered the spartan room and took a seat before the sturdy oak desk. Like Hortensia herself, the office was devoid of frivolous accoutrements or anything smacking of capriciousness. No shades of gray. Just black and white, right or wrong, and nothing in between.

"I'm sorry if I worried you, Hortensia, but I was perfectly safe at the Aurora."

"My dear, you spent the night under the roof of a notorious gambler, and a man who is your intended. That was highly improper and will surely set tongues to wagging."

"No one knows but you and Drucilla, and of course my friends at the saloon, and they're known to be very discreet. I don't believe my actions will be scrutinized."

Hortensia stood and began pacing the room. "What we do here is very important, Laurel. And we've been very pleased by your willingness to assist us in our cause. But your association with gamblers and prostitutes could ruin things for us."

Laurel stiffened at the rebuke. "Isn't my association with those people the very reason you hired me, Hortensia?"

The large woman paused before the window, nearly blocking out the morning sunshine. "I think it would be best if you stopped seeing Mr. Rafferty, Laurel."

"Stop seeing Chance? That's impossible, Hortensia." She'd sooner ask the sun to stop shining, the birds to still their songs. "Chance has asked me to marry him. And as his fiancée, I couldn't possibly abandon him to his vices. I'm sure you would agree that Mr. Rafferty is in need of saving more than any other man we've administered to thus far. Why, showing him the error of his ways will lead countless others to follow his example."

Laurel watched Hortensia closely and could almost see the wheels of practicality turning in her head. Hortensia Tungsten was nothing if not practical, and she would do whatever she deemed necessary to make a go of the Denver Temperance and Souls in Need League, even if it meant putting up with a scoundrel like Chance Rafferty.

"You say Mr. Rafferty has declared himself?"

Doing her best to keep her face impassive, lest Hortensia see the reply for what it was—a bold-faced lie—Laurel nodded, wondering if she'd be struck down for the telling of it. But she knew that even if Chance hadn't exactly declared himself, he was certain to now. Now that they'd made love. People didn't enter into those kinds of relationships lightly; she knew deep down in her heart that he cared for her, even if he hadn't said as much. Surely he would insist on making an honest woman of her.

The large woman folded her arms beneath her massive, sagging bosoms. "I guess under those circumstances it would be all right to continue your work toward reforming Mr. Rafferty. But there mustn't be any more clandestine meetings. Your relationship must be above reproach. The eyes of Denver are upon you, Laurel, and you must set an example of what is virtuous and good for others to follow."

After last night, her virtue was definitely a bit sullied, Laurel thought, but she still felt strongly that she could set a good example for others. After all, God loved all his childden, even the ones who weren't virgins. Besides, it wasn't as if she'd murdered someone, committed adultery, or blasphemed. She'd merely made love with the man she was totally and passionately in love with.

What could be wrong with that?

*   *   *

"You know what you're supposed to do?"

The bearded man nodded, holding out his hand for the rest of the cash. "The deal was for two hundred, Hazen. I want the rest of my money before I do your dirty work."

"I don't want any screw-ups, like the other night, you hear? I don't want anything left behind that can incriminate me."

Counting out the bills Al handed him, and satisfied that he hadn't been cheated, Shooter Davis smiled. "There ain't gonna be any screw-ups. I got my own reasons for getting rid of that little gal. And hurting Rafferty is just an extra bonus, far as I'm concerned. I didn't much like spending time in jail."

"You'd best lay low after the deed is done," Hazen advised. "I'll be the first person Rafferty suspects, and if he thinks we're in this together . . ."

The big man scratched his chest, making Hazen wince, for he knew Shooter was infested with lice and God knew what else. Shooter was dirty in every sense of the word, but he was perfect for the job Al had hired him for.

"If there's nothing else, I'll be getting back to my customers." Hazen swiveled about in his office chair and made to rise.

"Not so fast, Al," Shooter said, holding up his hand. "Ain't you forgettin' something?"

"I don't think . . ." He paused, remembering the rest of their agreement. "Pearl's mighty particular about who she beds, Shooter, but I think we can accommodate you."

Grabbing his crotch, Shooter rubbed himself, eager to plant his dick between Pearl's silky thighs, just like he'd dreamed of doing a hundred times over. Pearl had teased him, let him suck her tits, but she'd never fucked him, and that was something he wanted even more than Hazen's two hundred bucks.

She'd promised him a screw if he scared the little blond singer, but then he'd gotten arrested, and she'd never made good on their wager. He aimed to claim his winnings now.

"I want to poke her before I do the deed. Pearl knows how to make a man feel good. And I'm needing to feel good now, Al."

It had taken quite a bit of persuasion on his part to get Pearl to agree to bed Shooter. But the offer of a permanent seventy-five–twenty-five split was just too much of an incentive for the whore to resist. And Al knew Pearl wasn't all that particular about who she screwed.

For chrissake! If she did it with a porcelain dildo, she'd do it with just about anything. About the only thing Pearl liked more than a good fuck was a lot of money. Al and she were well matched in that.

"Pearl's upstairs waiting for you. Get your poke, then get out there and get the job done. I expect results for my money, Shooter. Don't disappoint me."

Laurel wished she could remain engulfed in Chance's arms forever, but she knew Hortensia would send someone to fetch her if she tarried too long on the porch. It had been difficult enough persuading the woman to allow Chance to escort her to lunch.

"I've got to go in, Chance. Hortensia watches me like a hawk."

"If you'd move back to the Aurora, we wouldn't have to worry about Mrs. Two-Chins spying on us."

"Ssh! Someone might hear you."

He snorted indignantly. "No doubt some old biddy's got her ear pressed to the door. Why don't we really give them something to talk about?"

Before she could protest, he captured her mouth, kissing her long and hard. When he finally released her, she looked stunned and well kissed.

"You're . . . you're going to get me fired. I told you Hortensia doesn't like our being together like this."

"Jesus, Mary, and Joseph!" He rubbed the back of his neck. "If I don't have you in my bed soon, I'm going to go crazy. What the hell do I care what the old blubber-ass says? I want you, angel. I want you now."

"It's only been two days since we were . . . together." Laurel's throat tightened at the exquisite memory. "And I promised Mrs. Tungsten that we would behave in a more circumspect manner. Kissing on the front porch of the boardinghouse in plain view of the entire town hardly constitutes circumspect behavior."

"Come back with me to the Aurora, angel. I'll light a fire and we can lie naked in front of it." He stroked her cheek. "You know you want to."

Laurel wanted to more than anything in the world. But just as she felt her resolve begin to weaken the front door opened and Gertie peered out. "Hortensia says she'd like for you to come in now, Laurel." The look of utter disdain the older woman shot Chance spoke volumes about what she thought of his unsuitable courtship. "It's rather chilly to be standing outside, don't you think?"

As hot as she felt at the moment, Laurel thought she could remain outside for days and never feel the effects of the cold. She sighed, "I'll only be another moment, Gertie."

There was a loud "Hmph!" then the door closed again, and Laurel gazed up at Chance, her face full of regret. "I've got to go in now. Perhaps tomorrow we . . ."

Disappointed, and extremely annoyed at having to take orders from a bunch of frustrated old biddies, Chance shrugged Laurel's hand off his coat sleeve. "Tomorrow doesn't always come, angel. Sometimes today is all we ever get."

Tears of frustration stung Laurel's eyes as she watched Chance walk away, and she felt like kicking in the front door and Gertie Beecham's teeth as well.

Being in love was hell, she decided. Being in love with Chance Rafferty was nigh on to impossible.

*   *   *

"I'll light a fire and we can lie naked in front of it."

Chance's words repeated over and over in Laurel's subconscious, and she moved fitfully in her sleep. Heat licked at her flesh, making her hot and sweaty.

Suddenly the quilt she lay beneath seemed entirely too heavy, and she kicked off the covers, taking a deep breath of crisp night air to cool herself down.

But the air was hot, and smoke filled her nostrils. Laurel bolted upright, covering her mouth at the sight of orange flames licking against the new draperies Drucilla had hung just two days before.

Fire! The word flashed through her mind. Screaming, "Drucilla!" she turned toward her roommate's bed. Its coverings were engulfed in flames.

"Oh, my God!" Without a thought for her own safety, Laurel grasped the quilt from her bed and began to beat at the fire eating through Drucilla's bedding. "Drucilla, wake up!" she shouted, coughing as the smoke burned her lungs.

But Drucilla did not awaken. Fearing the worst, Laurel felt for a pulse at the base of her throat. It was thready and weak, but it was there. "Thank God!" The young woman was still alive: apparently she had only been overcome by the smoke.

Smothering the flames as best she could, Laurel dragged Drucilla's body off the bed; it hit the floor with a thump. Making her way to the door in the thick, black, smothering smoke was nearly impossible, but Laurel kept moving one foot in front of the other, dragging the dead weight of Drucilla behind her.

Scream, her mind told her. *Scream loudly before we both die.*

It was the last thing she remembered before she passed out.

"Oh, thank the good Lord," Hortensia said when Laurel's eyelids fluttered open. "She's coming to. Get some water and a damp rag so I can wash some of this soot off of her," she told Gertie, who left immediately to do her bidding.

"Am I dead?" Laurel asked in a raspy voice she barely recognized as her own. She certainly felt dead. But she couldn't be, because she saw Hortensia staring down at her. Hortensia might have a pipeline to God, but Laurel didn't think it extended all the way up to Heaven.

"No, my dear, you're not dead. But you did have us terribly worried."

As memories of the fire flooded back, she asked, "Drucilla?" though the effort to talk proved costly, making her cough several times.

"She'll be fine, thanks to you. The firemen took her to the hospital. Drucilla was badly burned, but she'll live, because of your quick thinking."

Laurel breathed a sigh of relief, grateful that the woman had survived. "Is the house badly damaged?" She looked around, noting the familiar surroundings of Hortensia's office, and felt satisfied that everything appeared in order.

Hortensia shook her head. "Someone on the street noticed the smoke and called the fire department. Only your room was damaged."

Laurel struggled to sit up. "Was it the wood stove?" Drucilla was forever putting too many pieces of wood in the darn thing.

At the question, a guarded expression crossed the older woman's face, and Laurel immediately grew suspicious. "It wasn't the stove, my dear," Hortensia said, patting Laurel's hand. "I didn't want to worry you, since you're still incapacitated, but it looks as if the fire was deliberately set."

Shocked, Laurel began coughing again, and it took her a few moments to regain her composure. "The fire was set?"

"I'm afraid we make enemies in our line of work, Laurel. It isn't the first time some angry saloon owner or frustrated alcoholic has decided to take revenge on us."

An angry saloon owner . . . Al Hazen, she concluded. *Only he could be this blatantly evil.* "I've no doubt who it is."

Hortensia rose from her chair, a resigned expression on her face. "I suspected Mr. Hazen myself, but we have no proof, my dear. Whoever performed this nefarious act covered his tracks well."

"A snake leaves a small trail."

"That's true enough, but we must leave the investigating of the matter to the proper authorities. We're not vigilantes seeking vengeance, we're temperance workers. And we still have lots of work to do."

Laurel paled, for she knew that when Chance found out what had happened, he wasn't going to wait for any investigator's conclusions. He would jump to the same one she had. "It's not me you need to worry about, Hortensia. It's Chance. I'm worried what he'll do when he discovers what happened."

Hortensia sighed so deeply that her bosoms shook. "He's already found out. He was like a raving lunatic, Laurel. I'm afraid your concerns are justified. He's been pacing outside the office for the past thirty minutes.

"Chance is here? May I see him?"

"Only for a few moments. The doctor wants you to rest for the remainder of the day, and Mr. Rafferty's demeanor is not conducive to peace and tranquility."

"You know him well, Hortensia, for not knowing him long."

The older woman's smile was kind but thoughtful. "A man like your Mr. Rafferty burns hot and quick. Women are attracted to men like that, like moths are attracted to flames. But like the moth, if you venture too close to the fire, you're going to get burned.

"I may be an old woman now, my dear, but I was young once, and I've had my share of . . . fires." She blushed becomingly. "Unfortunately, I learned that fires burn out quickly, leaving only ashes in their aftermath. Be careful you don't get burned, Laurel."

CHAPTER 20

"Dammit, Laurel! You could have been killed. When are you going to stop all this nonsense and move back here?"

"Mr. Chance be right this time, Miss Laurel," Bertha agreed. "That Mr. Hazen ain't going to stop till you's dead. And, honey, I don't rightly think I could stand living if that happened."

Laurel had heard this argument many times since yesterday's fire. She smiled at the two emotional individuals, knowing that their harshness stemmed from concern rather than anger, then continued stirring cream into her coffee as she breathed in the tantalizing aroma of frying bacon.

Laurel had come to the Aurora for breakfast at Chance's insistence that Bertha wouldn't be convinced of her well-being until she looked upon Laurel's face herself and saw that she was all right. And hard as the black woman had hugged her, Laurel thought Chance had told the truth. Her ribs still ached from the heartfelt embrace.

"As you can both see, I came through the fire with nary a

singed hair. And I have no intention of giving up my work with the league. What would you have me do—go back to work singing in a saloon? That's not exactly a job without peril. Or are you forgetting that incident with Shooter Davis?"

The fierce light in Chance's eyes indicated that he remembered the incident with exacting clarity. He stood quickly, scraping the floorboards with his chair. "You're being unreasonable, Laurel. I can protect you here. But while you live at that boarding hotel, you're at the mercy of every lunatic in this city."

"You're the only lunatic, as far as I'm concerned, Chance Rafferty. I'm not coming back to work here and that's final."

Noting the pulse pounding at his temples, and fearing that Chance was about to say something he'd soon regret, Bertha grasped his arm. "Why don't you go fetch Jup and Whitey, Mr. Chance? I'm about done frying this bacon, and we'll be eating breakfast directly."

He stared at Laurel, seemed about to say something, but nodded in compliance. "Fine. But we're not finished discussing this, Laurel. Just remember that." He stormed out of the kitchen.

Bertha shook her head in dismay. "That man's got hisself a temper when it comes to you, Miss Laurel."

"He burns hot," Laurel found herself saying, remembering Hortensia's warning with some uneasiness.

"I guess you could say that, child," Bertha agreed, placing large ceramic platters of bacon and sausage in the center of the table. The pungent aroma made Laurel's mouth water.

"You know that man wouldn't be saying nothin' if he didn't care, don't you?"

"I know he cares, Bertha. But I'm a grown woman and I have to make my own decisions. And you know better than anyone why I made the decision I did."

The two women exchanged a meaningful look, then Bertha said, "He misses you, honey. We all do. And we's worried about your well-being. Jup was half crazy last night when he heard about the fire. And my poor Whitey started crying like a babe, thinkin' you was dead."

Tears filled Laurel's eyes at the image, but she blinked them away. "Please, don't make me feel any more guilty than I already do. Until Chance proposes marriage, I will continue my work with the league. And I'm not about to cower to Al Hazen's threats or attempts to intimidate me. My mama taught me to stand up to bullies."

"But, honey, how you gonna do that? You is just one little girl."

"I'm tougher than you think, Bertha. I stood up to Chance, didn't I?"

Bertha rolled her eyes heavenward and clucked her tongue disapprovingly. "Give me patience, Lord. This here girl is stubborn as the hind end of a mule."

"If you ask me, Bertha Tubbs, Chance is the one you should be praying for. He's the one who's stubborn as a mule; and twice as unreasonable as any normal man should be."

Her hands raised in supplication, Bertha shook her head. "If there is one thing I knows without a doubt, it's that you two young'ns deserve one another. And the good Lord help you both when you finally come together, 'cause there's going to be sparks flying in Heaven that day."

Having returned Laurel to the boarding hotel, Chance wasted no time in heading for the Silver Slipper to have it out with Hazen. If the pimp thought he'd escape unscathed this time, he had another think coming.

"Where's Hazen?" Chance demanded of the bartender as he stepped into the saloon, banging his fist on the bar. "And don't tell me he's left town, because I know the bastard's here."

Zeke Mullins nodded toward the stairs. "First door on the right. But he's not alone."

"Now why doesn't that surprise me."

As Zeke watched the angry gambler take the steps two at a time, he felt glad that Al would get the comeuppance he was due. For all the terrible things he'd done to Crystal and for his nasty treatment of Laurel Martin, Al deserved to be taken apart limb by limb, and Chance was just the man to do it.

Rafferty wasn't the kind of man to abuse women or tolerate it in others. And he wasn't the kind of man who would turn the other cheek when one of his own was threatened or mistreated. Zeke was counting on that.

Rubbing his hands together, the bartender chuckled to himself. Hazen was in for a big surprise. Zeke just wished he could see the bastard's face when Rafferty went bursting through the door.

Occupied in their lovemaking, neither Al nor Pearl noticed the tall man who crept stealthily toward the bed, until the cold silver blade of a knife was pressed against Al's derriere.

"My, my, what a charming sight, and such an interesting target."

"Chance!" Pearl exclaimed loudly, her eyes rounding at the sight of the knife and the man who held it.

"Morning, Pearl. Looks like you've landed on your feet again—or should I say your back." His look of pure contempt made Pearl wince.

Al froze like a deer caught in a hunter's gun sight, his face whitening to match the sheets he lay upon. "Rafferty, you bastard! What do you think you're doing here? Get the hell out of my room." With more courage than he usually displayed, Al suddenly flattened and rolled over, giving Chance an even more interesting target.

Ignoring the man's frightened gasp, Chance's look was deadly as he pressed the sharp tip of the knife against one of Hazen's testicles. "I know you were behind the fire at Costello's boarding hotel, Hazen, and when I get the proof I need, I'm going to see you put away for a long, long time. Or," he said, reconsidering, "I could take matters into my own hands now and castrate you for the evil deeds you've done."

Al shut his eyes and cringed in fear as the tip pressed deeper, making Chance laugh. "It's not easy being intimidated, is it, Hazen?" Lowering the knife, he took a step back. "You disgust me, you cowardly bully."

Hazen opened his eyes to see Pearl smirking at him, then leaned back against the pillows, trying to regain his composure—not an easy task with a madman pressing a knife to your genitals. "I don't know what you're talking about, Rafferty," he brazened out. "And if you don't get out of here, I'll summon the law."

Chance stepped forward again. "If you so much as look in Laurel's direction again, Hazen, I'll carve you up in such little pieces, your own mother won't recognize you." He trailed the knife blade along the inside of Hazen's thigh, delighting in the man's gasp of terror as he trimmed off several of his pubic hairs. "This will be my last warning to you. If any harm comes to Laurel, I'm going to hold you personally responsible."

"You're insane, Rafferty. Now get out of here!"

Chance stood fast, staring scornfully at the two lovers. The room smelled of sex, cheap perfume, and cigar smoke, and the thought of the two intimately together made his stomach turn.

"You've more to fear than this knife, Hazen," he said, looking pointedly at Pearl. "I'd be a little more discriminating where I put my dick. I hear the clap can eat away at your brain and make you crazy. Come to think of it," he added, pausing by the door, "maybe you've already got it. That would explain your psychotic behavior."

Chance slammed the door behind him, but the sound of his laughter lingered long after he was gone.

Ten minutes later, Chance stepped into the darkened Opera House and looked at the empty stage, remembering the audition of a frightened woman whose beauty far outweighed her singing talent. The image brought a queer ache to his chest, but a very different and inconvenient effect slightly lower.

Laurel's stubborn refusal to quit the temperance league had made him more determined than ever to take matters into his own hands. All Laurel needed was the right incentive, and he aimed to see that she had it.

"Howdy, Rooster," he said, stepping up behind the stage manager, who shrieked in fright and dropped the billboard to which he'd been putting a finishing touch; it smacked loudly as it hit the floor.

"Dammit, Chance! You nearly made me mess my pants. I didn't hear you come in."

"Come now, old friend. It hasn't been that long since Whitey and I were here listening to the auditions."

"Just since Laurel came to town, that's all," Rooster retorted, a knowing smirk on his lips.

"She's the reason I'm here. I guess you heard about the fire?"

Rooster nodded. "Flora Sue told me. She was nearly hysterical. Course, I had to comfort her."

Chance couldn't help but smile at the pleased look on the smitten man's face. "Of course. But I didn't come here to discuss your love life. Although I admit I'm looking forward to watching you make an ass out of yourself tonight at the big surprise engagement party you've planned for yourself and Flora Sue."

Grinning, Rooster asked, "Will Laurel be there? Flora Sue would be mighty disappointed if she wasn't."

"Laurel said she wouldn't miss it for the world." Though Chance wasn't sure how she was going to persuade the old battle-ax to let her attend a whore's engagement party. "It's Laurel I came here to talk about."

"Nothing's the matter with her, I hope."

Chance shook his head. "I want you to hire Laurel to perform here."

"Are you nuts? Witherspoon'll never hire Laurel. Never in a million years. Besides, why would you want that sweet thing around him? The old bastard's a lecher. He practically drools every time Flora Sue comes to visit."

"I need to protect Laurel from herself. She's going to get herself killed if she keeps working with those temperance women."

Rooster studied his friend closely. "Are you sure that's the only reason? Laurel's been pretty determined to shut you down. It'd make your life a whole lot easier if she stopped targeting the Aurora."

"Jesus, Mary, and Joseph!" Chance shook his head at the man's obtuseness. "It's her life I'm worried about, not mine. If she keeps on at Hazen, he's going to finish off the job he started with the fire."

"Hazen set the fire?"

"Probably not directly. But I'd bet a hefty wager that he's behind it. Al's not the type to dirty his own hands."

"Witherspoon's upstairs in his office, but I doubt you'll have any more luck than I did in convincing him to hire Laurel."

Chance grinned as if he had a dozen aces up his sleeve, and Rooster instantly grew suspicious. "If I didn't know better, Chance, I'd say you were playing with a stacked deck."

Patting his friend's shoulder, Chance replied, "Where Laurel's concerned, I'm leaving nothing to risk." And he hadn't. Witherspoon's gambling losses at the Aurora amounted to almost two thousand dollars. Men like Witherspoon, who lived off the good graces of rich wives, couldn't afford to have their indiscretions aired publicly.

Whoring, gambling, and the like wouldn't be tolerated by Mrs. Witherspoon, who'd recently donated a large sum of money to the temperance league. Chance figured that the old reprobate lived in constant fear of his moralistic, affluent wife finding out about his secret life.

He had Witherspoon right where he wanted him, which was why he hadn't called in his markers before now. If there was one thing a gambler learned at a young age, it was that he should always have an ace in the hole.

"Well, you're going to need all your luck where Witherspoon's concerned," Rooster said. "He ain't gonna hire her, I tell you."

"Don't worry. Just do your part when the time comes."

"Of course I will," Rooster agreed. Then he paused, scratching his head. "What part is that, Chance?"

Chance's reply was a confident grin.

"Congratulations, you two!" Laurel said loudly enough to be heard above the din. The Aurora was packed to the rafters with friends and well-wishers who had come to celebrate Rooster and Flora Sue's engagement.

Laurel hadn't seen the saloon this crowded since before . . . before the temperance league had come to town. She smiled guiltily as she raised her glass of champagne to toast the couple. "I couldn't be happier for you."

Flora Sue kissed her cheek. "You'll be next, doll baby. I just feel it in my bones."

Laurel gazed across the crowded room and saw Chance conversing with Crystal. She'd be the next to get engaged, not Laurel. Chance had about as much intention of proposing marriage as the temperance league had of giving up their quest to reform. That knowledge made her heart sink.

"Miss Laurel." Rooster tapped her on the shoulder. "I was wondering if I could have a word with you." He caught Chance's encouraging nod over Laurel's shoulder and shot back an irritated look of his own.

"You two talk to your heart's content," Flora Sue said. "I'm going to show off my engagement ring." Kissing Rooster's cheek, she disappeared into the crowd, leaving her fiancé with a sick smile on his face.

"Shall we make our way over to the stage?" Laurel suggested, noting the man's nervousness and wondering if all

prospective grooms reacted to marriage this way. For all
their braggadocio, men could be such cowards at times. "Perhaps it'll be quieter over there," she added.

Following her lead, Rooster summoned up all his
courage. Who would have believed that Witherspoon would
agree to Chance's proposal? Whatever Chance had on the
man had to be something downright dirty; Witherspoon
didn't bend to many men.

"You're looking awfully solemn for such a happy occasion, Rooster. You're not having second thoughts about marrying Flora Sue, are you? I know she loves you very much."

He shook his head emphatically. "Oh, no, Miss Laurel. It's
nothing like that. In fact, I have some good news for you."

"Good news for me?" Laurel asked, confused, then she
smiled playfully. "Don't tell me Mr. Witherspoon's had a
change of heart."

Rooster looked dumbstruck. "How'd . . . how'd you know?"

She rocked back on her heels and laughed lightly.
"Rooster Higgins, are you telling me that Mr. Witherspoon
wants to hire me for the Opera House?"

He nodded. "It's true, Miss Laurel. He told me so himself
just this afternoon. And I know how much it would mean for
you to perform there. Wouldn't it?"

Laurel's smile was so brilliant, it could have lit the room
without the help of electrified fixtures. "It's something I've
dreamed of my entire life." Suddenly she floated back down
to earth. "But what made him change his mind? He was
pretty emphatic when we talked last."

Rooster shrugged, trying to keep his face impassive.
"There's just no telling with Witherspoon, Miss Laurel. He's
contrary as they come." That at least was the truth. The man
changed his mind more often than Rooster changed his un-
derwear.

Excitement roared through Laurel's veins, and she blurted,
"I've got to tell Chance! I've got to tell Crystal and Flora
Sue!" With that, she pushed her way through the crowd.

Rooster, watching her, felt dirtier than horseshit on the bottom of a boot. But that was nothing compared to the way Chance would feel if Laurel found out the truth behind Witherspoon's magnanimous decision.

Spotting Crystal and Flora Sue, Laurel rushed toward them. She realized that they were having an earnest discussion about something important, because Crystal was throwing her hands up in the air and her face was twisted in anger.

Laurel didn't want to interrupt what looked to be a disagreement. On the other hand, she was full to bursting with the news of her impending employment at the Opera House and couldn't wait to tell her best friends. She inched closer, waiting for a break in their discussion.

"I can't believe Chance would do such a thing," Crystal said, shaking her head. "If Laurel finds out, she'll kill him."

Grinding to a halt behind a tall, heavyset man, Laurel grew increasingly uneasy as she listened to the heated exchange.

Flora's hands were fisted on her hips. "He did it for her own good. You know how caught up she is with that temperance league. And she's going to get herself hurt, or worse, if she continues working with them."

"How did you find out about this?"

"Rooster told me Chance paid him a visit at the Opera House this morning. Said he wanted Rooster to hire Laurel."

Shocked, Laurel covered her mouth to keep herself from screaming aloud all the vile things she thought about Chance Rafferty. She should have known he was behind Witherspoon's change of heart. The smelly old goat had made his feelings pretty clear when he'd refused to hire her those many months ago.

"Laurel would be terribly upset if she knew," Crystal said. "You know how much having an opera career means to her. She's not going to take kindly to Chance's interference."

"You are exactly right about that, Crystal."

Startled, both women turned to their friend, who looked angry enough to breathe fire.

Crystal held out her hand to Laurel. "I'm sorry, honey. I was hoping you wouldn't find out."

"As was Chance, no doubt," Laurel replied, her lips tight. "How long did he think it would take before Witherspoon threw me out on my rear? Or didn't he think about that when he went behind my back to find me a job?"

Flora Sue clasped Laurel about the waist. "Don't be upset, doll baby. Chance was only trying to protect you. And besides, he's blackmailing Witherspoon about something or other. It ain't likely the old coot's going to fire you."

That made things even worse, and Laurel felt her face growing red. "Where is he? Where's that scheming, no-good gambling man?" She scanned the crowd until her eyes fell on the laughing face of her supposed intended. He wouldn't be laughing for long, Laurel decided.

Despite Crystal and Flora Sue's best efforts to subdue her, Laurel burst through the crowd like a firecracker exploding. "Chance Rafferty!" she shouted, and the swarm of merry-makers quieted, separating to make a path for her, like Moses parting the Red Sea.

"Chance Rafferty," she repeated, stepping up to him. Drawing back her hand, she slapped him soundly across the face. A collective gasp rose from the crowd.

Chance stopped laughing, grasped Laurel's wrist, and said, all in the space of an instant, "What the hell was that for?"

"For interfering in my life, that's what."

His face still bearing the imprint of her anger, Chance shot Rooster a menacing look, and his co-conspirator quickly disappeared into the crowd.

A dropped pin could have been heard in the next moment, as Chance yanked Laurel across the room. "We'll discuss this without an audience, if you don't mind, angel. I don't like airing my dirty linen in public."

"Release me at once, Chance Rafferty," she demanded, but her pleas fell on deaf ears as he firmly led her up the stairs. Only when they were ensconced in Chance's bedroom, did he let go of her.

"I'd think you'd be thanking me, not slapping me. I thought you wanted to sing at the Opera House."

She was so furious that she couldn't even speak; and she had to breathe deeply several times to regain her composure. "Thank you? For humiliating me? For taking it upon yourself to interfere in my life? You've made me a laughingstock!"

"I was trying to protect you, not interfere in your precious life, goddammit!" he said, heading for the brandy decanter.

"Oh sure, have yourself a drink. That's what men like you do to solve their problems, instead of facing them square on."

Ignoring her, he swallowed the amber liquid and felt better for it. "And what do you do? March head-on into the lion's den and wait for him to chew your fool head off?"

"What I do is none of your business. It never has been."

"Everything you do is my business, goddammit. And don't you forget it. I've saved your ass more times than I can remember. I figure that makes it mine."

"Some women get a Prince Charming who rides in on a white steed and rescues them from the villain. But not me. Oh, no. Not me. I get an interfering, blackmailing, hard-drinking gambler, who ignores everything I've been working for and tries to destroy it, along with my reputation and my self-respect, all in one fell swoop."

"You wouldn't know a Prince Charming if one came up and bit you squarely on the behind." She stiffened, and his voice filled with entreaty. "Dammit, Laurel, I was only trying to help."

As he saw the tears trickling down her cheeks, Chance stepped closer to her. "Don't cry, angel. I can stand your anger, but not your tears."

"I'm not crying," she insisted, sniffing loudly and wiping her cheeks with the back of her hand. "And don't you touch me." She backed away from the hand he offered. "I'll never forgive you for this, Chance. Never in a million years.

Maybe you were concerned about my safety, but I think there's more to your interference than that."

"Laurel."

There was a wealth of apology in that one word, but she went on as if he'd not said it. "I wondered at your motives in courting me, and now I know. You thought you could sweet-talk me into stopping my work with the league. Knowing how much my singing career meant to me you thought you could force Witherspoon to hire me and that I would then quit the league, thereby leaving you and your saloon free of the temperance league's wrath." She was poking her finger at his chest now and hollering at the top of her lungs.

"Well, it didn't work, Mr. Rafferty. Your ploys to stop my work with the league didn't work. In fact, I intend to step up my efforts to shut down this place. Just see if I don't."

Chance's face reddened, his fists clenched as tightly as his lips. Laurel had misread every single one of his motives. He'd tried a hundred different ways to show her he loved her. True, he hadn't said the words, but a reasonable, intelligent woman would know just the same.

And he'd behaved every bit the Prince Charming of her fairy tales by trying to rescue her from Hazen and, more aptly, from herself.

But all he'd received for his efforts were ridicule and mistrust. Not unlike other times in his past when he'd tried to do the right thing, open himself—his heart—to others.

Well, no more. If Laurel wanted to declare war on him, then she damn well better be prepared for the consequences, because he had every intention of winning come hell or high water.

That was something Miss Temperance Worker could place a hefty wager on.

CHAPTER 21

After the night of "the big blow up," which is how Bertha and Crystal referred to Chance and Laurel's argument and resulting estrangement, liquor flowed freely at the Aurora. More accurately, it was free.

Having decided that profits didn't matter as much as winning his battle with Laurel, Chance made good on his promise to teach her and her band of do-gooders a lesson.

Free beer now accompanied sandwiches; whiskey was reduced to five cents a shot; and if a man really wanted to whoop it up at the Aurora, he arrived at midnight for the girlie show, which was touted as the closest thing to Sodom and Gomorrah this side of the Rocky Mountains.

Chance had searched the city for prostitutes willing to earn a few extra dollars dancing naked, save for a few strategically placed flowers and feathers.

Over the past two weeks the men of Denver had flocked to these entertainments and the promise of untold delights, while the women of the city, in particular those of the Denver Temperance and Souls in Need League, had grown more incensed with every passing day.

"I've called this emergency meeting to discuss what we can do about Mr. Rafferty's assault on decency and reversion to debauchery," Hortensia said, addressing the angry women who packed the auditorium. "As I have so often said," she looked pointedly at Laurel, who had the grace to blush, "the leopard does not readily change his spots. In Mr. Rafferty's case, it appears that he doesn't even camouflage them."

"Let's put him out of business," an overweight matron shouted. "My husband has been frequenting that disgusting show at the Aurora every night for a week, then coming home drunk and smelling of strange perfume. I say burn the place down."

A burst of cheers went up, and Laurel's face paled. "That's a bit harsh, don't you think, ladies?" She rose to her feet. "After all, innocent people could get hurt."

Drucilla, almost recovered from her burns, jumped up. "I was an innocent bystander who was hurt because of your illicit relationship with Mr. Rafferty. How dare you try to spare the lives of your lover and his friends? You're a trollop and should be kicked out of this organization."

The room grew ominously quiet as the two women faced each other. The hatred emanating from Drucilla Gottlieb was tangible, and Laurel thought that if words could kill, she'd certainly be dead by now.

Obviously, Drucilla was not the least bit grateful to Laurel for saving her life, and it was further evident that the scars on the young woman's arms and face were not the only ones she carried.

Deciding that to provoke this agitated woman would not be the wisest course at the moment, Laurel replied in a soft voice, "I'm very sorry you were injured because of me, Drucilla. It was never my intention that any harm should come to you."

"You should be sorry. You should be—"

"That will be quite enough, Drucilla," Hortensia interrupted in a voice that brooked no refusal. "I will make allowances for your vicious attack against Miss Martin because you are still recovering from a terrible ordeal, but the fact remains—Laurel did save your life. And she is doing everything in her power to shut down the Aurora, short of burning it to the ground, which is a totally unacceptable suggestion.

"Our leader, Miss Willard, does not advocate violence. We demonstrate through example and strength of character. We do not take the law into our own hands, nor do we target innocent men and women. That is not the WCTU way. Those of you who do not agree with our methods are free to leave."

Drucilla remained standing. "I am not feeling well and would like to return to my room at the hotel."

"As you wish, Drucilla. Perhaps while you are in your room you might wish to commune with our Lord and ask for His guidance and intervention into this recent ordeal, and perhaps His forgiveness."

Laurel watched the teary-eyed woman flee from the auditorium and sighed with sadness; she felt truly sorry for Drucilla. The woman was filled with inner demons, and Laurel wondered if anyone, including God, could ever exorcise them.

"Now," Hortensia began, clapping her hands to bring the room to order, "does anyone have any *other* ideas on how we can shut down Mr. Rafferty's saloon?"

Laurel rose to her feet once again. "I've been spending a considerable amount of time at the library, consulting various books on the law. It appears there is a statute that the founding fathers of Denver enacted many years ago, prohibiting public nudity and lewd and lascivious conduct. There is a little known and even lesser enforced law called the Denver Decency Code.

"I propose that we force the law and public officials to

shut down Mr. Rafferty's business if he does not comply with the Decency Code. And we won't stop with the Aurora; we'll target every saloon, gambling parlor, and brothel that does not strictly adhere to the letter of the law."

Hortensia beamed. "That's a wonderful idea."

"But the police are corrupt. The mayor himself frequents the saloons and gambling parlors. How are we going to accomplish such a difficult task?" Sue Ellen Turner asked. No longer employed at the Aurora, Sue Ellen had become a devout WCTU member and outspoken critic of vice and corruption.

"It's simple," Laurel said, smiling enthusiastically for the first time in days. "We shall take our case to the people. We shall take our case to the loudest voice this city has to offer: the newspaper."

The newspaper headlines over the next few days screamed for social reform and an end to Denver's vice and corruption: MAYOR CAUGHT WITH HIS PANTS DOWN AT THE SILVER SLIPPER; THE AURORA'S STARS NO LONGER SHINE; POLICE CHIEF'S WIFE LAYS DOWN THE LAW BY CRACKING HIM OVER HEAD WITH WHISKEY BOTTLE.

"Jesus, Mary, and Joseph!" Chance said, shaking his head as he read the latest edition of the *Rocky Mountain News*, and the fact that he was being touted as the Destroyer of Decency. At least they hadn't called him the Demon of Denver; that honor had gone to Al Hazen.

"It looks as if the Destroyer could use a friend long about now."

Chance, looking up from the newspaper as Gus Baldwin entered, was clearly disturbed by what had been written about him. "Friends are few and far between these days; I can tell you that."

Seating himself at the kitchen table, Gus poured himself a cup of coffee from the blue-speckled enamel pot. "You targeted the wrong woman for revenge when you went after Laurel, I'm afraid, Chance. No good ever comes of revenge. And Laurel's made a lot of friends in this town."

"She started it."

At the childish response, Gus wiped the smile off his face. "I would think you would know by now that Laurel is no simpering miss. Didn't you learn your lesson over that oil painting and stereoscopic device you were so intent on shoving down everyone's throats?" He shook his head. "At least you've made restitution by getting rid of the dancing girls. That little stunt really went beyond the pale, son."

"I thought you came here as my friend, Gus. You sound as judgmental as Bertha and Jup." The black woman had given him a tongue-lashing he wasn't likely to forget anytime soon, commenting on his ancestry, the stupidity of white folks in general, and the Lord's vengeance against sinners. According to Bertha, he was about to be smitten by a mighty blow of retribution. Chance heaved a sigh of regret. "Even Whitey took me to task over the 'nekked women,' as he terms them."

"Out of the mouths of babes, as they say," Gus commented.

"I just wanted to teach Laurel a lesson." Chance clanged the teaspoon against the sides of the coffee cup as he stirred the dark liquid around and around in an agitated fashion. "She made me mad with her holier-than-thou opinions and accusations."

"Crystal told me what happened at Rooster's engagement party. I'm glad now to have missed it. Sometimes this tuberculosis has its advantages."

"Yeah. Well, I've got a sickness, too, and I aim to get over it real quick. Laurel Martin is just plain bad luck. I curse the day I ever laid eyes on the woman." He remembered that day as if it were yesterday. How sweet and beautiful she looked, eating that gargantuan meal, her big blue eyes so full of innocence and self-determination. Who could have known that such a tempting example of womanhood would turn his life upside down, wreak havoc on his emotions, and rip his insides to shreds?

But that's exactly what his little angel had done.

Draping a comforting arm over Chance's shoulders, Gus said sympathetically. "You love her, don't you, son?"

Chance looked defeated, as if the woes of the world rested squarely on his shoulders, and he nodded. "That's the hell of it, Gus, and it's likely to kill me. I love Laurel so much I can't see straight anymore."

"Have you told her?"

Chance stared at the clergyman as if he'd lost his mind. "What? And give her something else to hold over me?" he shook his head. "No, sir. I'm keeping that bit of information to myself."

"You're making a big mistake, Chance. A woman can forgive a man a lot, if she knows he acted out of love."

"Yeah? Well, tell that to Bertha, Crystal, and Flora Sue. They all hate my guts."

"They're not the ones who matter in this, now are they?"

"I thought confession was good for the soul. So how come I feel like shit?"

Repressing a smile, and doing his best not to be offended by Chance's profanity, Gus replied, "God grants man wisdom, a heart, and soul, so he can think for himself and make the right decisions in life. Sometimes we choose poorly, and we are burdened with unhappiness and misery. But sometimes we choose wisely, and are rewarded with peace, contentment, and, most important, love."

"And sometimes God gives us no choice at all." Chance spoke the depressing thought aloud. Loving Laurel certainly hadn't been a conscious choice on his part. He'd sooner have been tarred and feathered than have fallen in love with that stubborn slip of a woman.

"That just isn't true," Gus said, shaking his head, trying to get through the stone barricade Chance had erected around his heart. "We always have a choice. It's what we do with it that shapes our destiny. Think about it, Chance, then choose wisely."

A bone-numbing wind whipped the thin cottonwood branches against the windows of the parlor, scratching the glass like fingernails raking a chalkboard, and Laurel shivered, grateful to be sitting in front of a roaring fire instead of delivering a speech to the Denver Historical Society's monthly Ladies' Auxiliary meeting.

Hortensia had graciously offered to substitute when Laurel, complaining of a headache and nausea, had informed her she didn't feel well enough to go. The influenza was making the rounds in the city, and Laurel feared she'd been bitten by the nasty bug.

Taking a sip of hot tea, which Mrs. Costello insisted would cure any ailment known to mankind, Laurel ripped open the envelope from her sister that had arrived that morning from San Francisco.

It had been months since she'd heard from Heather, and Laurel was eager to hear how her sister's governess position at the Montgomery mansion was working out. Heather was not one to follow orders graciously; she was more adept at giving them. And she wondered if she and Mr. Montgomery had butted heads over the raising of his children. Heather had very definite ideas when it came to rearing young'ns.

Dearest Laurie, she began, using the nickname from Laurel's childhood and filling her heart with homesickness.

Having received your last letter before the Christmas holiday made me feel as if I'd gotten a cherished gift from home. I'd been feeling lonely for you and Rose Elizabeth—I do miss you so—and hearing from my little sister was better than any gift you could have bought me.

Much has happened since last I wrote, and not all good, I'm sorry to say. Mr. Montgomery and I still have certain obstacles to overcome, but I won't go into that now.

Obstacles? Whatever did that mean? Laurel wondered, her brow furrowing as her mind searched out the possibilities. Heather was always so closemouthed about everything. Why didn't she just come out and say what the problem was, for heaven's sake?

Rose's last letter was filled with her continuing difficulties with the duke and the many problems they'd had with the farm. Apparently, they don't see eye to eye on a great many things, but that's not unusual when dealing with men.

Laurel knew exactly what her older sister meant. She and Chance didn't see eye to eye on much of anything.

How are things between you and Mr. Rafferty? This courtship you speak of sounds interesting, especially in light of your current employment with the temperance league. I'm sure it won't be long until you're writing to tell me of your marriage.

Tears slid down Laurel's cheeks, landing on the white vellum stationery and smearing the ink. After the horrible fight they'd had, and the newspaper articles painting him out to be the vilest of men, she doubted that Chance would ever speak to her again.

Not that she wanted him to, mind you.

But it certainly did get lonely with just a bunch of boring women for company, especially ones who didn't laugh, sing, look at the stars . . .

"Oh, Chance, I miss you so," Laurel whispered, staring at the flames in the fireplace and having the sudden urge to vomit. She took several deep breaths until the queasiness subsided.

Maybe her illness was a sign. Maybe God was trying to tell her something. Maybe she and Chance just didn't belong together. Or maybe she was just sicker than she thought.

Two days later, Laurel entered the Busy Bee Café to keep her luncheon engagement with Crystal. She should have canceled, as awful as she felt, but Laurel knew that Crystal looked forward to their weekly luncheons as much as she did.

Being with Crystal was like breathing fresh mountain air. No words of condemnation ever fell from her lips, and the young woman, having borne her own share of life's burdens, never sat in judgment on anyone.

Drucilla could definitely take lessons from Crystal. Laurel was sick and tired of her roommate's snide innuendos about her relationship with Chance, and she was definitely weary of hearing about Drucilla's near brush with death.

Though she knew she'd be cast down to hell for even thinking it, there were times when Laurel wished she'd never dragged the spiteful woman from that burning bed. Times like last evening, when Drucilla had been unusually nasty.

"What's happened to that fancy man of yours, Laurel? I don't see him hanging around here much anymore."

"That's really none of your business," Laurel had replied, trying to ignore Drucilla's sarcasm and concentrate instead on brushing her hair. They'd been moved to another room because of the fire, but unfortunately Hortensia had not seen fit to separate them, much to Laurel's regret.

"Men like that gambler of yours tire easily of women. It's the chase and the challenge that make life interesting for them. Once they bed a woman, they lose interest fast enough."

Laurel had jerked her head around at the insinuation. "How would you know, Drucilla? I doubt any man's ever paid that much attention to you."

Drucilla's spine had gone so rigid that Laurel thought it might snap in two. "I wouldn't want a man putting his dirty hands on me, pawing and petting my flesh." She shivered, as if the very thought of being with a man totally repulsed her. "I intend to remain virginal and pure for the remainder of my days."

Sorry or not about Drucilla's misconceptions of life, Laurel had had enough of her roommate's narrow-minded opinions and acerbic tongue. "That shouldn't be too difficult, Drucilla, considering the fact no gentleman ever comes to call on you."

At Laurel's remark the young woman had stormed out of the room, but not before assuring Laurel in a purely childish way that she would make her sorry if it was the last thing she ever did.

Sighing at the recollection, Laurel was grateful when Crystal finally arrived and seated herself at the table.

"Sorry I'm late, but Gus had me helping out at the church again. I'm sewing altar blankets, if you can believe that!"

"Of course I can believe it. You're the only one who ever doubted your abilities. I'm so happy you took my advice and agreed to marry Gus. I know you're going to be very happy."

"It was a difficult decision, what with my previous occupation and all. I don't want to bring shame on Augustus. I love him too much for that."

"And he loves you. So be happy and quit worrying needlessly."

"What I'm worried about at the moment is you, Laurel honey." Crystal reached out to feel Laurel's cheek, then she frowned, "You're so pale. And you look terribly unhappy. Have your troubles with Chance made you ill? You look white as clotted cream."

"I think I've got a touch of the influenza. I haven't been feeling well these past few days."

"The influenza! That sounds serious, honey. Have you seen a doctor?"

Having never put much stock in doctors—they sure hadn't done much to save her parents—Laurel shook her head. "I'm sure it'll pass in a day or two. I've been nauseated, unable to keep much of anything down, except for Mrs. Costello's tea."

A gnawing suspicion took root in Crystal's mind and began to grow. "Laurel honey, have you been feeling overly tired lately? Are your breasts tender when you touch them?"

Blushing, Laurel whispered rather emphatically, "I don't touch them!"

Crystal laughed. "I meant when you're taking a bath, silly. Surely you touch them then?"

"Well, of course I do, then. But what does that have to do with the influenza? Honestly, Crystal, sometimes you don't make a lick of sense."

Her face sobering, Crystal grasped Laurel's hand. "Laurel honey, we need to talk, but not here. I want you to come back to the Aurora with me."

Knowing exactly what her well-meaning friend was trying to do, Laurel shook her head. "Oh, no, Crystal. I'm not going to let you pull me into that trap. You've got 'matchmaker' written all over your face."

Crystal weighed her options, then decided to be blunt and to the point. "You may need a matchmaker more than you know, Laurel honey. I think you're pregnant."

CHAPTER 22

Pregnant. The word reverberated off the walls of Laurel's mind and heart, and she slammed the door to Crystal's room, then leaned heavily against it.

Looking down at her flat abdomen, then up at her friend, who stared worriedly at her, she said, "Pregnant? I . . . The thought never crossed my mind." Even though her breasts had been sore, and she had been feeling unusually listless of late, she'd just chalked it up to the influenza. How ridiculous her self-diagnosis seemed now, as did her own stupidity. The signs had been there; she'd just ignored them.

Leading Laurel to the chair by the window, Crystal poured a small amount of brandy into a glass and pressed it into Laurel's hands. "Drink this. It might bring some color back to your cheeks. You look white as a ghost."

With no thought to how the liquor might affect her, Laurel downed it in one gulp, coughing as the burning liquid seared her throat. "Tha-thank you," she said in a hoarse whisper.

Crystal took the chair next to her. "There's always the

possibility that you're not, Laurel honey, but from what you've told me, I'd lay odds on the fact that you're carrying Chance's child."

Laurel's hand went to her abdomen, and her eyes filled with wonder. "Chance's child." She smiled wistfully. "I never realized . . ."

"Honey, didn't your sister ever tell you the facts of life? Being with a man, like you've been with Chance . . . Well, it often results in a woman getting herself with child."

Remembering all the lectures she'd received from Heather on keeping her virginity intact, Laurel smiled self-deprecatingly. "I received plenty of information from my older sister, all except the facts that explained how a man's kiss made you feel all jittery inside, and how the touch of a man's hand on your breast made you forget everything proper you were taught." She sighed. Those were the things that should have been taught; those were the things that took an innocent young woman off guard and made her vulnerable to a man.

Crystal clasped Laurel's hand, needing to make sure the young woman realized the reality of her situation. The time for moonbeams and fairy tales was over. It was time for Laurel to face the harsh facts of life.

"I know you love Chance, honey, and I'm sure you're pleased to be carrying his child, but a woman faced with the predicament you're in needs to understand a few things. An unmarried mother is the same as a whore in folks' eyes. A woman who bears a child out of wedlock bears a bastard. And that woman is ostracized, ridiculed, and held in contempt."

Pain filled Crystal's eyes, and it was easy to see that she spoke from experience. "Respectable ladies will cross the street to avoid being near you, Laurel. They'll gather their children to them, to protect them from the wicked whore who played fast and loose with a man."

"But I'm not like that, Crystal! I love Chance. I wouldn't have made love with him, if I didn't."

"Honey, don't you think I know that? Your feelings were pure, but that's not going to change things. Unless Chance gives you the protection of his name, you're going to be considered a fallen woman."

"Chance isn't going to marry me, Crystal, and I don't want you telling him anything about this. You must promise me." She had no intention of trapping the footloose gambler into a marriage he didn't want, especially for the sake of a child.

"I promise, honey. But have you thought of all the consequences? Have you thought about what those temperance women will do when they discover you're with child? They'll toss you out on your rear without batting an eyelash."

Though Laurel hated to believe that, she knew Crystal spoke the truth. Hortensia couldn't afford to have the league's name smeared with scandal. And Drucilla would waste little time spreading the news of Laurel's downfall among the members. "I never realized how loving a man could cause so much difficulty." She hung her head. "My life appears to be ruined."

"It doesn't have to be, Laurel. There are ways to rid yourself of the child."

Her hand protectively covering the growing life within her, Laurel asked in confusion, "What are you saying?"

"A woman in my profession learns how to protect herself, honey. There were times when I found myself in the same predicament as you."

Laurel was shocked by the disclosure. "You never told me you had children, Crystal. Where are they? Why aren't they—"

"I don't have children, Laurel. I got rid of them."

"You gave your own children away? But, Crystal . . ."

"Dammit, Laurel," Crystal's voice was harsher than she'd intended. "How naive you are, honey. There are ways for a woman to rid herself of a child she doesn't want, or isn't able to care for. It's called an abortion, and it's done before the baby is even formed."

"When you say 'rid,' do you mean that I should destroy Chance's child?" At Crystal's nod, a look of abhorrence crossed Laurel's face. "I could never do such a thing. It's not right. It's his child, too, Crystal."

"But what if he doesn't want it, honey? What if he won't marry you? Think, Laurel. What will you do then?"

Crystal's questions bombarded Laurel, bringing tears of pain and uncertainty. "I . . . I don't know. Perhaps I can go back to Kansas."

"To live with your sister and a man she isn't married to? She's likely to end up the same as you, honey. From what you've told me, the duke isn't exactly thrilled with her presence."

That was the God's awful truth, and it stung like the tears behind Laurel's eyelids. Her choices were narrow to nonexistent, Laurel thought. If only Chance had loved her enough to marry her, then none of this would have mattered. But he didn't love her, and it did matter. She was a woman alone, barely able to support herself. How would she care for a small baby—a baby who would depend on her for its very existence?

"I know a woman who can help you, Laurel. Her name is Madam Eula, and she performs this operation for most of the prostitutes in the city."

Laurel's laughter was almost hysterical. "Well then, I guess I'd be in good company, wouldn't I?"

"Pregnancy is just another harsh reality of life that a woman must face. Men take their pleasure and women pay the consequence. It's been that way since the beginning of time."

"I can't lay all of what happened on Chance's doorstep. I had my pleasure, too. I could have said no, but I didn't. I'm as much to blame as Chance. It takes two to make a baby."

"But Chance will go on with his life as if nothing ever

happened, Laurel, while yours will change forever. Life's not fair, and it sure as heck's not equal, by any stretch of the imagination."

"I need time to think about all this, Crystal. I can't make such an important decision on the spur of the moment."

"Just don't take too long, honey. Madam Eula won't perform the abortion after too much time has passed; it's too dangerous."

Laurel rose from her chair to stare out the window at the darkening gunmetal sky. The gloominess matched her mood exactly; there wasn't one ray of hope, one glimmer of sunshine to hitch her future to. Everything was as gray as the reality of her situation.

Turning back to face her friend, she said, "I'll give you my answer tomorrow."

"How come Miss Laurel don't come visit no more, Chance? I miss, miss, miss her."

"Miss Laurel . . . miss Laurel . . . miss Laurel," Percy repeated, much to Chance's great annoyance.

Lifting a heavy wooden crate, Chance stacked it atop another and straightened, his hand pressed to his lower back. "We had a disagreement, Whitey. Laurel's mad at me."

"Yep. She surely is," Jup agreed, shaking his head sadly. "And I surely do miss her smiling face. Miss Laurel was like a ray of pure sunshine. Bertha's still grievin' over that child being gone."

Whitey handed up another whiskey crate to his cousin. "You shouldn't'a been mean to Miss Laurel, Chance. Bertha told me you was mean. Miss Laurel was my friend. Now I ain't got no friend."

Sighing, and wishing Bertha would keep her unflattering opinions to herself, Chance replied, "You've got me, Whitey. I'm your friend."

"But you don't teach me my letters, and Miss Laurel made

me feel like I was smart. She didn't do nasty stuff like Miss Pearl . . ." the big man blushed, "and she was always nice to me."

"I know, Whitey, but . . ."

"Miss Laurel used to read to me and Bertha stories from the Bible," Jup added, smiling in remembrance. "Why, once, when I had me a misery in my back, she made a hot mustard compress for me. Miss Laurel was always doing nice for others."

Chance's face filled with anguish. "She won't talk to me, I tell you! She hates me."

"Give her some tongue, babe. Give her some tongue, babe."

All three heads whipped around to stare at the parrot, who was doing a sprightly little dance on top of a whiskey crate. Jup was the first to respond.

"Seems like that bird finally has hisself a fine idea. Yessir! A mighty fine idea."

The burning look Chance shot the bird could have roasted him in seconds. He transferred that same look to his two companions, who were grinning like hyenas. "Are you nuts? Laurel'd bite my head off if I so much as tried to talk to her." There was no telling what she'd do to his tongue!

"Sometimes a man's got to swallow his pride and say he's sorry."

Whitey nodded at Jup's advice. "Tell Miss Laurel you're sorry, sorry, sorry, Chance. *Pleeeese.*"

At the pleading look on both men's faces, Chance rubbed the back of his neck, "Jesus, Mary, and Joseph! All right. I'll go and apologize."

Whitey beamed.

"I'll swallow my pride and say I'm sorry."

Jup grinned.

"I'll even stick my tongue down her throat if she'll let me."

Chance hardened.

"But I'm not, I repeat, *not*, riding over there on a goddamn white charger."

Though it wasn't marked as such, the weather-beaten building known as Madam Eula's to almost every prostitute in Denver, and a few society matrons as well, stood by itself on the edge of the tenderloin district, as if ostracized by the very people who made use of it.

A knot of apprehension filled Laurel's stomach as she approached the dilapidated home and stepped onto the sagging porch, holding on to Crystal's arm for support, moral and otherwise. After a sleepless night of soul-searching, she'd come to the dismal conclusion that Madam Eula offered the only alternative to her predicament.

"I'm so scared, Crystal," she confessed to her companion. "I've never done anything like this before." Her teeth chattered from the cold, and from the fear that filled her every pore.

"You'll be fine, honey. Madam Eula's not so bad. And after everything's said and done, you'll know you made the right decision—the only decision you could have made."

A stench so foul it made Laurel's eyes water greeted the two women when they stepped into the outer room, where they were met by a young black girl about ten years of age.

"Madam's busy. You all have to wait here a minute," she said in a sing-song voice, then skipped off as if she didn't have a care in the world. Her actions seemed incongruous with the seriousness of the occasion.

"That's Eula's daughter," Crystal whispered. "She's not quite right in the head."

Neither was she, Laurel thought, for coming to this horrible place to begin with. She had half-convinced herself to leave when a black woman weighing at least three hundred pounds appeared, wearing a bloodstained apron and carrying a basin filled with reddish brown water. The sight brought bile rising to her throat.

Balancing her burden on her hip, the woman nodded at Crystal, whom she recognized. "You be in trouble again, pretty girl? I thought I taught you how to stop the seeds from growin' before they took root by usin' the alum douches and the pisser."

Not knowing that such things were possible, Laurel's eyes widened.

"I haven't come for myself this time, Madam Eula. I'm here for my friend, Laurel!"

Eula nodded, set the basin on a nearby bench, and ushered the two women into the back room, where Laurel pulled up short, eyeing a bloodstained table with revulsion.

There were two curtained partitions for Eula's "patients" to recover after the procedure, and one drape was closed, indicating that it was presently occupied. Dirty medical instruments—the tools of Madam Eula's trade—lay waiting on an equally unsanitary counter for the next patient. A shiver trailed down Laurel's spine at the thought.

"You be that temperance woman, no? You be in fine fix if them proper ladies find out you's carrying a child, no?" Her dark eyes held more practicality than sympathy.

Laurel swallowed with great difficulty and nodded. "Crystal said I should talk to you to find out what's involved. I've never done anything like this before."

The woman studied Laurel, assessing her from head to toe. "Take off the coat and the dress. I need to examine you to see how much the baby has grown."

At Crystal's silent encouragement, Laurel did as she was instructed, feeling mortified that a complete stranger should see her in her underclothing.

What would her sisters say if they knew she had come to such a terrible, disappointing end? What would her beloved papa say? She'd been the one with such promise—"the golden girl," her papa had called her. Well, she wasn't golden any longer; she was tarnished goods now.

"Is the examination going to hurt?" she asked, unable to keep her voice from trembling or tears from moistening her eyes.

"Not as much as the operation, child." Eula chuckled, placing her hands on Laurel's abdomen. "You still pretty flat on the outside, but that don't mean nothin'. The babe could be larger than we think. I need to feel inside, too."

Glancing down at Eula's large hands, Laurel cringed. They were dirty, the fingernails jagged and caked with blood. Laurel shook her head, unable to tolerate the idea of Madam Eula touching her most intimate area with hands that had touched so many others. "No," she said, taking a step back from the woman. "I've changed my mind. I won't be needing your services after all."

"Laurel," Crystal chided gently, clasping her friend's arm. "Are you sure? I know you're afraid, but Madam Eula is very good at what she does. Remember what we talked about."

"I'm sure. I wasn't before, but I am now. I'm going to have Chance's baby and suffer any consequence that may result. It wouldn't be fair for me to make an innocent child suffer for my stupidity. And I can't bring myself to harm Chance's child. It's part of him, after all."

A deep frown etched the black woman's face. Time was money to Eula, and she hadn't made a dime yet. "Don't be wastin' no more of my time then. I got others to tend. You go on your way now, and don't be botherin' Eula again."

With apologies to the woman, Crystal pressed two dollar bills into her palm for her trouble, helped Laurel dress, and hurried them both out the door.

"I'm sorry, Crystal, but I just couldn't go through with it," Laurel said once they were outside again, gulping in huge breaths of fresh air.

Wrapping a comforting arm about her friend's shoulder,

Crystal hugged Laurel to her. "That's all right, honey. Madam Eula's not for everyone. We'll go back to Mrs. Costello's and put our heads together. Surely we'll be able to think of something."

Mumbling invectives under her breath about the foolishness of some folks, Madam Eula waddled to the curtained partition at the back of the small room and pulled back the drapery.

"You feel better now?" she asked.

The whore repressed her satisfied smile and nodded. "I'm fine, you fat bitch. Now help me up off this table. I've got important matters to attend to."

"You shouldn't be getting to your feet yet, Miss Pearl. It's only been thirty minutes since we took the child. I tol' you to wait another hour at least."

Pearl could almost savor the sweet taste of revenge on the tip of her tongue. When news of Laurel's pregnancy became public, she'd be ruined—dishonored—cast aside, as Pearl had been cast aside by Chance.

The knowledge that Chance and his little whore would finally get their just desserts made any discomfort she felt quite bearable, even worthwhile.

She smiled maliciously. *"Good things come to those who wait,"* Al had told her many times. Apparently Al was right.

CHAPTER 23

Chance approached the door to Mrs. Costello's boarding hotel with a knot in his stomach the size of a watermelon. The flowers he held—a bouquet of golden chrysanthemums that Bertha had tossed at him before he fled out the door—looked as if they might wilt under the severe turbulence they were being subjected to. Not because of the blowing wind, but because his hands were shaking so badly.

"Jesus, Mary, and Joseph!" he chided himself, feeling like a goddamn fool for being so nervous. Laurel was only a woman, after all. But she was damned important to a lot of people, especially him.

The knock at the front door brought Crystal and Laurel to their feet. Mrs. Costello was at the rear of the house preparing dinner, and most of the temperance workers were at a rally sponsored by Reverend Fodor's Episcopal church.

Support for the women's temperance movement had grown tremendously. Many of the local churches and newspapers had offered their support, both monetarily and in sponsoring various events the league held, and Laurel supposed that another reporter had come to ferret out the latest bit of gossip about what the women were presently planning. The Decency Code campaign had thrust everyone involved into the limelight—a spot Laurel definitely didn't want to be in at the moment.

"Let me get it, honey. You've had a trying morning." Crystal urged Laurel to sit back down, fully intending to bar admittance to any reporter who might be lurking outside the door. Laurel didn't need such aggravation at the moment. And neither did she!

Crystal pulled back the white lace curtain, smiled widely as she turned back to face Laurel, who once again had her nose buried between the pages of a romantic novel.

"You won't need to keep reading that mushy stuff, Laurel. Your very own Prince Charming has arrived, and he's brought flowers."

Laurel launched herself off the sofa, and the book went crashing to the floor. The pounding on the door continued, but it wasn't nearly as loud as the beating of her heart. "Chance is here?" She could hardly believe it. It was as if the fates had sent him to her just when she needed him the most.

Don't get your hopes up, Laurel, she told herself. But he was bringing flowers. And that was a good sign.

"Shall I answer it, or will you?" Crystal asked, grinning at her friend's rapturous expression. "He's likely to freeze his you-know-whats off if you don't make up your mind soon."

"You answer it," Laurel directed. "I need to compose myself before I see him. I don't want to appear too anxious. After all, I'm the one who stormed out on him."

Returning a moment later with Chance in tow, Crystal looked like a proud mama who'd just snared the biggest catch of the century. On the other hand, Chance looked blatantly ill-at-ease—almost nervous. It surprised Laurel to see the usually calm and composed gambler in such a state; it also gave her a teeny bit more self-confidence.

"Hello, Chance," she said, wondering if that breathy sound was her own voice.

Thrusting the bedraggled-looking flowers at her, Chance swallowed past the lump still lodged in his throat. "You're looking lovely as ever, angel."

An awkward silence followed, then Crystal laughed to break the tension and reached for her coat. "Well, three's a crowd, as they say. I guess I'll be heading back to the Aurora now. Gus is expecting me to have dinner with him this evening."

"Thanks for everything, Crystal. You're a good friend."

The two women stared meaningfully at each other, and Laurel's heartfelt gaze brought tears to a woman who hadn't shed them in years. "Take good care of her, Chance," Crystal whispered before disappearing out the door.

"Do I dare ask what that was all about? You two look as solemn as mourners at a funeral. Surely you can't be that sorry to see me, angel?" Grinning, he winked, and her heart flip-flopped.

The old Chance was back, and for some reason, Laurel found that knowledge comforting. "Not everything revolves around you, Mr. Rafferty. Would you care for some tea or hot chocolate?" she asked, offering him a seat. "I'm afraid we don't have anything stronger around here."

Chance remained standing. "I don't need liquor when I'm around you, angel."

His compliment brought a teasing smile to her lips. "Does that mean you're planning to shut down the Aurora? Hortensia will be pleased."

"I didn't come here to discuss business—mine or yours. That just seems to get us into disagreements."

"Then what did you come for?" she asked, sniffing the bouquet, pleased by the thoughtful gesture. "The flowers are lovely."

Not nearly as lovely as you, angel. "I came to apologize for everything that's happened between us."

"Everything?"

"I'll never be sorry for that, angel," he admitted, and a warm feeling infused her entire being.

"Neither will I."

He reached for her hand and engulfed it in his own, accepting her statement as one of forgiveness. "I was wondering if you'd like to take a walk with me to see the new church I've been building for Gus and his flock. It's almost completed, and I thought you might like to see what we've done."

She would dearly love to see the new church. But what if she had one of her queasy spells while she was out? How would she explain that to Chance without alerting him to her condition? She chewed her lower lip for a moment, then replied, "I'd love to. But I must warn you that I've been under the weather lately. A bit of the influenza, I'm afraid. I still might be contagious."

He stepped closer, until she could feel his warm breath on her face. "Is this something that can be caught from kissing? Because if it is, I'm willing to die for it." Removing the bouquet from her hand, he tossed it onto a nearby chair, bringing her close to his chest. "I've missed you, angel. More than you'll ever know." More than he'd ever realized was possible.

She buried her face against his sheepskin jacket, reveling in the familiar masculine scents of tobacco and aftershave lotion. It felt so right to be in his arms; it felt like coming home. "I've missed you, too."

He kissed her then, a long, slow, thoughtful kiss that made her toes curl heavenward. A kiss that sang through her veins like the finest aria from a Puccini opera. A kiss that said "forever" and made her hope for things that might be.

Caught in the rapture of their embrace, they didn't hear the front door open, but they did hear the outraged gasp. Breaking apart at once, Laurel's heart, which had been soaring high, suddenly plummeted to her feet.

Drucilla stood there, her lips puckered as if she'd been sucking a tart lemon. "Miss Tungsten will surely hear about this, Laurel. And she's not going to be pleased by your vile actions."

Chance took a menacing step toward the dour-faced woman, whose eyes widened in fear, but Laurel held him back. "Nothing you can do or say is going to deter Drucilla from having her revenge."

Drucilla's hatred was palpable, but Laurel ignored it saying, "Why don't you run along and tattle, Drucilla? It's what you do best."

As soon as the vindictive woman had stalked out of the room, Laurel reached for her coat. "If we're going to leave, we'd best do it now, before anyone else returns. I'm afraid Drucilla is going to make things difficult for me when Hortensia gets back from her meeting."

"Angel, why don't you . . ." At the look of misery on Laurel's face, Chance bit back his retort. Arguing about Laurel's leaving the league wouldn't serve any purpose now, and would just drive another wedge between them. "Why don't you fetch your scarf," he said instead. "It's cold outside."

Neither the biting February wind nor the muddy streets beneath her feet could dampen Laurel's spirits as they traversed the short distance to Reverend Baldwin's new church. Though the sun shone brightly, the air was wretchedly cold. But there was a warmth in her heart that no freezing temperature could dispel.

For the first time in weeks, Laurel felt free; unencumbered by difficulties. No obstacle seemed too big to overcome with Chance by her side, and she squeezed his hand to communicate her joy.

He looked down at her and smiled. "Are you cold? I guess I should have rented a buggy, but we're almost there."

"Don't be silly. I love to walk. And besides, the streets are congested enough without adding another conveyance to them." Every day seemed to bring new arrivals to the bustling metropolis known as the Queen City of the Plains.

Folks looking to make a new start, or to strike it rich with the lure of silver, flocked to Denver by the hundreds. Gold had founded Denver, but it was silver that had laid the foundation for wealth and culture in the frontier town. The population was expanding at an astounding rate. One had only to look at the city's skyline to see the multitude of church spires rising to the heavens to greet the throngs of new worshipers. For a city steeped in sinners, Denver had its share of pious Christians, too.

It was an odd mixture, much like Gus Baldwin's congregation of miscreants and misfits who sought the word of the Lord by day and the rattle of the roulette wheel by night.

"Well, here we are. What do you think?" Chance asked with pride in his voice.

Laurel stared in awe at the imposing, nearly completed brick structure. As churches went, this one was first-rate, and she told Chance so. "You should be prouder than a peacock, Mr. Rafferty. This is a splendid example of what caring people can accomplish in a short amount of time."

He shuffled his feet, embarrassed by the compliment. "I had help. Lots of it."

She squeezed his arm. "Can we go inside? I'm dying to see what it looks like. Gus must be bursting at the seams with excitement."

With his hand resting on the brass doorknob, Chance's face grew solemn. "He cried, Laurel. The day we completed the exterior of the building Gus cried like a baby." Chance had been at a loss for words that day, and Gus's emotional outburst had nearly brought tears to his own eyes. Good grief! He was becoming as dotty as an old woman, he thought.

"There's no shame in a man's tears. Especially a man as fine as Augustus Baldwin. Some people feel things more deeply than others, and aren't afraid to express their emotions."

Chance wasn't certain if her remark was directed at him, but he felt his cheeks color anyway. "Yeah, well . . . This is the new church," he said, pushing open the door.

The scent of freshly cut pine whirled about her as Laurel stepped into the vestibule. The floors had been sanded as smooth as a baby's behind, and the twenty rows of pews, ten on each side, were painted white, as were the pristine plastered walls.

A great deal of hard work had gone into the construction of the building, and Laurel could see Chance's fine hand in the exquisite stained glass windows, which filtered the sunlight into ribbons of subdued color.

"I'm so impressed," she said, reaching for his hand and kissing it in an emotional display of affection. "You've done a marvelous job. I'm so proud of you."

Her praise touched him as nothing else could have. No one, except for Gus, had ever thought to applaud him for his deeds. It was a good feeling to be recognized for one's efforts, especially when those efforts didn't center around a card table.

"It was just something that needed doing," he replied with a shrug.

"Is there no heat?" Though warmer than outside, the church was still chilly, and Laurel shivered, rubbing her arms to warm herself.

Chance shook his head. "Not yet. The coal-burning furnace I've ordered from San Francisco hasn't arrived. But we did install a wood stove in Gus's office, so he can continue to work. Would you like to go in there where it's warm?"

They moved down the aisle toward the front of the church, and Laurel envisioned them walking down the same aisle at their wedding. She'd be wearing a beautiful white satin gown adorned with hundreds of tiny seed pearls and a veil so long it would touch the rose petals at her feet. Chance would be decked out in impeccably tailored black formal wear, looking handsome, dashing, and incredibly Prince Charming–like. She sighed wistfully at the fanciful image.

"That secretive smile on your face has me wondering, angel, what could be so darned appealing about a church."

"Is this the door to Gus's office?" she asked hurriedly, pointing to the door on the left and purposely ignoring his comment.

They entered to find the wood stove emanating warmth from the fire Gus had laid earlier in the day, and Laurel rushed toward it, rubbing her hands together. "We're saved!" she said, laughing. "I think the cold's gone clean through to my bones. I know it gets as cold as this in Salina, but right now I can't remember when." The intense look in Chance's eyes made her blood much warmer than the heat coming from the stove.

"There's nothing like shared heat to warm a body up," he said, stepping closer, and there was a husky, earthy sensuality to his voice that made goose flesh rise on her arms. "I'll warm you up, angel, if you'll let me." He held out his arms, and she rushed into them, praying with all her heart and soul that he would finally declare himself.

"I've missed you so much, Chance. And I'm sorry for slapping you that day."

"Ssh," he said, kissing her lips as his hands moved to unbutton her coat. "That's all in the past. We'll start again."

Yes, she thought. *Let there be a new beginning for us and for the child growing within me.* "I know this sounds terribly sacrilegious, and I'll probably be struck down for saying it, but I want to make love with you."

His surprise lasted only a moment, and then he grinned. "You took the words right out of my mouth, angel."

The sun had gone down, casting the small room into shadows of darkness, and Chance lit the kerosene lamp Gus kept on his desk. "I want to see you when we make love. I want to look into your eyes and see your passion and your pleasure."

She caressed his cheek with great tenderness. "If you look hard enough, Chance, you'll see something else. You'll see the love I have for you shining from my heart."

"Angel . . ."

Scooping her into his arms, he carried her to the small bed

in the corner, which Gus often used when his illness got the better of him, and began to undress her. It took only moments to remove her clothing, but to Chance, who had dreamed of this so often, it seemed an eternity.

When they were both naked, he lowered himself to the bed and drew Laurel into his arms. "I think it's fitting that we make love in a church, because you're most certainly an angel that God has seen fit to send me." With that heartfelt declaration, Chance covered Laurel's lips hungrily, tasting and devouring the honeyed sweetness of her mouth.

His words, his kiss, set Laurel's blood rushing through her veins; everywhere Chance touched, her skin burned with exquisite heat. She wanted to melt into him, be one with him, be part of his life forever.

"God, Laurel, I can't wait to have you," he whispered, moving his hand down to cup her womanly place, pleased to find her wet and ready for him. Closing his lips around her turgid nipple, he suckled, first one breast and then the other, reveling in her soft moans of pleasure. "You're so sweet, angel. I've never known anyone like you before."

Laurel reached down to find his member hard and waiting, and she stroked it, guiding it to her entrance. "Take me," she whispered. "I need you so."

With one hard thrust he entered, and she cried out her ecstasy as her body welcomed, reveled, ignited.

Their joining was like putting flame to dynamite. The reaction was instantaneous and explosive. A choir of bells rang in Laurel's ears as she reached her climax and felt Chance's seed spill into her.

"Angel . . . angel . . . angel . . ." He chanted her nickname like a litany, kissing her fiercely, possessively. "I love you, angel."

Laurel's heart soared, and tears blinded her vision. "Oh, Chance! You don't know how long I've waited to hear you say that."

Still deep inside her, he brushed the hair from her forehead, placing tender kisses on her nose and chin. "How could you not know? You've made me crazier than any sane man should be. You've turned my orderly life upside down." He smiled widely. "And the worst part is that you've turned a perfectly good gambler into a do-gooder. You've ruined my reputation."

Chance's mock outrage made Laurel smile, and she wrapped her arms about his middle, hugging him close, and felt the awakening effects of his response. "You're hardly respectable, Mr. Rafferty. No respectable man is capable of performing quite so readily."

He arched one eyebrow. "And how would you know that, Miss Martin? I thought I was your one and only."

She pulled him down and kissed him hard. "You are. But have you forgotten that I've had the benefit of some very excellent and experienced tutors in Crystal and Flora Sue?"

He rolled his eyes, then gave her a wildly erotic smile. "Let's see just how much you've learned, angel."

An hour later, dressed and basking in the afterglow of their lovemaking, Laurel and Chance stood before the altar, their arms wrapped about each other.

"You've made me very happy, angel."

She heaved a sigh of pure contentment. "As you have made me." She still couldn't quite believe that he loved her. But Chance had said the words over and over again.

"I guess we've christened Gus's new church pretty good."

"Chance! You'll be struck down if you make any more comments like that."

"Probably. But I'll die a happy man." He tweaked her nose and laughed.

Her eyes sparkling with happiness, her voice filled with enthusiasm, she said, "Just think, Chance, we can be the first couple to be married in this church. We can ask Gus to perform the ceremony. We can—" She stopped abruptly at the horrified expression on his face. "What is it? What's wrong?"

"I never said we were getting married, angel."

"But . . . You told me you loved me. Naturally, I assumed . . ."

"Laurel, don't you see? A marriage between us would never work."

"Why not? We love each other."

"I'm not the kind of man who'd be content to settle down to a mundane kind of life, to be the kind of husband you need. I'm a gambler, for chrissake! I live above a saloon. And who knows how long I'll be able to hold on to that. Business isn't exactly booming."

He didn't mention the temperance league, but the implication was there just the same. "If I don't object to your line of work, why should you?"

"Practicalities aside, angel, I've always believed that marriage is a death sentence. It destroys whatever's good between two people. I saw it happen to my aunt and uncle. I don't want to lose what we have."

Disappointment and fear clutched at Laurel. Disappointment at Chance's reluctance to wed her, and fear for the future of her unborn child. If he didn't wed her, the baby would be a bastard. She could tell him about the child she carried, force him into a marriage of necessity, but her heart told her that would be wrong.

"Just because your aunt and uncle didn't get along doesn't mean we won't. I love you, Chance; you love me. As long as there's love between us, nothing else matters."

He shook his head at her naïveté. "That's just a fairy tale, Laurel. A pretty dream that has nothing to do with reality. Marriage has a way of bringing out the worst in people. I've seen it happen all too often."

"My parents were very happily married," she countered. "And look at Bertha and Jup. You couldn't ask for a more devoted couple." She clutched his arm. "Don't let your fears destroy our happiness, Chance. I want to be with you always, bear your children, be your wife."

The tears in her eyes were ripping his guts to shreds. "I

love you, Laurel. Isn't that enough? We can continue to be together. You'll move in with me. Nothing has to change."

"We can't have a relationship worth anything without commitment, Chance. Don't you realize that? I can't move in with you without the benefit of marriage, like some whore or kept woman. How could you even think I would?"

Her stubbornness annoyed him. "Aren't you being hypocritical, angel? Some of your best friends are whores. Some of the kindest, most caring women I know have walked the line a time or two. At least whores are honest and don't make demands on a man."

Laurel's face crimsoned. "Like Pearl?"

"I told you before, there was never anything between me and Pearl. We had a brief encounter that meant nothing to me. It was sex, pure and simple."

"Is that what we'll end up having, Chance? A brief encounter? Sex, pure and simple? I want more than that. I want a lifetime of love and happily-ever-after."

"I can give you the love, angel. But that's all I can give. I hope it'll be enough."

Laurel was silent for several moments. "You make no promises, and neither can I. I guess this is what you would call a 'draw' in poker. Nobody comes out the winner." But she knew deep in her heart that she'd already lost, for she could never be any man's whore, and she could never bring a child into the world to face ridicule and scorn.

"Win, lose, or draw, I'm in love with you, angel. Never forget that."

He kissed her long, hard, and thoroughly to prove his point. And he did so in spades. But Laurel knew that kisses weren't enough to sustain a lifetime, and the warmth of an embrace without commitment could turn cold at a moment's notice.

Marriage was the only solution to her predicament. And marriage was the one thing Chance wasn't offering.

CHAPTER 24

Hazen had wasted little time in spreading the news Pearl had overheard at Madam Eula's.

By noon the following day, Laurel was confronted with eight angry, disappointed stares as she sat at the luncheon table, not the least of which came from Hortensia, who'd been apprised of Laurel's alleged condition by none other than Drucilla.

"I hope you will put to rest these disgusting rumors which have been making the rounds, Laurel," Hortensia remarked. "I had the misfortune of hearing some disturbing allegations concerning a rather indelicate matter." She looked pointedly at Drucilla, who smiled maliciously at Laurel.

"Tell her, Laurel. Tell Mrs. Tungsten that you carry the gambler's bastard inside you."

A collective gasp rose at Drucilla's less than circumspect remark, and all heads turned in Laurel's direction.

Sipping slowly on her cup of chocolate, Laurel didn't respond at first, but Hortensia's look of disappointment and

Gertie's concern finally became too much to bear, and she set down her cup. "I will neither confirm nor deny Drucilla's assertion and these so-called rumors which have been circulating about me. My personal life is not open to public conjecture. I will, however, offer my resignation, effective immediately. I don't wish to bring notoriety to the league."

Pleased to no end by the announcement, Drucilla folded her thin arms across her equally sparse chest and said, "I always knew you were nothing but white trash."

"Drucilla!" Hortensia's slap came out of nowhere, startling the young woman and bringing tears to her eyes. "Since your mother isn't here to administer to you, I will. How can you be so cruel? Good Lord, young woman! Laurel saved your life."

Tears coursed down Drucilla's cheeks, which still bore the imprint of Hortensia's hand. "I should have been the spokeswoman for this group, but instead you chose her," she shouted, pointing an accusing finger at Laurel. "A saloon singer with a pretty face and winning smile. Well, see how far that smile gets you now, Laurel Martin. No decent woman in this town will deign to speak to you. You're no better than those whores you call friends." She ran out of the room.

"That girl's not right in the head," Gertie offered by way of apology. Laurel had her faults, but she'd been kind and steadfast in her work, and Gertie wished no ill-will toward her, despite her poor lack of judgment.

With a deliberateness in both action and thought, Laurel rose to her feet. "I'm sorry to have caused such dissension. I will pack my belongings and leave immediately."

Hortensia was truly aggrieved over the announcement. She saw great potential in Laurel, saw a little bit of herself at the same age, before life's harsh realities had sucked all the optimism out of her soul. She prayed that Laurel would be spared that consequence.

"But, my dear, where will you go? I'm sure everyone here

is in agreement that you should stay until you can work things out. We owe you that much for all the effort you've put forth for our cause."

Touched by the woman's kindness, and knowing what an awkward position she'd placed Hortensia in, Laurel smiled at her. "Unlike Drucilla, I do have friends. Perhaps they're not the most respectable in the eyes of the league, but they're loyal and kind, and they'll take me in with no questions asked, no condemnation."

Guilt rounded the oval table, landing undisguised on each lady's face. Minerva drew herself upright and asked, with no small amount of disbelief, "You're going back to the Aurora?"

Laurel nodded. "Yes. For the time being I'm going back where I'm accepted and loved for who I am, not what I could or should be."

The awful truth of Drucilla's words of warning hit full force later that day when Laurel and Crystal ventured to Hudson's Department Store to purchase a new nightgown, a hairbrush—Drucilla had tossed Laurel's into the water closet—and some other items Laurel needed.

The mustached gentleman whom Laurel had taunted so long ago stood in the doorway of the establishment, arms folded across his chest, barring their admission. "I believe you know the rules," he said, and the smirk on his face when he looked at Laurel told her he'd already heard the gossip.

"We'd like to enter, sir. I have some items to purchase," Laurel informed him in her haughtiest voice.

"We don't allow your kind in here, nor hers neither." He nodded in Crystal's direction. "You both thought you were so smart that day you marched in here. You especially," he said to Laurel, "pretending to be a fine lady when you're nothing more than a prostitute like your friend. You might have fooled me that day, but I know the truth about you now. Go away before I have you thrown bodily into the street!"

Laurel's cheeks flared red, and her eyes flashed blue lightning. "How dare you speak to us like that, you puffed-up, frog-faced man! We have every right to frequent this establishment. Our money is as good as the next person's."

"Mr. Hudson does not want your ill-gotten gains. He's a respectable businessman and a Christian. We don't want fornicating whores mixing with our genteel clientele. Now leave at once."

Crystal, who'd been silent till now, grasped Laurel's arm and said, "Let's get out of here, people are starting to stare."

Laurel gazed about to find curious eyes looking in her direction—narrow-minded eyes, suspicious eyes, cold and accusing. "But we have every right to shop here."

Crystal led Laurel back out to the sidewalk. "I was afraid this was going to happen, honey. Gossip spreads quicker than butter on hot toast. And your reputation was already suspect from your working at the saloon."

"But what are they so afraid of? I just wanted to buy a few personal items. I'm not contagious. I don't have the bubonic plague. I'm pregnant, for heaven's sake! A condition one can hardly catch by casual association."

Smiling at the remark, Crystal linked her arm through Laurel's, and they began walking back to the Aurora. "That's just the way folks are, honey. You get used to it after a while and learn to ignore the icy stares and condemning looks."

"I'll never get used to being treated like some rabid dog, Crystal. I refuse to remain in such a coldhearted city."

"Why don't you just tell Chance the truth? I'm sure once he hears about the baby . . ."

"No! Chance has made his feelings perfectly clear. I won't force him into marriage for the sake of a child. That wouldn't be fair to either one of us, and it wouldn't be fair to the child." Chance had been responsible for another human being all of his adult life. To learn that she was pregnant, that he'd be forced to assume unwanted responsibilities, would frighten him even more.

"But, honey . . ."

Laurel drew to a halt and looked earnestly into her friend's eyes. "Don't you see, Crystal? Chance would grow to hate us eventually. He'd feel trapped and grow resentful. I won't do that to him. I love him far too much."

"What will you do?"

Laurel shrugged. "I'm hoping and praying that some solution will present itself. Until it does, I'll remain at the Aurora and resume my former position, if Chance will let me."

"The man is putty in your hands, honey."

"Putty is easily molded. Chance is like a large block of concrete—rigid and unyielding to pressure."

"I tell you it's true, Chance." Rooster was breathing so hard that his face was red, and he leaned against the bar to steady himself. "Flora Sue heard it this morning from one of the girls. Hazen's been spreading the gossip all over town, and doing a bang-up job of it, I'm told."

Laurel was pregnant? He could hardly believe it. She'd never said a word about it yesterday at the church. Or had she? *"I want to be with you always, bear your children, be your wife."* No wonder she'd been so insistent on getting hitched.

"You don't look all that surprised, Chance," Rooster said, reaching for the whiskey bottle at his elbow. "Not for a man who just found out he's about to become a father."

"I guess it was bound to happen one day."

Rooster chuckled. "I guess this means you'll be getting married. Maybe we could have a double wedding. You and Laurel, me and Flora Sue."

"A baby changes nothing as far as I'm concerned, Rooster. I've no plans to marry, but I'll do right by Laurel and the baby. I won't run from my responsibilities."

Rooster downed his drink in one gulp, staring in disbelief at the man he'd called his friend for many years. "I never figured you for such a coldhearted bastard, Chance. That little girl must be frightened out of her wits, and you stand here talking about responsibility. *Shee-it!* I thought you loved her."

Chance's voice grew cold. "Mind your own business, Rooster. When I want your advice I'll ask for it. Now why don't you run along back to the Opera House. I'm sure you've got business to attend to."

Rooster picked up his bowler hat from the bar and brushed it off. "Guess I'd rather spend time in my own company than in yours anyway."

Chance heard the hurt in Rooster's voice and saw the indignation on his face, but he ignored both. Why was everyone so free with their advice? It was his life, for chrissake! And he'd live it as he saw fit.

He had his reasons for not marrying. Maybe they seemed foolish to everyone else, but to him they were as valid as his love for Laurel. And she knew how he felt. He'd tried to explain to her that day in the church why he couldn't marry her. Of course, she hadn't accepted his reasoning. She'd countered his arguments with fairy-tale dreams and happily-ever-after.

But once Laurel knew that he was aware of the baby, she would expect him to marry her, despite everything he had told her. Jesus! Everyone would expect him to do the honorable thing, the gentlemanly thing, once they found out she was pregnant.

Reaching for the bottle of whiskey, he upended it and took a big swallow, then wiped his mouth with the back of his hand. Whiskey always took the edge off a man's conscience.

So how come he was still feeling guilty as hell?

He didn't have time to ponder the answer, for Laurel and Crystal came bursting through the doorway, banging the door shut loudly behind them against the fierce wind.

"It's starting to rain," Crystal announced, unbuttoning her coat and hanging it on the peg to dry.

"Howdy, babe! My dick's hard." Percy squawked loudly in protest when Chance immediately threw a linen towel over his cage.

"Afternoon, angel. Did you enjoy your shopping trip?"

Laurel cast a cautioning look at her companion and shook her head. "We changed our mind about shopping, didn't we, Crystal?"

The red-haired woman looked at Chance as if trying to communicate something, then she shrugged. "Guess so. I'm going upstairs. See you later."

Frowning at her best friend's abrupt departure, Laurel removed her coat and placed it on the peg atop Crystal's.

"Did you two have a disagreement? I sense some friction in the air?"

"It's nothing. Just a difference of opinion." She kissed him tenderly on the lips. "It's good to be back."

He snaked his arm about her waist, noting the slimness of it, and wondering how long it would take for her condition to become noticeable. "It's good to have you back, angel, and I'm not just talking about your outing."

She knew what he meant. She felt the same way. But how long would she remain? That was the burning question.

"You look a little tired. You're not sick, are you?" he prodded, on one hand hoping that she would reveal her condition to him; on the other praying that she wouldn't.

"Why, no. I feel just fine." In fact, she felt wonderful. The morning sickness of the past few weeks had been absent this morning, and she truly felt like her old self again.

He kissed her cheek. "Oh, I almost forgot. Bertha said a letter arrived for you while you were out. She's keeping it in the kitchen for you."

"A letter?" Laurel couldn't keep the excitement out of her voice. "Do you know if it's from my sister?"

"No, but I'm sure Bertha's done a careful examination of

the envelope by now. She'll be able to fill you in on all the details."

She started to leave, then halted and turned back to face him. "Will I see you . . . later?" The seductive note in her voice made his heart lurch.

"If you mean, will I be coming up to your room?—The answer is yes. But I've got a few things to take care of first." He clicked open his gold pocket watch and checked the time. "Shall we say in about an hour? That'll give you time to read your letter and me enough time to settle up some accounts. Newt Lally's been hounding me for weeks about his butcher bill."

She blew him a kiss and disappeared toward the kitchen; and Chance felt a terrible sense of loss envelop him.

Now that Laurel was back, he would do everything in his power to make her stay. Everything, except marry her.

With the letter from Rose Elizabeth clenched firmly in her hand, Laurel climbed the stairs to her room, feeling a mixture of melancholy and joy at Bertha's ecstatic reaction to the news of her pregnancy.

"Me and Jup's going to be grandparents!" The older woman's face had glowed with pleasure. "Ain't that somethin'? I's so happy I could cry," she'd told Laurel. And then she had lowered her massive bulk into one of the kitchen chairs and sobbed like a baby.

Laurel had no idea how Bertha had found out but it didn't really matter. It wouldn't take long before everyone knew she was carrying Chance Rafferty's child. Everyone . . . including Chance.

What would his reaction be? she wondered. Happiness? Anger? A little of both? She sighed, wishing things had worked out differently between them. Chance would have made a wonderful husband and father if he'd just given himself half a chance, given them both an opportunity at happiness and happily-ever-after.

Shutting the door, and shrugging off her depressing thoughts, Laurel sat on the edge of her bed and tore open the envelope. Rose Elizabeth's familiar scrawl was a welcome sight.

As she read, she discovered that Euphemia Bloodsworth, Salina's town gossip, had become totally enamored of the Duke of Moreland, baking him cakes and inviting him over for tea. That revelation made Laurel smile, for Euphemia's blood was reportedly made of vinegar and certainly never ran hot, as Rose was suggesting.

> *The house is all but complete, and I've set aside a lovely room upstairs, just in case you get it in your mind to come for a visit. I truly hope you will. I've missed you so. And Alexander has assured me that he wouldn't mind in the least if I invited you to spend some time with us.*
>
> *Spring is just around the corner, and you know how lovely it is here that time of year. Please take some time off from your work with the temperance league and come visit. Trust me, I can use all the moral and familial support I can get right about now.*

Laurel's heart started beating rapidly. The answer she had sought from divine intervention had come by way of Rose Elizabeth's letter: She would go home to Salina!

"When the good Lord closes one door, he always opens another," her dear mama had said. Laurel breathed a deep sigh of relief. Her child wouldn't have to be branded a bastard. She could fabricate a story of her husband's tragic and untimely death. Widows were respectable, often cherished members of a community; welcomed with open arms.

Rose Elizabeth would have to know, of course. It wouldn't be fair to impose on her and the duke's hospitality without telling her the truth. But Rose would understand. She was a very pragmatic and practical woman, wise beyond her young years.

"Thank you, Rose Elizabeth," she whispered, clutching the letter to her breast, her eyes brimming with tears of gratitude.

She would miss her friends here in Denver. She would miss Chance most of all. But she had a baby to think of now. She couldn't put her own wants and needs ahead of what was best for her child.

Laurel Martin was going to be a mother. The naive girl from Salina, Kansas, who had stardust in her eyes and dreamed of fairy tales and Prince Charming, was no more. The new Laurel would be mature, businesslike, practical . . . like her sister Rose. Never again would anyone chide her for being out of touch with reality. Never again would she indulge herself in what-ifs and foolish desires. Tomorrow Laurel Martin would set her new life in motion.

But today the old Laurel would indulge herself in just one more fantasy. Today Laurel Martin would store away enough memories of loving Chance to last her a lifetime.

Weary and heartsore, Chance paused before Laurel's door and sucked in his breath, trying to control his emotions.

He felt guilt over Laurel losing her position with the league—that weighed heavy on his shoulders; but the news that she had gone to Madam Eula's to seek a remedy for her condition filled him with shock and disappointment.

He couldn't blame her for wanting to get rid of the baby. He hadn't offered her any alternative, any support. But in the deepest recesses of his soul he was glad she hadn't gone through with it. Though he didn't relish being a husband and father in the traditional sense, the child she carried was conceived out of the love they had for each other. And that love would survive, sustain them through the years, as no worthless marriage certificate could.

And if he publicly acknowledged the child, as he planned to do, then it wouldn't be labeled a bastard, wouldn't be thought of as unwanted. His own legitimacy certainly hadn't prevented him from being unloved and unwanted.

Chance entered the room, then stopped dead in his tracks at the sight of Laurel reclining against the pillows, wearing a white lace gown so sheer that it left nothing to the imagination. "Jesus, Mary, and Joseph!" he said, slamming the door behind him. "What if it hadn't been me?" The thought was too unsettling even to consider.

Laurel laughed seductively, and the pleasing sound rippled along his spine. "What took you so long? I've missed you." She patted the bed.

Chance didn't need a second invitation, and he began to strip out of his clothes. His fingers paused on the bone buttons of his shirt, and he retraced his steps to lock the door. "There—now we won't have to worry about being disturbed."

As he removed his shirt and tossed it onto the chair, Laurel's eyes feasted on the muscled planes of his naked chest. Unable to resist, she slid off the bed and moved toward him. "You're a very handsome man, but I suppose you know that." Her hands moved over him, her fingers exploring the dark pelt of hair, then trailing over his rock-hard abdomen, while her tongue made circles around his nipples. "Mmmm," she said. "I can see why you like doing this to me."

He sucked in his breath, surprised by her aggressiveness, and wondered if this was one of the things she'd learned from Crystal and Flora Sue. "God, Laurel, you're killing me!" he choked out, feeling his member swell painfully close to bursting.

Laurel's hands moved down to the fastening of his pants. "I want you, Chance." There was an urgency in her voice he hadn't heard before as she unbuttoned the copper studs on his jeans, but he was too caught up in the moment to pay it any mind.

Sweeping her into his arms, he carried her the short distance to the bed. "I love you, Laurel. I love you so much it hurts."

"Then show me," she urged, pulling the nightgown up and over her head to reveal her nakedness. "Show me now."

"Jesus!"

Chance lowered himself onto the bed and pulled her into his embrace. Clasping her head between his hands, he kissed her with all the longing and love his heart contained, then trailed his tongue down her neck, her chest, savoring the sensitive, swollen nubs of her breasts.

"Chance," she moaned, her head lolling from side to side. "Please! I want you."

Cupping her mound, he moved the heel of his hand over the sensitive bud of her femininity until she squirmed restlessly beneath it. "You're torturing me!" But it was sweet torture.

His head moved lower, his tongue entering to taste the nectar of her womanhood, and Laurel thought she would die from the pleasure of it. Over and over he flicked the rigid bud, teasing and tormenting, until she cried out; "Stop! I can't take any more."

Positioning her legs over his shoulders, Chance entered her, moving deep within her core. "Take it, angel," he demanded, sliding in and out, harder and faster. "Take it all."

"Oh, God! Oh, God!" She climaxed instantly, as did Chance, who promptly collapsed on top of her.

Sated, they lay back against the pillows; nestled in each other's arms, and in that moment Chance felt more complete than he'd ever felt in his life. "I love you, Laurel. I always will."

His tender words brought tears to her eyes and a heaviness to her heart. "Chance, I . . ." She wanted so desperately to tell him about the baby, but in the end she couldn't bring herself to do it. "I love you, too."

"Things will work out for us, angel. You'll see."

Laurel's heart ached for all that could be, but wouldn't, and she caressed his cheek.

I'll miss you, she said silently.

CHAPTER 25

"Why didn't she just rip out my guts with her bare hands? It would've had the same result." Slurring the maudlin words, Chance leaned heavily on his forearms, shaking his head as he clutched the note Laurel had left behind.

She was gone. She'd left for Kansas on the noon train, and there was nothing left for him now but regret and self-pity. Her departing words were firmly embedded in his memory:

> I'll miss you, Chance. I've waited longer to leave than I should have in the hope that you'd reconsider and ask for my hand in marriage. I'm truly sorry that your fears had to come between us. I love you, but it's over between us. I have a child to consider. I have to make a new life for myself.
>
> Take good care of yourself. And take care of Bertha, Jup, and Whitey. They'll need you now more than ever.

"Is Chance sick?" Whitey asked, a worried look on his

312

face as he stared down at the body slumped before him. "He sure looks sick, sick, sick."

Augustus sighed dispiritedly and shook his head, wondering why some men were such blind fools. Thank the good Lord he'd had sense enough to propose marriage to Crystal. He couldn't imagine what his life would be like without her.

"Your cousin isn't sick, Whitey. He's corned . . . drunk, I'm afraid."

"Laurel!" Chance cried out suddenly, banging his fist on the table, then sweeping his arm forward to knock the glasses there onto the floor. "Laurel, come back, goddammit!"

Whitey looked at Gus with what seemed to be a deep understanding in the depths of his blue eyes. "Chance is sad because Miss Laurel left. Why did Miss Laurel leave, Gus?"

Wrapping a comforting arm about the man's shoulders, Gus offered a suggestion he hoped Whitey would take. It wasn't up to him to explain the workings of the heart; he had enough trouble with the soul. "Why don't you go ask Bertha to brew a pot of coffee? That might help to make Chance feel better." Though Gus doubted that the cook was going to care much how Chance felt. She'd called the gambler an assortment of colorful, derogatory names upon learning that Laurel had left—names that had made Augustus's ears turn red in embarrassment.

"Do you think he'll be all right, Augustus?" Crystal asked, feeling both heartsick and furious at seeing Chance so upset. "I've never seen him drunk before."

"Women have that effect on a man," Rooster piped in, eyeing his friend with distaste. "But I say he deserves the heartache and the headache he's going to have come morning. He never should have let that little girl leave without asking her to marry him. I never thought Chance Rafferty would act like a coward, or be such a goddamn fool. Pardon my French, Reverend," he added as an afterthought, smiling sheepishly.

"Just you remember that, Rooster Higgins," Flora Sue

cautioned. "I expect to be standing up at the altar any day now."

The banging on the door brought a frown to the bartender's face. "We're closed," Bull shouted, waving the patron away. "Death in the family." They all stared at the desolate look on the gambler's face and nodded at the veracity of the pronouncement.

"He'll grieve for a while yet," Gus said. "Let's get him up to bed."

The next morning Chance woke up with the worst hangover of his life, a tongue fuzzier than a three-month-old orange, and a mind clearer than a mountain stream.

He was going after Laurel, he'd decided. He was going after the woman he loved; he was going to marry her; and he was going to be the best damn husband and father this world had ever laid eyes on.

But first he was going after Al Hazen. That man had a lot to answer for: the fire that almost killed Laurel; all the beatings and cruelty Crystal had endured at his hands; the destruction of Laurel's reputation and position with the league.

The bastard would not go unscathed, Chance vowed.

"Bertha," he bellowed, strutting into the kitchen like a cock into the henhouse. "How's my favorite woman this morning?" He walked right up to the angry cook, despite the frying pan she clutched, and kissed her on the cheek, making her gasp.

"Is you touched in the head or just plain stupid? I done told you yesterday that I ain't talking to you no more."

"Not even if I bring Laurel back and marry her?"

Her eyes widened, and she dropped the cast-iron skillet to the floor, splattering bacon grease and almost crushing her toes in the process. "Is you touched, or is it me, Mr. Chance? I thought I heard you say you was going after Miss Laurel."

Hugging the large woman to his chest, he kissed her

soundly on the lips. "That's what I said, Bertha my love. I'm going to make an honest woman of Laurel. After I rid this town of Al Hazen."

Bertha's elation fizzled faster than curls in the rain. "I ain't saying he don't deserve his comeuppance, Mr. Chance, but you gots more important considerations right now. You gots to get Miss Laurel back."

Grabbing a slice of hot, crisp bacon off the plate, he took a bite and grinned. "Leave everything to me. I've got a plan to end all plans."

"Hmph!" she said with no small amount of skepticism, crossing her beefy arms over her chest. "Men is always makin' plans, makin' war, makin' love, but they never does what they's supposed to when they's supposed to. Why'd you let her leave, Mr. Chance? That girl loves you somethin' powerful."

Her question made the pulse at his temples start throbbing again, and Chance rubbed his forehead, trying to ease the pain. "I was scared. Scared of marriage. Scared of fatherhood. Scared of bringing change to my life. But you know what I discovered I was most scared of, Bertha?" She shook her head. "I was most scared of living my life without Laurel. I love her, Bertha; I really do. I was just too stupid to realize how much."

The black woman started to cry, and Chance threw his arm about her shoulders, trying to console her. And that's how Crystal and Flora Sue found them.

"What'd you say to her, Chance Rafferty?" Crystal demanded, advancing on him like an avenging angel, her eyes flashing fire. "Isn't it bad enough you made Laurel's life miserable? Now are you trying to ruin Bertha's as well?"

Bertha and Chance exchanged grins, then Chance grasped Crystal's wrist and said, "Come on. I'm going to need your help before I can go after the woman I love." Wide-eyed and speechless, Crystal darted a confused look at Flora Sue and Bertha as she followed Chance out the door.

Shaking her head, Flora Sue stared after the departing cou-

ple. "Is his brain pickled or what? I know he had a lot to
drink last night, but that's no excuse . . ."

"Oh, hush, Miss Flora," Bertha chided, a smile of pure
pleasure on her face. "That boy knows what he's about. And
it's about time, too!"

The train came to a screeching, smoke-belching halt, and
Laurel cursed the fates that were conspiring against her
reaching her destination.

Trains were definitely not her favorite mode of transporta-
tion. Her back ached from sitting upright all night in the uncomfortable seat, her stomach churned from the disgusting
meal she'd been served, and now the conductor was saying
something about flash floods and impassable tracks and Lord
knew what else.

This was definitely the worst trip she'd ever taken. Certainly the saddest. There hadn't been a moment when she
hadn't thought of Chance and how much she missed him. If
only . . .

*Stop it, Laurel! You've played the fool long enough. It's
time to grow up now.*

Her conviction was sorely tested when the child across the
aisle stuck out his tongue at her, and Laurel was tempted to
respond in kind. Only the fact that his mother appeared to
outweigh her by some three hundred pounds kept her from
reacting.

"Patience and kindness are always rewarded, Laurel,"
her mama had always said. But Laurel was having some
rather serious doubts about her mama's platitudes and pre-
dictions at the moment, and wondered for the thousandth
time what everyone back in Denver was doing.

Dressed in her gaudiest, lowest-cut red satin gown, Crystal
approached the Silver Slipper Saloon with a great deal of

trepidation. If Chance's plan was going to work, she had to convince Al that she was finished with the polite, respectable side of life and was ready and willing to resume their former relationship.

She swallowed at the idea of letting Al touch her again. She had absolutely no intention of sullying her relationship with Gus, but she was going to have to be convincing enough to make Al believe that she missed him and still desired him.

She had to make him trust her.

It would have to be the performance of her life. But she'd pretended before with sweaty miners, with rich, egocentric bankers, and with cowboys out for a night on the town. She'd convinced them all that she enjoyed their rutting, uncaring abuse of her body. She prayed that she'd be able to convince Al, as well.

Pearl would be a problem. She knew that the possessive woman had her hooks sunk tight into Al, that the whore had replaced Crystal in Al's bed. Pearl would definitely be a problem. But after the way Laurel had described Pearl's cruel treatment of her, Crystal thought it was one complication she'd rather enjoy fixing.

"Well, Crystal! I'll be damned. What brings you back here?" Zeke Mullins smiled with genuine pleasure. "We sure have missed your pretty face around here."

She patted the bartender's cheek, noted his blush—Zeke had always been such a dear man—and pasted on her most engaging smile. "Is Al around, honey? I've come for a little surprise reunion."

As quickly as it had appeared, the smile melted off Zeke's face. "You're not going back to him, are you, Crystal? You know what he's like."

"Don't worry about me, honey. I can take care of myself. Now where is he?"

With a look of disappointment, Zeke pointed to the stairs. "He's still in bed, and he ain't alone."

Though her smile was full of self-confidence, Crystal's stomach was churning enough to make butter. "Why, knowing Al the way I do, Zeke, I suspected as much." With a wink, she picked up her skirts and said, heading for the stairs, "Wish me luck."

Ordering her hands to quit shaking so pitifully, Crystal paused before Al's room and took a deep breath, then knocked three times before she had a chance to change her mind.

She heard the squeak of bedsprings and a few muffled curses, then the door was yanked open. Pearl stood in the threshold, wearing little more than a frown and a stained satin wrapper, looking for all the world like the whore she was.

It could be me. Crystal forced herself not to cringe at the thought and smiled haughtily. "Is Al here? I'd like to speak to him." She didn't miss the hatred in the whore's eyes.

"Who is it, Pearl?" Al's gruff voice carried into the hallway.

Pearl's smile was malevolent. "It's your old whore, sugar. She says she wants to talk to you."

Crystal's eyes narrowed slightly, but brightened when they landed on her former pimp and lover. "Hello, Al. It's been a long time." She saw the pleasure in his eyes before he had a chance to conceal it, and she breathed a sigh of relief. Al still wanted her.

Belting his flannel robe, Al turned to Pearl and said, "Take a hike, I've got company."

The whore turned on him, hissing like a snake ready to strike. "Why, you . . . !" But at the ominous look of warning he cast her, Pearl cut off what she was going to say and brushed past Crystal, nearly knocking the younger woman into the door.

"I do believe I've upset Pearl. And that was never my intention," Crystal said, removing her shawl and allowing it to slip gently through her fingers onto a nearby chair. "You're looking well, honey. I've missed you."

"What's the matter? Ain't the reverend sticking it to you enough?" Al laughed at his vulgar jest, and Crystal wanted to scratch his eyes out, but instead she laughed, too, hating herself for what she was about to say.

"Gus is sickly." She ran a red-lacquered fingernail over his bare chest. "A woman like me needs more of a man. Gus can't satisfy me."

He took her in his arms and kissed her roughly, and Crystal thought she was going to retch. "No man can please like I do, babe. You should know that by now."

She broke out of his embrace. "But it looks like you've found someone who can please you, Al." She added just a hint of jealousy to her words.

"You mean Pearl?" His look was almost incredulous. "She can't hold a candle to you, babe. But a man's got to have release, and she is a whore after all."

Good old Al. Always loyal to the end. And vicious. She'd noticed the bruises on Pearl's face and arms.

"So if I was of a mind to come back here, I'd be welcome?" she asked, her eyebrow raised in question.

Al couldn't hide the elation he felt. "You know there's never been anyone for me but you, babe. But what brings about this sudden change of heart? I thought you had given up whoring and the like. Word has it that you're looking for respectability." He practically sneered the word, as if it were something vile. And to Al, Crystal guessed, it probably was.

"I've had my fill of respectability. Those temperance bitches dealt Laurel a dirty deal, forcing her to leave, just because she went and got herself with child."

"I guess Rafferty's pretty upset she's gone." That thought obviously pleased Al to no end.

Crystal shrugged. "Chance is like most men. He liked the fun but not the responsibility. Although . . ." She paused for dramatic effect, patting the sides of her hair. "Chance has been acting a bit odd lately."

"What do you mean—odd? I always thought the bastard was damned peculiar. He built a goddamn church, for chrissake!"

"Well, maybe Laurel's leaving did have more of an effect on him than he's let on. He's been talking about adding on to the Aurora, bringing in whores to work, redecorating the place to make it more elegant."

Crystal almost laughed aloud at the horrified expression on Al's face. Her former employer didn't have anywhere near the resources to compete with Chance. And if Chance carried through with his plans, it would put Al right out of business.

"I doubt he'll do all that," he said to reassure himself.

Her eyes widened innocently. "Don't know about that. He's fixing to have a big poker game tomorrow night. Winner take all."

Al scoffed. "So? The bastard fancies himself the best poker player in Denver, when everyone knows I am."

She walked slowly to the window and glanced out, trying to keep her voice steady and devoid of emotion. "Chance's game is going to be really big, from what I hear. Some rich swells from Frisco are coming to town for it. But then, the Aurora would be a definite lure to most—"

"The Aurora?" Al closed up the space between them and grabbed her arm roughly, spinning her around to face him. "What are you saying—that Rafferty is putting up the Aurora as part of the pot?"

She nodded, wrenching her arm from his grasp and rubbing it to restore the circulation. "Chance figures it'll be a big draw. Though Bull told me he has no intention of losing it."

"The smug bastard." The wheels in Al's head began turning, and Crystal could almost see them through the greed reflected in his eyes.

"Can anyone get into this game?"

"I . . . I guess, Al. But the stakes are very high. I'm not sure you'd have enough money to convince Chance that you're serious competition."

"I've got the Silver Slipper. If Rafferty is fixing to bring in whores, he'd probably love to get his hands on this place."

Mock horror crossed Crystal's face. "But, Al! What if you lost? What would you do then?"

He laughed, as if losing were inconceivable, totally impossible. "I've no intention of losing, Crystal. There are ways for a gambler to win, if he's clever." He smoothed the ends of his mustache, contemplating victory.

"You mean cheating?" She could barely hide the disdain in her voice. Al was such scum. What madness had made her think she'd loved him?

"Never mind. You just go on back to the Aurora and tell Rafferty that I'm interested in getting into the game."

"But, Al! What about you and me? Don't you want to . . . ?" her eyes strayed to the bed, but she couldn't bring herself to say the word.

He looked at the bed, at her, then shook his head, and Crystal felt greatly relieved. "We don't want Rafferty thinking anything's different, babe. You go back to the Aurora and pretend everything's just hunky-dory between you and the reverend." He pulled her into his embrace and kissed her hard. "Once I get my hands on the Aurora, I'll set you up as madam there. With your expertise at fucking, and mine at business, we'll grow rich, babe. Just think of it. You and me, together again."

Crystal did think of it, all the way back to the Aurora. And with every step she took she cursed Al to hell and back, praying that Chance was as good a poker player as he claimed, and hoping upon hope that after tomorrow night, Al Hazen would be out of her life forever.

CHAPTER 26

Tick, tock, tick, tock. The regulator clock on the wall ticked off the seconds.

Drip. Drip. Drip. The sweat from Hazen's brow fell unnoticed onto the Steamboat playing cards he held in his hands.

The deed to the Aurora rested in the center of the green felt-covered table, beckoning, tempting, like the most provocative of sirens.

Looking at the four kings in his hand, Hazen couldn't keep the satisfaction he felt from lighting his dark eyes. One more card would be dealt—an ace. He'd already substituted a stacked deck to assure his win tonight, so he knew that the trump card would fall into his hands. Then the Aurora and all it represented would be his, and Rafferty would be a beaten man. Victory was in the palm of his hand.

He glanced at his opponents. Rafferty looked unruffled, cool under fire, as he sat across the table studying his cards. But that was part of his expertise, and Hazen had expected no less. The other man who remained in the game didn't appear nearly as confident. His hands shook, and he'd drunk more whiskey than a good poker player should.

Playing poker was like making love: You needed a clear head and a steady hand to reach a satisfying conclusion.

"You in or out, Hazen?" Chance prodded, a cheroot dangling carelessly from the corner of his mouth. "You haven't made your bet yet." His face remained passive, giving no clue as to what he thought.

The kings in Hazen's hand filled him with confidence, and he grinned cockily, reaching into his coat pocket to retrieve the deed to his saloon. he tossed it onto the pile of money and the deed that already rested there. "I'm in, Rafferty. What about you, old man?" Hazen asked the other player.

The white-haired gentleman glanced at Hazen, then at Chance, and shook his head. "Game's too rich for my blood, gents." He folded his cards and leaned back, waiting.

A hush fell over the smoke-filled room as the two enemies faced off for the showdown. One more card would be dealt. One card would declare the winner.

Chance thought about the telegram in his coat pocket that Rooster had sent several hours ago. Laurel's train had been delayed indefinitely, giving them the extra time they would need, and he smiled inwardly, grateful that Rooster had taken care of all the arrangements.

The element of surprise was on his side with both Laurel and Hazen. Now it was time to play his trump cards.

Shoving the deck toward the older man, Chance said, "Would you mind doing the honors, Bat? I wouldn't want there to be any doubt as to the honesty of this game."

Bat Masterson, former lawman and gambler, smiled smoothly at his longtime acquaintance. "Why sure, Rafferty. It'd be my pleasure. I doubt Mr. Hazen here is going to doubt a man of my reputation." The Buntline Special strapped to his hip backed up his implied warning.

A momentary panic seized Hazen, and his starched collar suddenly felt two sizes too small. *Bat Masterson!* Why hadn't he recognized that slick son of a bitch? But then, why should he worry? Masterson was an old man. He didn't even have the skill to remain in the game. That realization restored Al's confidence, as did the ace that was suddenly delivered to him.

He leaned back, smirking. "I doubt you'll be able to beat this hand, Rafferty." He spread the cards out in front of him. "Read 'em and weep." He reached for the pot, but Masterson grabbed his arm.

"Not so fast, Mr. Hazen. We haven't seen what Mr. Rafferty's been dealt."

With a nod at the former lawman, Chance fanned out the cards in his hands, laying them down atop the pile of winnings, and Hazen's face registered disbelief before turning purple with rage.

"That's impossible! You couldn't have been dealt that hand."

"Ten, jack, queen, king, ace of hearts, Hazen. A straight flush beats four of a kind, even ace high."

Hazen tried to grab the deed to the Silver Slipper, but Chance was faster and snatched it up. "Uh-uh, Hazen. The deed is mine. I think all these good folks will agree that I beat you fair and square."

The crowd murmured their approval, while Crystal squeezed Gus's hand and smiled widely. "It appears Chance has beaten you, Al," she said, not bothering to hide the joy in her voice or keep back the laughter that bubbled up.

Hazen's face whitened as understanding dawned. "You whoring bitch! I'll kill you for this." He attempted to rise from his chair, but Masterson circled his neck with his large hand.

"Is that any way to talk to a lady, Hazen? I think you should apologize."

"They're in on this together. I was cheated, robbed!"

"You're the one who attempted to cheat by substituting a marked deck, Hazen. Did you think you were playing with some country bumpkin? Did you think I wouldn't smell the con?" Chance laughed. "The funny thing is, Hazen, I substituted a clean deck for your marked one and beat you all the same. You can check the cards if it'll make you feel better."

The irate pimp swept the cards to the floor. "The only thing that's going to make me feel better, Rafferty, is seeing you dead. You and that slut who carries your child."

The silence in the room grew ominous.

His face taut with anger, Chance's voice turned glacial as he rose to his feet. "I'll meet you outside, Hazen. It's time you and me had this out once and for all."

The crowd drifted out into the street and formed a torch-lit ring. The temperature hovered around the freezing mark, but the excitement of watching two adversaries pummel each other heated their blood to a fever pitch.

Hazen struck first, catching Chance right below the left eye, and a roar of approval rose up. "Five dollars on Hazen," somebody called out.

"I'll take that bet," Bat Masterson said with a confident smile. "But let's make it more interesting by doubling it."

Chance landed a powerful blow to Hazen's midsection, and the man doubled over in pain. The usually reserved reverend screamed out his approval. "Bash his face in, Chance. Give that no-good . . ."

"Augustus!" Crystal chided, placing a restraining hand on the clergyman's arm. "You forget yourself." Before Gus had the opportunity to apologize, Crystal turned her attention back to the fight, shouting, "Kill 'im, Chance. Kill the bastard."

"This one's for Crystal," Chance said, smashing his fist into Hazen's face.

Al screamed, clutching his nose as blood spurted everywhere. "You broke my nose, you bastard!"

"Excellent," Masterson commented.

Hazen lunged for Chance, but Chance was quicker and sidestepped the attack, jabbing a punch to the man's ribs. "That's for Laurel. And this one, too." His clenched fist caught Hazen beneath the chin, knocking him senseless to the ground. "Get up, you bastard. Get up and let me kill you."

"No, Chance!" Augustus called out, stepping down off the sidewalk and into the street to place himself between the two opponents, fearful that Chance would actually kill the pimp. "He's had enough."

"Is that true, Hazen? Have you had enough? Or shall I break the rest of your ribs?"

On his back in the mud, Hazen looked like the whipped dog he was. He held his hands up before his face and nodded. "I've had enough."

"If I see your face in this town again, Hazen, I'm going to finish what I started here tonight. Do I make myself clear? Denver isn't big enough for the both of us."

Hazen nodded again, and Chance turned toward his friends. "Come on," he said, linking his arms through Crystal and Gus's. "We've got a wedding to prepare."

Chug, chug, chug, chug. Chug, chug, chug, chug. The monotonous sound of the train's steam engine became a litany as Laurel stared out the filthy window of the passenger car at the unrelenting low hills of the plains. They rolled in waves like an ocean, and the only relief from the dreary landscape was the occasional buffalo bush or sagebrush, or an unexpected patch of wildflowers.

Interestingly enough, the town they'd soon be pulling into for water and provisions was called Monotony, and Laurel was more than eager to reach it. She needed to stretch her legs to get the blood circulating back into them and to relieve the pain in her lower back from sitting such long hours.

The flash flood had delayed the train in River Bend for

more than two days, and they were just now crossing the border into Kansas. It would be a welcome sight to see Fort Ellsworth, Laurel decided, for Salina lay not many miles beyond it.

Turning her attention to her swollen ankles, she sighed. She had a mind to write the folks at the Kansas Pacific Railroad just to let them know how poor she thought their service was. It wasn't right for passengers to have to . . .

"Monotony!" the conductor called out, marching down the aisle toward the connecting door to the next car. The brakes screamed as the train rolled slowly to a halt.

The obese woman seated next to her, who Laurel now knew as Helen, cried out, "My goodness gracious! Land sakes alive. I ain't never seen such a thing in my life."

Curiosity getting the better of her, Laurel craned her head to look out the window, and what she saw made her mouth drop open in disbelief. Blinking several times, she wiped at the window, just to make certain it wasn't an illusion. Then she smiled.

Chance was seated atop a snow white stallion dressed in, of all things, black formal evening attire. In one hand was a bouquet of red roses, in the other, a box of candy.

"Who on earth do you suppose that man is making such a fool of himself over?" Helen asked, shaking her head, as well as her chins, and sighing wistfully. "That is one lucky woman, if you ask me."

Speechless, Laurel spotted a three-piece orchestra, also arrayed in formal attire, playing what sounded like a piece from *The Barber of Seville*. Next to them stood Rooster and another man she didn't recognize. They were holding up a white bedsheet on which had been painted: Laurel, will you marry me? I love you!

Tears flooding her eyes, Laurel jumped to her feet like a shot, unmindful of her swollen ankles, the fat woman's astonished gasp, or the other passengers who were now staring at her as if she'd taken leave of her senses.

"Excuse me," she said, elbowing her way down the aisle toward the door. "Excuse me. This is my stop."

Chance waited patiently, hoping Laurel had seen the effort he and Rooster had put forth on her behalf, and wondering if his irritated, chafed crotch was going to endure one more minute seated atop the goddamn horse.

He'd taken the train part of the way, then had ridden the huge beast, which he'd borrowed at a railway station, at breakneck speed to reach Monotony before Laurel. Horsemanship not being one of his strong suits, his butt had taken the brunt of the journey, and he now felt pain in every single one of his gluteus maximus muscles. The flowers he held were slightly wilted, as was his enthusiasm, due to his aching butt, but he aimed to persevere and greet Laurel just as he and Rooster had planned.

He smiled at his friend, knowing he would never have been able to pull off this wild scheme without Bartholomew Rooster Higgins, Gus, Crystal, and the others.

Friends were special. Family was indispensable. And love was the one thing no one could live without. Especially not him, and certainly not without Laurel.

As soon as Laurel's foot hit the boardwalk, Chance dismounted and waited, hoping she'd find it in her heart to forgive him for all the stupid things he'd said and done and the callous way he'd treated her. She looked radiant and more beautiful than he remembered and when she smiled at him in that glorious way that only she could, his heart expanded two sizes in his chest.

Chance spread his arms wide to receive her, and Laurel rushed into them, showering him with kisses, squeezing his midsection tightly, as if to convince herself that this wasn't just an illusion that would soon disappear.

"Chance. Chance. I love you so. I can't believe you went to all this trouble for me." Through her tears she smiled at Rooster, who was wiping his eyes with his handkerchief and sniffing loudly.

"Afternoon, Miss Laurel," he said.

"Do I look enough like Prince Charming to qualify, angel? I love you, Laurel. I want you to be my wife and stay with me always."

Laurel's tears began anew, and she pressed her face into Chance's shirtfront. "Yes!" she whispered, then repeated louder, "Yes! Yes! Yes!"

"God, Laurel, you've made me the happiest man on the face of this earth."

"Are you certain, Chance?" she wanted to know, looking up at him. "I know how you feel about marriage and babies."

"Not any longer. I can't wait to get married. In fact, I've arranged for us to be married as soon as we return to Denver. Bertha, Crystal, and Flora Sue are making all the arrangements, and Gus is going to perform the ceremony."

Using Chance's sleeve for a hankie, much to his dismay, Laurel wiped her nose. "I can't believe this is happening."

"Believe it, angel." He kissed her passionately, to an exuberant chorus of passenger well-wishers who now lined the platform. "Now that I've got you, I'm never going to let you go."

"Are we going to ride off into the sunset on the back of that white horse?" she asked, and he heard the wistfulness in her voice.

Swallowing a groan, for he knew the pain that awaited him on the back of the horse, Chance nodded, wanting to give her fairy tales and happily-ever-after. "What kind of Prince Charming would I be if we didn't do that?" He lifted her onto the saddle, then mounted behind her.

"Shall we find a room at yonder castle, my fair lady?" he whispered into her ear, nodding toward the dilapidated hotel in the distance. "I'm in the mood for a hot bath, a warm bed, and a willing woman. And not necessarily in that order."

"Chance Rafferty," she chided in mock offense. "Prince Charmings do not lure innocent maidens into dens of iniquity and sully their virtuous reputations. It just isn't considered chivalrous."

"Jesus, Mary, and Joseph! I don't give a tinker's ass about being chivalrous. I intend to get you into that bed, strip every inch of clothing off your delicious little body, and make mad, passionate love to you."

Laurel sighed, feeling happier than she'd ever felt in her whole life. There were things she and Chance needed to talk about, like how they could turn the Aurora into a profitable, first-class restaurant and dinner theater that served no hard liquor but only fine wines instead.

Yes, there were many important things they needed to discuss. But all those would come later. Much later. Now, she intended to make love with the man she loved.

Nestled in Chance's embrace, Laurel thought she could die now and go to Heaven happy. She wasn't sure anything in life could be better than making love with someone you loved as much as she loved Chance.

Well, maybe one thing, she reconsidered, patting her abdomen softly.

"Chance." Laurel ran exploring fingers over the soft mat of hair on his chest, and smiled when he groaned.

"Jesus, Laurel! Can't we wait a little while? We've already done it five times. I'm a little wore out."

She kissed his cheek. "There's something I want to tell you, Chance. Something very important."

He grinned, tweaking her nose. "I know—you love me and think I'm the best lover in the world."

She laughed. "Certainly the most conceited, but definitely the best." At his pleased look, she added, "I just wanted to prepare you about the babies."

He jerked to a sitting position. "Babies?"

She nodded.

"Jesus, Mary, and Joseph!"

"I think I'm carrying twins."

It was actually Helen, from the train, who'd deduced as much. A midwife of some repute, Helen had delivered dozens of sets of twins during her career, and had proclaimed after a brief external and auditory examination of Laurel's abdomen that she would indeed deliver twins. Of what sex? Helen hadn't been bold enough to predict. But some sixth sense told Laurel that they were going to be big strapping, handsome boys like their papa.

Chance shook his head, unwilling to believe it. "Two babies? I think you've made a mistake, Laurel. In fact, I'm pretty damned certain you've made a mistake." There was no way in hell Laurel could be having twins. He was potent, but not that potent!

Kissing him softly on the lips, Laurel's eyes filled with joy, mirth, and boundless love. "Care to place a bet, gambling man? I think this is one wager you're going to lose."

Placing his hand on her abdomen, he stared at her body in wonder, his eyes softening as he imagined Laurel nursing their child—okay, two children—then he hugged her fiercely. "I've already made the biggest gamble of my life, angel, and won."

Please Turn the Page

for a Preview of

PRIM ROSE

BOOK THREE IN THE DAZZLING

FLOWERS OF THE WEST

TRILOGY

COMING WINTER, 1997

CHAPTER ONE

Salina, Kansas, Late Summer, 1883

"Damn, damn, and double damn!" Rose Elizabeth tapped her foot impatiently against the rotting boards of the railway platform as she waited with no small amount of dread the arrival of the westbound train from New York City.

It was cursed hot; she was sweating like a pig; and there wasn't a cloud in the sky that held any promise of rain for relief.

"It's surely going to be something having a real live English duke living here in Salina," Skeeter Purty, the station manager, remarked, scratching his whiskered chin. "I reckon it could put this here town on the map." The wad of chewing tobacco he spit missed its mark, landing just short of the brass spittoon near his rocker.

Rose's head jerked around, and with narrowed eyes she stared in disgust at the brown gooey mess on the platform, then at the old man himself, wondering if he'd been secretly nipping at the bottle of corn liquor he kept hidden in his desk drawer and thought no one knew about. She had half a mind to turn the old fool in to the sheriff, though she doubted Morris Covington would do anything about it. Mo had a hollow leg himself when it came to drinking whiskey.

Liquor had been banned in Salina and elsewhere in Kansas for the past two years, though that didn't stop old-timers like Skeeter and Morris from imbibing when they got a hankering, which was often.

"In case that feeble mind of yours ain't workin', Skeeter Purty, I am not one bit happy about that damned duke coming here, and I'm doubly damned unhappy that he's stealing my farm out from under me." She crossed her arms over her chest, and her toe went into double-time.

The old man rocked back and forth, and he spit twice more, unfazed by Rose's sharp tongue. Rose Elizabeth had about the sharpest tongue in the whole state of Kansas for someone of such tender years. Some folks said she could cut a man down to size without raising much of a sweat, her tongue was so keen.

The townsfolk had taken to calling her "Prim Rose" behind her back, because like her namesake, Rose was about as thorny as they come, and not the least bit prim and proper like a young lady should be.

" 'Pears to me, Rose Elizabeth, that your sister wanted that farm sold off. Your pa, too. God rest his soul. 'Pears to me that you was lucky to have found a buyer so quick, and a rich one at that."

Rose felt in her pocket for the cursed telegram that had arrived from the duke's English business factor, and she railed silently at the fates that had brought her to this day. Alexander James Warrick, the Duke of Moreland, would be arriving on the noon train. *"Please be prepared to greet his lordship, show him every possible courtesy, guide him to his new residence, and familiarize the duke with the lay of the land,"* the telegram dictated, like she was one of his dukeship's royal flunkies.

"We'll just see about that!" No one dictated to Rose Elizabeth, except perhaps her older sister Heather, who, much to Rose's great dismay, had had the unerring good sense to insist that their local land broker, Mr. Walker, advertise their farm for sale in the *New York Times* and other large city newspapers.

Well, despite her bad luck that the duke's business factor had seen the ad for their land and had talked the stuffy old goat into buying it, she had absolutely no intention of following Heather's highhanded orders that she hightail it to Mrs. Caffrey's School for Young Ladies in Boston once she turned over the farm to the new owner.

She didn't need refining, and she certainly didn't intend to abandon Ma and Pa's graves to a total stranger—a damned Englishman, and a duke to boot!

Whatever could Heather have been thinking of? Rose knew perfectly well that it had been her pa's idea to sell the farm. Ezra Martin wanted better for his three girls.

But to cast them off to parts unknown . . .

Send them out into the cruel, strange world to seek husbands . . .

She shuddered. It was perhaps the most impractical idea Ezra had ever concocted, and he'd hatched some doozies in his lifetime. And for Heather and Laurel to have gone along with him was, in her opinion, even more ridiculous.

Just because Heather had this undying desire to illustrate for a big city newspaper, and Laurel, who had the voice of a tree frog on her best day, had taken it in her head to become an opera singer in Denver, was no reason that she, Rose Elizabeth, should be forced out of the home she loved, off the land that was so much a part of her, to travel to a dirty, depressing city so she could get refined and become a schoolteacher.

Indeed, she couldn't think of a worse fate. Unless, of course, it was being hitched to some smelly old English coot like the Duke of Moreland.

He was probably short and squat and looked like a toad. And with that reminder, she reached into her other pocket to make sure Lester, her pet bullfrog, was all right.

The duke was probably a dandified gentleman who had absolutely no idea about running a wheat farm, and he was probably so arrogant and mannered that the sound of a good belch and a few well-delivered swear words would send him into a fit of the vapors.

Rose smiled at that notion.

"Rose Elizabeth, praise the saints! Don't you have something better to wear than that old threadbare dress to greet the duke? Why, he's royalty, young lady."

Groaning aloud at Euphemia Bloodsworth's high-pitched voice, Rose turned to cast Salina's most notorious gossip and resident spinster a thin smile. In fact, it was so thin you'd have been hard-pressed to find it, if your eyesight wasn't one hundred percent accurate. "Good afternoon to you, too, Miss Bloodsworth."

"Old Beaknose," which is how the Martin sisters had always referred to Euphemia behind her back, moved over to where Rose was standing.

"I don't mean to interfere, my dear," she said, and Rose's eyes rolled heavenward, "but I feel it's our duty to show his lordship that we aren't just a bunch of country bumpkins. As founder of the Salina Garden Club and Ladies Sewing Circle, I feel obligated to put our best foot forward." She smoothed the folds of her black taffeta gown adjusting her white crocheted shawl.

Wondering how the woman could stand to wear such stifling garments in the summer heat, then remembering that Euphemia supposedly had vinegar in her veins instead of blood, Rose replied, "We are a bunch of bumpkins, Miss Bloodsworth. And I don't think we should be trying to fool the duke into thinking any different. I certainly don't intend to put on airs and pretend to be something I'm not. My foot's staying firmly planted on good old Kansas soil."

Euphemia shook her head in disgust. "The other ladies of the welcoming committee will be joining me shortly, Rose Elizabeth. Perhaps the duke won't notice how provincial you look dressed in that faded blue gingham gown. And really, Rose Elizabeth, you know how checks make a body look . . . Well, you should take care to minimize your propensity to pudginess."

Rose's cheeks reddened in embarrassment, as they always did when someone had the insensitivity to comment that her figure wasn't as pleasing as those of her two sisters. She'd been cursed with a curvaceous body, a "pleasingly plump figure," her ma had always called it. But though she'd been cursed, she wasn't about to starve herself or make herself into something God hadn't intended. As long as no one called her a "plump little partridge," which was the nickname her pa had always used, she'd be able to put up with just about any of their stupid remarks.

"Leave the girl alone, Euphemia." Skeeter rocked forward and rose to his feet. "Rose looks just fine. There ain't nothin' wrong with the way she's dressed, far as I can see."

Rose flashed the station manager a grateful smile, firmly convinced once and for all that he had indeed been tippling at the whiskey bottle.

Skeeter and most of the other bachelors in Salina kept their distance from Miss Bloodsworth and did their best not to engage the spinster in conversation if they could help it. Because to Euphemia Bloodsworth conversation, no matter how innocent, no matter how mundane, was an indication of interest. And an indication of interest to a spinster of Miss Bloodsworth's years was tantamount to a full-fledged proposal.

"Why, Mr. Purty," Euphemia advanced on the man, "how very gallant of you to come to Rose Elizabeth's defense. Though it was totally unnecessary." She pursed her lips into what was supposed to be a smile, reminding Rose that she should pick up some lemons from the grocer while in town. "I'm sure Rose knows that I was only being motherly. Since she was orphaned at such a tender age, I've always done what I could to step in for dear departed Adelaid."

And she'd very nearly given poor Ezra a heart seizure every time he'd had the misfortune to run into the old wind-bag in town. The widower had been at the very top of Euphemia's eligible husbands' list before his demise last May.

Having absolutely no intention of placing his name under Ezra's scratched-out one, Skeeter stepped back. "I'd better mosey on in and check to see if there's been a telegram sent. Train shoulda been here by now." He clicked open his pocket watch and scratched his thinning head of hair in bewilderment. "Can't figure out what's causin' the delay." But he sure as hell was happy to have an excuse to leave for a spell.

Rose Elizabeth watched Skeeter depart, and she had half a mind to run after him. Skeeter was, for all his shortcomings, a friend. And though he tried her patience on many occasions, he was kindhearted and harmless for the most part. Except when strong drink took hold of him. But even snockered, Skeeter was a better companion than Euphemia. Being alone with the spinster for any length of time was not an amusing prospect.

Where the hell was that damned train? Maybe his "Most Royal Pain in the Butt" wouldn't be as bad as Euphemia's endless array of questions.

"You must just be so excited to be entertaining a member of royalty." Euphemia's face flushed with pleasure.

"It just gives me the runs to think about it, Miss Bloods-worth. Why, my bowels have been in an uproar ever since I heard about the duke's arrival." At least that was the truth, Rose thought.

Gasping, Miss Bloodsworth's hand flew to the cameo brooch at her throat. "Really, Rose Elizabeth!" She drew herself rigidly erect. "Proper young ladies don't mention such things. It isn't seemly. I can see that your father and sister were justified in wanting to send you back East to attend finishing school. You've many rough edges to smooth out, my dear.

"You may not be aware of this, but I was a graduate of

Mrs. Caffrey's. Though it wasn't called by that name back then. I guess you can see what proper guidance can do for a young lady."

Biting the tip of her tongue, Rose decided once and for all that she was never going to attend Mrs. Caffrey's, or any other finishing school for that matter. The prospect of turning out like Euphemia was enough to curtail enrollment at the most prestigious of learning institutions.

"Don't see much use in finishing schools, Miss Bloodsworth. Aside from teaching a body to poop silently and cutting an orange with a knife and fork, I can't really see the benefit of them." At the choked sound the woman made, Rose Elizabeth chuckled inwardly.

"I . . . I must go and see what's keeping the welcoming committee. Please don't let the duke leave without meeting all of us." Euphemia ambled off the platform with more agility and speed than Rose had thought possible.

The whine of a locomotive could be heard in the distance. Rose's brown eyes sparkled with mischief, and her lips curved into a smile. Perhaps getting rid of his dukeship was going to be easier than she'd originally thought.

She had every intention, as the telegram requested, to show his supreme portliness the lay of the land. She was certain that when she was finished with him, she'd have also shown him exactly which way the wind blew.

The welcome mat at the Martin farm was going to be just a teensy bit smaller than what she was sure the Duke of Moreland expected.

The train pulled into the Salina railway station amid the screeching of brakes, belching black smoke, and a large number of curiosity seekers who had come to see what a real member of English nobility looked like.

Euphemia, along with her welcoming committee comprised of Sarah Ann Mellon, whose husband owned the mer-

cantile, her daughter Peggy, whose bustline matched her sur-
name, and who "welcomed" just about anything wearing
pants, and Abigail Stringfellow, wife of Horatio T. Stringfellow, mortician and sometime dentist, waited anxiously for
the duke to descend from his private Pullman car.

All four were waving wildly at the train, smiling like hyenas, and making perfect fools of themselves in Rose Elizabeth's opinion. Why anyone in these United States would
welcome British aristocracy with open arms, when it had
taken this country so long to get rid of the pompous devils,
was beyond her understanding. As her mama used to say,
"There was just no accounting for taste."

Skeeter sidled up next to her, looking a mite perplexed by
the whole turn of events. "I confess I was excited at the
prospect of meeting the duke, but now I ain't so sure. 'Pears
to me he's gonna be the center of attention for a right good
while. The way them ladies are carrying on, don't know if
that's such a good thing."

Rose stared into the crowd to find Marcella Tompkins
waving as wildly as everyone else. Folks in Salina knew that
Skeeter had a crush on Marcella, and that one day he was
fixing to ask her to marry him. "I doubt Marcella will be interested in anyone as shallow as the duke, Skeeter," she reassured the older man with a pat on the arm. "He's sure to be
as homely as my Lester and not nearly as smart."

Skeeter let loose with a loud guffaw, slapping his knee,
and Rose Elizabeth followed suit. But her laughter soon died
on her lips when her eyes fixed on the tall, incredibly handsome gentleman emerging from the train.

Impeccably dressed in a well-cut suit of black worsted
wool, which contrasted dramatically with his snow-white
shirt and head of flaxen-blond hair, he was surely the finest-
looking man Rose Elizabeth had ever laid eyes on. In fact,
she was quite certain she'd never before seen such a fine
specimen of a man. And she knew damn well that there

wasn't one like him in Salina, and probably in all of Kansas. A sinking feeling formed quickly in the pit of her stomach.

"Do you think that's him, the duke, I mean?" Skeeter asked, impressed in spite of himself, his complexion paling considerably. "I'd best go see how Marcella's faring. She might find this heat too unbearable, considering how delicate she is and all." In the blink of an eye, he disappeared, leaving Rose alone to face her fears and her worst nightmare.

Alexander James Warrick, the Duke of Moreland, was not the supreme portliness she'd been expecting. In fact, she doubted if he had a spare ounce of flesh on his muscular physique.

"Damn, damn, and double damn!" she cursed, pasting on an uneasy smile as he approached.

"Miss Martin?" He held out a gloved hand to her, and she stared stupidly at it, as if it were some foreign object out to do her harm—it was definitely foreign—then she gazed up into his very aristocratic face, which was void of anything resembling a smile. "I'm Alexander Warrick, late of Sussex, England." His tone was imperious, and she knew without a doubt that this man was used to issuing orders and having them obeyed.

Rose Elizabeth grasped his hand in what she hoped was a firm handshake. "I'm Rose Elizabeth Martin, presently of Salina, Kansas, of these United States of America," she mimicked, and several of the townsfolk laughed. "Where'd you stow your gear, your dukeship? We'd better get a move on if we're going to reach the farm."

The duke glanced in bewilderment at the redheaded giant who appeared suddenly out of nowhere to stand beside him.

"Now don't be selfish, Rose Elizabeth," Euphemia scolded with a silly giggle as she came to stand before the couple. "The rest of us would like to make his lordship's acquaintance."

The duke opened his mouth to speak, but Rose Elizabeth butted in, not allowing him the opportunity. "It's my responsibility to see that the duke gets settled in, Miss Bloodsworth

. . . ladies." She smiled spitefully at Peggy, who she knew was in a perfect snit. They'd been unfriendly rivals for years.

"Perhaps the duke will invite all of you out for tea and crumpets after he learns his way around *my* home." That shouldn't take him too long, Rose thought, considering the soddy only consisted of three rooms, and none of them very large. She couldn't wait to see the duke's expression when he saw his new "castle" for the very first time.

Conveying his apologies to the group of men and women who had come to greet him, the duke issued orders to the man at his side, who Rose assumed was one of his servants, then clasped her upper arm rather firmly and led her off to the side of the platform where he could speak to her in private.

Alexander's gaze slid over the woman, and he wasn't overly impressed by what he saw. She was taller than a woman ought to be, and definitely a bit more well-rounded than he liked, but it wasn't her physical attributes that put him off. It was her damnable big mouth!

Who did this annoying chit think she was anyway? He bit the inside of his cheek to keep his temper in check. Obviously she had no respect for simple courtesy, and no respect whatsoever for his superior position and intellect.

Americans! he scoffed silently, then wondered for the millionth time since beginning this wretched journey what had possessed him to purchase a wheat farm in Kansas, and cursing the fates, and that devastating scandal, that had forced him from his home.

"Don't ever presume to speak for me again, young woman," he said finally. "You've overstepped your bounds."

He removed his leather gloves and slapped them against his left palm, and Rose had the distinct impression that Alexander James Warrick was trying to intimidate her. Fortunately she wasn't easily dissuaded from her goals. And getting rid of Alexander Warrick was definitely her main priority for however long it took.

"Custom dictates that I take charge, your royal highness,"

she called him, hoping to annoy the duke further, and was gratified to see that the vein in his neck pulsed like oil gushing from a well.

"The telegram I received from your business factor stated that I was to greet and guide you to your new residence. If that's being presumptuous, your dukeship, then I guess I am." She smiled sweetly at him and was immediately rewarded with a dark scowl.

"Where is your conveyance, young woman? I'm tired, and I am in need of a bath and a hot meal."

"Really? Well, if you'll just follow me, your royalness, the farm wagon's out behind the station." She couldn't wait to see how he would manage to fit his rather well-developed backside into the old tin tub. No doubt he had a porcelain, or even a gold one, back in England.

"I hope this wagon has a cover. It's deuced hot in this Kansas."

"This is nothing, your dukeship. Wait until the temperature really starts to sizzle. Why, you'll think your drawers are on fire for sure."

Years of breeding kept Alexander from commenting on the chit's lack of decorum, but they didn't keep his eyebrows from arching up to meet his hairline. "If I didn't know better, Miss Martin, I would think that you were trying to scare me off."

Rose shrugged. "Just trying to be honest about things. If you don't want to know the truth . . ."

"And are you a great teller of truths, Miss Martin?" Somehow, he thought not. Her lack of response only proved to confirm his opinion.

They had been riding in silence for almost two hours, when Alexander mopped the sweat off his brow with a pristine linen handkerchief and said, "This is a strange land. I can't ever remember seeing anything so lacking in vegetation or so blasted flat." It was a harsh, unforgiving land, save for the fragrant wildflowers that bloomed in great profusion. Heat, wind, and miles and miles of nothingness stretched out before him. Erect windmills stood forlornly against the monotony of the azure sky, and tall-stemmed prairie grass swayed gently in the breeze.

"My pa used to say that if you stood at one end of Kansas, you could probably see all the way to the other. Of course he was just joshin'. Kansas ain't really that flat." Rose Elizabeth smiled at the memory, knowing that her father's love for the land flowed staunchly through her veins. "Pa also said that living here cultivates patience, a hide so thick you couldn't stick a knife through it, and a considerable sense of humor. Kansas ain't for everyone, that's true enough."

He winced at her fracturing of the English language. "I suppose not, but you seem quite taken with it."

"You've got to be born to this land to love it. Foreigners, such as yourself, don't usually fare well here."

"Indeed?"

She nodded. "Especially Englishmen. They're the worst of the lot, I'm afraid. With no great abundance of trees to speak of, no pretty green hills, no babbling brooks at every turn, like there is in England, Kansas is just too alien a place for most Englishmen to adjust to."

"You seem quite familiar with my ancestral homeland."

She clucked her tongue to prod the mules along. "I can read, your majesticness."

He cast her a sidelong glance of pure irritation. "Alexander will do quite nicely, Miss Martin."

"I guess you might as well call me Rose Elizabeth, or Rose, if that's easier. That's my name."

"Ahh," he said. "That explains it then."

She looked at him, and her brow furrowed in confusion. "Explains what?"

"Why, the thorns of course." He smiled for the first time, and Rose's breath caught in her throat. Lordy be, he was a handsome devil. It was just plain sinful for a man to possess such long thick lashes and eyes the color of robin's eggs.

"On Richmond Hill there lives a lass more bright than Mayday morn; whose charms all others maids' surpass—a rose without a thorn."

"Why, you're a poet, your imperial highness," Rose quipped to hide her embarrassment. "Let's hope you're as poetic about your new abode." She pulled the wagon to a halt at the end of the lane leading down to the sod hut, waiting for the duke to catch a first glimpse of his new home. His white-faced, eye-popping reaction was everything Rose Elizabeth could have hoped for.

"Bloody hell! Bloody blasted hell!"

THROUGHOUT THE NEXT YEAR, LOOK FOR OTHER
FABULOUS BOOKS FROM YOUR FAVORITE WRITERS
IN THE WARNER ROMANCE GUARANTEED PROGRAM

WIN A ROMANTIC GETAWAY FOR TWO

To show our appreciation for your support, Warner Books is offering an opportunity to win our sweepstakes for four weekend trips for two throughout 1996.

Enter in February and March to win a romantic spring weekend to Hilton Head, South Carolina;

Enter in April, May and June to win a gorgeous summer getaway to San Francisco, California;

Enter in July and August to win a passionate fall trip to the blazing mountains of Vermont;

Enter in September, October, November and December to win a hot winter jaunt to Sanibel Island.

To enter, stop by the Warner Books display at your local bookstore for details or send a self-addressed stamped envelope for an application to:

Warner Books
1271 Avenue of the Americas
Room 9-27B
New York, NY 10020

No purchase necessary. Void where prohibited. Not valid in Canada.
Winner must be 18 or older.

WARNER BOOKS. WE'LL SWEEP YOU OFF YOUR FEET.